P9-BBU-217

Beach
Colors

Beach Colors

SHELLEY NOBLE

WILLIAM MORROW

An Imprint of HarperCollins*Publishers*

BEACH COLORS. Copyright © 2012 by Shelley Freydont. All rights reserved. Printed in the United States of America. No part of this book may be used or reproduced in any manner whatsoever without written permission except in the case of brief quotations embodied in critical articles and reviews. For information address Harper-Collins Publishers, 10 East 53rd Street, New York, NY 10022.

HarperCollins books may be purchased for educational, business, or sales promotional use. For information please write: Special Markets Department, HarperCollins Publishers, 10 East 53rd Street, New York, NY 10022.

FIRST EDITION

Designed by Diahann Sturge

Library of Congress Cataloging-in-Publication Data has been applied for.

ISBN 978-0-06-210308-6

12 13 14 15 16   OV/RRD   10 9 8 7 6 5 4 3 2 1

To Maggie Cousins and Julia Cauthorn

Acknowledgments

Writing a novel is a long, solitary journey. It is mostly a personal and private endeavor, but at some point you have to let go, and if you're lucky the light at the end of the creative tunnel is peopled with those who will take the story on its next journey and make it into a book.

Special thanks to:

Pearl Wolf, devil's advocate and cheerleader, for letting me brainstorm, act out, and question until it made sense.

Irene Peterson, first reader, sounding board, and idea maven with an incredible eye and ear for what works.

My agent, Kevan Lyon, for seeing the potential in this story, for her enthusiasm, and for her insistence on honing the manuscript until it became just what I meant it to be.

My editor, Tessa Woodward, for treating the story gently and making it better.

For the whole team at HarperCollins, for making me feel welcome, for designing this beautiful cover, and for the crash course on effective social networking.

My writing friends at Liberty States Fiction Writers, always ready with a good laugh or a swift kick, and tons of good advice, thanks for your unwavering support.

My nonwriting friends, who cheerfully let me drag them to look at the salt marshes at noon, then again at sunset; who aren't embarrassed when I talk to strangers in department stores; and who don't get annoyed when I stop conversations to jot down an idea. And, mostly, for just being you.

And to my readers, who are the reason this book exists.

The porch steps were hot. Margaux Sullivan hopped from one foot to the other while she searched the beach for her friends.

It was the last day of summer. Sunlight floated on the water like a million diamonds. Lazy pinwheels of white filled the sky. Across the Sound, Long Island stretched like a green thread on the horizon. It felt like time would last forever. But tomorrow the houses would be closed up, and the Selkies would be separated for another winter.

Margaux's stomach clenched. This year would be different. Margaux and Grace were both returning to Hartford with their families, but Brianna was moving to New York. They might never all meet here again.

Stupid. Of course we will. The Selkies will always have each other.

She shielded her eyes against the sun and found the others standing at the water's edge. Brianna posed for the lifeguard, pretending to ignore him, while he practically fell off his seat to get a better look. Grace stood in the water trying not to giggle.

The lifeguard was tall, dark, and handsome, but Bri's mother told her not to fraternize with him because he was a townie. Bri didn't listen.

Margaux had her own tall, dark, and handsome young townie. Well, he wasn't really hers. He was much older and they'd never even spoken. But they had sat across the same table at the library every summer since she was ten—him frowning over his books—her copying dresses from the latest fashion magazines. It was *almost* like a date. Only he wasn't there this summer, and now she was sorry that she'd never asked him what he was studying.

The screen door slammed behind her and her brother, Danny, ran past her and jumped down to the sand.

"Hey, Magsy. Want a ride to the library?"

"No thanks. I'm busy. And it's Margaux."

Danny grinned back at her. He pushed his motorcycle helmet over unruly red curls and made a bow. "Madame *Ma-a-argaux*." Then he reached up and scrubbed her hair. "Magsy." The pencil stub that was pushed through her equally unruly curls fell to the steps.

She slapped at his hand but he dodged away. "See ya, Mags." He ran around the side of the house. A minute later she heard his new Honda 500 roar to life. Margaux pulled at her hair. It had taken her ten minutes to get it to lie flat, and now it was every which way again. She picked up the pencil and shoved it behind her ear.

Brothers could be so annoying. She put two fingers to her lips and whistled. Brianna and Grace looked up and started walking toward her. They met halfway and turned as one toward the jetty at the end of the crescent beach.

Brianna led the way, walking ahead as if she were already leaving them. They climbed up the rocks of the jetty, barely paying attention, they had climbed them so often. Then down again to the cove. The tide was in and they had to splash through the water to reach the path that led through the woods.

Margaux lagged behind. Things were changing and she

wasn't sure she was ready. She knew some people outgrew the beach, but not the Selkies. Even when they got too old to explore and write secret messages and go crabbing—Margaux would never be too old to go crabbing—the beach would still be a part of them. Would live in a special place inside each of them.

She felt a flutter of nerves. Today they were leaving something of themselves behind—just in case.

It was cooler beneath the pines and scrub oak. Silently they walked along the narrow path, nearly grown over with rhododendron and fern.

When the path veered off, they ducked under the gnarled tree limb, climbed over the rotten log, and stopped at the entrance of the Grotto. They had discovered it that first summer, an outcropping of rocks and a ledge of granite that formed a shallow cavern. It became their secret hideout where first they made magic potions, or hid from pirates, and later, talked about boys. They had grown older; the sapling whose roots spread over the rock had become a tree.

But the Grotto never changed. It was a magical place that could make dreams come true.

Brianna flipped on her flashlight, crouched down, and ducked beneath the ledge. One by one, each took her place, sitting cross-legged in a circle, knees touching, while the flashlight cast their shadows eerily against the rough stone.

Brianna reached into her string bag and pulled out a Tupperware container. She placed it in the center of the circle, lifted off the top, and glancing at the others, slowly reached back into the bag and pulled out the pink plastic diary where, that morning, each had made her last secret entry. Solemnly, she placed it in the Tupperware container. She closed the lid and sealed it tight.

They gathered around the fissure in the rock wall. Brianna shoved the box inside, and they covered the opening with three large smooth stones.

"The Selkies forever," Brianna intoned in her throaty voice. They crossed their hearts, licked three fingers, and raised them in the air.

"The Selkies forever."

Nick Prescott stood on the dark rocks of the jetty, careful not to get his new uniform wet or scuff the polish of his new boots. Tomorrow he would be in Fort Dix, New Jersey. Private Nick Prescott.

For the past two years, he had watched his friends get on with their lives while he stayed behind. The money he'd saved for college dwindled away while he tried to take care of his mother and brother. But now it was his turn.

He would miss the shore. Even though his family only owned a cape in town, he was proud to have grown up here. He wished he could say the same for his brother, Ben.

He was down there now at his lifeguard post, flirting with the blonde. He just didn't get that they would never accept him. No matter how many times Nick told him. They were summer people. But Ben wouldn't listen.

Nick watched the girls join another girl. His heart tightened—just a little—when he saw her halo of red curls. She had been his talisman ever since the summer after his father died. Then she was just a kid, sharing his table at the library. Drawing pictures with the tip of her tongue pressed to the corner of her mouth as she concentrated. Pushing curls out of her face with an impatient hand. He could hardly wait until school was out and she came back to sit across from him.

Only this summer was different. She had grown up, become one of them, and that put an end to everything.

He would become a history professor someday. The army would pay for his education. And she would become—he didn't know. He just knew that she would always be a summer person, and he, just a townie.

One

 Margaux Sullivan stood unmoving and listened to the echoes of her failure. Only a week ago, her Manhattan loft had been thrumming with energy, excitement, and caffeine, as twenty-five pattern cutters, drapers, and seamstresses worked round the clock to prepare M Atelier's latest collection for the event of the year. New York City's Fashion Week.

Now it was just an empty space. The finished pieces carted away in cardboard boxes. The long worktables cleared of everything but a few forgotten scraps of fabric. The mannequins repossessed, the brick walls bare except for the row of five-by-three-foot photographs of Margaux's award-winning fashions that her creditors left behind.

The asymmetrical black moiré satin sheath had been her first CFDA award winner. The black wool tuxedo had made the cover of *Vogue*. *Marie Claire* had called the black tulle ball gown—not a fluffy evening dress, but cutting-edge stark—"Tulle with a Bite."

The models stared back at her, caught in time, sleek and scowling. *This dress will make you thin, this will make you beautiful, this will make men adore you.* Black, unique, and powerful. They'd promised to make Margaux's dream come true.

And it had come true. Ever since that sticky summer day when she'd discovered a bridal magazine in the Crescent Cove library. She'd opened its shiny pages to brilliant white, palest pink, creamy ivory. Pearls and veils and promises—and she thought, *This is what I want to do.*

For the rest of the summer, she rode her bike to the library almost every day to draw and dream. During the school year she took art classes and every summer she returned to the library to copy the latest magazines. She majored in design in college and interned in New York, and gradually worked her way up to owning her own workshop.

It had been a long fierce climb, but she'd made it. She was successful, envied, happily married. But it was just an illusion. While she worked unceasingly to establish herself as one of New York's top designers, her loving husband had siphoned off their assets and disappeared.

The bank had taken everything else.

All she had left was her car and her reputation. The car was paid for, but her reputation wouldn't be worth a two-martini lunch once the news got out that M Atelier had gone belly up.

Margaux felt her chin quiver. *Not now.* She had one more thing to do before she broke down and howled at the moon.

She slipped the business card out of her pocket and picked up her portfolio. She stepped into her secretary's office. "Guess we're the last two."

Yolanda looked up from a soggy Kleenex. Margaux thrust the business card toward her. "Liz Chang at DKNY has been threatening to steal you for years. Here's her number. Call her."

Yolanda took the card. "She'd take you, too."

Margaux shook her head. "Don't worry about me. I'll be fine." She'd thought about hiring herself out again. But the thought stuck in her gut. She couldn't do it. It was too humiliating. And she wouldn't give her competition the sastisfaction of seeing her grovel. Not yet, anyway.

"Good luck." Margaux turned to leave and came face-to-face with the most recent photo of herself. An awards dinner at the Plaza. Tall, sleek, her impossibly curly auburn hair gelled, sprayed, and pulled back into a classic French twist that an earthquake wouldn't ruffle. Her black evening gown, one of her own designs, had stopped conversation when she'd entered the room. She was holding a glass of Taittinger's champagne and smiling. At the top of her game.

And now the game was over.

She walked across the long expanse of wooden floor to the elevator, her heels tapping in the deserted room. She stepped inside and closed the grate; listened to the rhythmic creak as the ancient elevator descended to the ground floor one last time, stood as it clanked at the bottom, then pushed open the door to the street.

The air was thick with car fumes and the noise of living. Handcarts filled with goods rattled up the sidewalk. Garbage bags lined the curb. Men late for appointments shouldered past slower pedestrians. An old woman stuck her mittened hand out at Margaux. "Help an old lady?"

Margaux couldn't even help herself. She no longer belonged here, had no place here, no business, no apartment, no income.

There was only one place she could go.

Nick Prescott glanced up as the blip appeared on his radar. Resignedly, he tossed his *History of the Ostrogoths in Italy* onto the passenger seat beside him. He should be sitting in his office correcting final exams, not hiding in the trees waiting to ticket some unsuspecting speeder.

Nick flipped on the siren, pulled the cruiser onto the tarmac, and took off after a bright blue sports coupe going at least sixty. The tourist season hadn't even begun, and already the summer people were breaking the law.

The car slowed and pulled to the sandy shoulder of the road. Nick followed and stopped several yards behind it. He noted the make, model, and license plate—New York—of course. Connecticut was their weekend retreat of choice.

As he got out of the cruiser, he slipped on his sunglasses

and unsnapped his holster. He'd been out of the army for ten years, and until six months ago, he never thought he'd ever use a firearm again.

A woman sat behind the wheel, the window was open, her hair was windblown. Auburn, deep, rich, like burnished mahogany. A color that as a boy stopped him in his tracks. It stopped him now, even while his rational mind told him it couldn't be her.

He took a breath and stepped up to the car. "Ma'am."

She looked up at him with wide, serious blue eyes. Eyes the color of a sunlit sea.

He'd know her anywhere in spite of the years that had passed. Felt the same jolt of connection he'd felt twenty years before. It hadn't changed, hadn't softened or diminished. And was still just as one-sided as it had always been. She had no idea who he was. "Do you know how fast you were going?"

"Fifty-five?"

"Sixty."

"But . . . that's only five over the speed limit."

"It *was*—a mile back. But you've entered Crescent Cove and it's thirty here."

A worried expression flitted across her face. "I didn't see the sign."

"Driver's license."

She riffled through an expensive-looking handbag and came up with an even more expensive-looking wallet.

"Take it out, please."

She jimmied the license out of the plastic sheath and handed it to him. Her fingers trembled a little.

"Margaux Sullivan."

She jumped as if the sound of her own name was a surprise. He frowned at the license, mainly to keep from staring at her.

She clutched the edge of the window. Her nail polish was chipped. She definitely had been biting her nails. The cuticles, too. Not something you'd expect from a hotshot New York fashion designer. And though she had turned into a beautiful woman, there were dark circles under her eyes and she looked drawn, not just model-thin. It made her eyes larger, vulnerable.

If this is what the big city did to you, she could have it. He studied her license. "New York City."

"Yes."

"Around here, Ms. Sullivan, we stick to the speed limit."

"I do, too," she assured him. "I just didn't realize I had entered the town limits."

"Uh-huh. Registration."

She fished in the glove compartment and handed it to him.

He took a look, then handed it back and pulled out a citation pad from his back pocket. It was his job after all.

"Officer," she pleaded.

"Chief of police."

"What? What happened to Herb Green?"

"Retired."

He didn't want to give her a ticket. Not with the way she was biting on her bottom lip. His heart was pounding and the sun beating down on his neck felt like a third-degree burn. He wanted to take her hand and tell her that whatever was making her look so unhappy would go away. He would make it go away. But he didn't. She'd been speeding, not five miles over, but twenty-five over. Ignorance was no excuse.

He handed her the ticket. "Drive carefully."

When she eased the Toyota onto the road, he pulled out behind her. He stayed behind her all the way into town, down Main Street to the other side of town where it joined Shore Road. He followed her until she turned through the chain-link gate of Little Crescent Beach. She was on her way home, and that open gate might as well have slammed shut behind her.

He jammed on the accelerator and sped away. For a few minutes he'd been young again. Just a townie boy with an ordinary dream. Not an ordinary man with no dreams left.

★ ★ ★

Margaux gripped the steering wheel in an effort to keep from shaking. She didn't have the money to pay for a speeding ticket. She barely had enough to pay for gas. When she'd slid her card into the gas pump on the way up, she prayed that it wouldn't be denied.

She drove slowly down Salt Marsh Lane, staring straight ahead, not even glancing at the summer house her best friend Bri's family owned, or at the cottage Grace's family rented each summer. She blinked away tears so close to the surface they hurt, but she resisted the urge to speed toward sanctuary. Most of the cottages were still boarded over from the winter, but small towns had a way of noticing things. It would be hard enough facing everyone without having to explain why she'd come running back or why the police had followed her home.

When the lane reached the beach, it curved to the right. Three houses later, Margaux turned left into the parking niche at the back of the Sullivan beach house.

She took her suitcase and a bag of groceries out of the trunk and dumped them at the back door. She didn't go inside but took the path between the houses to the beach, scuffing through the sand, her head bowed, letting her shoes fill up with the heavy grains and her hair blow wild in the salt air.

She knew exactly when to look up. The perfect moment for that first full view. The blues of the water reaching up to the sky. The white sand stretching to each side in a graceful curve, like a smile.

When she was a kid, she would throw her arms open to the sea, let it take her troubles away. No matter how sad or angry or hurt she'd been, the waves could wash the feeling away. Could make her problems seem not so bad.

Margaux was older and wiser now and knew the waves couldn't fix what was wrong in her life, but at least they might give her some temporary respite.

There was one family on the beach, clustered beneath a

bright umbrella near the empty lifeguard station. Farther along, two figures crawled over the rock jetty looking for crabs.

She sat down on the porch steps, closed her eyes, and lifted her face to the sun. Spots danced on her eyelids, the waves murmured in her ears. She concentrated on breathing and gradually her body began to relax. The knots in her shoulders eased. Her stomach gave up its churning, and she drifted back to a place where each day was a promise, and joy was just waking up to the cries of the gulls.

She lost track of time, maybe she dozed. When she opened her eyes again, the sky had turned from blue to mauve and the sun sat like a fiery fat beach ball on the horizon. The crabbers were gone. The family gathered up towels and their cooler and trudged up the beach toward home.

A solitary gull strutted near the water's edge, his bill jackhammering the sand in search of food. A wave rolled in; he swooped into the sky and was swallowed by the dusk.

Margaux was alone.

Lights began to come on in the condominium complex two coves away where her mother lived. Was Jude sitting on her balcony watching the sunset? Could she see Margaux? And what would she think if she did?

Would her failure become one of those moments printed indelibly on the memory, linked forever with these steps, this porch. Posing for pictures in her white First Communion dress. Chasing sand crabs that Danny had dumped on Jude's lap to proudly show off his catch. Louis's proposal. Dad, Jude, and her sitting together the Sunday after Danny died. And sitting with her mother, years later, when Henry Sullivan followed his son.

From deep inside the house the telephone rang. Resolutely, Margaux stood and climbed the steps to the porch. A rectangle of wood hung from a nail beneath the porch light; its black letters spelled out *The Sullivans*. She lifted the sign. Paint flakes drifted to the floor; a spider, disturbed from sleep, scuttled beneath the cedar shakes. She extracted the house key and let the sign fall back into place.

The lock was stiff and she had to lean against the door to open it. But when she stepped over the threshold, she stopped, suddenly terrified. What had she been thinking? How could she come back like this—jobless, husbandless, childless. How could she face Jude with her boundless compassion and unfailing optimism.

The phone continued to ring. She groped her way across the dark foyer and picked up the receiver.

"You're there," said Jude's familiar voice.

"I'm here."

"I saw you from my terrace. Why didn't you let me know you were coming? I would have aired the house."

"It was a spur-of-the-moment thing."

"Are you free for dinner?"

"Sure, but let's eat here."

"Deke's? I can pick up food and be there in an hour."

"Deke's would be great." Margaux replaced the receiver and closed her eyes. She didn't think clam rolls were exactly what she needed to salvage her life. But maybe her mother could help.

Jude slid the glass doors shut and called Deke's Clam Shack.

"Holy cow," said Deke O'Halloran. "The only reason you'd be eating fried is if Mags was home."

"She's home," Jude said, trying to keep the worry out of her voice. It wasn't like Margaux to show up unannounced. It wasn't like her to show up at all. She hadn't been back in years.

"Twenty minutes," Deke said. "I'll put on a fresh batch."

Jude hung up. When she'd seen the figure sitting on the front steps of the beach house and recognized her daughter, her heart leapt to her throat. Something it hadn't done in a long while.

Margaux never told her the real reason she and Louis had stopped coming to the shore, though Jude suspected it had nothing to do with how busy she was. She'd just about given up hope of them coming again, but she kept the house clean anyway—just in case. Jude had been disappointed but not surprised when Margaux called to say she'd filed for divorce. She didn't say why, only that things weren't working and that she could handle it.

Jude was proud of Margaux's strength. She had always known what she wanted, worked hard to get there. But that strength had become brittle in the last few years and Jude was worried. Strength ebbed and flowed, but brittle would break.

Well, whatever it was, they would see it through together. She glanced at the clock. Time to go. And on her way, she'd stop by the church to light a candle to the saints; her daughter had come home.

Margaux sat at the kitchen table, running her bare toes across the old linoleum floor, scratched from years of sandy feet. She was tired, she wanted to be alone, to stay in this cozy old kitchen while its dark maple cabinets and wallpaper of watering cans and ivy created a cocoon of safety around her.

But she knew that was impossible and when she heard the familiar *beep-beep* of Jude's Citroën as it pulled into the drive, she dragged herself from the chair and went to meet her.

Jude bustled through the door, carrying a greasy paper bag and a six-pack of Budweiser. She was trim and fit, a few inches shorter than Margaux with the same auburn red hair. She was sixty-two but she had a new hairstyle that made her look years younger. She put down her parcels and opened her arms. Margaux walked into a hug. Her mother's cologne mingled with the smell of fresh fried clams, and the aroma was enough to make her cry.

Jude gave her a squeeze. "Let's eat. Deke'll kill me if the clams get cold. He put on a fresh batch just for you."

Margaux pulled away. "You told him I was here?"

"Well, of course." Jude frowned. "Shouldn't I—"

"You have a new hairdo. It looks great."

"Whole town does. Even Dottie, if you can believe that. New girl. From Brooklyn of all places. Bought the old Cut 'n Curl across from the marina. And a sheer genius." She smiled at her own joke. "By the way, Dottie said she better see you at the diner first thing tomorrow morning."

"Dottie knows, too?" She'd hoped to hibernate for a while, but now that was impossible. Dottie's Diner was the local gossip exchange.

Jude opened the bag and placed two foil-wrapped paper cartons on the table. "I was supposed to meet her for girls' night. Had to call to tell her I wasn't coming." She flipped the tab of one can, then stopped and peered at Margaux. "Is there a reason you don't want people to know you're here?"

"No." Margaux sat down at the table.

Jude sat down, too, but she didn't take her eyes off Margaux. "Is something wrong?"

Margaux shook her head, nodded.

Jude handed her a napkin. "Eat. Then we'll talk. There's nothing in this world that can't be fixed."

Margaux picked up her clam roll. It was so stuffed with succulent clams that a handful fell out when she bit into the roll.

They ate in silence. When Margaux had scooped up the last clam bit, Jude put down her beer. "Now tell me what's happened."

Margaux took a breath but the words stuck in her throat. She took another breath. "In a nutshell. While I was climbing the ladder of haute couture, becoming famous and building a nest egg so we could start a family, Louis stole everything. Savings, investments, everything, then dropped out of sight. I've lost the apartment, my business—"

"What? No. This can't be."

"He—" Margaux's voice cracked; a tear escaped and rolled down her cheek. She sucked in air. "They repossessed everything. Patterns, machines, fabric, even the drafting paper. I only had enough credit left to pay my staff.

"And my designs. They shoved them into cardboard boxes and took them away. What could the bank possibly want with them?"

She felt a hand on her shoulder and she turned into her mother and held on for dear life. "I've lost everything. How could Louis do this?"

And how could she have been so stupid not to notice before it was too late?

"Why didn't you call me? I could have transferred funds, sold the condo."

"It was over before I knew what was happening. Besides, I couldn't ask you to bail me out. It wouldn't have done any good. We're talking about a couple million."

Jude pulled away abruptly. "I'll call a lawyer I know. We'll stop this."

"I have a lawyer. She had the court freeze whatever assets were left. There wasn't much. She has a forensic accountant trying to trace the money, but they may never find it, if he still has it."

Margaux groped for a napkin. "You hear about this kind of thing all the time and you think, That could never happen to me. I'd never be so stupid. And look." She held out her hands. "Everything I dreamed of, worked for. Gone. I was on the brink of making it big, and now, zip, nada, nothing." The thin control she'd been holding on to for the last few weeks broke and she cried, sobbing in big gulps and not caring. "I would have given him half—money, property—more than half. I only wanted one thing and he took that, too."

Jude pushed a wild strand of hair from Margaux's cheek. "What?"

"My future."

"Oh, Margaux. It only seems that way now. You were right to come home."

Margaux sniffed. "Where else could I go?" She hated herself for sounding so needy, so incapable, but she'd used up every reservoir of strength just getting through the last two months.

"No place else in the world. You've got family and friends and a home. You'll create more designs, make more money, and someday you'll meet someone to love and have a family with."

"Mom, I'm thirty-four."

"Thirty-four is nothing. Women have children into their forties these days."

"There won't be anyone else."

"Of course there will be. It's early days yet."

"There wasn't for you."

"No." Jude smiled. "You're exhausted. Things will look better when you've rested. Why don't you come stay at the condo with me tonight?"

"Thanks, but—" Margaux shook her head.

"Or . . . I could stay here."

"No. I just need to sleep. You go on home. I'll be fine."

"Are you sure?"

"I'll be fine. I promise."

Jude gathered up their trash. "Okay, but call me if you change your mind. Doesn't matter what time. I mean it."

"I will." Margaux walked her to the car.

Jude kissed her good night. "Dottie's for waffles. I'll pick you up at nine."

"Mom, I can't."

"Sure you can. You don't want to hurt Dottie's feelings and you need to eat."

Margaux gave in. It took more than she had to resist. By tomorrow she'd be able to hold herself together. For a while anyway.

Jude beeped as she rounded the curve and Margaux went inside. She was numb with shock, with pain, with sheer exhaustion, but she knew she wouldn't be able to sleep. It seemed like she hadn't slept in years, and the stairs to her bedroom seemed to stretch forever.

She walked through the parlor and out the front door.

She hesitated at the bottom of the porch steps. The beach was dark, the sand eerily illuminated by the sliver of moon. She took a step and the sand shifted beneath her feet. Another step, another shift. Another . . . and another until the sand turned wet and hard. Another and another until she stood ankle deep in the cold water of the Sound.

She looked into the darkness, opened her arms, and gave in to the pull of the tide, strong, relentless, its siren call singing her home.

Two

 Nick waited for the printer to spit out his last report. He was drowning in paperwork, something he hadn't bargained for when he agreed to take the job of police chief. And the season was just beginning.

But a job was a job and this one paid regularly and had good benefits. He needed both.

He pressed his fingertips to his eyes. The skin was rough. He'd been spending every spare minute doing chores for his mother or moonlighting at Jake McGuire's woodworking business. By next month, he wouldn't have time for any of that. His entire force of seven would be working overtime dealing with congested traffic, illegal fireworks, fender benders, sunstroke, stolen purses . . . The list seemed interminable.

When the printer clicked back to Power Save, Nick scooped up the pages and tossed them into the outbox.

He stretched to ease the stiffness in his back, then pushed himself out of his chair. God, he felt more like eighty-eight than thirty-eight. And he still had to do the shopping and drop the groceries off at his mother's before going home.

Out of habit, he reached into the desk drawer for his copy of *A History of the Ostrogoths in Italy.* Though if he was learning anything about the Ostrogoths, it was through osmosis. He'd barely opened the book in weeks.

He tucked it under his arm, turned out the lights, and closed his office door. The public area was empty except for Dee Janowitz, the night dispatcher, and his deputy, Finley Green, who was perched on the edge of the switchboard.

Finley stood up, unfolding like an accordion, six feet of sinew and charm. He grinned at Nick. "Dee here tells me you made a stop and search today. And there I am sitting down in the hollow all day, and nobody even rolled through the stop sign."

Nick grunted. He didn't want to think about Margaux Sullivan. "A stop, not a search. It was just some tourist, driving over the limit."

"I heard it was Jude Sullivan's daughter," said Dee, giving him the I-was-dispatcher-here-when-you-were-in-diapers look. "Nick, how could you?"

Hell. Somebody must have been driving by and seen him. He'd been too floored to notice. "Just doing my duty, ma'am." He flicked two fingers at his forehead. "I'll have my cell if you need me, Finley. See you on Monday."

He drove to the Cove Market at the edge of town, pulled a basket away from the outside rack, and pushed it through the automatic door. He went straight to the cereal aisle.

He tossed a box of Lucky Charms into the cart, knowing his mother would click her tongue and put them on a top shelf where she hoped they would go unnoticed. Connor loved Lucky Charms and a kid, especially one who had been through what Connor had been through, deserved some sugar in his life. Nick added a box of All-Bran as atonement.

He wielded the cart into the next aisle. Maxwell House, dish detergent, Mop & Glo. He grabbed a bag of potatoes from the produce section and sped toward the checkout stand.

The cashier, a plump thirtyish woman whose name tag read *Hi, I'm Cindy,* pursed her lips as she scanned the Lucky Charms. "Breakfast is the most important meal of the day, Chief. I hope you're planning to have these with milk."

"Shi— I'll be right back." He sprinted off. Sprinted back with a gallon of milk. She finished ringing him up; he packed the groceries and wheeled them out.

"Enjoy your breakfast," she called after him.

He drove back through town to the Cape Cod where he'd grown up. His mother was standing at the side door, waiting for him.

"Sorry I'm late, Ma. Lots of paperwork."

She tried to relieve him of the groceries but he fought her off. She was small and fine boned. Lately it seemed she had grown more delicate, and tonight she seemed frail. He swore at himself for not being able to help her more.

"Sit down, Nicky. I've got a plate warming in the oven."

"I'll just wash up." He started rolling up his sleeves on his way to the door.

He stopped by the bathroom, then looked in on his nephew. Connor was lying on his side, his Shrek night-light illuminating his face. He sighed in his sleep and for a split second he looked just like Ben. Nick leaned his forehead against the doorframe trying not to think about his brother, or to remember. Then he gently closed the door, leaving it ajar in case Connor became frightened in the night.

When he returned to the kitchen, his mother was standing on tiptoe, pushing the Lucky Charms onto the top shelf of the cabinet. He took it from her and set it between the All-Bran and the oatmeal on the bottom shelf. He heard the oven door open and close, and when he turned around, a plate covered with aluminum foil was sitting on the table.

She lifted the foil away and a finger of steam curled into the air. "I hope it didn't dry out."

He sat down. "It looks great. Thanks." Pot roast swimming in gravy. Chunks of potatoes and slices of carrots and green beans.

She poured him a glass of milk and he smiled at her. He'd

been thinking what he really needed was a double shot of Scotch.

She poured herself a cup of coffee and sat down across from him while Nick dug into the roast.

"Karen Ames called today."

"The school psychologist? What did she want?"

"She's scheduled an appointment for Connor on Thursday with the therapist she recommended."

"Ma, we discussed this. We're not sending him to a special school."

She nodded. The little wisps of hair that always sneaked out of her bun lifted in the air. Hair, he noticed, that was more white than honey these days.

"They just want to do more tests."

Nick stopped with the fork halfway to this mouth. "No." He pushed the forkful of beef into his mouth, chewed slowly, hoping he would be able to swallow it.

"He'll be a year behind the other children as it is. There's a nice school out on the highway. Deke and Peg O'Halloran's daughter goes there."

"Cecilia is mentally challenged. Connor is not. He's—"

"Traumatized."

"Quiet. He's just quiet. The summer will be a perfect time for him to get to know other kids. We sent him to school too soon after . . ." He couldn't even say it. "After he came here." Nick had made a lot of mistakes in his life but he wasn't going to rob Connor of a normal childhood in a normal school. "I'll set up some playdates, maybe we can send him to day camp. I'll take him to the park, down to the beach—"

She reached across the table and laid her hand on his. A little bird hand, a feather's touch. He felt a stab of panic, that there would be a time in the future when she would be gone, and he would be left to take care of Connor by himself.

"Nicky, you're exhausted."

"I'm fine, Ma. Just a little tired."

"You stop here every night," she said as if he hadn't spoken. "Spend weekends with Connor." She turned his hand over. "And I know you're working for Jake McGuire, though I don't know when you find the time."

He gently pulled his hand away and picked up the paper napkin next to his plate. "I like working with my hands. It's relaxing."

"And what about your schoolwork?"

Nick thought of the history book lying on the passenger seat of his police car. "It's an Internet course. There's no time limit." It didn't matter. He had already written the Denver college where he taught to say he wouldn't be back in the fall.

"I'll take him to the kiddie shrink, but Connor needs to go to school with normal kids." His appetite was gone, but he forced down the rest of his dinner. His mother would be hurt if he didn't. He carried his plate to the sink; she took it out of his hands.

"I'll do this. You go on home and get some sleep."

Gratefully, he dried his hands. "Thanks. And thanks for dinner."

She walked him to the door and they stood for a moment looking out. The street was dark, there was barely a moon, and the stars were sprinkled like confetti through the sky.

"What would make a mother leave her child?"

"She was . . . overwhelmed . . . perhaps."

"Selfish."

"She may come back."

"She may, but she sure as hell won't take Connor away from us."

"Nicky."

"Sorry, Ma, but I won't give him back, not after how she left him."

His mother placed a hand on his sleeve. "You know best, Nicky."

They stood for a while longer, just looking into the night. Nick sighed. "Margaux Sullivan is back."

"Is she? Jude will be so pleased. We were talking about her just the other day."

"You talked to Jude Sullivan?" How much could they have in common? They might be close to the same age, but his mother was working-class. The years had worn her down. Jude was sophisticated, still young-looking and vital.

"Of course. We're on the flea market committee together."

"I'd forgotten."

"How did she look?"

"Margaux?" He swallowed. "Fine . . . I guess. She looked . . . okay."

She smiled. "You're tired. Go home." She reached up and kissed his cheek, then patted the place as if sealing the kiss there.

"Tell Connor I'll see him at supper tomorrow, then Sunday we can play some ball maybe."

He cut across the front yard and began the three-block walk to the marina and his apartment over the Cut 'n Curl—Le Coif, he corrected himself. Even though Linda, the new owner, had changed the name and put up a cutesy sign, it would always be the Cut 'n Curl to Nick.

He always left his police car in his mother's driveway. It made him feel better about leaving them alone. Not that there was much crime in a town the size of theirs, but you never knew. He enjoyed starting and ending each day with a walk. It was surprising how little exercise he got as a policeman. And if there was an emergency, his truck was parked at the marina.

Once the summer was over, things would be better. The antiques dealers and art galleries that had sprung up around town drew hordes of shoppers on the weekends. But for the other five days of the week, they would enjoy their sleepy little beach town, forgotten until the next summer rolled around.

Then he'd catch up on all the things he would have to let

slide during the tourist season. Connor would settle in; get used to living with his grandmother; he'd go to school, make some friends. And maybe by next summer Nick would have a new teaching job closer to Crescent Cove, and he could afford a house large enough for the three of them. But first he had to get through the next three months.

The beauty parlor was dark, but he could see light coming from Linda Goldstein's apartment on the second floor. Fortunately, his attic apartment had its own entrance, even if he had to climb a deeply pitched outside staircase to get there.

He hung his uniform neatly in the closet and went to bed—but not to sleep. His mind became a treadmill, his thoughts exploring the same territory over and over and never finding a solution. How to support his mother. How to make Connor whole again. How to finish his master's while working fourteen-hour days. How he would ever be able to pay for a private school if Connor had to be sent there. How to make up for the things he'd done and hadn't done. His mind roiled and his body tensed until he thought he'd never fall asleep.

When at last sleep came, he was thinking about the reappearance of Margaux Sullivan.

Margaux awoke to darkness, wondered where the hell she was, remembered. She was at the beach house, asleep on the couch. And she remembered why she was here. Panic surged up. She forced it down. She'd deal with it tomorrow. Tomorrow when she was stronger. Tomorrow in the sunlight.

She rolled off the couch and padded upstairs to her old bedroom. She climbed into bed, pulled the quilt up, and fell asleep in her clothes.

When she awoke again it was light. A square of blue filled the window and sunlight cast warmth across her face. She was home, in her own room.

She pushed the quilt away and sat up, perched on the side of the bed, her hands pressed between her knees. Home, because her life was in shambles. Her hard-earned career down the toilet. Her marriage a farce. Because of Louis.

She didn't want to think about him, but every morning since he'd left, she'd awakened with his image in her mind. She didn't love him. Not anymore. Hadn't for a while. Now she hated him.

And hate tied you to a person as surely as love. She had to cut him loose, excise him out of her feelings if she was ever going to be able to start again.

Just the thought of starting over made her want to climb back in bed, pull the covers over her head, and sleep forever. But that wasn't an option. She had to sever herself from the past and move forward. And she had to start now.

She forced herself to her feet, rummaged through her suitcase, and found a pair of black yoga pants and knit top. Everything in her suitcase was black. But hell, black had made her famous. Her spring designs had knocked them on their designer-clad asses; the next show would have guaranteed her a place with the movers and shakers.

A mewl of pain escaped from deep inside her and she clapped her hand over her mouth to stop it. Not now. Not ever. This was the first day of the rest of her life. Clichéd, but true. She had to get it right this time.

She tossed her slept-in clothes toward the closet and put on a new set of black. She went downstairs and was mystified to see that it was almost nine o'clock. She had slept ten hours.

She barely had time to wash her face before she heard Jude's distinctive *beep-beep* in the driveway. She quickly pushed her fingers through her hair and ran outside to meet her.

They drove along Shore Road to Main Street where the old Esso station had been converted into an Exxon self-service island. The white clapboard library, where she had spent hours studying drawing books and the latest fashion magazines, had a fresh coat of paint.

In those days, she didn't know about cutting edges and predicting trends, industry spying, and advertising spots. She just loved to draw. Wedding gowns, seascapes, miniskirts, pieces of driftwood. It had been a long time since she had drawn for the sheer fun of it.

Now there were deadlines, budgets, competition. Knocking out one design after another. Changing them when the costs ran too high or the silhouette looked too derivative. Always staying one step ahead of everyone else.

She'd come a long way from *Modern Bride* and *Seventeen*. Maybe she had gone too far.

As they drove through town, Jude pointed out the new stores that had opened. The whole town had a trendier look Margaux hadn't noticed on that hateful drive yesterday with the new chief of police riding her bumper.

Jude pulled into a parking space in front of a store that had been Thelma's Foundations, but was now a coffee bar called In Your Cups.

"What happened to Thelma's?"

"Went out of business."

"And the old hardware store?"

"After they built the Home Depot on Route 1, Mr. Oglethorpe said it wasn't worth the trouble of staying open. His son, Roy, moved the store to the end of the block near the boardwalk. It's smaller, but he carries basic hardware, beach stuff, and arts and crafts."

Margaux sighed. "It's all so different."

"The important things are the same."

Margaux wasn't sure how she felt about all this newness. At least the diner appeared to be unchanged.

It had started life as an old railroad car with a row of booths along one side, a counter along the other, with a concrete-block kitchen added onto the back. They'd built an addition when Margaux was a teenager. She could remember sitting in a booth with her best friends, Grace and Brianna, eating French fries with gravy, as they yelled to each other over the noise of construction.

Margaux lagged behind as Jude opened the door. The whole town had been so supportive of her, proud of her accomplishments. How could she ever tell them she'd let them down. Especially Dottie, who was Jude's best friend and Margaux's godmother.

Jude nudged her inside.

Dottie was standing behind the counter dressed in her usual pink uniform, talking to a man wearing jeans and a T-shirt. She was still as skinny as ever and had on the same color of lipstick she'd used ever since Margaux could remember.

But her hair was different. For years she had worn it in a high French twist that could be recognized "a block away on a moonless night." Her new style, a brighter shade of strawberry blonde, was cut short and curled around her face. It made her look ten years younger.

Dottie saw them, threw both hands in the air and squealed "Magsy!" loud enough to be heard to the town line. "It's about time you came to see us." She flew out from behind the counter and wrapped her arms around Margaux, shaking her back and forth like a puppy tugging at a stick.

"Let me look at you." She pushed Margaux back and grinned. "You look good. Hey, Nick. Look who's here."

The man at the counter stood up and slid on a pair of mirrored sunglasses as he turned to face them.

Margaux stepped back, right into Jude, as she registered the glasses, then the rest of the man. Even without the uniform, there was no mistaking him. Close-cut dark brown hair that might curl if ever allowed to grow longer than a regulation cut. No idea about the eyes. But she'd recognize that jawline anywhere, made even sharper by the close shave. He was tall and broad enough to intimidate even a hard-edged New Yorker.

Jude gently eased Margaux off her foot. "Morning, Nick."

His mouth twitched.

Margaux couldn't call it a smile, but it sent a shiver of something—apprehension?—down her spine.

"Morning, Jude."

"Do you remember my daughter, Margaux? She was a few years behind you in school."

The chief nodded stiffly in Margaux's direction. "Ms. Sullivan."

Despite the sunglasses, she knew he was giving her the once-over. Not in the way men usually did, but rather as if she might be packing a weapon.

He dropped a handful of change on the counter. "Thanks for the coffee, Dottie. Ladies." He dipped his head again and strode toward the door. He seemed to block out the sun as he passed.

"What's up with him?" asked Jude.

"I don't know, guess he had to get to work. Come on. I saved you a table." Dottie grabbed two menus from beside the cash register and led them to a booth by the front window.

Margaux slid into the near side in time to see the chief get into a white Ford pickup and drive away. If he was going to work, why wasn't he wearing a uniform?

"Do you two know each other?" Dottie asked.

"Huh? Not exactly. He gave me a ticket on my way into town yesterday."

"Why that scoundrel. Did you tell him you were a Sullivan?"

Margaux shook her head. "I didn't have time. He steamrolled right over me. But he knew I was a Sullivan. It's still on my driver's license. And I wasn't even speeding except that I had come into town and didn't know it. I didn't see the sign."

"That's 'cause the Morrison boys ran into it with their four-by-four. Tore it clean out of the ground. They haven't replaced it. I bet if you go to court, you can have it overturned."

"I don't think so," said Margaux. She had no intention of

throwing herself in the chief's path any more than necessary. He was way too intense for her comfort level.

"Herb's wanted to retire for years, but could never find a replacement," Dottie said. "When Nick came back last winter, he saw a perfect opportunity and turned in his badge. The council appointed Nick interim until they find a new chief. I don't think he really enjoys the job."

"He seemed to be enjoying it yesterday." The truck was headed toward Shore Road. Margaux just hoped she didn't keep running into him each time she left the house.

Dottie smiled at her. "He doesn't have time for much fun. It probably did him good to see a gorgeous young woman speeding by. Now, what are you having for breakfast? We've got Belgian waffle with fresh strawberries."

Margaux put down the menu she hadn't opened. "That's fine."

"What about you, Jude? The same?"

"Don't tempt me. I had a clam roll last night. I'll have a poached egg on a slice of rye toast."

"At Deke's? He must have been thrilled."

"Takeout. Margaux was tired."

Dottie nodded. "We'll get you up and running in no time. Be right back." She went off toward the kitchen, barking out their order.

"You're dieting?" asked Margaux. "You've never dieted in your life."

"That's because I never needed to. It's almost summer and your mother wants to look good in her swimsuit."

She looked great to Margaux. She frowned as an unwelcome thought entered her mind. Was Jude trying to impress someone in particular? She dismissed the thought. There could never be anyone for Jude but her father; she was sure of it.

Dottie returned with three mugs of coffee and scooted in with Jude. "Breakfast is on its way. So, Magsy, is this a weekend visit or are you planning to stay for a while?"

"Uh . . ." Margaux glanced at Jude and wondered what she had told Dottie.

A waitress placed plates on the table, several of which they hadn't ordered: a platter of bacon, scrambled eggs, and a bowl of whipped cream.

"Dottie. I'll have to go on a diet myself if you feed me like this."

"Darling, you could use a few pounds. I don't know what all this allure of thin is about. I've been skinny all my life, and I got more razzing than I care to remember. Guess I was just born a couple of decades too early."

"Tom doesn't seem to mind," said Jude.

"How *are* Tom and Quinn?" asked Margaux.

Dottie threw her hands in the air. "Tom retired last year and he's driving me crazy. Yesterday I found him up on a ladder measuring the back of the house. Says he wants to put in a Florida room. A Florida room in Connecticut. Go figure. Quinn is managing to graduate from high school, don't ask me how, and barring any unforeseen disasters, he'll hire on with the fishing fleet in the fall."

Dottie drained the last of her coffee. "I gotta help with the breakfast crowd. You plan on staying a good long time. We'll feed you and pamper the daylights out of you." She leaned over and brushed a quick kiss across Margaux's cheek.

"You're gonna be fine." She waved back over her head and pushed through the double swinging door of the kitchen without slowing down.

On their way back to the beach house, Margaux asked Jude to stop by Oglethorpe's Hardware. While Jude and Roy chatted about the upcoming flea market, Margaux quickly chose a box of pastels, some watercolors, a sketchbook, and some drawing pencils.

Roy insisted on throwing in a plastic paint palette and several good-quality paintbrushes free of charge. "We've got our share of famous people buying up property about here these days, but you're the first one we ever produced ourselves. And we appreciate it."

Margaux thanked him and accepted the brown paper bag of supplies he'd carried to the door for them. She couldn't tell him how really thankful she was. Her cash was reaching red alert, her credit barely breathing.

Jude drove Margaux back to the beach house but didn't come in. "I have to go to New Haven. I'll be gone late, so you'll have to have dinner on your own. I'd cancel but it's really late notice."

"That's fine. I brought some food from the city—and there's always the Cove Market. It's still there, isn't it?"

"Sure is. Stay busy and don't mope. Things are going to work out fine."

"I know," said Margaux with as much conviction as she could muster. "And I have plenty to do." She held up her bag of supplies. She just hoped inspiration struck and made the expense worth it.

"Good. And try to have a little fun. Skilling's is open late tonight. They still make your favorite flavor."

"Good idea. I've missed their ice cream."

"And Grace Holcombe is practicing law in town. She asks about you all the time."

Margaux nodded. She knew Grace had returned to live in Crescent Cove; she'd been the only one of the three who had no aspirations to see the world and become famous. Over the years, Margaux had let the friendship slide, but she knew Grace wouldn't hold it against her. She just wasn't ready to face her old friend yet. "I'll be fine."

"See you tomorrow then. I'll pick you up for Mass at eight-forty."

Mass? Margaux hadn't been to Mass in years. "I don't have anything to wear."

"It's the shore. Just don't wear cutoffs." Jude backed out of the driveway and sped off down the street. She beeped as she rounded the corner.

"I don't own any," Margaux said into the quiet street.

She went inside, suddenly aware of being alone. Really alone. And really at loose ends. It was Saturday. She was at the beach. But she hadn't taken a Saturday off in years and didn't know what to do.

Her cell phone was sitting on the table, but she didn't open it. No one had called her in days. She was already forgotten.

Determined not to succumb to depression, or self-pity, she dumped her supplies on the table, took out the sketchpad, and two graphite pencils, and went out the front door to the porch. The porch was bare, the chairs and a love seat stored away for the winter. The waves looked inviting, but the water would be too cold for a swim, besides she didn't have a suit.

She walked down the wooden steps to the sand, testing each tread as if it were July when they would be hot enough to burn the bottoms of your feet. But of course they weren't.

She hadn't been here in July in years. Not since the summer after Brianna moved away. She wondered where Bri was now. She'd had a successful career as a model but they'd lost touch over the years.

She turned northward to where the sandy beach ended at the jetty. Its massive boulders rose above her head. She climbed to the crest and stopped to take in the view. The salt air was bracing. The sea stretched out to the horizon where it met the sky in a seamless wash of blue, and she had it all to herself . . . and her sketchbook.

Below her on the north side of the jetty, a tiny pebbled beach was enclosed by woods that grew right down to the water. The underbrush grew so dense that you had to wade through the water to get to the beach and the little path that led to the outcropping of rock that had once been their secret hideout.

Margaux wondered if a new generation of kids used it now.

Or were secret places a thing of the past? She was half tempted to take a look, but it would be like trespassing without the others.

Behind her and beyond Little Crescent Beach, she could just see the masts of the sailboats moored at the town's marina. And the turret of the old Gothic house at the end of Crescent Point. Somewhere below it was the town beach and boardwalk, whose metallic organ music you could hear wafting from the carousel on quiet summer nights.

She sat down on a flat boulder. The jetty had always been her favorite place to sketch or do nothing. To just lie back against the warm stone, surrounded by shades of blue and green and gold while ideas drifted in and out of her lazy mind and colors swirled into kaleidoscopes of magic light. Sometimes Bri and Grace would join her and they'd talk about their futures. Or spy on the townie boys who swam in the cove. Sometimes, she'd rush home to paint.

She looked down on Little Crescent Beach and the Sullivan house nestled in the semicircle of houses, a little shabby but much loved. Margaux had never understood why Jude moved from the beach house to the condo. When she asked, Jude said that she was tired of tracking sand into the kitchen.

Now, as she looked at the house, Margaux thought she knew why. Jude couldn't stand to live there alone. Couldn't bear the memories that came when you were least ready for them. Margaux had felt her own. Bad memories were hard enough, but it was torture to be haunted by the good.

What would happen to the house now? If Danny had lived, it would have gone to his children. Now, it should go to her children. But she had no children.

Would their house one day be sold to strangers, become a blank slate without memories? Would it be torn down and replaced with condos like the one Jude had moved to? What happened to memories of a place when the place was gone?

All the wishes in the world wouldn't bring back the slam of

the screen door, or the creak of the porch steps. Or the smell of fish smoking on the grill. The beat of the pine tree on the windows when a storm blew in. The sound of Danny's motorcycle; her father's laughter. Where would those memories linger if not in the Sullivan house? Would they die in the same place as disappointed dreams?

Not if she could help it. Margaux opened her sketchbook and began to draw.

Three

 Nick hoisted the bundle of oak planks onto the shop table, pulled off his work gloves, and wiped sweat from his eyes. He'd changed into shorts and an old T-shirt after he left the diner but the workshop was stifling. "That's the last batch," he yelled over the whir of the table saw.

Jake McGuire gave Nick a thumbs-up, killed the saw, and pulled off his protective goggles. He was a couple of inches shorter than Nick, wiry but strong. His hair was darker, almost black, and longer and he was constantly egging Nick to let his grow to a "human" length. They'd played basketball together in high school, and if Nick had a best friend it was Jake.

Jake looked over the latest shipment of boards. "I really do appreciate the help, man. I know it's your day off, but it's my busy season."

"And mine is coming up. So use me while you can."

Jake clapped him on the back. "That's good for today. It's hot as hell, let's go rustle up a couple of beers."

Nick followed him out of the converted garage that was McGuire's Custom Woodworking and Design and across the lawn to the house Jake shared with his father, a Cape Cod similar to Nick's except that with eight children and a score of grandchildren it was a jumble of additions. They snagged two bottles of beer out of the fridge and went out to the backyard where they stretched out in two rusty aluminum chaise lounges.

"So how's the job search going?" Jake asked.

Nick snorted. "It isn't."

"Are you even looking?"

"Nope. I can't get anything with as much salary and benefits as I have as the chief of police. Not until I finish my master's anyway."

"I thought you were going to finish this spring so you could apply for the tenure position in Denver."

Nick shrugged. "Not going to happen this year. I've already withdrawn my name from the candidates' list."

"Hell, Nick, I'm sorry."

Nick sat up. "It doesn't matter. I couldn't leave Ma to look after Connor. And I can't just uproot them and move them somewhere else. She's lived here most of her life. And Connor's just getting used to a new place."

"Maybe you could find something around here."

"I already checked out local colleges. None of them can pay what I need." Nick took a long drink of beer. "Hell, I don't even know if this job is enough."

"Enough for what?"

Nick stared into the woods that surrounded the property.

"Enough for what?" Jake repeated.

"Nothing."

"It must be something or you wouldn't have clammed up. Bad habit of yours, Nick. Had it ever since we were kids."

Nick picked at the beer label. Jake could probably advise him on what to do, but he hated to have to admit even to Jake that he was out of ideas. "I might have to send Connor to the Eldon School. Or someplace like it but less expensive. He didn't fit in when we tried to send him to kindergarten. The school psychologist is worried about him coping in a regular classroom."

"Diagnosis?"

"Dammit. He's shy. He doesn't like loud noises. His father's dead, his mother ran off. What do you call that?"

"Hey, I'm not the enemy."

"Sorry. It's just that school starts in less than four months, and I don't know what to do."

"It's a good school. Deke and Peg's little girl goes there. Ask them about it. And you can get state aid." Jake held up a hand. "Don't get all hot under the collar. It isn't charity. It's given to everybody."

"Public school doesn't cost extra. He needs to be with kids that aren't . . ." Nick searched for a word. "Handicapped."

"Listen, Nick, I know it's hard to swallow, but the Eldon kids are great. I teach art there twice a week. And yeah, they're a challenge, but it's worth it. Lord, you've never seen kids get so enthusiastic and so covered in paint so fast. They're kids. Not freaks."

"Jesus, Jake. I know that. I'm not a Neanderthal. But Connor isn't handicapped, he's just emotionally scarred. He needs a safe haven, normalcy, not to be around kids who will never be like other kids."

"You'll figure it out."

"Yeah. Sure." Nick glanced at his watch.

"What? Got a hot date?"

"Do you?"

"Nah." Jake sighed and braced his elbows on his knees. "We're both sad cases, you know that?"

"What happened to the girl that runs the Sun and Surf shop? The way she was chasing you all winter, I thought—"

Jake gave him a look. "Nothing happened. She's a sweet kid, but she's just that. A kid. She's twenty-two, I'm thirty-eight. Not for me. I'm waiting for my soul mate."

"Good luck with that one." Nick said it lightly, but he empathized. He was waiting for his soul mate, too, and he was afraid she'd just driven into town.

There was no chance in hell of that working out.

"I'm thinking about trying to get the carousel up and running for next summer."

Nick looked at his friend, surprised. "I thought you'd given up on that."

Jake took a swig of beer. "Dad's not doing so great. He misses the work, even though he wasn't doing much business the years before we closed down. He'd like to see it running once again."

"Shit. I had no idea things were like that. He looked fine last time I saw him."

"He is fine. It's just that his heart is slowly giving out. He doesn't seem to get any pleasure out of life the way he did before Mom left. I was a late baby. There's six years between me and my youngest sister. He was over forty when I was born, maybe it just took the starch out of him."

Over forty, Nick thought. Pretty soon Nick would be forty, too old to even think about having a family other than the one he had now. "Did you ever think we'd end up back in Crescent Cove?"

"Yeah, actually, I did." Jake gestured with his beer bottle. "Name a place more beautiful than this."

Nick couldn't. He'd seen the world, thanks to the army. Some of it was incredible, some of it horrific, but he'd never found a place he'd liked more than here.

"You know, the whole time I was in the army, I hardly ever thought about Crescent Cove. It was exciting to see new places. Meet new kinds of people. I was lucky, I saw very little action." Luckier than his brother had been.

He finished peeling the label off his bottle, trying not to think of Ben, dead. Trying not to remember him in happier times before all his trouble began. He crumpled the label in his fist.

"Cut it out."

Nick glanced at Jake. "What?"

"When you get that look, I know you're thinking about Ben and blaming yourself. You should get over it. It wasn't your fault. He was a hero. He gave his life for his country. It was his choice."

"No it wasn't. I forced him to go."

"You did what you thought was best. Ben was on a collision course with disaster. You were gone those last couple of years and didn't see how wild he'd become, but the rest of us did. You had two choices: enlist him or let them send him to jail."

"Maybe jail would have been better."

"You think he would have come out a better man? Think again."

"At least he would be alive."

"He re-upped when he could have come home. He said himself that the army had made a man out of him. Sending him may have been your decision, but staying was his. Respect that."

Nick's throat was tight.

"You were barely more than a kid yourself. Faced with some heavy choices. Why don't you cut that kid a break?"

Because that kid was as dead as Ben.

"Ben was a soldier. He died with honors. You can be proud of him."

"You're right. Thanks." Nick forced a smile, though his heart was wrung dry. He'd never told Jake the real story behind Ben's death. He hadn't told anyone. Not even his mother.

"So stop obsessing about the past. Start thinking about the future. And if opportunity knocks . . . I hear Margaux Sullivan is back in town."

"I don't think so."

"Why the hell not?"

"I don't even know the woman."

"You knew the girl."

"Only from a distance. She didn't exactly hang out with the likes of you and me."

Jake shrugged. "Times change."

"Yeah, they do. I gave her a ticket on her way into town."

Jake barked out a laugh. "Damn, you are a glutton for punishment."

"I'm an idiot."

"That, too. You want another beer?"

"Thanks, but I told Ma I'd be by for dinner. And I thought I'd get in a quick swim down at the cove before I have to be there."

"Swimming, huh? Maybe do a little spying on a certain girl who just came home like we did in our misspent youth?"

Nick gave him a sardonic smile. "Just swimming. Want to come?"

"Hell no. It's still May; it might feel like summer, but that's because there's a storm coming. Always gets hot and muggy right before it hits. The water will still freeze your balls. Ask me again mid-July."

"I'll be too busy to swim in July."

"Then go for it." Jake's eyes twinkled. "Maybe it'll get your . . . mind off a certain person who just blew into town. Or if that doesn't work, go for it."

"In my dreams." Nick snagged a towel out of the truck and cut across the lawn to the woods where a path led down to a secluded cove. He knew he'd have it to himself. Hardly anybody swam there, even when it was warm, even when he was a kid. Mainly just the local boys and most of them had moved away.

When he reached the tiny pebbled beach, he sat down, unlaced his boots, and pulled them off. He dropped his watch into his shoes and tugged his T-shirt over his head.

With the woods on one side of the shore and the rock jetty on the other, separating the cove from Little Crescent Beach, he was completely alone. He stepped into the water and sucked in his breath. Cold all right. Bracing. Just what he needed.

Margaux had completed several pages of sketches when a two-masted sailboat appeared at the end of the Point, leaving the marina. She turned to a fresh page and captured it with fast deft strokes of her drawing pencil.

She scooted around on her butt in order to follow it out to sea, but a nearby movement caught her eye. A man stepped out of the woods and onto the pebbled beach, disturbing her concentration, not to mention her peace and solitude.

She shrank back, not wanting to disturb or be disturbed, but she didn't stop watching him. He sat down and took off his shoes. Then he pulled off his shirt and stood up.

Margaux blushed at herself for her unabashed voyeurism and the curiosity that made her wonder if he was going to shed his shorts, too. Her mouth went dry as he stretched his arms wide as if he were exalting in being free from the bonds of clothes.

He was amazing, not the lithe, gym-defined model of *GQ,* and not the sculpted freak of bodybuilding. But something so strong and masculine she couldn't look away.

He didn't strip, but walked into the water until it was waist high, then dove into the waves, as graceful as a dolphin.

A shiver ran up her spine and she was hit with a deep primal longing that shocked her, even as she recognized him. She shouldn't be reacting this way to a man she didn't even know and who she probably wouldn't like if she did. She shouldn't have that kind of feeling about anyone. She was still married, even if she was married to a lying, cheating, absconding . . . but she didn't want to think about Louis.

She wanted to watch the chief of police swim through the calm waters. His head popped up several yards farther from shore. He shook himself, at home in the water. And she wondered how he ever became a law officer. He belonged in the wild, free and—

She brought herself up sharp. *You are losing your mind.* Yeah, she had every right to, but not over a man she'd hardly ever seen, much less talked to. How could she be thinking like this? She never had these kinds of thoughts when she was working. Not even about her husband.

The realization hit her like a tidal wave. When had she stopped loving Louis? Long before he'd stolen her life. When had he stopped loving her? If he ever had. Because how could someone who loved a person, even if that love had faded, how could he have done that to her?

And how could she be sitting here indulging in totally inappropriate thoughts about a stranger?

She ordered herself to get up and skulk away before he came back, but she didn't move. He swam parallel to the shore with strong, graceful strokes. She only got a glimpse of his head and sometimes his shoulders as he cut through the water, but it was mesmerizing.

She didn't know how long she watched, but suddenly he straightened in the water, his head bobbing out of the waves; then he dove again and disappeared beneath the surface.

It was her chance to get to the other side of the jetty out of sight, but she sat still, holding her breath, waiting to see where he'd reappear. And jumped when he rose out of the water not ten feet away.

He stood there with the water sluicing down his body, looking toward the shore, tan and muscular and— He turned, saw her, his movement arrested like a startled stag.

And she was getting way too fanciful. He was a guy, nothing more. Right, so why was her heart racing like a bad case of stage fright. He cocked his head slightly, either a question or an acknowledgment of her presence. He began moving toward her but stopped when he was knee deep in water.

"I was just, uh . . ." Her brain froze; there was a gaping silence.

"Enjoying the view?"

Was she ever. But was he flirting with her or talking about the landscape?

"I was sketching." She held up her sketchbook, realized he might think she was drawing him and said hastily, "The sailboat." She pointed toward the water, knowing full well the sailboat had dipped out of sight at least ten minutes before.

"I see."

Even though his face—strong jaw, sculpted cheekbones—remained passive, Margaux swore she could see amusement in his eyes. And she could actually see his eyes; they were a deep rich chocolate. He was more approachable with those smiling eyes and she smiled back in spite of her intention to act aloof.

He started wading toward her, came to stand right below her, which put his head on the same level as her butt. She shifted her position, which she realized wasn't much better.

"We seem to be running into each other a lot," she ventured. God, where was the sophisticated woman she'd been only days ago?

"It's a small town, remember?"

"Of course I remember, it hasn't been that long since I've been back."

"No? How long?"

She shrugged. It really was none of his business and besides she couldn't concentrate with him standing so close to her. *Get a grip, he's the chief of police.*

"A few years, five maybe—eight—ten. And I certainly didn't expect anyone to be swimming. You must be freezing."

"What, you could tell by the goose bumps?" His mouth quirked up on one side.

She looked at his arms. They were covered with goose flesh. Her eyes drifted to his chest. They shouldn't have. He was very buff and the cold had made everything tight.

He hoisted himself onto the boulder, biceps swelling as they took his weight. Margaux moved back. To keep from getting dripped on, she told herself.

"Swim here a lot?" she asked weakly.

His face broke into a true smile and Margaux's stomach did a little butterfly two-step. Was this the same uptight cop who'd given her a ticket? Maybe he had a twin. An evil twin who was making her feel things she hadn't even considered for a long time. And had no right to be considering now.

"Ever since I was a kid."

Margaux nodded. She really needed to keep the distance between them. But she just felt like smiling.

"We used to climb up to these rocks and watch the summer girls lying out on Little Crescent Beach."

"We did that, too," Margaux blurted. "Watch the townie boys, I mean." She jerked her head. "But over on the other side."

"I know." He moved closer.

Margaux's breath caught, her senses alert, but he merely leaned past her to peer at the Crescent Beach side of the jetty.

He moved back into his own space and Margaux felt a traitorous stab of disappointment.

"You were one of those girls?"

"Yes," she said without thinking. "I mean. You knew we were watching you?"

"Of course. Teenage boys have radar when girls are around."

Margaux tried to think back. Surely she would have remembered him. But the past had melted into an impression, all soft lines and pastel colors. She couldn't pick him out from the others, she couldn't even remember how many there were.

"And never the twain shall meet," he said.

"A cliché."

"Kipling."

"I mean how you're using it. Town people, summer people. We're not so very different."

"Right. You should look at it from this side of the jetty—a townie's point of view."

"My father was a townie."

"But you weren't."

He was right. *Townies, summer people*. She was neither. She didn't belong here. She should never have left Manhattan. Without warning, dark panic swelled inside her, threatened to drown her.

"I have to go." She stood up abruptly, which was stupid because now the rock was wet where he'd dripped all over it. Her foot slipped and she fumbled to save her sketchbook.

Nick sprang to his feet, grabbed her arms, and steadied her.

They were standing so close that when she looked up, her hair brushed his chest. His muscles flexed, Margaux's skin tingled, and she felt that ache deep inside her. Neither of them moved. She was standing half risen on her toes, but she couldn't tell if Nick was holding her there or whether she had raised herself in order to offer her mouth.

She was definitely going stark raving mad, but she didn't care.

She tried to grab hold of her rational self, shake it awake. This was so wrong. How could she be standing here so close to another man, someone she didn't even know, and feel drawn to him? Want to lose herself in him—in someone. It had been too long.

Her eyes swam with unexpected tears. She blinked hard, trying to stop them from overflowing.

"Margaux, what is it? Are you hurt?"

He was holding her tight and she wanted to give in to his strength, but she couldn't. She had to be strong—but on her own terms—on her own. Her life, her livelihood depended on it.

"Margaux, tell me."

She shook her head, a tear flew off and landed on his shoulder. He flinched as if he'd been burned.

"I'm sorry," she mumbled. "It's nothing. Something flew in my eye. I'll be all right in a second." But her mouth twisted.

"Let me see." His hands moved from her arms and he lifted her face up, peering into her lying eyes. He lifted her eyelid.

His hands were gentle, so unlike the rest of him, hard, unyielding, and powerful.

"I don't see anything."

She sniffed. "Tears probably washed it out. That's what

they're for, right? Washing things away?" She laughed unconvincingly. "Thanks."

"No problem." His hands had moved back to her arms as if he thought she might float away if he let go. But she was caught in one of those time stretches; seconds or minutes passed, Margaux didn't know or care. She just knew she wanted to stay right where she was, give in to the strength of this stranger and feel safe if just for a few minutes.

His hands eased around her back and he pulled her closer, lowered his head.

Margaux closed her eyes.

"No. Sorry." He dropped his arms so quickly she almost stumbled. "If you're okay, I'll, uh . . . It's been nice to see you . . . again. Enjoy your sketching." He slid back into the water and looked up at her, a slight frown creasing his brow, his eyes deep and dark.

"You might want to put some sunscreen on. Your nose is turning pink."

Margaux's hand went unconsciously to her nose.

He turned and splashed back to the little triangle of pebbled beach, snatched up his shoes and shirt, and headed up the narrow path.

Margaux stared after him, feeling deflated and more alone than ever. She watched him until he was swallowed by the trees. She was rattled; alarmed at her reaction to this man she'd met once and who'd given her a speeding ticket. Horrified at the ease with which she fell under the spell of the moment. At what she was feeling.

Desire.

She sat down, her mind reeling. She had forgotten what desire felt like. Why now?

Maybe it was seeing him in all his unnerving masculinity or sitting so close that his dark eyes seemed to pierce her soul. Or because . . . She stopped herself. She was not going to follow that train of thought. It was out of the question. Ridiculous to even contemplate. How could she feel desire when her life was in shambles?

It must be some kind of fatal attraction. Because he was nothing like her ideal man. Too rough, too muscular, too . . . heavy-handed. The chief had no finesse, not in body or personality. He was there; a presence, uncompromising. And she didn't need that kind of man, she didn't need any kind of man. God knows she'd had a husband for better and definitely for worse and she certainly didn't plan to go down that road again.

And besides, she'd cried in front of him. Hopefully he'd bought the old insect-in-the-eye bit.

It was not that big of a deal, she tried to convince herself. She'd just have to tough it out next time they met. If they had to meet at all.

Of course they'd meet. Even with the additional summer people, Crescent Cove was too small a town not to run into each other all the time.

She wouldn't burst into tears every time she saw him. He'd just caught her in a fragile moment.

Hell, she never had fragile moments. And she'd be damned if she'd start now. She'd overreacted a little bit and who could blame her. It had been a long time since she'd looked at a man as a man, not just as a mannequin to drape clothes on or to accessorize the models who wore her designs. But a flesh-and-blood, virile, sensual experience . . .

She glanced once more to the path that led through the woods and touched her flushed cheek.

She yanked her hand away. It was just a little sunburn. "Ugh," she growled. She was here to reinvent herself and salvage her career, not to flirt with the local cops.

Disgusted with herself, she sat down and opened to a new page of her sketch pad, determined to work. She drew a picture of a person, a man, a merman, rising from the sea to claim his love. And he looked just like the chief of police.

Oh for heaven's sake. She ripped the page out, but there was nowhere to throw it away. She carefully stuck it between the pages of her sketchbook.

Nick didn't even bother to put on his boots, he was in such a hurry to get away. And now he was paying for it. His feet were tender from the winter and the ground was covered in debris. But he didn't stop until he was back in the truck, then he just sat behind the wheel trying to analyze what had just happened.

His entire teenage life he'd waited for Margaux to grow up, to become the person he hoped she would be. She was only about ten when she'd first sat down at "his" table at the library and began copying pictures of dresses out of magazines. It didn't seem to occur to her that he might want the table all to himself.

Maybe she hadn't even noticed him, she was so focused, even as young as she was. He was already spending lots of time at the library. He came almost every day after school and before his job at the marina. She was only there in the summers, so he knew she was a summer person.

All winter he sat at that same table with the vague sense of comfort that she would be back the next year. Then his father died and his life and his future fell apart. Even though he knew he wouldn't be going to college, he still went every day to study. He could have cried when he saw her walk through the library door the next summer. That at least was the same.

He started the truck engine. It was stupid to think about those days. She'd grown up and he'd finally gotten his chance to get an education.

Now they were both back. And what had he done? Made some stupid comment about the view when all he wanted to do was take her in his arms and make her love him. Hell, they'd been sitting right next to each other. Standing so close that her hair tickled his chest. His hands were still alive where they'd touched her arms. And he couldn't think of an intelligent thing to say. He was an idiot.

It was small consolation that she'd been just as flustered as he had been. More so. Not at all the cold, in-charge, remote woman he expected. It just made her more enticing.

And then he'd screwed it up by making her cry. He didn't get it. He could tell she was skittish as soon as he saw her. She'd practically levitated off the rocks when he sat down beside her.

But the crying thing. He went back through the conversation. They'd just been talking about the past. Teenagers spying on each other. That wasn't so bad. But those were real tears. He didn't believe she had something in her eye. He'd upset her when he wanted nothing more than to hold her, keep her safe. Hell, he'd almost kissed her. That had been close. And would have been a disaster. He was the chief of police and she was a private citizen. *He was that boy in the library and she was his talisman.*

He backed out of the McGuires' driveway, feeling emotions he shouldn't be feeling. He tried to force them back where they'd lurked for years. He didn't want them out again, didn't even want to name what he felt. Because that would put him right back standing on the jetty all those years ago, knowing that was as close as he'd ever get.

Jude smiled across the candlelit table at Roger Kyle. The tiny restaurant was quiet, with only the low murmur of conversation, the tinkling of china and crystal, and the muted strains of a string trio as background to their conversation.

Roger was an old and dear friend. She and Henry and Roger and his wife, Alice, had spent many wonderful times together. They had become closer during Alice's long battle against cancer; they were at the hospital the day she died. And Roger had been there for her when Henry died years later.

The two of them had kept up their friendship, often met for dinner, to go sailing or to a museum. She knew Roger had once hoped for more than friendship. But Jude couldn't imagine waking up to anyone other than Henry. He would always be her husband, even in death.

She had tried. She was still a young woman when she was widowed. Even Dottie, her closest friend and confidante, had urged her to remarry. She had dated several men, but Roger was the only one she continued to see through the years.

They were both getting older. Roger's hairline had receded. His hair, once the color of corn silk, had turned to white. Sailing, his passion, kept him fit, but the sun had crinkled the skin around his eyes and mouth. She didn't think of him as old, just mellowed like a good cognac.

Time had changed her, too. Though Linda had put life back into her fading hair, and exercise kept her muscles toned, she felt her years. She hadn't noticed it until today, worried about her daughter, the only thing she really had left of Henry.

An involuntary shudder passed over her. Roger looked up, their eyes met. She reached for her wineglass, but Roger's hand closed over hers and held it poised above the table. Then he drew it toward him and lightly kissed her fingers.

"I'm sorry, Roger. I'm not very good company. I just can't stop thinking about Margaux. She's so unhappy."

"Margaux's lawyer sounds up to snuff. It's pretty hard to hide money these days, even with offshore accounts or in Geneva." Roger smiled and released her hand. "I know what I'm talking about. I didn't work in the governor's office for thirty years without learning a thing or two about nefarious dealings."

"I have some savings," Jude said. "I could sell the condo. It wouldn't be close to what she lost, but it might be enough to start over again."

"Do you think Margaux would let you do that?"

Jude shook her head.

"It's an altruistic gesture, but the condo wouldn't bring nearly what it's worth in this economy. There are small business loans set up for just this kind of thing." He looked at her from beneath eyelashes bleached almost colorless from the sun. "Unless you'd like to sell and live somewhere else . . ." The sentence trailed off, leaving the question in the air. "No. Don't say it. You know you have a standing invitation and that's the last we'll say on the subject."

After dinner, Roger kissed her good night and put her into the Citroën.

"Drive carefully and call me when you get home." He stood watching from the parking lot as she drove away.

There was always a part of her that wanted to turn around and stay. Maybe once Margaux was free and her life was back on track, Jude would think about changing her life. But she knew she wouldn't. Every time she tried, something held her back. And that thing was Henry. She couldn't bear to say goodbye.

Four

 The carillon was ringing as Jude and Margaux pulled into the parking lot across the street from St. Michael's Church of the Ascension. The priest stood at the red arched doors, greeting his parishioners, his thick white hair gleaming halo-like in the sun above a gray cassock.

"It's Father Timothy," said Margaux.

"Who did you expect? Come on. You'll want to say hello."

Margaux smoothed the skirt of her black linen dress.

"You look fine," said Jude. She was wearing a jade green pantsuit and looked twenty years younger than she was. "And if anybody asks you about Louis, just say he's a lying, cheating snake and you're better off without him."

"Mom," Margaux whimpered. "I can't go in there."

"Magsy, it's the twenty-first century. Even Catholics get divorced."

"I can't. I'll meet you afterwards."

"No you won't. Father Timothy's seen you. You can't sneak away now."

Margaux reluctantly let Jude guide her across the street to the church. What if the priest asked her when she had last been to confession? She hadn't confessed in at least ten years, and there was too much she'd have to tell if she started now.

But Father Timothy just smiled and said, "Welcome back."

They walked down the aisle to the front of the church to their regular pew, the same pew Sullivans had used for three generations. Margaux acknowledged everyone's nods and smiles, but she didn't slow down. By afternoon everyone in town would know she was back. She prayed, really prayed, that no one would ask her why.

The service began. Gratefully, Margaux settled back in her seat and the next hour passed in a blur. Margaux stood, knelt, and sat at all the right times. At least most of the time. Jude only had to nudge her once when her mind wandered. So she was surprised to find everyone rising to their feet and the processional music fill the air.

She vaguely remembered Father Timothy talking about forgiveness. That's when she'd tuned out, she realized. She wasn't ready to forgive. It might be a long time before she could think of Louis without wanting to tear him limb from limb.

Outside, knots of people stood on the grass chatting. Father Timothy was standing with a spare little woman in a lavender suit and old-fashioned hat, clasping a pair of white gloves in one hand. A small boy stood next to her, holding on to the strap of her purse.

Jude guided Margaux toward them.

Father Timothy beamed at Margaux when they reached the group. "So good to have you with us."

"Thank you, Father," Margaux said meekly, feeling like a child again.

"Have you met Mrs. Prescott? One of our most faithful parishioners. Adelaide, this is Jude's daughter, Margaux."

"This is Margaux?" Mrs. Prescott said. "I wouldn't have recognized you." She exchanged smiles with Jude, one of those one-mother-to-another smiles. "Are you home for long?"

Good question, thought Margaux, and gave a noncommittal shrug.

"We'll take her for as long as we can get her," Jude said breezily. "Adelaide makes the best zucchini bread in town."

Mrs. Prescott smiled and shook her head, pleased at the compliment.

"And this is Mrs. Prescott's grandson, Connor."

"Hi, Connor," Margaux said, looking down at the boy.

"Hi." The boy's response was hardly more than a puff of air. He pressed closer to Mrs. Prescott and peeked out at Margaux from behind her skirt. He was a beautiful boy with dark expressive eyes beneath dark brown curls that just begged to be brushed off his forehead.

Father Timothy excused himself and joined another cluster of parishioners. Mrs. Prescott said goodbye and led her grandson across the street. As they reached the parking lot, Connor looked back at Margaux. She waved; he pressed closer to his grandmother and they disappeared into the maze of cars.

"Dottie's for brunch?" Jude asked as she and Margaux headed back to the car.

"Not today. I need to get groceries and I think I'll head over to Skilling's later. I never made it yesterday." And she didn't want to take a chance of running into the chief of police at the diner. She was pretty sure she'd had an erotic dream about him last night. Just as she was pretty sure that was a venal sin. The sooner she got back to the solitude of the beach house the better.

Nick was frowning when he came to a stop in front of his mother's house. He was thinking about Margaux Sullivan. He'd been thinking about her for two days. He'd even gone by the station today hoping that paperwork would keep his mind off of her. It hadn't.

Maybe an afternoon at the ball field will do the trick. He got out of the truck. Connor was waiting for him at the front door, his face pressed to the screen, and Nick forgot all about Margaux.

The door opened and Connor, wearing Ben's old high school baseball cap, struggled through the opening. Nick's throat tightened. He quickly pushed aside the memories the hat evoked and grinned at his nephew. His skinny arms were wrapped around two bats, the new red Louisville Slugger that Nick had bought him, and an old heavy wooden one for Nick. Two mitts, one small and new, the other old and beat-up, were wedged under his chin. He held a baseball in each hand.

Nick's grin widened even as something sad pulled at his heart. This was Ben's son, not his. Ben should be taking Connor to the park, just as their father had taken Nick and Ben years before.

Connor was trying to hold the door with one shoulder. His face screwed up in concentration as he struggled to ease the door shut and keep all the equipment balanced at the same time.

One mitt slipped out from under his chin. He grabbed for it and dropped the baseballs. The other mitt popped into the air and the bats clattered to the wooden stoop. One of the baseballs bounced down the steps and came to rest in the grass.

Connor was all arms and legs trying to catch everything at once. The screen door slammed and Connor froze. Slowly he straightened up, the baseball equipment forgotten. His bottom lip quivered, then his face crumpled.

Nick rushed across the lawn and took the steps in one leap. "Hey, big guy." He scooped Connor off his feet. "Ready for some batting practice?"

Connor didn't make a sound, but tears rolled down his cheeks.

"It's okay. It was just the door." Nick pulled the boy close and held him tight.

Connor was wrapped around him like a little monkey, his head burrowed into Nick's shoulder, his body trembling. He smelled like peanut butter and kid and seemed too fragile for a six-year-old. Nick rested his cheek against the boy's hair. Dark and curly like Ben's, like his, like their father's, rest his soul.

God, he felt like crying himself. He had come back to help his mother with Connor, to make things better, to fix the things he'd screwed up. He was failing.

He cleared his throat. "Hey, Connor. It was just the door. Guess the spring came loose again. I'll fix it when we get back." He'd wrench the damn thing off its hinges if he had to. He slid Connor down his side, picked up a ball, and put it into the boy's hand. He had to close the small fingers around it. He retrieved the other ball from the grass, then picked up the bats and mitts.

"Let's get this gear in the truck." He smiled down at his nephew. "Race you!" He took off at a dog trot toward the street, looking back over his shoulder.

Connor stood where he left him.

"Come on, Connor. We're outside, you can make noise."

Connor looked back at the closed door, then took a slow step, then another. Nick ran in place, pumping his arms, lifting his knees. Being ridiculous. Connor watched him, his expression worried. Nick ran in a circle around the boy. He ran backwards, panting, his tongue hanging out like one of Connor's silent cartoon characters. Then Connor's mouth popped into a gap-toothed smile and he bounded for the truck.

Connor won and they sat in the truck, grinning at each other and breathing hard. They both needed more exercise.

Nick leaned over and fastened Connor's seat belt.

"That was fun," he whispered.

The words were said so quietly Nick could barely hear them. How would the boy ever survive in school if he startled at every loud noise, only talked in whispers. It had been a disaster when Nick had registered him for kindergarten mid-year. The other kids made fun of him. The teachers were too busy to give him extra help.

The pediatrician checked him out. He was fine physically. The school psychologist ran a bunch of tests. Couldn't find anything wrong. She talked with Connor, she talked with Nick, she talked with his mother, with all of them together, and none of them could figure out why he wouldn't talk louder. And Connor wouldn't, or couldn't, tell them.

Nick cupped a hand to his ear and said in an old codger voice. "Eh?"

"That was fun," Connor whispered.

Nick moved closer until their heads were almost touching. "Eh?"

He heard Connor take a deep breath. "That was fun." But it was still a whisper.

Disappointed, Nick mustered a smile and pulled the brim of Connor's cap over his eyes. "Let's play some ball." He started the truck.

The kid spent too much time in the house with his grandmother. He was pale and thin. He had the natural grace of his father, but he didn't know how to do little boy things. He didn't jump on the bed or race through the house whooping like an Indian. He didn't even laugh out loud at the muted cartoons he watched. If Nick turned the television up, Connor just turned it down again. And he cried when the screen door slammed.

The doctor was right. Connor needed something that Nick couldn't give him, but it wasn't a special school. Connor needed a father and a mother. And Nick couldn't give him either.

"Uncle Nick?"

"What, sport?"

"Are you sad?"

"No way. I was thinking that after baseball, we'll stop at Skilling's for some ice cream. What do you say to that?"

"Okay."

An hour later, Nick turned off Shore Road into the graveled parking lot of Skilling's Ice Cream stand and pulled into a space in front of the wooden building. Baseball had been a bust. Connor's arms got tired right away. And Nick couldn't get him to run, not even to first base. He hoped to hell ice cream would salvage the day.

There was a crowd at the stand. There always was. Skilling's was probably the last place in Connecticut you could still get real homemade ice cream.

They took their place at the end of the line. Nick leaned over, close to Connor, and asked, "Know what you want?"

"Chocolate with sprinkles."

Nick smiled. That had been his favorite, too. It seemed like somebody else's life, his childhood was so remote. He looped his arm around Connor's shoulders and pulled him close. "Good choice."

They stepped up to the window. Connor's nose barely came up to the sticky sill. The teenage girl on the other side smiled at them.

"Hi, Chief. What can I get for you?" She peered down at Connor. "Are you the chief's deputy?"

Connor shook his head. Nick gave him a nudge.

"He's my uncle."

The girl looked at Nick. "What did he say?"

Nick swatted at a fly and felt sinking disappointment. "He's my nephew."

The girl looked back at Connor. "What would you like?"

"He'll have a chocolate cone with sprinkles," said Nick, too tired to even try to get Connor to speak at an audible level.

A blue sports car pulled into a space next to the truck. There was only one blue sports car in town that Nick knew of. He tried not to look but he couldn't help himself.

She was walking toward them, looking up at the board that listed the ice cream flavors. She paused for a moment reading, her head cocked up, her neck stretched like a baby bird taking food . . . *or a beautiful woman reaching up for a kiss.*

"Chief?"

"What?" The image dissipated.

"Do you want some ice cream?"

Margaux Sullivan had made her choice and was standing right behind him. His mind went blank. "Oh, uh. Chocolate with sprinkles."

Nick took out his wallet while the girl moved off to get their cones. He was acutely aware of Margaux, but he should probably pretend he hadn't noticed her. Pretend that his heart wasn't knocking like an engine with a bad carburetor. Yeah, like that was possible.

He was being ridiculous. He couldn't just ignore her. First of all, he was the chief of police. Secondly, he'd just dripped all over her at the cove the day before. Had held her close enough to feel her breath on his skin. He'd seen her cry. Surely that called for some kind of acknowledgment.

He turned around. Smiled, at least he meant to smile. It felt more like a grimace.

A quick half smile in return and she looked away to scan the menu board.

Connor tugged at his pants leg.

"What, sport?"

"Why is that lady wearing black? Did her daddy die?"

Nick cringed. Even though he whispered, Margaux had to have heard him. She had. Her cheeks turned pink. It hadn't been sunburn yesterday. She was blushing.

Margaux looked down at Connor. "Guess I'm not dressed for the beach, huh?"

Connor shook his head.

"That's because I'm from the city. We wear black there."

"Why?" he breathed.

Margaux moved closer to hear him. She was practically kneeling at Nick's feet. Not that she noticed. Her attention was focused on Connor. All Nick got was the top of her head, those bright wild curls corkscrewing in the sunlight.

"Hey, buddy, I bet our ice cream is ready." He turned Connor toward the counter. "Sorry he bothered you."

She stood. "He didn't bother me. I guess I better get out my beach clothes, though."

"No. You look fine. I mean you look . . . you look good."

"Thanks." She dipped her chin. He stared at her. He couldn't seem to take his eyes away. "Um, I think your ice cream . . ." She dipped her chin again.

"What? Oh." He turned toward the service window, glanced back at her. "Nice to see you."

He pulled out a ten-dollar bill and shoved it through the window. Took the ice cream, handed one of the cones to Connor and hustled him to a picnic table at the side of the building. He should probably have asked her to join them. No, that would be stupid. Why would she want to have ice cream with him and a kid?

A couple of minutes later, Margaux Sullivan picked her way across the gravel toward her car, licking a double pistachio ice cream. As he watched, she backed out of the parking place and slowly drove off toward Little Crescent Beach. And Nick was hit by a feeling he hadn't felt in a long time. Regret.

This was getting weird, Margaux thought as she drove away. She was prepared to see him in town occasionally. But three for three was too much. She couldn't even go for ice cream without running into the man. And his kid, she added. The same kid she'd seen at Mass. Connor Prescott. Nick Prescott.

Now she knew what the chief of police's hair would look like if he let it grow. *Like his son's, you dolt.* Her face heated all over again. She'd been having thoughts about a married man . . . with children. At least one.

Ice cream began to drip down her wrist. She licked it off and a smile crept to her lips. She'd never have figured him for a chocolate-with-sprinkles kind of guy.

The smile disappeared. The kid thought she was in mourning. A kid that young shouldn't know about mourning. But he was right.

She was mourning. Not for a father or a brother, not anymore, not even for her marriage, but over her life. And that had to stop.

The sun scudded behind a cloud, seconds later the sky turned dark. The first raindrop fell as she turned onto Salt Marsh Lane.

By the time she reached home, it was coming down in sheets. Nobody had said anything about rain.

Head tucked, she raced to the back door, dumped her ice cream in the trash, then stood in the middle of the kitchen floor, soaked to the skin. She slipped out of her espadrilles and headed for the stairs and a change of clothes.

She opened her closet door. Her city clothes were lined up neatly across the rack. She was looking at black, black slacks, black shirts, black dresses, black. She pulled out the top two drawers of her dresser but she already knew what she would find there. Black—lingerie, camisoles, blouses. All black.

The kid had nailed it, she looked like a bird of prey.

She was sure there must be some hand-me-downs or forgotten clothes in one of the closets. The Sullivans never threw anything useful away. So what if they might be a little out of date, a little faded.

It didn't matter. No one in the business knew where she was and no one at the shore cared that she wasn't dressed in the latest style.

She hit pay dirt in the bottom drawer of the dresser. There was a pair of shorts, not high-fashion, but still in wearable condition. Two pairs of stone-washed jeans and a pair of cutoffs. How about that, she *did* have cutoffs. A faded bikini that would do in a pinch. And three T-shirts with advertising across the fronts.

She went back to the closet. Rummaged in the corners where she remembered seeing a red Windbreaker and rehung it front and center.

She got down on her hands and knees and crawled into the closet, groped along the floor until she came up with a pair of pink flip-flops which she threw out into the middle of the floor. Her hand hesitated over a paint-splattered pair of sneakers, then she tossed those out, too.

She was backing out of the closet when her elbow caught the

edge of a large brown portfolio. It had been pushed to the very back corner and forgotten.

She dragged it out and carried it to her bed.

It was her first portfolio, dusty and a little frayed at the edges. She sat down on the spread and just looked at it, half curious, half hesitant to look inside. Carefully she untied the black ribbon that held it closed and opened the flap. She tipped it toward the bed and a sheaf of sketch papers slid out.

On the top was a primitive self-portrait. She picked it up and shook her head. It did resemble her in a Grandma Moses sort of way, except the hair was a deep chestnut, long and totally straight instead of red and curly. In the corner was one of her early signatures.

She put it aside and looked at the next. This was a seascape. The jetty was depicted in muddy grays on the left of the canvas. Little people dotted the bright yellow beach that spread across the bottom of the canvas.

The next was another seascape, this time in a storm. The beach glowed almost white as if lightning had just lit the sky. Whitecaps jumped out at the eye from a midnight blue sea. Waves too large for the Sound, except in a hurricane, crashed on craggy rocks in a fireworks display of spray.

"Not bad," Margaux murmured to herself. The painting, as naïve as it was, drew her in, made her wonder what was happening just outside the frame. She riffled through the rest, each getting a little more proficient. The landscapes contained more people, and the people wore more colorful outfits.

She was taken by surprise by the white wedding dress. It was one of her first fashion renderings. No landscape, no crowd of people. Only one model, one dress, with a wide billowing skirt and a train that ran off the page. It had a princess neckline with little dots Margaux thought must be seed pearls.

She remembered the day she'd drawn it. She'd been at the library looking over the newest edition of *Modern Bride*. She must have been ten or eleven. She always sat at the same table and pretended it was her studio. Except there was this older kid who always sat across from her. She didn't mind. He just read these big fat books and hardly ever moved or made a sound.

She'd seen that dress in the magazine and pulled out her sketchbook and copied it. The model had Brianna's long blond hair.

Margaux smiled and looked at the next sketch. A flounced dirndl of large red, magenta, and pink flowers. The colors should have clashed, but they didn't. Just popped the skirt off the page.

Beginner's luck, she thought as she looked through several more designs.

She'd come a long way since those early days, but she felt akin to that young girl who'd created them. Colorful. Bold. Optimistic. Joyous. This is where she had started. This was what she was, not the cold, aggressive look she had become.

Where was her joy? She'd become so serious, so competitive, so intent on staying on top that she'd lost the joy of designing.

The realization hit her hard. Had that lack of joy been partially responsible for her losing everything?

No, she argued back. *Louis is responsible for your losing everything. You would have recaptured the joy. Maybe when the fall show was over.*

Now, she wouldn't have that chance.

She returned the sketches to the portfolio, tied it together, and put it back in the closet. Joy was fine, but it didn't pay the rent.

Five

 It continued to rain through the night and Margaux opened her eyes the next morning to a rain-speckled window. She watched dumbly as the drops ran in rivulets down the pane; listened to the continuous *splat-splat* on the overhang beneath her window and closed her eyes again.

Nothing had changed. She was at the beach house, broke and out of work, and now it was raining. For a few moments while sketching out on the jetty, she'd felt almost optimistic. When she went to bed last night, she thought she might be on the mend. She fell asleep with colors dancing in her head. But this morning it was gray again. And the energy she'd felt had dissipated. She couldn't seem to muster the energy to get out of bed.

Nor did she want to. She just wanted it to all go away. To go back a few months and make things different. To go back a few years and make things different. Do anything to keep herself from being where she was now.

She pulled the covers over her head. Maybe the next time she woke up, life would be better.

The next time she woke up, she had to pee. She pushed the covers back and, shivering, trotted across the hall to the bathroom then climbed back in bed. Pulled up the quilt. Put the pillow over her head . . . and stayed awake. She turned over, cleared her mind, but it just filled up again.

A branch brushed steadily against the cedar shakes of the house. Its *swish-swish* gradually became a tormenting mantra. *Stupid, stupid, stupid.*

Stupid to have missed the signs that Louis was not her loving husband. Stupid to not keep total control of her business. Stupid to not notice the missing money. Stupid. Stupid. Stupid.

She stared out the window, the view blurred by the rain. And stupid to sit here and do nothing.

That was the trouble with being a high-achieving, workaholic A type; it was nearly impossible to sit back and do nothing. Even when she had nothing to do.

She got up and dragged on a pair of jeans she'd found the day before, surprised to find that they hung loosely on her. Not many thirty-four-year-old women could boast of still being able to fit into clothes they wore in high school. Of course most women hadn't had their life destroyed in one massive screwup.

She pulled an old T-shirt over her head and looked down to the word scribbled across her chest. *Nirvana.* If only. There wasn't a pair of socks in sight so she stuffed her bare feet into the paint-smeared sneakers and went to the bedroom door.

A glance over her shoulder told her she was in big trouble. The organized, neat-as-a-pin person she had been was MIA. Her clothes from the night before were lying where she'd left them on the floor by the bed. The dress she'd worn to Mass was crumpled on the seat of her desk chair. The quilt had fallen half off the bed and the sheet was twisted into a knot.

She turned her back on them and went downstairs.

She made coffee and stood with her forehead pressed to the window, looking out at the windswept beach. The lifeguard stand rose like a forlorn sentinel, clumps of seaweed twisted around the wooden stilts. A sheet of newspaper tumbled across the sand. Whitecaps chopped up the surface of a gunmetal gray-green sea.

The coffee grew cold in her mug. She flopped down into the

chintz easy chair and ran her index finger around the outline of a huge faded cabbage rose.

The telephone rang. She let it ring. It would be Jude wanting to have lunch, wanting to be there to support her daughter. But Margaux couldn't face her right now. It would almost be easier if Jude ranted and railed at her, blamed her for failing. Margaux could deal with that. She deserved it.

But nothing ever ruffled her mother's composure or her optimism. Even when Danny died, she went on with life, grieving deeply but inwardly, while she arranged the wake and the funeral, greeted mourners, comforted Margaux and Henry as if a piece of her hadn't died with her son.

Margaux had been young enough to think she could make up for Danny's loss. Be the best she could be, make her parents proud. Of course, she didn't realize until later that they would be proud of her no matter what she did.

A shudder racked her body; she drew up her knees and clung to them. God help her, she'd even married Louis thinking of her parents. She thought he could make her family whole again. He even looked a bit like Danny.

But he wasn't Danny, he wasn't even the man she thought she'd married.

The telephone rang again. She counted the rings—five, six, seven, eight. Then quiet.

She wasn't being fair. Jude would worry. She pushed herself out of the chair and called Jude back.

She answered on the first ring.

"Hi, Mom," Margaux said, forcing a smile into her voice. "Can you believe this weather?"

"It's supposed to last for a couple of days. Do you want me to come over? I'll bring lunch. Or we could go out."

"Thanks, but I'm set for food and I'm really busy right now. I'll call you later, okay?"

"Okay, but call my cell phone if I'm not here."

Margaux scribbled the number on the telephone pad.

"Call me."

"I will. Bye."

She didn't call Jude back that day or the next. She didn't answer the phone, but she turned on lights so her mother would know she was okay.

Two days passed, the rain kept up, Margaux's spirits plummeted. Her mind raced at night, but when she tried to think of a plan during the day, that same mind went blank.

She found a copy of *Wuthering Heights,* but even her favorite story couldn't keep away her demons. Unfortunately, Heathcliff looked an awful lot like the local police chief. She cried anyway and couldn't decide if it was for Cathy and Heathcliff or for herself.

She ran out of milk and drank her coffee black. She ate dry toast. She finished *Wuthering Heights.* Mostly she just sat in the chintz chair and stared out the window to the shore.

By the third day of rain, Margaux began to go stir-crazy. She caught herself doodling on the telephone pad. It was a drawing of the window, the column of the front porch and the beach beyond. Funny, she hadn't even been aware of what she was doing. She put the tablet back on the table and realized there were sheets of paper on the floor around her feet.

She leaned over and picked up the closest one. The couch and blanket chest that doubled as a coffee table. She reached for another. The floor lamp, its light falling onto the throw pillow, *Bless This Home.* Another sketch of the oval rag rug, the details picked out in shades of gray with her No. 2 pencil.

She slid off the chair, gathered all the papers up, then spread them out on the blanket chest. She'd drawn the whole room. The old television set. The escritoire with its curved Queen Anne legs. The fireplace surrounded by speckled bricks.

She had no memory of drawing any of them. And they were all defined in shades of gray. Like the day. Like her designs. Like her life.

The light was yellow, the couch a goldenrod tweed, the cabbage roses were pink and green with yellow sepals that had been much brighter many years ago. The rag rug had hints of blue, green, orange, lavender. They were faded, but not gray.

There was nothing black-and-white about this room. There was nothing black-and-white about the shore. Even the clouds and the gunmetal sea weren't gray. They had shades of mauve and pink and midnight blue.

She'd just bought pastels and watercolors a few days before, but her creativity had defaulted to black and white.

She couldn't remember when she hadn't designed in black. Sure there was the occasional silver detail, a hint of gray, but all her designs came from the same palette. She was known for her stark designs; black had catapulted her into the limelight.

But the designs in her old portfolio proved she hadn't always been that way.

Which was the real Margaux? The cutting-edge, black, Tulle-with-a-Bite designer or the fun, vibrant, colorful designer of her girlhood? Margaux had no idea, but suddenly she knew she had to find out.

She bounded up the stairs two at a time, tore open her closet door. She tugged her suitcase out of the closet, opened it onto the floor. She wrapped her arms around her New York clothes, lifted them out of the closet and dropped them hangers and all into the suitcase, snapped it shut, zipped it up, and rolled it down the hall to another closet and out of sight.

She was left with a bright red Windbreaker. She sat down on her bed, her hands clasped between her knees, and stared into the closet.

Besides the Windbreaker, she had two pairs of faded torn jeans, a few stretched-out T-shirts, and flip-flops. She couldn't make do with that, but she'd be crazy to buy clothes when she didn't know where her next penny much less paycheck was coming from. On the other hand, she had to start over sometime. And shopping for clothes was as good a place as any.

She'd be frugal. Besides, she doubted if Crescent Cove

Clothiers carried two-hundred-dollar jeans. She'd start with just a couple of pieces to augment her two pairs of jeans.

She shrugged into the Windbreaker and stopped to check herself out in the dresser mirror. The Windbreaker had a certain retro charm, but her hair . . . It stuck out like a rusted scouring pad and clashed terribly with the red of the Windbreaker. She tried to run a brush through it but it was no-go.

She found a hair elastic and forced the wild frizz into a ponytail. She looked around for a baseball cap to camouflage the rest. She found one in the foyer closet, next to a huge blue and white UConn umbrella.

She tucked her ponytail through the hole and pulled the cap down hard over the rest. She snatched up the umbrella and her purse and hurried out to the car.

She had to lean forward to see past the wipers and through the fog and rain. Slowly, she drove toward town.

In summer, the rain drove everyone from the beach into the shops, the movie house, the bowling alley. But today without the summer people, downtown was virtually empty.

That was fine by her. She found a parking place right in front of Crescent Cove Clothiers. They were having their end-of-winter sale and she bought a pair of khaki trousers, a green sweatshirt with a picture of a palm tree on the front, and two packages of crew socks.

Clutching her shopping bag under the umbrella, she jogged two doors down to a new store in town. They sold two-hundred-dollar jeans. They also appeared to be going out of business. Prices were slashed; the slashes were slashed. Even the price of the two-hundred-dollar jeans.

She bought several T-shirts in various colors, a blue pin-striped tailored shirt, a pair of navy blue capris, and another sweatshirt, this one in magenta. At the last minute she snagged a skimpy knit dress in shimmery moss green.

The salesgirl was ecstatic. Margaux was their only customer.

Margaux was pretty pleased, too. Her whole shopping spree

had come to less than eighty-five dollars. She couldn't think of a single thing in her wardrobe that cost less than eighty-five dollars. Underwear maybe.

Her stomach rumbled, and for the first time in days, maybe weeks, she was hungry. She turned automatically toward Dottie's diner but checked herself. She loved Dottie and didn't want to hurt her feelings, but her new state of optimism was too fragile to test in public.

She turned down Barton Street where she saw a sign that looked like it might be a sandwich place and took temporary respite from the rain beneath one of the green awnings that seemed to have sprouted up around Crescent Cove. Two large barrel planters were filled with geraniums and a sandwich board by the door announced *Granny's Attic Memorial Day Sale.*

Memorial Day was nearly a month away, but Margaux couldn't blame them for getting an early start. There didn't seem to be a lot of foot traffic in Crescent Cove, off season, especially down the side streets, especially in the rain.

The drops began to let up and she hurried toward her destination.

There was no green awning over the next door. No flowers, just a window with black lettering, *Grace Holcombe Attorney-at-Law,* and in smaller letters, *Real Estate Agent.* Margaux jumped back. How stupid of her; she knew Grace's office was on Barton Street. But she wasn't ready to see Grace. She looked like hell. Her hair was frizzy.

Stop making excuses. Grace wouldn't care what she looked like. With any luck she might not even be in the office. But she refused to skulk around just to avoid her. She hadn't seen Grace in years, and now she felt guilty for not making the effort to stay in touch. They'd been best friends, for hell's sake. Some kind of friend she was. But then the telephone worked both ways. Grace could have called her.

Well, there was no time like the present. She opened the door to the law office and stepped inside.

She would have known Grace anywhere. She was just an older version of the wiry, nearsighted kid she'd been when they'd met twenty-seven years before. She was still petite, though her blue-black pigtails and severe bangs had been replaced with a sleek face-frame hairstyle. Her long thick lashes were no longer hidden behind thick, black-rimmed glasses.

Grace had followed them around one summer, looking so plaintive, that Margaux and Brianna finally took pity on her and let her tag along. She spent the rest of the summer explaining to them why they were lucky to have her as a friend and promised them that when she was a lawyer they could come to her for free.

Margaux smiled. None of them thought they would ever need a lawyer in those days. Margaux hadn't even been sure what people hired lawyers to do.

Now she knew all too well.

Grace looked up from her computer, squinted at her, and blinked several times.

"Mags? Margaux?"

Margaux nodded. Grace jumped up from her chair and raced around the edge of her desk, but drew herself up short just before reaching Margaux.

"I can't believe it. What are you doing here?"

Margaux's mouth went dry. She shrugged. "I know I look frightful, but I just wanted to see you." She gave Grace an awkward hug.

"You look . . . great." Grace looked around the tiny office. "Here, sit down." She reached for a chair. A pile of papers slid to the floor. "Oh hell. I'll put the closed sign up. Let's go to lunch. But not Dottie's. I want you all to myself."

"Good. I'm starving. There's a place at the end of the block that looks nice."

Grace flipped a sign over, grabbed a huge overstuffed purse, and scuttled Margaux out the front door.

"I bet you're a good lawyer," Margaux said as she was force-marched down the sidewalk while trying to hold the UConn umbrella over both of them as well as her unwieldy bunch of shopping bags.

"Thanks. I am, but not a very busy one at the moment."

"That's where the real estate part comes in?"

"You got it."

Margaux shook her head. Leave it to her childhood friend to figure out how to eke out a living in a small town whose populace would rather argue over a beer at Deke's than go to court, and who for the most part had owned their homes for at least two generations.

They went to a cute little bakery called Cupcakes by Caroline. Grace had always had a sweet tooth; it looked to Margaux as if that hadn't changed either. Grace was packing a few extra pounds. Well within the normal limit, Margaux reminded herself. She was just used to anorexic models.

It turned out that Caroline, who was definitely packing a few extra pounds, also served lunch as well as cupcakes, homemade bread, cookies, and a variety of pastries. They chose a table in a brick alcove and ordered the special. Salad niçoise and mint iced teas.

"I loved that spread in *Vogue* last year," Grace said, reaching for a fresh breadstick and slathering it with butter. "I bought two copies. There was a run on them at Dingley's Drugs. I had to go all the way to one of those mega bookstores on the highway. I took a copy to Brianna—"

"Brianna was here?"

"Still is. You *have* been out of touch. She moved back seven or eight years ago. Long story." Grace looked pensive for two seconds before she was off and running again. "Oh Lord. Remember how you used to dress her up in your fashion concoctions?"

"I remember, unfortunately. You guys were good sports to put up with me."

"Remember the wedding dress you made out of your grandmother's tablecloth?"

"How could I forget? Bri stole her mother's negligee to use for a veil and we went outside to take pictures. Then the lifeguard laughed at her and she got all huffy and snatched the negligee off and tore the strap."

Grace's face sobered.

"What?"

"You know the lifeguard?"

"Yeah, skinny guy, kind of cute, and had it bad for Brianna."

"He died."

"That's terrible. How?"

"In one of those wars—Iraq, Afghanistan. Nobody was real clear on the details. It happened a couple of years ago. Brianna was upset. Not that she'd seen him in ten years or ever did anything more than giggle in front of him. But you know Brianna. She's sensitive."

Margaux knew. Brianna could go from Little Miss Sunshine to Lady Macbeth in a heartbeat. She'd been a successful model. Then her name had dropped out of the public eye, and Margaux had lost track of her.

"I didn't know she'd moved back. What happened?"

"I'll let Bri tell you. She bought that big farmhouse near Skilling's Ice Cream. The one that used to have horses. She's renovating, little by little."

"A huge job if it's half as bad as I remember."

"Huge," Grace agreed.

A young waitress brought their salads. Grace dug in but Margaux had lost her appetite. "I've been a terrible friend."

Grace looked over her fork of tuna. "Nah, just unmindful. We kept expecting you to come home for a visit and you never did. Then life happened. But what the hell. We're all here now."

By the time the waitress cleared their plates, both salads

were gone, along with two Key lime cupcakes and two skinny cappuccinos—to make up for the cupcakes—and they were chattering away like they'd never been apart.

Grace looked at her watch. "Yikes. We've been here two hours. I have to be in court." She pushed her chair back. "How long are you staying?"

The inevitable question. Margaux hesitated. She'd made it all the way through lunch without divulging her true situation to Grace. Which was easy because they'd been reminiscing about the past.

"Well. I'm not sure." And suddenly she didn't want to be keeping secrets anymore. She took a breath and plunged in. "I'm getting a divorce. My husband cleaned me out, I've lost my business, my studio, everything. I'm here because, dear Grace, I have no place else to go."

Grace sat down. "Shit. Do you have a good lawyer?"

Margaux smiled in spite of the stinging in her eyes. "A shark, but she isn't cheap. She's working on spec so far."

"Well, I'm cheap if it comes to that."

"Thanks. Still doing pro bono work?"

"Of course. I have a case this afternoon. But what are you up to Saturday? I'm pretty sure Brianna is free. We could spend the day doing something."

"Or nothing. Come to the beach house."

"Like old times?"

"Happier times."

"Sounds like a plan. You want me to call Bri?"

Margaux nodded. "Tell her to bring her swimsuit in case it stops raining." She frowned. "I don't suppose she's gotten fat or anything, has she?"

Grace laughed. "Like that was the worst thing in the world." She patted her midsection. "But no. She's just as thin as she ever was."

"Rats," said Margaux, and they both laughed.

"Like you can complain."

"I know, I've dropped a few pounds with all this mess."

"You find the beach umbrellas, we'll bring steaks and fix-ings, wine . . ."

"And cupcakes," they said together.

It was a full-fledged downpour when they came out of the café. The wind drove heavy sheets of rain across the street at an oblique angle. Margaux dropped Grace at her office and hur-ried back to her car on Main Street.

Lightning cracked and thunder boomed almost simultane-ously. She sprinted across the sidewalk. Another crack of light-ning. She dove into the front seat as the air filled with ominous rumbling. That had been really close, already she heard sirens slicing through the downpour. She backed the car out and pro-ceeded cautiously down Main Street.

She'd only gone a block when she saw the reflection of red and yellow lights ahead. A cop in a yellow slicker motioned her to turn. A tree lay across the street. Wires were down. All cars were being rerouted.

Only there didn't seem to be any other cars. As she drove down a back street toward the shore she began to think it was downright spooky, as if she might be the last person on earth.

The rain pelted the windshield. The Toyota shuddered in the wind. Margaux hunched over the steering wheel, but even with the defrost pumping out hot air and the wipers on high, she could barely see the road in front of her.

It happened so fast she had no time to brake. A tiny figure darted into the street. Her mouth opened in a silent scream. She swerved to the right, hit the brakes, and slammed into the curb.

"If it doesn't stop raining," Dottie said, looking morosely out the diner window at the rain-swept street, "we'll have moss growing on our butts."

"Hmm," Jude said. "Why the heck doesn't she answer the phone?"

"Maybe she went to the mall. Hell, if you're worried you should go over there."

"I don't want to be one of those overbearing mothers that hovers and fusses and gives unwanted advice."

"You?" Dottie snorted. "There's a difference between being supportive and being a buttinsky. And you have never been or ever will be the latter."

"Sometimes it's hard to understand that when you're on the receiving end."

"There is that," Dottie said.

But Jude wanted to do something. She knew how it felt to be lost. When Danny died, she had kept going because Margaux and Henry needed her. But when Henry died, Margaux had Louis, and Jude had crawled into bed and stayed there until Dottie drove up to Hartford and yanked her onto her feet and back into living.

She thought that Margaux was going through her own kind of grieving.

"Hell, she's better off without that conniving son of a bitch. He was never my favorite person. Who can like a man who turns up his nose at fries with gravy?"

Jude laughed in spite of her mood. "You were right."

And so was Henry. He had taken an immediate dislike to Louis, but she thought it was just a father's jealousy. It was their first Christmas without Danny. Louis was miserable the entire week—the cold, the sand, the old plumbing. And it made Henry crazy. He loved Christmas and he missed his son.

That night as they lay side by side, he pulled her close and whispered in her ear, "I don't think that young man's right for our Magsy."

"Nor do I," she whispered back. "But if she loves him . . ."

"Then we'll have to love him, too." Then he kissed her. They snuggled under the covers, and fell asleep, encircled in each other's arms.

Jude ran her tongue over lips that felt suddenly dry. It had taken thirteen years, but Louis had proved them right in the end. She was just glad Henry wasn't here to see it.

Rain always brought a new set of problems to the shore, and three days of rain taxed Nick's small staff to the limit. Lightning had struck a transformer, plunging a quarter of the outlying town into darkness for nearly six hours. Then there were a slew of fender benders, a heart attack, a flooded bridge, and several drifting boats.

Nick didn't have much time to eat or sleep. He had even less time to think about Margaux Sullivan, which was fine with him.

Two evenings in a row, his mother called frantic with worry. Connor had wandered off. So Nick, instead of going home, cruised the neighborhood looking for a small boy. The first night Nick had found him standing in the rain, at the corner of his street. He told Nick he was waiting for him to come home from work.

The second night, the fog was so thick that Nick drove past him twice even though Connor said he'd waved to him. Nick's blood ran cold. Connor could have been killed. It didn't soothe Nick to find him sitting at the kitchen table drinking hot cocoa when he finally returned to the house.

Connor's wanderings were something new. The whispering and starting at loud noises, Nick could handle; his mother was there for the nightmares, but this new thing was out of their control. What if he wandered onto the highway, got lost in the woods. Or worse, picked up by some psychopathic predator.

And now a tree had fallen across Main Street, bringing down several lines with it. He was standing in the rain cursing the power company for being slow to respond when his cell rang. He looked at caller ID. His mother and he knew what she was going to say.

"Yeah, Ma. Okay, calm down. When did you see him last?" Nick cursed silently as a hundred disasters shot through his mind. A felled tree, lightning, a car, a live wire. Connor was missing; he could be lying hurt somewhere, he could be— He put Finley in charge and left the scene.

Margaux sat clutching the steering wheel, her heart pounding. It had been a child, a child out alone in this weather. His parents should be shot. And where was he? She looked out the window but couldn't see him. She hadn't hit him. She was sure of that.

But she couldn't just drive away. She forced open the door; the wind snatched it out of her hand. The rain hit her so hard she thought it must be sleet. Leaning into the rain, she searched the asphalt to make sure no small body lay broken there. Peered across the street and saw him standing beneath a tree, as frozen as a statue.

Lightning flashed, Margaux screamed and ran toward the boy.

But the thunder sounded far away. Thank God, the storm was moving off.

She knelt down beside him. "Are you hurt?" She had to yell to be heard over the rain and wind.

His head was bowed, but he shook it, no.

"Are you lost?"

He nodded. And looked up.

It was the chief's kid. Connor Prescott. How could this be? Surely they wouldn't let their kid out in the rain.

"Remember me? Margaux? We met at church."

He looked at her with those big eyes and she saw that he was shivering.

"I know you're not supposed to go with strangers, but I'm not really a stranger. I'm Jude Sullivan's little girl. Will you let me take you home?"

He nodded and held out his hand.

She took it. Small and cold and trembling. She hurried them across the street and into the car. But before she drove away, she reached into the backseat and grabbed her new sweatshirt.

She pulled it over the boy's head and helped him to thrust his arms into the sleeves. Then she buckled his seat belt.

"Do you know where you live?"

He said something.

She leaned closer. "Where?"

"At Nana's." It was a mere whisper.

"What's the address?"

He shrugged.

"Phone number?"

He shrugged again and his bottom lip began to quiver.

Weren't people supposed to teach their children to know these things? Especially a police chief.

She grabbed her cell phone and called Jude. It was hard to make herself heard with the storm blocking decent reception. But finally Jude understood, gave her the address, and said she would call Adelaide Prescott to let her know he was safe.

The Prescotts lived just a few blocks from downtown in a neighborhood of gray-shingled capes. All the lights were on. As Margaux pulled into the driveway, the side door opened and Mrs. Prescott came out grasping an umbrella above her head.

Margaux quickly got Connor out of his seat belt, then ran around to the passenger side and lifted him out of the car. He was cold and clammy and shaking convulsively. With Mrs. Prescott trying to hold the umbrella over them, Margaux carried him into the house.

"He's all right," she said before anything else. The older woman's pallor was ghastly. "Really. Some dry clothes and some soup and he'll be good as new." At least she hoped so.

Connor was still clinging to her so she carried him down the hall to a bedroom that looked like it had belonged to a teenager. Mrs. Prescott handed Margaux a large towel and Margaux began stripping off his wet clothes while his grandmother rummaged in drawers for dry ones.

Together they had him dry and warm and within minutes he was sitting at the kitchen table with a cup of hot chocolate.

"Are you sure you won't let me give you something dry to wear? At least a cup of coffee? I called Nicky."

"Nicky?" asked Margaux, getting a sudden sinking feeling.

"He's the chief of police, they had an emergency, but he's on his way home. I'm sure he'll want to thank you."

He's on his way home. "Thanks, but I really have to go. Bye, Connor, and no more running out in the street, okay?"

The boy looked up, a chocolate mustache framing his upper lip. He smiled and nodded his head.

She turned to leave. Her fingers made it to the doorknob before the door flew open, pushing her back into the room, and she came face-to-face with Nick Prescott.

He was dressed in a gray rain slicker, his hair was dripping into his face. He stopped dead as he recognized her.

"He's fine," she said, and eased around him to the door for a quick getaway.

Nick rushed toward the table but pulled up when Connor shot Margaux a frightened look.

"Easy, he's okay," she said quietly, hoping to make her point. All that intensity was scaring the boy, even if it was because Nick was scared.

Nick stopped, walked more slowly toward Connor's chair, and knelt down beside it. "Hey, buddy, you can't—" He pushed a curl from Connor's forehead. "I was worried about you."

"Margaux found me," Connor whispered, and wrapped his arms around Nick's neck.

Margaux didn't wait to hear more, but slipped out the door into the rain.

She made it to her car before the kitchen door opened and Nick ran out.

She braced herself while the rain pelted her shoulders and face and drenched her already drenched clothes.

He came to a stop in front of her. "Thank you. Just . . . thank you."

"You're welcome," she said.

"I don't know what I'd— Jesus, what am I thinking? You're all wet."

Margaux laughed, whether from pent-up nerves or from the irony of his statement.

"I didn't mean— I meant—"

"I hope you meant I should get out of the rain."

He looked up as if he just became aware that it was pouring. "Right." He grabbed her door and yanked it open. She got into the driver's seat.

He looked in after her, then shut her door. He stood in the driveway while she backed out, then shot both hands through his dripping hair and walked slowly into the house.

Six

 Margaux opened her eyes to a sunny morning. *Thank you thank you thank you.* A new day, the sun was out, her friends were coming tomorrow. Surely life was looking up. She pushed back the covers and opened the window. Crisp and cool but not a cloud to be seen.

She spent the morning cleaning house, something she hadn't done in years. She scrubbed counters and polished furniture, ran the vacuum. While she was busy, she hardly thought about the uncertain future that loomed ahead of her. She knew she should make calls, take a job with one of the big designers, and slowly climb back to the top.

But even now, pride kept her from picking up the phone. She'd paid her dues, worked unceasingly to attain her dream, only to have it brought down by a man she trusted and thought she loved. She wouldn't make that mistake again.

Whenever the underlying panic erupted and threatened to drown her, she thought of her friends coming tomorrow and she felt better.

When the house was clean, she wandered to the front porch rail. There were several intrepid sunbathers on the beach getting an early jump on summer. A few doors away, beach towels were draped over the rail of the Doyles' front porch. Mr. Doyle stood on the steps smoking a cigar and looking out over the water. Two doors down, Sarah Thompson was planting zinnias along the front of her house.

Life at the shore.

Her life for now, and it was time she embraced it. She went inside and called Jude.

"The grill? Probably in the shed."

The shed's hinges were a little rusty—everything rusted in the salt air—but the door opened easily enough. The inside was filled with mountains of tarp-covered shapes. Things hung from racks on the wall and from the ceiling, but there was no grill in sight.

Margaux stood in the opening, stymied. Normally at this point, she would have given up the search, gotten in the car, and driven to the nearest hardware store to buy a new one. But those days were over. She wasn't even sure she had enough gas to get to town, much less the money to buy a grill.

She ducked under a cloud of cobwebs and went inside.

Beneath the first tarp, she found a wicker chair and dragged it into the yard. It was painted white with a rounded back and blue-striped cushions; it looked so comfortable, evoked so many memories, that she was tempted to sit down. She pushed it aside and went back into the shed.

She heard the *beep-beep* of Jude's Citroën. She stuck her head out of the shed; this time she forgot to duck and got a face full of spiderweb.

Jude got out of the car.

"Hi, Mom," Margaux said, picking the gossamer spiderweb from her face. "You didn't have to come."

"I can find it faster." She ducked into the shed. "It's probably behind the love seat. Grab that other end. We might as well get out the porch furniture now. It's almost summer."

They carried the love seat and two chairs around to the porch.

"There," Jude said, slapping her hands together and standing
back to look at the furniture. "Just like—summer," she ended
lamely.

Margaux knew she was thinking of the days when all four of
them had sat on the porch, happy and content and not suspect-
ing the tragic change that lurked ahead.

"Let's go find the grill."

Jude smiled distractedly, but led the way. They found the
grill at the back of the shed. Margaux rolled it outside. "It looks
pretty beat-up."

"Just let the fire burn off all the gunk and it'll be fine. What
are you going to grill?"

"Bri and Grace are coming out tomorrow. They're bringing
steaks."

"How wonderful. I'm sorry I'll miss them."

"You're invited to drop by."

"Can't. I'm going sailing."

"Sailing? You're kidding. You can't swim."

"Yes I can. Learned at the Y three years ago."

"And did you learn to sail there, too?" Margaux asked, peering into the shed looking for the grilling utensils.

"No. I'm going out with Roger Kyle. He taught me."

Margaux stopped, looked at Jude. "Roger Kyle?"

"You remember Roger and his wife Alice. Your father and I
used to go out with them a lot, back before . . . Now that Alice
and Henry are gone . . . well, Roger and I meet occasionally
just to stay in touch."

And her mother was explaining way too much. Which
meant there was a lot more she wasn't saying. But it wasn't
Margaux's business what her mother did, or whom she saw.
Roger Kyle was a nice man. But he would never—Jude would
never.

She found the utensils, then went back into the shed and
tossed out the beach umbrellas. Behind them, her old bicycle
leaned against the back wall.

She rolled the bike out into the sunlight. "Look what I found."

"Oh Lord. I didn't know we saved that."

It was a purple mountain bike with a big wire basket and a flat front tire. Spiderwebs clung to the seat and a rust spot was creeping down the crossbar. But the Bon Jovi license plate on the back had escaped unharmed.

"I was thinking I needed some exercise. This should do it." Not to mention it would save on gas.

Margaux went back inside the shed and found the air pump. It was hanging from a peg on the wall. The Sullivans might be pack rats, but they were organized pack rats. "A little soap and water and WD-40 and it will be as good as new."

"Please practice before you decide to ride it down Shore Road."

"Think I've forgotten how to ride a bike?"

"I just think you should practice before you go into traffic."

After Jude left, Margaux went inside to clean off the dust and spiderwebs. One look in the bathroom mirror told her that either it was Halloween or she needed some serious repair work. Why hadn't Jude said something? Her hair was a wreck, but that was just the first catastrophe. There were dark circles beneath her eyes; the skin was drawn across her cheekbones. Her face looked like it had never seen a makeup brush. She leaned into the mirror. Damn, she had a freckle.

In her business, image was everything and it was about time she did something about hers. And her first stop would be Jude's "genius" on Marina Street. Even if it turned out to be a disaster, it couldn't be worse than this. She could always get it fixed when she got back to New York. And if the cut was decent, at least her friends wouldn't feel sorry for her.

The Cut 'n Curl took up half of the first floor of an old white Victorian house across the street from the marina. Margaux almost drove past it. It had been newly painted a soft mauve.

Shutters and porch were moss green, edged with a fine detailing in burgundy. White gingerbreading ran beneath the roof and the eaves of the porch. To the left of the entrance, a huge bay window overlooked the street and marina. On the right, a painted wooden sign hung above the porch rail. *Le Coif* was scripted out in gilt letters.

Margaux just hoped the stylist was as good as the paint job.

She parked across the street in front of the seawall that ran along the cove that gave Crescent Cove its name. Below it was a small marina, used mostly by locals, with one gas pump, a bait shop, and no amenities other than some benches where old-timers sat and reminisced.

Margaux got out of the car, crossed the street, and climbed the steps to the porch. A sign in the door's oval window read, *I'm in.*

"Terse but to-the-point," she muttered, and pushed the door open. Above her head, chimes played the "Toreador Song" from *Carmen.*

The foyer was softly lit from an overhead chandelier. In the center of the oak floor, a shag rug depicted a smiling Elvis Presley. The smell of ammonia and hair products permeated the air.

Margaux looked into a door on her left. The room was empty but filled with morning light. She was just about to try the door on her right when it opened and a woman, dressed in a *Beauticians Do It with Style* T-shirt, black leggings, and chartreuse bunny-fur slippers, stepped out. She was about five feet tall, with black spiked hair shot with gold streaks. An open paisley smock flapped around her calendar girl's figure and she held a mug filled with yellow liquid.

She stopped when she saw Margaux, peered out from behind cat-eye glasses, and screeched, "Holy moly!" in an unmistakable Brooklyn accent. The liquid sloshed out of her mug onto the floor. She rubbed the spot away with her toe.

"Chamomile, good for the wood. Linda Goldstein," she said, pumping Margaux's hand. She immediately released it, pulled her glasses to the tip of her nose, and peered over them.

Margaux was about to turn and run when the hairdresser grabbed her by the elbow and pulled her inside a room crammed with salon equipment.

A long Formica counter ran across the far wall. A huge bank of mirrors partially obscured the windows behind it. Three sinks were attached to the back wall, each with a padded reclining chair facing the room. A display of hair care products was lined up across the marble mantel of the fireplace left over from the original parlor. It was the same layout as the Cut 'n Curl, but somehow, it looked brand-new.

Linda flicked a switch beneath the counter and a marquee of lights flared to life around the mirrors. She turned to frown at Margaux.

"Damn, don't know if you need a hug or a cut first. Let's go for the hair. It'll be the easiest fix. I know hair. Whatever else is making you look like you do is beyond me."

She nudged Margaux into the salon chair, then whirled it around to face the mirror. She stood behind Margaux, lifted and dropped her hair, batted it with her fingers, capped it close to her head.

"Uh-huh. Beneath that frizz, I see a good cut. Fifth Avenue? Jacques Cotille or I don't know my hairdressers. Surprised you, didn't I?"

"How did you—yes, it is."

"Not your fault. Not Jacques's either. Good cut, but not for the shore. Too short or too long. If you get what I mean." She grabbed a fistful of Margaux's hair. "Too thick. In this humidity, the bulk's gotta go. Lucky for you, you came to the right place."

Unconsciously, Margaux reached up to smooth back her hair.

Linda expelled a gust of air. "Well, that's a good sign. Whatever's wrong, it isn't so bad if you're worried about your appearance. What I say is if you have the right outfit and the right hairstyle, the rest is a piece of cake."

"There's nothing wrong," Margaux said defensively.

Linda pulled her glasses down to look over the rims at Margaux. "What? You always walk around looking like you just lost your last cabana boy?"

Margaux barked out an involuntary laugh.

"That's better."

"Okay, do whatever you think best. I'm in your hands."

Linda guffawed. "You know the rest of the joke that goes with that punch line?"

Margaux laughed. "No, but I can imagine."

Linda took out a pink plastic cape and snapped it in the air. "All right, Mags. You don't mind if I call you Mags, do you? Used to be this girl in beauty school, her name was Margo. She was a first-class *beyotch,* nah I take it back, there was nothing classy about her."

"How did you know my name?" asked Margaux, wondering if Linda was actually a lunatic impersonating a beautician.

Linda shrugged. "Crystal ball? Or is it because you and Jude have the exact same color hair. Hell, if I could bottle it, I'd retire."

She motioned for Margaux to follow her to the sink.

"Sometimes I cut curly hair dry, but this"—she pushed Margaux into the reclining chair and took her hair in both fists—"this could give me a hernia."

She began humming as she lathered Margaux's hair. Her fingers moved from her scalp to the base of her neck and she massaged the tight muscles there. Margaux gave in to the experience and began to relax. After a lukewarm rinse, she wound a towel around Margaux's head and held it while Margaux moved back to the counter.

With a magician's flurry, she pulled the towel off, tossed it over the back of the adjacent chair, and lined up several scissors and razors on the counter.

Margaux swallowed and hoped for the best. It would always

grow out again. And it couldn't look worse than it did already . . . she hoped.

Linda combed out her hair with quick jerky movements. She parted the bottom layer of hair and pinned the rest to Margaux's head.

Just breathe, Margaux told herself.

Linda picked up a pair of scissors and snipped at the air.

"What are you going to do?"

"Hell if I know. Get out the garden shears?" She patted Margaux's caped shoulder. "There, there, don't worry. Think Rodin and a block of stone. I'll just start hacking away until something comes to me." Linda snorted and took a gulp of tea that had to be cold by now.

Margaux closed her eyes while a comb raked down the length of hair. She felt a tug, heard a snip.

Linda parted out another section and clipped the rest back. "When was the last time you had this thinned?"

"I don't. It looks better in the city." Margaux couldn't believe that she was apologizing for her two-hundred-dollar cut. "I know how to look good. It's my business to look good. I'm usually . . ." She wound down. Usually what? Whatever it was, she wasn't that now.

"That's the reason I left in the first place."

"What is?" asked Margaux, totally not following the non sequitur.

"Too much freaking stress, too much hard edge. Always being on, never relaxing for a second. A person needs a place to blossom, am I right? Take me. I was a hard-assed dynamite hair designer. I could turn out a classic do asleep with my eyes closed. Then one day I got a wake-up call when two of my appointments showed up at the same time. And damn me, they looked exactly alike. I was ready to pack in the scissors. I mean Pete and Repeat. Who needs that shit? Life is too short. Am I right?"

Margaux opened her mouth.

"I stood on my feet three hundred fifty-one days of the year just so I could spend two weeks on my butt at the beach. Last year, when I was up here for the summer, I thought, What the shit. A little change of pace, a little ocean view, freaking-freezing-in-the-winter air. A new me. So I stayed. People have to have their hair cut no matter where they live. Job security. It's great to be needed. Makes you fit in right off the bat."

Margaux couldn't imagine this brazen-mouthed Brooklynite fitting in with the quiet seaside residents. Her mouth would have most of them running in horror if her personality didn't, but no one had said a bad word about her.

"And I get to experiment."

"Experiment? How so?"

"What? Don't you trust me?"

An hour later, Linda handed Margaux a mirror and spun the chair around.

"Am I good, or what?"

Margaux stared. It had shape. It softened her face, made her look less harsh. "You're better than good. You're a genius."

Margaux shook her head; strands swirled across her face. "It moves!" she exclaimed. "What did you do? Am I going to be able to do it myself?"

"I just thinned and feathered and layered and prayed. Lightning didn't strike and your hair looks great."

"It does. How much do I owe you?"

"How 'bout twenty bucks."

"Are you kidding? Do you know how much this cut would cost in New York?"

"Yep, two hundred, two-fifty. That's what I used to charge. But like I said. That's why I left. So now I gouge the tourists all summer so I can do what I want for the rest of the year."

Margaux paid her twenty and left a twenty-dollar tip. She might be broke but that didn't mean she had to cheat people who still had a living to make.

Linda just gave her a look and stuffed both twenties down her shirt.

Margaux glanced at herself in the mirror. Who would have thought it? Right here in the back roads of Connecticut—a mouth like Joan Rivers, a figure like Marilyn Monroe, and a genius like Vidal Sassoon. It was amazing and the new haircut really raised Margaux's spirits.

Linda handed Margaux a tube of hair product. "Use that when it's raining. On the house."

She walked Margaux out to the foyer. "You don't know anyone who wants to rent a retail space?" She lifted her chin toward the open door Margaux had seen on her way in.

"I live upstairs, but I rented this out to a couple of aliens from the sixties last summer. It opened and tanked before Labor Day. A glorified head shop. Remember those? Well, these guys couldn't sell a hookah to an opium addict. Pitiful. Knew it was a mistake from the beginning. They kept snagging my clients coming and going. I was glad to see the back of them. But it's been vacant all winter. I wanted to get a nail place in or some kind of spa thing, but hell, nobody's starting up businesses these days."

"Don't I know it," Margaux mumbled, mostly to herself.

Linda narrowed her eyes at Margaux. "Doesn't mean they couldn't if they had product."

"Sorry, I don't know of anybody. I just got back myself."

"How long you staying?"

"I'm just doing some R and R."

"Yeah," said Linda, and walked her out to the porch.

"Well, thanks again." Margaux started down the steps just as the chief of police came around the corner.

He looked up as if he'd heard her, their eyes met, and for what seemed like an eon, neither of them moved. She was vaguely aware that Linda was quietly warbling the theme from *Beauty and the Beast.*

The chief moved first. He began walking toward her.

"Gotta run," Margaux said, and sprinted across the street to her car.

Nick stared after the retreating figure. He'd almost walked straight into her before he recognized her because that wild lush hair was now sleek and shiny.

A classy cut, he guessed, but it made her look more like the unapproachable New York fashionista that she was. Not that he should care. He had no intention of approaching her at all.

And it was obvious by her reaction that she had no intention of letting him approach her, even if he wanted to. Which he didn't and wouldn't. Unless she broke the law.

Before he could slip away, he was flagged down by his land-lady. She was dressed like a suburban house frau in some kind of god-awful printed coat and green furry slippers. But she was a crass New Yorker who kept him in stitches, not an easy feat these days.

"Yo, my man, whatcha got to smile about?" Linda gave him her trademark toothy grin.

"Your shoes."

"Huh."

"Was that Margaux Sullivan who just left?" Stupid question. He knew it was.

"Well, that answers *my* question. And my answer gives you the answer to your question."

Nick laughed. "Has it ever occurred to you that a simple yes or no might do the trick?"

"Nope. Where's the fun in that? Did you come to hit me up for a cup of coffee?"

"If you're offering."

"Come on. I'll see if I can rustle up a slice of twenty-year-old fruit cake to go with it."

Nick followed her inside. The smell of baking had awak-ened him that morning. His apartment was right over Linda's kitchen, and whenever she cooked, Nick got the aromas. Baking won out over stuffed cabbage any day.

"So what are you doing home in the middle of the day?" She took a bag of coffee out of the freezer.

"Having lunch and making some phone calls."

Linda put a finger to her chin. "Let's see. You always have lunch at Dottie's, so you must be making calls that you don't want anyone else to hear." She ran water into the coffee carafe and began filling the coffeemaker.

She was not only funny, she was damn astute.

"Connor ran away again last night. I have to make an appointment with the kiddie shrink."

"The kid needs a mother."

"Uncle is the best I can do."

"How long have you had a thing for Margaux Sullivan?"

Her question caught him totally off guard.

"I don't."

"Uh-huh."

"I don't even know the woman."

"Then how come you were standing on the sidewalk looking like you were about to go down on one knee?"

"You're nuts. I was just surprised at her new hairdo. Nice, by the way."

"Thank you, I must say I outdid myself. So?"

"So what?"

"You know, being obtuse does not make a man sexy."

"Oh hell, Linda, I gave her a speeding ticket on her way into town. She nearly ran over Connor last night and brought him home. I thanked her; I would have thanked her again, but she cut out. She doesn't like me much. And I have no feelings about her whatsoever. So don't even start with me."

Linda guffawed. An over-the-top reaction that let him know she wasn't buying any of it.

"I was just surprised to see her at the Cut—at Le Coif."

For once Linda didn't have a sassy comment. Just turned around with the empty coffeepot in her hand and studied him.

"Uh, the coffee?"

"Yeah, right." She replaced the carafe and turned on the coffeemaker, then leaned against the counter facing him. "Didn't you know her when her family *summuhed* here."

"No. Summer people didn't mix with us townies."

"Poor you. I'd get out my violin but I had to use it for firewood."

Nick tried not to smile, he wanted to be pissed off at her for asking too many questions. Questions he really didn't know the answers to. But he couldn't.

"One day that mouth of yours is going to get you into trouble."

"Oh, promises, promises."

The coffeemaker spit out its last puff of steam; Linda filled a mug and handed it to him. "Now where did I put that fruit cake?" She placed a plate of freshly baked cookies in front of him.

Nick took one and bit into it.

"When was the last time you had sex?"

Nick choked on the cookie, coughed out cookie crumbs. Linda whacked him on the back.

"Jesus, Linda. What the hell kind of question is that?" He hoped to hell she wasn't going to proposition him. When he first moved in, they kind of danced around the possibility until she figured out he wasn't interested. As it turned out, she wasn't offended or really disappointed. Linda had her pick of men in the town. She hadn't really been interested in Nick. It was more of a habit with her.

"Every night I listen for sounds of *amore* coming from your apartment and I get zip, nada. The only action I hear is you turning the page of some old history book." She sighed heavily. "Why Nick, are you blushing?

"I was just kidding. I don't hear a thing. Ever. The history book was just a good guess. But what I haven't heard, or seen, is some beauty sneaking down the stairs in the middle of the night. And you're home every night, ergo . . ."

"Linda, I don't have time to even meet women. Much less date them. And if I ever do start, I won't bring them here, knowing you've got a glass pressed to the ceiling."

"Aw, you're no fun. If I promise not to listen or spy, will you get a girlfriend?"

"On my next day off." Nick stood up, snagged another cookie, and headed for the door.

"Aren't you off this Friday?" Linda called after him.

Seven

 Margaux watched from the kitchen window as a red Dodge came to a stop behind the house. She quickly dried her hands and ran outside to meet her friends. Grace hopped out of the car and waved as Brianna emerged more slowly from the passenger side. Her long legs unfolded to the ground and she seemed to stretch in slow motion, tall and lean with golden hair piled nonchalantly on the top of her head. As poised and beautiful as ever.

And then she grinned. "Mags!"

Brianna held out her arms and Margaux fell into her hug, nearly knocking her over. "I can't believe you're here."

Brianna laughed, low and throaty. "I've been here. I can't believe *you're* here. Group hug." She opened one arm to make room for Grace. They laughed and exclaimed and cried until finally Bri pulled away.

"We all look fabulous, haven't aged a bit, and are just ecstatic to be together again. But enough already. The ice is melting."

She reached over them for a bag of ice which she handed to Margaux. Reached in again and came out with a large thermos. "Watermelon martinis." She walked off toward the kitchen door.

"Is she limping?" Margaux whispered to Grace.

Grace nodded. "A long story, she'll tell you after a martini or two."

Grace hoisted a box of groceries out of the trunk. "Steaks, potatoes, salad, chips, dip, cheese, crackers, olives—and cupcakes. Close the trunk, will you?"

They bustled about the kitchen, putting away food, getting down glasses, grinning and shaking their heads each time they passed. And by the time everything was put away, they were the Selkies again.

"Lunch or beach?" asked Margaux.

"Beach," Bri said.

Grace rolled her eyes.

"Oh come on, both of you could use a little vitamin D and I have a great sunscreen."

They went off to separate bedrooms to change into their suits. As soon as Margaux was ready, she went downstairs to get the pitcher of fresh-squeezed lemonade and round up a stack of beach towels.

Grace was already on the porch, sitting on the railing, wearing a white tailored shirt that came to mid-thigh.

"Is there a suit under there?" asked Margaux as she handed her the pitcher of lemonade.

"Yes. Is there one under there?" She nodded to Margaux's knee-length bathrobe.

"Afraid so."

"Hey, where are you?" Bri called from the house.

"Out here," Margaux called back.

"Don't stare," Grace said quickly before the screen door opened and Bri struck a pose in the doorway. She was wearing an oversized T-shirt with a voluptuous torso in a string bikini printed on the front.

"Ta-da."

"Very chic." Margaux adjusted the towels, picked up the beach umbrella, and marched off to stake a place in the sand.

It took several minutes to spread out towels and unload beach bags. None of them seemed too eager to be the first to take off her beach cover-up.

"Okay," said Bri. "On the count of three, we strip." She grinned satanically. "In order of age."

"Okay," Grace said, obviously relieved.

"Youngest first."

"Not fair."

"Tough." Bri pointed to Grace with a finger whose manicure was showing signs of wear, then to Margaux, then to herself. "*Un, deux, trois.* Ready?"

"I have nothing to hide . . . much." Grace slowly unbuttoned her shirt and slipped it off. Beneath it was a navy blue one-piece with low-cut legs and a square neckline.

"I have a sedentary lifestyle," she said defensively.

"You look great," Margaux said.

"You look just like a lawyer in a swimsuit," Bri said, and turned to Margaux.

"Oh, all right." Margaux untied the sash and let the robe fall to the sand.

Grace sputtered. "Strawberries?"

Brianna groaned. "And ruffles. Wait a minute. I remember that suit. You were twelve or something."

Margaux pulled a face. "I found it in the dresser. I guess I'll have to buy a new suit next time I'm in town."

She and Grace both turned toward Bri.

"Are you ready?"

Margaux thought she heard a subtle tremor in her friend's voice.

Bri pulled the T-shirt over her head. Her suit was not even a bikini, it was almost nothing. Just three tiny patches of gold with three tiny strings holding them together.

"Jesus Christ Almighty," said Grace. "Do you want us to get arrested for indecent exposure?"

Brianna grimaced. "Too much?"

"Too little," said Grace.

"You want to trade?" Bri reached for the minuscule string around her neck.

"No! Can you imagine if any of my clients saw me wearing that?"

"You'd have to hand out those little numbers like they have at the deli."

"I don't think so."

Brianna turned to Margaux, one eyebrow lifted. "Well, what do you think?"

"I—" The suit was amazing, but Margaux hardly noticed it. She was staring at the long ugly scar that stretched from Brianna's thigh to ankle.

"Where on earth did you get it?"

"The suit or the scar?"

Margaux swallowed. "Both."

"The Lido for the suit. The store on Canal Street, not France." Bri lowered herself to her towel and began to slather on sunscreen. "The scar I got in France.

"So just to get it out and over with, this is how it went. I was living the good life, yukking it up with the rich and famous, parties, drugs, alcohol, men. You know the drill. The particular man I happened to be with at the moment was drunk and driving his Aston Martin too fast. He took an *S* turn and skidded out of control. He walked away from the crash. I wrecked my body and ended my career.

"Fortunately his family was willing to pay to keep me from suing and the newspapers from having a field day. I took the money and came home . . . eventually."

"Eventually?"

"After a stint in rehab and another in the loony bin. Old news."

"Not to me."

"If it's any consolation, she didn't tell me either." Grace poured lemonade into a plastic tumbler and handed it to Brianna. "And it wasn't a loony bin."

Bri took the glass. "Next best thing."

"Why didn't you let us know?" asked Margaux.

"I was too ashamed." Bri gave them a twisted smile. Tears sparkled in her eyes, making her look even more beautiful.

"To tell your friends? We could have been there for you." Except Margaux had been too busy building her career to have been able to help Bri. As it turned out, she hadn't even been able to take care of herself. "I've been a terrible friend."

"No," Bri said. "Just busy getting ahead—like the rest of the world."

"And here we are right back where we started."

Grace frowned at Margaux. "You make it sound like a bad thing."

"It turned out okay for me," Bri said. "I bought a house right outside of town, I went to college and got a degree in business, and I'm in the process of adopting two little girls from China."

"Wow, that's amazing. No man in your life?"

"Nope." She took a sip of lemonade. "This lemonade is delicious. Just like Jude used to make."

"I learned it from the best," Margaux said. "So what about you, Grace? Any great loves? Beside the law?"

"Just the law. Domestic disputes, traffic tickets, and the occasional foreclosure."

"Oh, don't be so modest," Bri said. "Last year some developer tried to buy up the boardwalk. Okay, so the area has seen better days, but McMansions for rich people? It's our only public beach. Anyway, our little friend here hustled her butt up to the state assembly and had them put a stay on the sale."

"Good for you. So where does it stand now?"

"Limbo," Grace said. "Which is as good a place as any when it comes to jurisprudence."

"In the meantime, she had the town council apply for historic designation. Seems the carousel is over a hundred years old."

"Our carousel? Does it even run?"

"No. But it's still there," Grace said. "And that's enough to garner interest in saving it."

Margaux sighed. "McMansions on the boardwalk. Is no place sacred?"

"Evidently not." Brianna leaned back on her elbows. "So, Mags. I heard you closed M Atelier. What's up with that?"

Margaux glanced at Grace. Grace shook her head.

"Grace didn't blab. I read it in the trades. They didn't say why."

"Thank God for that."

"So what happened?"

"Oh God." Margaux dropped her head to her hands.

"Come on. Out with it."

Margaux looked up. "The short version. Louis stole every cent I had, then disappeared, the bank foreclosed on my apartment and my business. I'm finished."

"Shit." Bri sat up. "Shit. That rat bastard. Do you need a good lawyer? I just happen to know of one."

"I already offered."

"I have one. She's a shark."

"With sharp teeth, I hope."

"I'm counting on it," Margaux said.

"So do you have a plan?"

"To start on my tan." Margaux lay down and for the next few minutes life was good.

"This is great," Grace said on a yawn. "Being back together."

"Hmm," agreed Margaux. "Thank God for friends."

"Hmm," said Grace.

"I wasn't sure I still had any."

Bri sat up. "Are you kidding me? We're the Selkies. We swore to be friends forever. Remember?"

Grace opened one eye. "Not really."

"Sure you do. We wrote down our dreams in a diary and buried it in the Grotto and swore to be together forever."

Margaux sat up. "I remember. It was the summer before you moved to New York. Do you think it's still there?"

"Wouldn't that be a kick? Let's find out." Bri struggled to her feet.

Grace lifted her head. "Are you sure we want to go there?"

Bri looked down at Grace, hands on her hips. "Figuratively, yes. Literally? I might need some help getting over the rocks. It'll be fun." She leaned over and hauled Grace to her feet.

"Come on, Mags. Don't you want to see what we wrote?"

"I guess."

Bri struck off toward the jetty. Grace and Margaux fell in behind and they walked up the beach as they had hundreds of times before, climbed up the rocks of the jetty, picking out hand- and footholds as if twenty years hadn't passed. Except that every now and then they had to stop to help Bri over a difficult place.

"This used to be a lot easier," Bri grumbled.

"We used to be younger," said Grace. "And there used to be cute boys swimming on the other side."

"Maybe there still are."

"No," Margaux said.

Bri gave her a look. "Something you want to tell us?"

"No. I mean, do you really want to spy on twelve-year-old boys?"

"I was hoping they'd grown up by now. Oxymoron, I know."

"I thought you were done with men," Grace said.

"I am, but it doesn't mean I don't like to look. Come on."

Please don't let Nick Prescott be there, Margaux prayed. He'd probably think she brought an audience. She gave herself a mental kick. She was approaching middle age, not puberty, she really needed to get a grip. But still she sighed with relief when they reached the crest of the jetty and the cove was empty.

"What are you smiling about?" asked Grace, huffing to stop beside her.

"Me? Was I smiling? Just remembering, I guess."

"Yeah. The good old days." Brianna started down the other side.

Grace scrambled after her. She might be used to Bri's injury, but Margaux noticed that she stayed close enough to help if she started to fall.

The tide was in and they splashed knee deep through the water to reach the pebble beach. Brianna led the way up the narrow path. She yanked her T-shirt away from a brambling vine. "I don't remember it being quite so—wild."

They walked single file until the path ended in a tiny clearing.

"Where's the Grotto?" asked Grace.

"Probably behind that tree." Margaux pointed to a lopsided pine. It was at least two feet in diameter and grew at a sharp angle. The roots lay like coils of gnarled rope over the rock and disappeared beneath the rotting leaves that covered the ground.

"Don't tell me that's the little runt we used for our pirate flag."

Margaux had forgotten that. The days when they were still young enough to play pirates and had made a skull and cross-bones from one of Jude's best handkerchiefs.

"It used to be so little."

"So did we," Bri said.

"You were never little," Grace said.

"That's okay. You were short enough for both of us."

"Yeah. That was before I hit five-two."

Bri barked out a laugh and stepped past them to peer through the tangle of roots and branches.

Margaux and Grace crowded behind her.

It wasn't a real cave, but a deep hollow carved into the rock. Just big enough for three young girls to sit tailor-style, knees touching, and swearing to be friends forever.

"Well, I can't go in there," Bri said, stepping back. "Grace, you'd better go get it."

Grace gave her a look. "Now, suddenly you're going to start crying infirmity."

"Oh hell, but if I get stuck you'll have to drag me out." Bri crouched down.

"No. I'll go." Grace stepped through the vines and disappeared.

A screech echoed from inside. A chipmunk skittered out and shot into the underbrush.

Grace ran out. "What was that?"

Brianna laughed. "A chipmunk. We'll all go."

It was a tight squeeze and they had to squat down to get beneath the overhang. Margaux knew Brianna must be terribly uncomfortable.

Grace peered around. "So where's the diary?"

"Too bad we didn't bring a flashlight," said Brianna. "But I think . . ." She twisted around and stretched out one arm. Something clinked. "Well, I'll be damned. The cairn," she intoned in a sepulchral voice.

"Cairn?" asked Margaux.

"A mound of rough stones used as a memorial."

"Let me guess. English 101," Grace said.

"History of the Irish 202."

Margaux squinted at the back of the cave and saw the rocks each of them had placed to hide the diary.

Brianna took the first stone and moved it to the side. "Okay, Mags."

Margaux removed the second stone.

Grace went next.

They peered into the crevice.

"Now what?" asked Margaux. "I'm not sure you should stick your hand in there."

It was too late. Bri's arm disappeared up to the elbow. There was a scraping noise; the sound of dirt and pebbles rolling away. Brianna withdrew her hand and lifted a plastic Tupperware container into the light.

A hush fell over the Grotto. The air was so still Margaux could hear the faint buzz of a skill saw in the distance.

Brianna thrust the Tupperware at Margaux. "I say we read this over a martini." She scrambled awkwardly back to the daylight, Margaux and Grace at her heels.

They retraced their steps through the cove and over the jetty.

"I hope this isn't going to turn out to be one of those Pandora's box–type things," Margaux said, clutching the container to her chest as they strode across the beach.

"Nah. It was before we became so jaded," said Bri.

"I'm not jaded," Grace said.

"No, alas, you're not, but hope springs eternal."

Grace made a face at her.

"Happy hour," Bri announced as soon as they reached the porch.

They went straight through the house to the kitchen. Margaux placed the container on the kitchen table while Bri made the martinis and Grace opened bags of nuts and chips, and spooned dip into a bowl.

By the time they carried everything out to the living room, Bri had refilled their glasses and half the chips were gone. Margaux pushed aside the pencils and sketches that littered the top of the blanket chest and placed the diary in the center. Grace arranged the drinks and hors d'oeuvres.

"Hmm," Bri said, picking up the stack of sketches. "The lamp, the couch, the rug, the window. Is this some kind of therapy?"

Margaux shook her head. "I was just doodling. Waiting for the muse to return."

"Huh," Bri said, and took a sip of her drink. "The thing I've learned about muses is that you can't wait for them to act. Sometimes, you have to grab them by the hair and beat them into submission."

"You have a muse?" Grace asked incredulously. "She could probably sue you. I know a good lawyer." She grinned and flopped back on the couch and Margaux realized they were all getting a little tipsy.

She and Bri sat down and they all looked at the Tupperware container.

Brianna took a sip of her martini. "Who's going to open it?"

"You are," Margaux said.

"You're the oldest," Grace said.

"Don't remind me."

"And it was your idea," added Margaux.

"Like I said, don't remind me." Bri took another sip of martini and set her glass down.

"We vowed to meet in twenty years to see if our dreams had come true. Seeing how it's been nineteen-plus years—"

"Maybe we should wait," Grace said.

"So maybe none of us is in the best place to talk about dreams coming true, but, hell, aren't you curious?"

"I'm not sitting around wondering what it says for another year," said Margaux. "We started this, let's finish it."

Bri eyed the plastic diary as if it were the Lost Ark of the Covenant.

Grace slid the container toward Bri. "You got it out. You read it."

Bri cut her a look but reached for the Tupperware. She lifted the edge of the rubber top and pulled it off, revealing a square pink book closed with a golden lock.

There was an audible sigh from all three.

She held it for a moment, then pushed the brass button on the side. Nothing happened. She threw it onto the coffee table. "It's locked."

"Oh, for crying out loud. Give it here." Grace took the diary from Bri. "Mags, you have a paper clip somewhere?"

"Probably." Margaux found one in the writing desk. Grace unfolded it, stuck it in the keyhole, and with one twist, the lock flipped open. "You didn't see that." She handed the diary back to Bri.

"Here goes." Bri opened the diary and read. "This diary is the property of the Selkies. Anyone caught reading these words will answer to us."

Grace chuckled. "Hard to believe we were ever that young."

"Speak for yourself." Bri turned the page. "August 31, 19— well, forget the date." She flipped several pages over. "Grace."

"I object," countered Grace. "Go in order."

"Overruled," said Bri. " 'Grace Holcombe, age thirteen. I'm going to be an attorney when I get out of college. Not the kind that makes lots of money, but the kind that will help bring justice to the world.' "

"Okay, stop, stop." Grace grabbed for the book. Bri snatched it away and continued to read with it held out of Grace's reach.

" 'It doesn't matter if a client can't pay. If I believe in their case, I'll help them. The crooks of the world won't have a chance if they come up against me.' Favorite color: pink." Bri burst out laughing. "Pink? You were going to right the wrongs of the world and your favorite color was pink?"

Grace threw a peanut at her.

"Pink aside, you seem to be right on target with your dream of being a poor bleeding-heart attorney."

"Thank you."

"Favorite food: Skilling's hamburgers. Favorite boyfriend: Larry T? I thought you were going steady with Bobby Covington."

Grace laughed. "I plead the Fifth."

"Okay. Margaux." Bri lifted both eyebrows at her. "Are we quite ready? 'I, Margaux Sullivan, have a dream.' "

"Oh shit, I didn't write that."

"Yes, you did." Bri turned the book around. "See, right here. 'I, Margaux Sullivan, have a dream. To design clothes that will make people who wear them feel good about themselves. I have a long way to go, but I'll get there.' "

"Favorite color: Granny Smith apple-peel green. How

poetic. Favorite food: tacos. Boyfriend. What? I can't even read this. It's just scribble."

"I kept changing my mind." Margaux sighed. "I can't even remember any of their names. Your turn."

"I think I need another martini."

"Oh no you don't," Grace protested. "You're not going to start slurring your words just when we get to you."

Bri turned the page and read silently.

"Out loud!" Grace and Margaux cried together.

" 'I, Brianna Boyce, will set the world afire'—shit—'I'm going to New York and sign with Elite Management. Watch for me on the runways of Paris, Milan, and New York.' " Bri's voice wavered. "Well, I made it . . . and lost it."

"Me, too," said Margaux. "I guess that's something. Just to get there."

"Yeah," Grace said. "But did it ever occur to you that dreams are just that—dreams."

"Is that legalese for 'we really screwed up'?" asked Bri.

"No. Just keep reading. Which of your many boyfriends did you put down. Or did you put them all down?"

"Ben," said Bri.

"The lifeguard? You never even talked to him, just giggled whenever he was around."

Bri shrugged, a gesture of loss. "I know and now he's dead. You just never know . . ." She trailed off into silence.

"No you don't," Margaux said, suddenly wondering what happened to the boy in the library, what he was doing now and if his dreams had come true.

Bri stood up, swayed slightly. "Time to cook the steaks."

They finished the pitcher of martinis while Bri manned the grill and Margaux and Grace made salad and kibitzed from inside the screen door. They ate in the kitchen and polished off a bottle of wine over dinner, then donned sweatshirts and moved to the porch where they stayed up until the wee hours.

Margaux told them the long version of her crash and burn;

Bri described her stay in a Swiss sanatorium. Grace listened to it all just as if she was in a courtroom, but swore there was nothing much to tell about her life.

"Not to worry," Bri told her. "Your time is near. The Selkies are back and ready to rock and roll."

It was nearly three when Bri stood up and announced, "I'm going to bed. I have to get up early to feed the animals."

Margaux squinted one eye at her. "You have animals?"

"Two dogs, a barn full of cats—I stopped counting at six—four chickens, a rooster, and a goat."

"A goat?"

"Her name is Hermione."

"You named her?"

"Well, I'm not going to eat her."

"What about the rooster?"

"Merv."

"Grace, is she telling me the truth?"

Grace nodded. "Afraid so."

"I can't even begin to imagine."

"When I'm a little more set up, you'll have to come see for yourself. 'Night." Bri yawned and headed for the stairs.

Margaux stood, too. "Wait a minute. What are we going to do with the diary?"

"Take it back?" Grace suggested.

"In the middle of the night?"

Bri looked around the room. "We could put it in the blanket chest. We might want to read it again. If Mags doesn't mind."

"It's okay with me, though it is kind of weird, being the keeper of our hopes for the future, especially now that it *is* our future."

The three of them clustered around the blanket chest and lifted the lid. The chest opened in a whiff of cedar to reveal a stack of folded blankets. Grace placed the diary on top.

"The Selkies forever," Brianna intoned. She licked three fingers, held them in the air, and yawned.

"The Selkies forever," Grace and Margaux repeated.

Margaux closed the chest and they began returning things to the top. Bri picked up Margaux's sketchbook. "What's in here?"

Margaux shrugged. "More of the same. Furniture, the beach, sailboats."

"Mags, I don't want to be pushy, but shouldn't you be working on next season's line? I understand the need to cleanse the palette, but to hell with waiting on that muse you were talking about. You and I both know the fashion world doesn't wait for inspiration."

"Yes, I do know. But like I told you, I don't have jack, not even a spool of thread. There's no way I'll get anything out by fall."

"Maybe not, but spring surely."

"Impossible."

"Excuse me? You two went to Catholic school. What did the nuns always say?"

Grace groaned. "Can't was killed in the battle of tried."

Margaux heaved a sigh. "They obviously didn't know the fashion industry."

"You just figured that out now?" Bri jabbed her finger at her forehead. "Hey, maybe that's where you got your inspiration."

"Where?"

"From the nuns, all those black-and-white habits."

Margaux rolled her eyes.

"Just a thought. And now, good night."

As she tossed the sketchbook onto the trunk, a piece of paper slipped from the back pages and wafted to the floor. Before Margaux even realized what it was, Bri leaned over and picked it up. She glanced at the page as she started to put it back in the sketchbook. "Wait a minute. What—or should I say who—is this?"

"I was just doodling."

"What is it?" asked Grace, sliding around the chest to peer at the drawing of Nick Prescott, merman.

"It's nothing really." Margaux reached for the drawing.

Grace studied the sketch, her eyebrows dipping in concentration. "He looks familiar. Except for the tail."

"He does," Bri agreed. "Really familiar."

"I was just being fanciful. I was out on the jetty and just let my imagination run."

Bri looked at the sketch. "You know, he really, really looks familiar. Let me think."

Margaux slipped the merman sketch from her fingers, stuck it in between the pages of the sketchbook, and tucked the book under her arm before she nudged Bri and Grace out of the room.

"Really familiar," said Bri as they climbed the stairs to bed.

Margaux awoke six hours later to bright sunlight and a hangover. She was a one-glass-of-wine-a-night girl and she had overindulged—overate, overdrank, and overconfessed, bigtime. She forced herself to sit up and sat on the edge of the bed waiting for the pounding in her head to stop.

After a few minutes, she realized it wasn't nearly as bad as she anticipated. She put on sweats and tiptoed across the hall. She peeked into the other bedrooms; the beds were made and there was no trace of Grace or Bri.

She went downstairs to the kitchen where she found coffee and a note. "Had a fabulous time. Thanks for having us. We love you. Now get your butt in gear and go to work. See you soon. Bri and Grace."

Can't was killed in the battle of tried. They were right. It was time she got off the pity wagon and started fighting her way back to the top.

Eight

 The house seemed empty with her two friends gone. It wasn't the kind of house that did well with empty. It had always been the hub of beach activity; her parents and their friends, Danny and his friends, then Margaux and the Selkies.

The emptiness just accented what she knew and Bri had pointed out. She was procrastinating and she couldn't put it off any longer. She had to start working on new designs. Every day she was away from New York, her presence became weaker. The industry had a short memory, and it was too easy to slip into obscurity.

But the mere thought of what it would take to get back what she lost made her sick to her stomach. Made her hands tremble, made her mouth go dry.

Can't was killed in the battle of tried.

Bri was right about the nuns influencing her. Not with their black habits, but with their work ethic. It had helped her rise to the top. And it would help her again.

She'd need a place to work where the light was good. The living room looked south, but the porch shaded it from the sun. All the bedrooms were filled with beds, chairs, and bookcases. Only her parents' room got full light and she didn't have the heart to move things to make room for her easel.

She even looked into the room she and Louis had shared on their few trips to Crescent Cove.

At first she stood at the closed door, afraid to open it. She had pushed her soon-to-be-ex-husband almost out of her mind since she'd been here and she didn't want him intruding again. Didn't want to unleash any demons that might be lurking there. But when she finally turned the knob, nothing happened. It was just an unused room, with a chenille spread covering the bed, mismatched end tables, and a rag rug made of undershirts.

Margaux sank down on the bed, the scene of their last beach house fight. When Margaux said she wanted to start a family and Louis refused. He liked their life the way it was and children would only interfere. Margaux had been floored. He'd known from the beginning she wanted children; he said he wanted them. He'd lied about that, too.

She stood up. She'd been wrong. There were demons here, the ones she'd brought with her. She crossed to the window, opened it, and let the wind blow them all away.

At that moment, she remembered Linda asking, "Do you know anyone who wants to rent a retail space? Cheap?" and looking into the bright deserted room at Le Coif.

She could design and construct there. If it was still available and Linda would accept a fee Margaux could afford.

And out of her sense of loss and futility, something rose— not a phoenix—something smaller, newborn, like a baby chick cracking out of its shell. And for the first time in weeks, Margaux felt a spur of excitement.

She dressed, ran a comb through her hair, grabbed her purse, and went outside to her car.

The gas gauge read empty. Or near enough to have to buy gas, and that was one expense she could curtail, especially with the prospect of rent ahead of her. She had a perfectly nice purple bike. Plus riding to town would give her much-needed exercise, since a gym was out of the question. She pumped up the tires, threw her purse in the basket, and climbed on.

She wobbled up Salt Marsh Lane and nearly fell off when she hit a crack in the asphalt. Undaunted, she straightened out the wheel and made the turn. By the time she reached the gate, she was cycling like a pro, though she did have second thoughts about tackling Shore Road.

But it was only three blocks until it turned into Main Street. She waited for a minivan to pass, then crossed the road to ride with the flow of traffic. Hugging close to the shoulder, she pedaled into town and came to a stop in front of Le Coif a few uneventful minutes later.

She propped the bike against the side of the steps, making a note to find a lock before the tourists arrived.

The front door was locked. Of course, it was Sunday and Linda would be closed. Margaux could wait until Monday, but she was stoked and impatient, and she didn't think Linda would turn her nose up at a potential renter even if it was Sunday.

Margaux rang the bell and waited.

"Hang on. I'm coming." Linda hurried across the street, not dressed for church, but wearing a flowered sarong and a black Cyclones hoodie zipped up to her neck. A magenta bandanna covered her head, and she was carrying a giant yellow beach bag that bounced against her thigh as she trotted across the cobblestones.

She stopped a few feet away and gave Margaux the once-over. "What? Everything looks fine."

Margaux shook her head until her hair flew. "Everything is perfect. I came because I was wondering if you still have that room for rent?"

Linda's frown brightened into a toothy grin. "You interested?"

"Maybe. Short-term. For a studio, just while I'm here or until you can rent it out permanently. If . . ." God, she hated having to say this. "If I can afford it."

"You can afford it," Linda said, searching in her bag. "Here, hold this."

She thrust a paperback book at Margaux. *The Duke Takes His Wife.* On the front cover, a Fabio look-alike and a buxom brunette were clasped in a fierce embrace. "And this." A huge black and red beach towel followed the book. "And this."

A bottle of suntan lotion? "You were on the beach?"

"Yeah. Not as warm as yesterday, but I couldn't get out yesterday. I worked my as—feet off until dark. Saturday is a big day. Gotta look nice for church and Sunday brunch. Voilà." She pulled out a key ring, gave it a yank, and the bungee cord it was attached to snapped in the air.

Margaux stepped back just in time to avoid being hit.

"One of my great ideas. I was going to attach the key ring to the bag with the bungee cord. That way I wouldn't always be looking for my keys. It woulda worked too except I never attached it. The road to hell is paved with good intentions, but what a party."

She opened the door and led Margaux inside.

The room was just as sunny as she remembered it. And it was completely bare, except for a pile of coat hangers in the corner, a few crumpled sheets of paper, and lots of dust. A big bay window looked out onto the marina and three large windows faced west. It would get morning and afternoon sun.

It was perfect.

"There's a powder room under the stairs for my clients that you can use. The kitchen's in the back of the house, you can access it through the hall. Just don't eat all my Cocoa Krispies."

"Oh, I wouldn't use your—"

"Sure you would. Don't worry. We don't have to be best friends. We can just pass like ships in the night." She shot her hands past each other to demonstrate. "But you might as well be comfortable while you're working."

This was moving way too fast. Something Margaux suspected happened with Linda a lot.

"What are you asking for it?"

"Hell, it's been vacant for eight months, what can you pay?"

Margaux stifled a laugh. "I'm not sure how long I'm going to be here."

"Good enough. Follow me."

She took off down the hall. Margaux followed meekly behind her.

The kitchen was a large airy room, painted a brilliant canary yellow with oak cabinets and a light pine table and chairs.

"So you want coffee? I have to cut off my supply on cutting and perm days. Don't want to get jittery fingers and cut off something I shouldn't. But on Sunday? I shake, rattle, and roll all day. Nothing better than a strong cup of joe."

"I'd love some."

They sat at the table, a plate of chocolate chip cookies between them.

"If you're worried about security. Don't be. I got the chief of police living up on the third floor."

Margaux's cup rattled. "The chief of police?"

"Yeah," Linda said, eyeing her speculatively. "If you're not an escaped felon, that should be good news."

She wasn't a felon, but she sure as hell didn't know about Louis.

"Plus he's a hunk. So even if you don't need the security, he's nice to come home to."

"You?"

"Hell no. He lives like a monk. Plus he isn't really my type. I like willowy effete men."

Margaux choked on her coffee.

"Okay. I lied. I flirted with him a little bit when I first got here. No chemistry. You know what I mean? Plus I like a guy who can walk on the wild side. Nick lives the letter of the law."

"I thought maybe he was married. I met Connor."

"Connor is his nephew. Nick's brother was killed in the war.

Mother ran off. Nick got the kid. Couldn't be in better hands. He's a little strange."

"Nick or Connor?"

Linda snorted out a laugh. "Both. Connor doesn't talk much and when he does he whispers. Spooky, but a sweetheart. Nick is just plain old strange. He works, he takes care of his family. He studies. *C'est tout.*"

"He sounds perfect." Margaux caught herself. "I mean a man who works hard, takes care of his family, and tries to stretch his horizons?"

"Know what you mean. The only horizons most men stretch is with their secretaries or some bimbette they pick up at a bar."

Margaux had to laugh; she'd been thinking pretty much the same thing. She wondered if Louis had also been having affairs while he was stealing her money. And she was shocked to realize she didn't care.

"But don't worry. He won't bother you unless you want him to." Linda made a face. "Probably not even then."

Just as well, thought Margaux. "It's absolutely none of my business, but why does Connor whisper?"

Linda reached for a cookie. "Nobody knows. Kid won't tell them, just clams up when they press him. Like I said, weird. Now about the rent. How about a hundred a month?"

"A hundred? That's highway robbery."

"Okay, how about fifty?"

"I mean, I'd be taking advantage of you."

Linda pulled her glasses down and peered at Margaux over the rims. "Fifty bucks, and that's my last offer."

"Twenty-five a week. If I stay longer than a couple weeks, we'll renegotiate. And if you're able to rent it out permanently, I'll move out without notice."

"Done."

Margaux handed Linda twenty-five in cash and they sealed the deal with a second cup of coffee and a chocolate chip cookie.

"I'll move in tomorrow if that's okay. And I'll clean out the place, so you don't have to."

"Works for me."

Linda walked Margaux to the porch and watched as she wheeled her bike down the front sidewalk to the street. "Bon Jovi!" she screeched, pointing to the bike's license plate. "This is going to be great."

Margaux only hoped she wasn't getting into something she'd regret. Linda was nice but Margaux couldn't have her interrupting all the time. And though twenty-five dollars was more than reasonable—it was a downright steal—she didn't really have any money to spare. On the other hand, she couldn't do better than to pump what she had into jumpstarting her comeback.

To celebrate, she rode to the Cove Market and bought a quart of milk, a bunch of bananas, a head of lettuce, a tomato, a loaf of twelve-grain bread, and a half pound of hamburger.

The grocery bag fit nicely in her wire basket and she felt very content and a little eccentric pedaling through town on her purple bike. She got a few looks and a couple of waves. One from Roy Oglethorpe, who was coming out of Harry's Newsstand. And one from the woman that ran Cupcakes by Caroline.

She was actually feeling inspired as she rode toward Shore Road. She waited to make sure no cars were coming before she crossed the street and headed for home.

Moments later, a car sped past her. The bike wobbled, she gripped the handlebars fighting to keep the bike under control as it rattled beneath her. A police car, siren screaming, raced after it. It created a blast of hot wind that buffeted the bike. Margaux instinctively wrenched the wheel away from the road, but the bike began to skid on the rocky shoulder. Margaux hung on, praying fervently that she wouldn't go down.

She managed to turn toward a grassy verge just before the

bike slid out from under her and she toppled off the side. She hit the ground and lay there too stunned to move.

The cruiser's radio crackled. Nick automatically tossed his book onto the seat and started his engine when Finley's voice came over the radio.

"Chief, I'm in pursuit of a red convertible, New York plates, speeding east on Shore Road. Lonnie's on backup. But I've got a cyclist down. She's on the south side of Shore Road, west of Skilling's Ice Cream."

"I'm on my way. Did you call an ambulance?"

"I don't think it's that serious."

"Okay. I'm two minutes away." Nick flipped on his siren and sped toward Shore Road. He slowed as he reached the location Finley had given him, and scanned the side of the road for any signs that the cyclist was still down or injured.

He saw nothing until the top of an auburn head popped up from the drainage ditch that ran alongside the road. Nick cursed and jumped out of the cruiser with his heart racing and a prayer on his lips. *Please let her be okay.*

She sat on the ground, the side of one leg caked in mud. The bike lay several feet away, half submerged in the drainage ditch.

Nick bent down beside her. "Are you hurt?"

She gulped in air, shook her hands, flicking bits of mud onto his uniform, and rolled her wrists.

"Thank God, no. They seem okay."

"Have you tried to stand?" Nick asked, exasperated that she only thought of her hands.

She shook her head and started to shake.

"What happened?"

"I was riding my bike—with the flow of traffic," she said between chattering teeth. "This car sped past. It had to be going ninety. But I held on until you whizzed by. Then I lost control and fell off."

"It wasn't me. It was my deputy." And he was going to kill Finley when he saw him. "I came because he called it in." Nick tried to calm down, but his temper exploded. "Did you ever think that riding along Shore Road might be dangerous?"

She shrank back. "I used to ride along here all the time. All the kids did."

"You're not a kid."

"You don't have to remind me." She struggled to stand up. Nick steadied her as she put weight on shaky legs.

She eased away from him.

Nick was still holding her arm; he didn't let go. "Maybe you should just rest for a minute. Make sure nothing's broken."

"Nothing's broken. Oh no."

Nick grabbed for her, afraid she'd been premature in her judgment.

She shook him off. "My bike. And my groceries."

The bike was half submerged in mud, weeds, and sea grass. There was a carton of milk crushed under the frame; spilled milk ran in white rivulets in the mud. What looked like a loaf of bread had suffered a similar fate. And what the other stuff was Nick couldn't begin to guess.

She started down into the ditch, but Nick pulled her back.

"Allow me." He kicked off his shoes, pulled off his socks, and rolled up his trouser legs. With a resigned sigh, he slid down the side of the ditch and stepped into the mud.

The bike was stuck fast and it took several minutes before Nick could pull it back to dry land. There wasn't much he could do about the groceries. The bread was smashed. Something that had been ground meat was leaking muddy water. He tossed it back into the ditch and climbed out. He managed to salvage her purse and toss it into the basket.

He dragged the bike up the slope to firm ground and lowered the kickstand.

She was staring at his legs. He looked down. He was covered in mud up to his shin bones, the folds of his trousers were caked with it.

"You, too," he said.

She looked down and gasped. "My new capris!"

It wasn't just her capris, it was one whole side of her, including hair and face.

He didn't know which was in worse shape, the bike or its owner.

"And my bike. Is it wrecked?"

Nick squatted down to get a better look at the bike. The frame seemed undamaged, but the front tire was totally blown out and the sprockets were twisted out of shape. "Bike seems okay, but you'll need a whole new wheel."

"How am I going to get it home?"

"I'll drive you."

She looked at his cruiser, then down at her muddied clothes. "Thanks but I'd better walk." She kicked up the stand and began to roll the bike down the road on one wheel. It was a hopeless endeavor.

He went after her and grabbed the handlebars. There was a momentary standoff, with both of them holding the handlebars and neither giving way. He was so close to her he could have leaned over and kissed her. Of course that would have been totally inappropriate. Not to mention stepping back into a time when he was young and rash enough to do something like that. Not to mention she'd probably sue.

"Get in the car. Don't worry about the mud. I'll put the bike in back and drive you home." He wrestled the bike from her and carried it around to the trunk.

He secured the bike, walked back, and opened the door for her.

She didn't move.

"You can walk if you want to, but I'm driving your bike back to your house."

Her eyes flicked to the seat.

He remembered the *History of the Ostrogoths*. He leaned past her and tossed it onto the dashboard. Without a word, she climbed in.

On the way to Little Crescent Beach, Nick tried desperately to think of something to say. He didn't want to lecture her on the dangers of bike riding. He wanted to talk about all the things he'd imagined talking about when he'd been young and clueless. But that time was gone, and besides, making idle conversation with a person who was about to fill in an accident report seemed ludicrous.

They didn't speak all the way to the beach house.

She jumped out of the car as soon as he pulled up to her house. He told himself not to get further entangled, just get the bike out of the trunk and drive away. Let Finley come back for her statement.

She walked toward an outdoor shower at the corner of the house and he followed her. She turned it on and stuck a leg under it. But when she switched to the other foot, Nick heard her intake of breath. She yanked her foot out of the shower spray.

"Let me take a look at those abrasions." Nick knelt down and gently washed the muddy water away. Her shin was beginning to bruise. The side of her calf was covered with fiery scratches.

"I'll get the first aid kit out of the cruiser."

"You don't have—" She stumbled as her ankle gave way. Nick scooped her up and carried her toward the house.

"I'm okay. Just a little shaky. Put me down."

He grasped the doorknob and maneuvered her through the door into a mudroom. He didn't stop there but carried her into the kitchen and deposited her in a chair at a Formica table. The room was old-fashioned and cozy, not at all what he expected.

She tried to get up.

"Stay," he said, and went back outside to get the first aid kit.

He stopped at the outdoor shower to wash off his own feet and calves, then carried the kit into the house. She was standing at the sink, attempting to clean her arms and face, but only managed to make it worse.

He turned her around and marched her back to the table. He wet a wad of paper towels and placed the kit on the table before pulling out another chair and sitting down in front of her.

She flinched when he lifted her foot, but he thought it was as much from surprise as pain. He rested her foot on his thigh while he inspected the abrasions more closely.

"This might hurt a little."

Nine

 How on earth had she ended up sitting at her kitchen table with her foot resting on the Crescent Cove police chief's hard, muscular thigh. She'd already seen it up close and personal at the cove, but the sight was nothing compared to— she tried to ease her foot away.

"Sorry. Did I hurt you?"

She shook her head. His hands were rough and callused, but remarkably gentle, which seemed odd since the rest of him was so intimidating.

He took her ankle and dabbed the damp towel up the outside of her leg to her knee.

Margaux sucked in her breath.

"Sorry, almost done."

Thank God, Margaux thought, because even the pain didn't prevent the path her thoughts were taking.

"That's much better, thanks. I'll be fine." This time she pulled her foot away.

He straightened up and began returning things to his first aid kit. He suddenly seemed as anxious to leave as she was to have him leave.

Nick stood up and pushed his chair beneath the table, fumbled with the clasp of the first aid kit. Suddenly the inviting kitchen was way too hot. He grunted something, grabbed the kit, and headed for the door.

It wasn't until he was sitting in the cruiser that he remembered the accident report he hadn't taken. He'd have Finley come by tomorrow. There was no way he was going back in there.

He hadn't felt this socially inept since he'd been seventeen and socially inept, sitting across the library table from her, wishing like anything that she'd say something to him. Just notice him.

Which was stupid because she'd only been thirteen. An ocean of difference at that age.

Or any age, he reminded himself. *Just drive away, jackass.* He started the engine. He didn't mean to look back, but couldn't stop himself. She stood at the door, her hand on the knob. She looked so forlorn. Vulnerable. Something he hadn't noticed before.

He was so tempted to go back, but he merely lifted his hand and drove away.

He didn't look back again; he was too busy trying to see the road and fighting feelings he didn't know existed. Not in him anyway. Not for a long time.

Margaux watched Nick drive away, then turned her back on him, determined not to give him another thought. But she thought about him anyway as she packed up her art supplies for the move to Linda's.

She was in the kitchen, contemplating dinner and ruing the loss of her ground beef, when there was a knock at the kitchen door.

She could see the silhouette of someone on the other side of the screen door. A large someone. A flutter of anticipation shook her. It wasn't fear, because she recognized the owner of those wide shoulders.

She hurried to the door. Nick Prescott stood outside, a bag

from the Cove Market in one arm. And a bouquet of flowers in the other. He'd changed into jeans, black T-shirt, and
Windbreaker.

Margaux held the door open for him. He walked straight
inside, put the grocery bag on the table, and handed her the
flowers.

"Compliments of the Crescent Cove Police Department
with our sincerest apologies."

Margaux took the flowers, embarrassed to realize that she
was blushing. Hopefully he wouldn't notice.

"You didn't have to do this."

He nodded brusquely. "The least I—we could do. I'm not
sure I remembered everything." He began unpacking the groceries. "Milk, bread, hamburger . . ."

Margaux rushed to stop him. There was something too intimate about watching him unload her groceries.

"I'll get those." She reached for the carton of milk he was
holding. Their fingers brushed. Electricity jolted down to her
toes. She snatched the carton away and shoved it into the refrigerator.

The chief was already heading for the door.

"Do you have to go back to work?" she asked, kicking herself simultaneously for the words. What did she think she was
doing?

He hesitated, looked back over his shoulder. "I'm off duty
but on call in case there's an emergency."

"Do you get a lot of emergencies?"

He turned to face her. "Always, but more so in the summer."

"Which is right around the corner."

He nodded, almost warily.

"Well . . . Maybe I could whip up a meal or something," she
said tentatively. "There's a decent bottle of wine." She shrugged
and added, "Since you brought me groceries."

"Are you asking me to dinner?"

No, she thought. "Yes," she said. "To show my apprecia-tion." Geez, what happened to that sophisticated business-woman from the city?

Nick's eyes narrowed and Margaux burned with chagrin. Did he think she was flirting with him? Propositioning him even? He was single and he probably had women chasing him all the time.

"You don't have to do that."

Margaux shrugged. "I know. It's no big deal." She couldn't tell whether the whole room vibrated with unspoken ques-tions, unsure emotions, or the desire to flee.

"Okay," Nick said. "Thanks."

The room seemed to exhale. "Do you like eggs?"

Margaux stood at the stove sautéing mushrooms, peppers, and onions while Nick uncorked the wine.

He handed her a glass, and tucked a stray strand of her hair behind her ear. It was such a natural gesture that Margaux hardly acknowledged it until Nick asked, "Did Linda strong-arm you into letting her cut your hair?"

Margaux started and flipped a piece of mushroom onto the stovetop. "Sort of. But it needed it."

"I thought it looked fine."

She gave him an incredulous look. "You saw it. It was out of control with the humidity. And I hadn't had time lately to get it done in the city." *Because my life was falling apart and the last thing I was thinking about was my hair.* Though maybe Linda was right, if you cared about what you looked like, things couldn't be that bad.

She glanced at Nick. "Are you're saying I shouldn't have?"

Nick considered her for a moment and Margaux wished she'd never asked.

"No. It's nice. It's just so tame."

Margaux took a sip of wine and raised an eyebrow.

Nick smiled. His whole face softened and for a second Margaux forgot the intense by-the-book policeman. "That's not a bad thing. I liked it both ways."

"Very diplomatic."

"No, really."

Margaux held up her hand. "Don't dig yourself in any deeper."

Nick rested his elbow on the countertop. They both watched the sizzling vegetables like they were the most fascinating things in the world.

The silence lengthened. It wasn't uncomfortable, at least not to Margaux. She glanced sideways at Nick. She couldn't tell how he felt.

"Dottie told me you were in the army."

"I was."

Margaux remembered that Nick's brother had died in the war. She immediately backed off.

"That's how working-class people get an education."

The bite in his voice surprised her. "And did you? Get an education?" And did that sound condescending or what?

"I have a degree in history."

"Which explains the book about the Ostrogoths."

He shrugged.

She poured the egg mixture into the pan. It would be a long night if he didn't loosen up.

"Are you planning to stay long?" he asked.

The question caught her off guard. "Why?"

"Just making conversation. Not the third degree."

"I'm taking a little vacation. I've been working really hard and needed a break." And that didn't sound convincing even to her. Designers on their way up didn't take vacations. Fortunately Nick probably didn't know that.

"Are *you* back here for good?"

He didn't answer and Margaux opened the oven door and

slid the pan onto the rack. She set the timer. "Just a few minutes. I'll make a salad." She rummaged in the fridge, trying to
think of something else to talk about.

"I don't really know. This is just an interim position until
they find a permanent replacement for Herb Green. I needed
the job for . . . well, I have responsibilities."

Taking care of his nephew and mother. Margaux had an
overwhelming desire to put her arms around him. "I admire a
man who doesn't shirk his responsibilities."

Again they settled into silence. Nick sliced tomatoes for the
salad. Each slice exactly the same thickness. Margaux smiled
to herself. A man that neat could drive you nuts. On the other
hand, not every man would make his family first priority.

Margaux wondered why he wasn't married. If he'd ever
been married. She was just curious. She was married and look
where it had gotten her.

"I'm in the middle of a divorce," she blurted. The timer
went off and she turned back to the oven with relief. Maybe
she should stick her head in and never have to face Nick or
anyone else again.

When she placed the egg pan on the top of the stove, Nick
was holding out her glass of wine. "Do you want to talk about
it or is it none of my business?"

"Neither. I don't know why I even said it." She took the
glass and gulped down a mouthful.

"You just wanted to set the record straight."

"I guess."

"Margaux. It's an omelet, not a commitment. But I can
leave." He set down his glass.

He was so prickly and he was going to leave. And God help
her, she didn't want him to. "How are you at getting an omelet
from the pan to the plate?"

He visibly relaxed and reached for the spatula. He divided
the omelet and slid each half onto a plate, filled their glasses

with more wine, and held her chair while she sat down. He made her run-down kitchen as elegant as any New York restaurant.

Margaux speared a bite of omelet, glanced at Nick, and realized he was waiting for her to begin. Their eyes met over their forks. Margaux smiled to herself. She certainly hadn't expected good table manners, which she realized now was a stupid assumption. She had a feeling that all assumptions about Nick Prescott might prove to be wrong.

He was sitting across from her like he belonged in her kitchen. As if the kitchen and maybe Margaux had been waiting for him all along. Which was absurd. She ate her bite of omelet, trying to figure out why she was feeling so . . . right.

He didn't seem to mind the absence of conversation. It was restful for a change. She didn't often cook; she never had the time and she mostly dined out where dinner was more about networking and deal making than enjoying food. But she hadn't forgotten how, and she'd made one pretty mean omelet tonight.

"This is good," Nick said, reflecting her own thoughts.

She laughed. "Are you surprised?"

"No, I just thought that working in fashion, you probably don't have a lot of time to eat, much less cook."

Worked in, she thought. "I was Jude's daughter before I was a fashion designer. The Sullivan household was always a place of celebration, especially on the holidays, food, family, friends." She sighed. "Then I left for school and my brother Danny was killed . . ."

"I remember. I'm sorry."

"You knew Danny?"

"Not really. My mother wrote me when it happened."

She waited for him to say something about his own brother, but he only looked around. "This kitchen feels like it's seen a lot of family gatherings."

"That it has." And maybe it would again.

When they finished eating, Nick started to carry the dishes to the sink, but Margaux stopped him. "I can also load a dishwasher. Sit. I'll make coffee."

They took their cups into the living room. Margaux glanced around the room. Sketches were strewn across every surface. Luckily, she'd hidden the merman sketch in the trunk with the diary.

Nick picked up a sketch from the coffee table. She craned her neck to see which one it was.

"I was just messing around with some ideas."

"A lot of ideas. You've been busy." Nick returned a pencil sketch of an evening suit and picked up a pastel of the sun setting behind the marina.

"Just filling the time."

"Jude said you had a really successful exhibit, or show, at Fashion Week in New York."

"Yes." It should have skyrocketed her into position for the fall Fashion Week. Instead she'd been catapulted out of the business completely.

"Are you cold?" Nick stepped toward her, concern in his eyes.

"What? No. Why?"

"You were shivering."

"No. Just—" He was standing close enough that she could feel his body warmth. Another shiver ran through her. Maybe she was cold, had been cold for a long time, and hadn't even noticed until now.

Nick reached out his hand and a deeper emotion invaded his eyes. But before Margaux could guess what it was, his beeper went off.

Nick groaned. "Sorry." He checked the number, opened his cell phone, and pressed speed dial. He listened for a minute and hung up. "I have to go. Someone set several boats adrift down at the marina. Kids, probably. They're starting early this season. Finley said to be sure and apologize for him."

She followed him to the back door.

"Thanks for dinner."

"Sure. Anytime." Which was a stupid thing to say. They shouldn't be having dinner together. They shouldn't be doing anything together.

Nick wasn't really making a move to leave. She was pretty sure they were thinking the same thing. There was an awkward moment while some unseen force drew them together.

She looked up at him, expectant. Nick dipped his head. But his lips bypassed her mouth and kissed her cheek.

"Thanks again."

And he was gone. Margaux heard the truck start up and drive away while she stood at the screen door, surprised, disappointed, and feeling better than she had since her first fashion award.

She turned back to the kitchen. Two plates, two wineglasses. She had to fight really hard to keep this particular fantasy at bay.

She began loading the dishwasher; the telephone rang.

"Was that Nick Prescott's truck I saw driving away?"

"Hi, Mom. Yes, it was."

"I'm not prying, but is everything okay?"

"Yes. My bike had a flat tire and he gave me a ride home."

"That was nice of him. The other reason I called was that I want to come over tomorrow morning and go through the attic. I thought I'd donate some things to the flea market."

"If you come early, I'll help."

"Great. See you tomorrow."

Margaux hung up, thanking her stars Jude hadn't come in person to see the state of her leg, and making a mental note to wear long pants tomorrow.

It was nearly midnight when the last boat was spotted on the rocks of Crescent Point and towed back to the marina.

The night guard managed to catch one of the perpetrators, a boy from a neighboring town and home from prep school.

He refused to name his associates, which Nick was sure would make him popular with his friends. Nick had Finley haul him off to the jail to wait for his parents.

Linda's kitchen light was still on when he finally crossed the street from the marina, exhausted, wet, and shivering. It had been a long day and longer night. And he hadn't even been on duty.

Dinner with Margaux had faded to a dim memory. He knew they'd eaten in the kitchen, talked about some things, but for the life of his tired mind, he couldn't remember what they'd said.

Instead of going straight up the stairs to his apartment, he went around back and knocked on the kitchen window.

Linda opened the door right away.

"Yo, Chief. You look like a drowned rat." She tossed him a towel.

"Thanks. You know you shouldn't open your door to strangers. Especially late at night."

"Well, kiss my butt. I didn't think we were strangers."

"You didn't know it was me."

"Of course I did. Who else would be knocking on my door at midnight? Not my freaking fairy godmother, that's for sure."

Nick started to tell her that safety was a serious issue, but he was just too tired.

"Sit down. I'll get you coffee. It's fresh-brewed. I've been keeping the home fires burning. And I knew it was you 'cause I saw your freshly mowed hair as you walked past my window. Though I gotta say, the wet look becomes you."

Nick scrubbed his hair and face and sat down at the table while Linda poured him a cup of coffee, something he did not need.

He drank it anyway.

"Just so you know. I rented the hippie's space."

"Oh God, what is it this time?"

"You'll like this one. I'm sure."

"A fortune teller?"

"You want to know what your future's gonna be? It isn't a fortune teller."

"Then who is it? Did you get references? Have you checked out their financial situation? You don't want to get stiffed again."

"Hey, I only lost a month's rent with the hippies and I gained a pound of yak butter they left in the fridge."

Nick chuckled and drained his cup. "Thanks for the coffee and the perspective on life." He stood and headed for the door.

"Sweet dreams," she called after him.

"You, too." As the door closed behind him, she started singing. She was in full voice when he trudged up the steps to his apartment.

"Everybody's looking for someone."

Ten

 The ceiling was creaking. Margaux opened one eye against the morning sun. She closed her eye again, turned over, and pulled the sheet over her head. Moments later a loud *thunk* above her made her sit up. She looked at the clock. Eight-thirty.

Jude was in the attic, and Margaux had overslept, probably because she'd stayed awake for hours making plans for her new studio. Which was better than walking around shell-shocked, which she'd been doing for months now.

She pulled jeans over her healing calf, put on a sweatshirt, and went into the hallway.

The attic stairs were pulled down. Margaux made a quick trip to the bathroom, then climbed the rickety wooden steps, holding on with both hands until she could peer into the attic.

Dim light pushed its way past a dirt-streaked gable window. A single lightbulb hung from the ceiling, turning stacks of old magazines, end tables, and other objects into phantasmal shapes.

Jude stood in the middle of the room bent over a torn cardboard box. A jumble of old books spread out around her feet.

"Morning," Margaux said.

Jude yelped and turned around. "Good morning. Did I wake

you?" she asked. "I was trying to be quiet, but the box broke."
She held up a torn piece of cardboard.

Margaux climbed the last few rungs and stepped into the
attic. She brushed her dusty hands on her jeans and sneezed. "I
haven't been up here in ages."

"Neither have I. Where did we get all this old junk?"

"When did a Sullivan throw anything away?"

"True. Well, today we turn over a new leaf. Quinn Palmer
will be here with his truck at eleven. I just hope we're finished
by then."

"Where should I start?"

"You don't have to help." Jude's voice sounded hollow in the
musty, dead air.

"I don't mind. And don't sell that dressmaker's dummy. I
may need it. Have you seen my easel or the drafting table?"

"The drafting table is probably over by that gable."

Margaux squeezed through the forest of forgotten objects
toward the window.

"Found it, but it's buried under a bunch of stuff that looks
like it should go to the flea market." A white Victorian étagère
with one curve of molding broken off, a steamer trunk with
a missing strap, a stack of *Life* magazines from 1972, and two
mismatched mahogany end tables nested together.

She hauled them out and piled them near the opening to the
stairs.

It took both of them to pull an old trestle sewing machine
across the wooden floor.

"Are you sure you want this to go?" asked Margaux. "Wasn't
it Grammy's?"

Jude considered the machine. Margaux could see that she
was torn between keeping the past and letting go. She felt a
little like that herself.

"Or at least have an antiques dealer look at it?"

Jude let out her breath. "No. It might fetch a good price

from a collector at the flea market. And it will go to a good cause."

"What is it this year?" Each year the town put on a flea market and carnival to raise money for a special project. One year it had paid for refurbishing the historic village school-house. One year they had sponsored three children to the Special Olympics.

"We're donating the proceeds to help clean up the old board-walk. It's really gone to seed. The arcade went out of business last summer. The old dance hall has been boarded over since that big nor'easter years ago. Even Seamus McGuire had to stop running the carousel after his heart attack."

"That's too bad."

"It's a darn shame, letting a big chunk of history just fall away. But fortunately, a developer expressed interest in buying it to build an apartment complex or some such. Suddenly, after years of ignoring what they had, the townspeople were up in arms. Now there's a move to Save the Boardwalk."

"Sounds like it'll cost a fortune."

"It would if we wanted to gentrify it, put in chichi restaurants, and draw hordes of tourists. Good for the local economy maybe, but bad for our quality of life. As it is, we just want to make it a fun, viable place for families to enjoy. Like it used to be, only better. Okay enough chitchat. The sewing machine goes, unless you want it."

"No thanks. Too slow for my needs, and since I don't have anywhere to keep it—" She broke off.

"Now don't you worry. This is your house for all intents and purposes. I always meant for you and Louis to have it. Now I thank my lucky stars that I didn't sign it over to you."

"God, I might have lost this, too." Margaux's knees went weak.

"Well, you didn't, and there is no way that so-and-so can get his hands on it even if he tried. So don't give it another thought. Let's see if we can pull that little slipper chair out to where Quinn can get it."

Margaux squeezed in behind the chair. She shoved it but it didn't budge.

"It's caught on something. Hang on." Margaux wiggled the chair but it stayed put. "If you can move that big suitcase, I think I can slide it out."

Jude lifted the suitcase out of the way. Something rolled across the floor. Jude dropped the suitcase. Margaux's breath caught when she recognized the candy-apple red motorcycle helmet resting at her mother's feet. Danny's motorcycle helmet.

Neither of them moved, then slowly, Jude bent down, picked it up, and cradled it to her breast.

"Mom."

Jude shook her head.

Margaux came out to where Jude stood motionless, just holding that helmet, and Margaux thought her heart would break.

They stood close but not touching.

Finally Jude said, "Not this." And carefully placed the helmet back on the chair.

"Why don't we go make some coffee and let Quinn help us with the rest?"

Jude shook herself like someone coming out of the water, or out of a dream. "I'm sorry, honey. You haven't had a cup yet. That's a good idea. Let's go down."

"You go ahead," Margaux said. "I see my old easel in the corner. I'll just get it and come right down."

Jude stepped down onto the ladder. When her head disappeared, Margaux picked up the helmet and carefully placed it out of sight. Then she grabbed her easel and followed her mother downstairs.

Quinn and his friend showed up in a rusty black pickup while Jude and Margaux were in the kitchen having their coffee.

"Yo, Mrs. Sullivan. Hey there, Margaux," he said.

"Hi, Quinn," Margaux said, trying not to look shocked at the snake tattoo that curled out of his rolled-up sleeve. "I hardly recognized you. You're so, um, tall."

"Six-one. This is Darren." Quinn gestured to the second boy, who slouched behind him.

"Hi, Darren."

Darren, shorter and stockier, grunted. Margaux interpreted it as hello.

"So where's the stuff?"

Nick watched Connor on the other side of the glass window at Monroe Elementary School. He was sitting at a child-size table across from the child psychologist. Dr. McKinnon was a tall man, barrel-chested, and Nick wondered how the small wooden legs of the chair held beneath his weight. His knees were tucked up to either side, drawing his khaki trouser cuffs up and revealing the argyle pattern of his socks.

He seemed to be chatting amiably with Connor, who was building some kind of arch with blocks. It was strange, Nick thought, how Connor could be so jumpy at times, and yet docile at others. He didn't cling when Mrs. Ames, the school psychologist, introduced him to McKinnon. He went happily enough when the doctor took him down the hall to the "puzzle" room to play.

It was Nick who wanted to draw him close, cling to him, beg them not to take him, to hurt him, to make him feel any more alien than he already felt.

Now, Nick sat in the padded chair, hands gripping the wooden arms. Wondering what they were looking for. Hoping that Connor didn't make a mistake, even though Nick, a college-educated man, couldn't figure out what they were doing.

His mother sat in the chair next to him, her hands folded demurely in her lap. She could have been at church or bingo night for all the emotion she showed. Nick felt his knee begin to jiggle and consciously stopped it. He didn't want to appear nervous, but he was scared as hell that they would find something wrong.

He didn't know how parents dealt with that kind of tragedy. He should probably talk to Deke and Peg O'Halloran. Their daughter, Ceci, had brain damage from lack of oxygen at birth. She was a sweet kid, but at ten she'd already outgrown her IQ.

At least Deke and Peg had each other. And faith. Nick had himself and he didn't much believe in God these days. It wasn't that he'd love Connor less if there was something not quite right, he just didn't know how he'd be able to juggle all the things necessary to give him a decent quality of life.

Dr. McKinnon laughed. Connor was smiling, but Nick knew he wouldn't be making any noise. Just those puffs of breath that posed as a laugh. It was like the cartoons Connor watched, the volume down so low that only the picture pulsed in the room.

Finally, the doctor stood. He shook Connor's hand and the two of them went out the door to the hall. Best of buds.

Nick braced himself for the doctor's opinion.

The door opened and the doctor came in. "I dropped Connor off in the playroom. There are other children there and Mrs. Delacorte and her aide are with them."

Nick was halfway out of his chair, but his mother put her hand on his and he sat back down.

Mrs. Ames ushered them to the other side of the room where several chairs were placed in a semicircle.

She sat down beside Nick's mother. Dr. McKinnon pulled a chair out so that he was facing them and sat down across from Nick.

"Connor is a very bright little boy."

Nick let out the breath he'd probably been holding since they arrived, but he didn't relax. He sensed the "but" that was to follow.

When the doctor didn't continue, Nick blurted out, "So does this mean he can go to public school?"

Hell, he would home-school the kid if he had to. Except that he already had a full-time job even if it was only temporary until the next election. Plus he had a part-time job with Jake. When would he have time to teach Connor?

"I'm concerned about his social skills."

"Jesus, the kid just lost both parents. He's living with a grandmother he'd never seen until a few months ago, in a town he'd never heard of." Nick stopped, took a breath, aware that he'd just lost his cool.

"I understand your frustration, Nick. But these things take time. And most children Connor's age have already spent several years in preschool and kindergarten and other social environments."

Nick felt his options sinking away. He wanted what was best for his nephew, but he just couldn't believe that sending him to a special needs school was going to help him adapt to a normal life. "So what are you suggesting? There's nothing wrong with his brain. Hell, the kid reads the newspaper."

"Yes, but mental readiness is not the only factor in sending a child to school."

And Connor started at loud noises, spoke only in whispers. Now he'd begun running away, looking for something or someone.

Nick rubbed a hand across his face. He was losing this battle. His mother was ready to do anything the doctor said. She was making rumblings about returning to work as a seamstress when Connor began school in September. So far he'd been able to talk her out of it, but if they had to pay for private school, he would need the extra income.

His mother had worked all her life, and Nick would be damned if he'd let her go back just when she should be enjoying retirement. He hated thinking about her having to work all day, then come home and have to take care of Connor.

Connor got a government check. They'd just have to make things work.

"Your mother told me that he was taken out of pre-K."

Nick's mind—his whole body—was coiled tight. "The teacher said he didn't participate and that she didn't have the staff to accommodate a boy . . . that shy." Those weren't exactly her words. It was something more to the effect that Connor was antisocial and unapproachable.

But he wasn't antisocial, he just didn't know how to be social. And he hadn't always been that way. What the hell had his mother been doing with him before she called to tell Nick she'd left him with a neighbor and gave him a Fort Bragg address where he could pick him up.

He'd gone personally to talk with the neighbors and anyone who knew the family, trying to get any information he could. All he learned was that Connor had gone from a bright, quiet, but friendly kid to something near comatose. They didn't think he'd been abused. Later examinations had confirmed this. But something had happened, not just the death of his father. And it happened before his mother took off with "some man," as her next-door neighbor described it.

He'd signed the necessary papers, packed up Connor's clothes, and brought him to Crescent Cove. He thought things would get better, but they were hanging on a thread.

God, he hated that bitch and hoped she had a miserable life wherever she was.

"I asked Connor how he liked school."

Nick waited for the big blow.

Dr. McKinnon smiled slightly. "He said it was fine."

The same thing he'd told Nick after he was sent home. Nick looked at the school psychologist, who was looking, as always, calm and nonjudgmental. She gave him a reassuring smile.

Nick wanted to shake them both until they came up with what was wrong with the kid. "There are still three months before school."

McKinnon nodded. "We can wait and see. He doesn't display any of the usual indicators of post-traumatic stress or Asperger's."

Nick flinched at the doctor's words. He didn't want to hear about PTSD. He'd heard enough. Read enough. Learned enough after Ben's death. He could have told them Connor didn't have that or Asperger's. He'd researched every possible cause for his behavior. There were some scary possibilities, but they weren't what Connor had.

"That's good. Right?" God, he hated the sound of his own voice. The need for reassurance.

"It isn't bad."

He hated how McKinnon refused to say anything outright. Nick wanted facts. He knew invasion and armistice dates. The reasons for the War of the Roses. The number of members of Parliament. Could quote the Declaration of Independence. He wanted to know what was wrong with Connor.

"One option is to send him for more testing. I have a colleague at Yale who is excellent with nonadaptive behavior."

He'd been tested and tested, they hadn't found anything physically or mentally wrong with him. That left emotional, and all the testing in the world couldn't fix that.

"No more tests. You said yourself he's bright, he doesn't have classic symptoms, he just doesn't talk loud. And he won't get any better if we keep dragging him around like a lab rat." Nick stopped, appalled at his outburst.

The doctor looked as unruffled as if Nick had agreed with him. "I was about to say pretty much the same thing. Try to involve him with other kids. We'll give it some time. See if they can draw him out. And see if maybe he'll open up about why he doesn't talk out loud."

Nick nodded. In spite of the air-conditioning, he felt sweat trickle down his temple. He wiped it away. No sense in trying to hide it from the doctor. McKinnon was pretty astute. He had to hand him that.

"I'm also concerned with how this is affecting you."

Nick just looked at him.

"Nick?"

What was he supposed to say? Thank you for your concern? Shut the hell up, my mother is sitting right here? Jesus. He had to get out of there.

"It's natural to feel a sense of frustration, helplessness, even resentment in these situations. It can take its toll on the family."

"I'm just trying to get us through this. Give Connor a place where he feels safe. Loved." He couldn't believe he was saying this stuff to a shrink.

"Mrs. Ames says you had to give up your teaching. Your life in Colorado."

"It was my choice."

"And?"

"That's all. It was my choice and I made it. End of story." And end of session. He stood up. "Thank you for your time, Dr. McKinnon." He stuck out his hand. Businesslike, firm.

The doctor smiled slightly before he took it. "Thank you for coming. I've made another appointment with Connor for next Thursday. I'd like you to be here if that's possible." Nick started to explain that the summer season was just starting, that he was understaffed and overworked, but he was tired of fighting. "Sure. I'll be here."

He moved to the door, fumbled with the knob with a sweaty hand, and yanked the door open.

A young woman in jeans and a bright blue T-shirt was walking down the hall holding Connor by the hand. She looked about twelve, but he knew she was a teaching assistant. Nick didn't know if Mrs. Ames had called down to tell them they were finished or if Connor had been too much for the girl to deal with.

He strode down the hall and took Connor by the hand.

"Bye, Connor," the girl said with a smile and a wave.

"Bye," Connor whispered before Nick whisked him down the hall toward the parking lot.

They'd brought his mother's old Buick and Nick lifted Connor into the backseat and strapped him in, then he helped his mother to climb in the front seat. He really needed to get her a more manageable car.

He thought about Jude's little Citroën, but couldn't see his mother driving anything so cute. Or wearing a perky hairdo. Or any of the things Jude represented. There was a world of difference between the two women. He wished it could have been different.

He dropped them off and picked up the police cruiser, turning down lunch because he had to get back to work. He wouldn't be getting any more time off until the fall. The prank at the marina last night had just been the overture.

He drove back to his apartment to change into his uniform. As he turned the corner onto Marina Way, he saw Quinn Palmer's truck parked at the curb outside. He and Darren Whitcomb were carrying boxes into the house. The new tenant must be moving in.

He was mildly curious, but didn't have time to check it out. He ran up the stairs to his apartment, and ten minutes later he came out dressed for work and carrying a peanut butter sandwich for his lunch.

He pulled out of his parking space just as a bright blue coupe drove by.

Eleven

"This is perfect," Margaux told Linda as they stood in the doorway of Margaux's new studio. Her drafting table was set up in the bay window. Her paints and pastels were lined up on a bookshelf she'd brought from the beach house. Her easel was placed in a corner.

The door opened and the "Toreador Song" filled the air.

"Go forth and create," Linda said. "Us mere mortals have to paint some hair. Coming, Mrs. Fortuna."

Margaux stood in the middle of the room. Light streamed in through the windows. The walls were white and there was crown molding along the ceiling. It was a good space.

Small compared to her loft space in New York. But then, she was just starting out . . . again. Somehow that fact didn't bother her as much as it should.

What had she said in the diary? She had a dream. To design clothes that would make people feel good. Now she realized she hadn't even been thinking about the people who would wear her creations. Just about which models to use in order to wow the industry.

Her work had become about the design, not about the actual clothes. It was gratifying in a remote way—to be on top, to be the one others copied. It was exciting, exhilarating, and yet somehow empty.

But where did you go after New York and Paris? Crescent Cove? Brianna was probably the only woman in the area who could pull off an M Atelier design. To do what? Go out and feed her chickens? Her goat?

And where did she start? *Clothes to make people feel good about themselves.*

She spent the next few hours sketching and tossing. None of her usual designs appealed to her. Yet nothing appeared to replace them. She knew she was in trouble when she found herself doodling the masts that rose over the marina wall.

She tore off the page and aimed it at the corner of the room. She was collecting quite a pile of rejects, though a few had survived and were clothespinned to a fishing line she'd strung along the west wall.

She leaned back in her chair and stared out the window at the street, the marina, the salt marshes, the point, the Sound.

She placed another sheet of paper on the drafting table, let her hand move, trying to let it roam free without her mind pushing it into what she knew. The outline of a dress emerged, not sharp and angular, but soft and gauzelike. She reached for her pastels, let her hand guide her head for once.

Blues on blue with bits of white, whimsical. She had to force herself not to interfere, but let it grow. She scalloped the hem and wrapped a flowing scarf around the model's neck. Then she leaned back and took a look.

She laughed. It looked like the old Margaux. The young Margaux actually. And she liked it.

She pinned it to the fishing line and stepped back to study it. She liked it. But would it sell?

As she stood there, the front door opened and the "Toreador Song" echoed through the house. Someone went into the salon. Margaux picked up a lighter shade of blue pastel and added another swirl to the skirt.

She felt movement beside her and looked down to see Connor Prescott, standing close and gazing at her sketch. It was as if he materialized out of thin air. His grandmother or uncle must be close by.

"Hi," she said.

"Hi," the boy breathed. He smiled up at her and went back to looking at her dress design.

She bent down beside him. "Well, what do you think?"

He looked from the sketch to her, his big brown eyes so sweet it was heartbreaking.

"It's the ocean," he said.

Margaux looked back at the dress sketch. "It *is* the ocean. You are so smart."

He said something. She leaned closer.

"I like you."

"Well, thank you. I like you, too."

"Connor. Connor, where are you?"

Margaux stood up, and Connor pressed close to her.

"Connor!"

"He's in here," Margaux called, her hand going instinctively to the boy's shoulder.

Nick stepped into the doorway and froze. He looked tired and harried, but he wasn't looking at his nephew. He was looking at Margaux.

Linda pushed him through the door. "Did I mention that Margaux is my new tenant?"

"No, you didn't." Ignoring both women, he stepped toward his nephew. "Connor, you can't run off like that."

Connor cowered against Margaux.

"Sorry," Margaux said. "He was giving me his advice about my new sketch."

"What?" Nick looked at the row of sketches hanging along the wall.

"The blue one. He said it was the ocean."

"Well, dee and tarnation," Linda said. "It *is* the ocean."

Nick looked from the sketch to Connor to Margaux and shrugged.

Linda guffawed out a laugh and Connor shrank even closer to Margaux.

"Sorry he bothered you," Nick said.

"He didn't." Connor felt good nestled against her side. A longing erupted deep inside her and she gently pushed the boy away.

Linda squatted down by Connor. "You two doing manly things this afternoon?"

She nodded and listened to words Margaux couldn't hear. "Going to Deke's?" Linda grinned wickedly. "You know Connor. Margaux was just telling me how she wanted to go to Deke's."

Margaux shook her head.

Nick shot a fulminating look at Linda.

Connor took a deep breath. "Can she go with us, Uncle Nick?" And out of the blue, he took Margaux's hand.

"Ms. Sullivan is too busy—"

"Connor, sweetie, I can't—"

"She'd love to go. Don't worry about a thing. I'll lock up." Linda practically shoved them out the door. "Have a good time and don't let Margaux eat all the clams."

Connor's shoulders shook with a silent giggle as they walked to the street.

Margaux tried to pull back when they reached the sidewalk, but Connor held on tight and pulled her toward Nick's truck. She looked at Nick and shrugged.

He turned to Margaux. "Do you mind? I just have to drop off some lumber first."

"No," she answered slowly. "But you don't need to be polite. Linda was just being—"

"Linda. I know, but Connor wants you to go."

"And you always do what Connor wants?"

He frowned.

"That wasn't a judgment."

"He never asks for anything much."

"I'd love to go."

Nick lifted Connor into the cab and helped Margaux in after him. There was a bustle about whose seat belt belonged where and Margaux and Connor giggled a lot while Nick watched stoically.

The man had no sense of humor.

At last they were strapped in and ready. They left town, passed the entrance to Little Crescent Beach, and turned into the next side street. The street dead-ended in a clump of trees. Nick pulled the truck to a stop at the last house.

Connor unbuckled his seat belt. Nick opened the door and Connor scrambled over Margaux and slid down to the ground.

"Jake has a tree swing," Nick explained.

They watched the boy race across the grass. He was several yards away when he came to an abrupt halt. Slowly he turned back and looked at Nick, then Margaux. His excitement drained away to something else. Fear? Pain?

Nick's breath caught, then he expelled a sigh. Margaux got a sense of total defeat. It was as if Connor had stopped himself from having fun. Because he expected to be yelled at? Nick was intense and serious, but she could tell he loved the boy. And she also saw his face when Connor lost his enthusiasm and slumped into quiet. It wasn't anger or disapproval she saw, but sorrow, bone-deep unhappiness.

"You do what you need to do, I'll do swing duty." She struck off across the grass to where Connor stood.

"Wow, that's some swing," Margaux said, taking him by the hand and leading him toward the tire that hung by a rope from an old maple tree.

He came willingly, but his lip trembled.

She dropped down beside him. "What is it, sweetie? Do you want me to push you?"

He nodded.

"Cool." She lifted him up and he stuck his legs through the tire opening. "Hold on tight." She pulled the tire back and gave it a push. He pumped his legs and smiled a big gap-toothed smile. Margaux waited for the *"whe-e-e"* kids were supposed to make when they swung higher, but it didn't come.

The swing died down a bit and Margaux gave it another push.

Nick came across the lawn.

Margaux pushed the swing.

After a few minutes, Nick said, "Thanks for coming."

"Wouldn't have missed it," she said.

They went back to watching Connor.

When the swing died down again, Nick walked over to Connor. "Last time, buddy, it's time to go."

Connor immediately stopped pumping and slid out of the tire. No whining, no dawdling. He just came to stand by Margaux and Nick.

They headed back to the truck. Halfway there, Margaux saw what looked like a path going into the woods.

"Is that Little Cove beyond those woods?"

"Yeah."

"So that's where you came from. Is that how you guys always came to the cove?"

Nick frowned. "Yeah. A friend of mine lives here."

"We always wondered where that path led to, but we never went any farther than the Grotto."

"The what?"

"Grotto. It was our secret hideout."

He grinned, the first truly amused expression she'd seen from him all day.

"Would you like to walk down to the cove?"

"Yeah, I would. If you don't mind."

"Fine by me. Connor's never been down there. He might like it."

Connor had stopped to dig a soda cap out of the ground.

"Connor, come on, we're going for a walk."

Connor immediately stood and hurried toward them.

Beneath the trees was cooler than in the sun and Margaux shivered, probably from excitement, which was silly because it was just a normal path. One she knew very well from the other end. And she couldn't for the life of her figure out why they had never followed it to its beginning.

The path was too narrow to walk side by side. It was rutted and overgrown as if never used. Roots grew over the earth and fern leaves slapped against their ankles as they walked, and only a few patches of dappled sunlight made its way past the trees.

Nick led the way. Margaux walked right behind Connor. Even so, he kept looking back as if making sure she was close by.

The path curved unexpectedly and Margaux knew they were near the Grotto.

She almost walked past it, it looked so different from the other side. It was completely hidden. No wonder the boys had never discovered them.

"Wait," she said. "There it is." She felt a little weird about showing it to strangers, but she didn't think Bri and Grace would mind, and she bet Connor would be impressed with a secret hideout.

Connor and Nick both stopped. Ignoring Nick, she crouched down next to Connor. "Do you want to see the secret hideout my friends and I had when we were kids?"

He nodded, his eyes round. She motioned for him to follow her. "It's over here."

The underbrush had already been trampled where they had visited the Grotto the week before. She stopped when she was at the edge of the overhang. "There it is," she whispered. Connor leaned over and peered inside.

She could feel Nick standing behind them.

Connor said something. It sounded like "cool."

"You have to duck-walk to get inside."

"Look before you step," said the voice of authority behind her.

"Aye, aye, Captain," Margaux said automatically.

She heard Connor's puff of laughter.

The two of them duck-walked inside and crouched beneath the ledge. Connor grinned up at her.

Nick braced his hand against the overhang and peered in at them.

"You really didn't know about this place?" Margaux asked.

"Nope. I guess we were too anxious to get to the cove to swim to pay much attention."

"And to spy on the girls?"

"That, too." He smiled. Once again it transformed his face. Made him seem human and even approachable.

Which was a good thing, since she probably shouldn't be out in the woods with a man she didn't know. Of course, she had Connor to protect her. The thought made her smile and the three of them kept smiling until Nick pulled away.

"We'd better get going."

Connor duck-walked out and stood up, Margaux followed him and gladly accepted the hand Nick held out to help her up.

"I was shorter in those days," she explained.

They continued down the path until a triangle of blue appeared between the trees, and suddenly they were standing on the pebbled beach, blue water spreading out before them, the color of Margaux's latest design.

Twelve

 They spent half an hour skipping stones on the water, though neither Connor nor Margaux was very good, even after Nick helped them with their technique. But they laughed a lot, at least Margaux did, and she thought Connor did because his whole body vibrated when something funny happened.

Nick did seem to lighten up a bit, but Margaux was beginning to think he never unwound completely. Maybe he didn't even know how. Which was a shame.

They took off their shoes, waded across the cove, and climbed the rocks of the jetty where Margaux pointed out her house to Connor. She felt Nick tense beside her and realized that he was looking at the old lifeguard stand and she cursed herself for making the suggestion.

The sun was beginning to head toward the horizon as they retraced their steps back to the truck. Margaux had spent more time than she'd planned with them and she knew she should use that as an excuse to get out of going to Deke's. She was aware of how people would jump to the wrong conclusions.

But it had been so long since she'd just had fun that she brushed her good sense aside. So instead of asking Nick to drop her off at the marina when they drove back toward town, she stayed quiet and concentrated on the passing scenery.

They turned onto the bumpy road that led through the salt marshes to the narrow bridge that was the only access to the Crescent Cove beach and boardwalk.

One minute they were on a paved street flanked by stores and houses, the next they were surrounded by delicate stalks of marsh grass that swayed and shimmered in the breeze. All around them the fragile tips reflected peridot and amber from the setting sun.

Margaux gasped. "Stop, please."

The truck screeched to a stop. "What is it?"

"Can you wait just a minute? I'll be right back." She was already getting out of the truck.

An idea had exploded in her head. She had to get a better look, engrave the subtle colors in her brain before memory dimmed them into gray.

"Or go ahead, I'll meet you at Deke's."

Near the bridge, a wooden platform jutted a few feet into the sanctuary. She walked out to the end. All around her, shades of green, gold, and silver glimmered and changed with the light or with a passing cloud. She let her peripheral vision melt the grasses into a myriad of shades, tones, and luminosity, all combining to create a sea of living color.

She heard a car door shut, the patter of feet behind her, and turned to see Connor running toward her. As he reached her he opened his arms, his eyes wide and dark and lonely.

She caught him up, swinging him onto her hip and pointing out to the marsh. "Look at that. What do you think, Connor? Shall we make a dress the color of salt grass?"

He nodded, then pointed toward the horizon. An egret lifted out of the grass, its white wings spreading against the blue sky and flying across the sun until it was merely a silhouette.

"And an egret, too," she said. "You are such a smart boy."

He'd seen what she had been missing. It was out there, vibrant and alive. Had been surrounding her all along, but she hadn't seen it. She had been too busy reacting—to her impending divorce, to losing her job, to something she couldn't name until now as she gazed at the marshland. Fear. She was afraid. To let herself come out in her designs, to face life alone, to let herself be attracted to a man with whom she had nothing in common. To find joy again.

It was calling to her, that missing something. Somehow she had to capture it and bring it back into her life again.

As she stood there with Connor, she wasn't seeing marsh grass. She saw silk chiffon, shimmering in the lights of the runway. It was a stunning idea. Could she translate these colors from nature to cloth?

The sun flared from behind a white cloud as it settled toward the horizon. But Margaux was seeing a gown of red, gold, pink, mauve, a train the colors of sunset fanning out behind it like the sun itself.

Nick came up beside them. "What are you doing?"

"Seeing color," Margaux said, and laughed. "Isn't that right, Connor?"

Connor nodded and wrapped his arms around her neck.

Suddenly she was aware of how crazy she looked, of how she'd picked up Connor without thinking. She let him slide down her hip and peeled his arms from her neck.

"Sorry, I got a little carried away." She turned back to the truck. Nick took Connor's hand. Connor reached for Margaux's hand and he skipped between them until they reached the road.

They were quiet as they drove over the bridge to the boardwalk. It wasn't a true boardwalk. The walk was actually asphalt, though big chunks had heaved out of it over the last decade and weeds grew up in the cracks. At one time it had been the center of local life in Crescent Cove.

She and her friends sometimes came over to play the games at the arcade or ride the carousel and reach for the golden ring. They'd eat fried dough and buy clam rolls from Deke's father.

Sometimes they'd come to watch the beach movies, scooping out the sand to make pillows for their heads.

Nick pulled to a stop in the parking lot. Everything but Deke's looked closed now. The arcade was boarded over. The smaller stores were dark. The Seaview Motel, the only motel in Crescent Cove, had closed years ago. But it still sat behind the parking lot, a one-storied, sky blue, concrete bunker, deserted and unused.

They got out of the truck, and Connor ran over to the rail fence that surrounded the parking lot. He pointed across the beach to the point of land that jutted into the Sound like a fallen stalactite.

"What's that?" he breathed.

"It's Crescent Point. On a moonless night, if you go to the very end, you can see the whole Milky Way."

He looked up at Margaux and screwed up his face.

"Not the candy, goose. But stars that look like milk in the sky."

"I want to see it." His whisper carried a little louder than before, but Margaux might have imagined it.

She wanted him to see the Milky Way, but she wasn't about to intrude into Nick's territory.

"I'm sure Uncle Nick will bring you when the moon is a sliver." She raised her eyebrows, but Nick wasn't paying attention, he was looking into the mid-distance halfway between her and Connor, oblivious. "Isn't that right, Nick?" she said louder.

He actually jumped. "What? Sure?"

Connor pointed to Margaux. "You, too."

She definitely heard him then. Nick was looking at him, too. She shot him a warning look not to make too much of the tiny breakthrough and risk pushing him back into silence.

"Okay," she said tentatively. "We used to go out there when I was a kid." It was the most popular necking place in the area.

"See the big house with the turrets, the round things on the side? We thought it was haunted."

"Really?"

"Yes, but it turned out that these really nice people lived there. And they used to rent out cottages that looked just like they belonged in a fairy tale." She turned to Nick. This time he was watching her. "Do the Vanderhoefs still live there?"

Nick nodded.

What was wrong with him? He'd just started easing up and now he was remote and unapproachable again.

"You hungry?" Margaux asked.

Connor nodded.

The three of them walked across the street to Deke's.

"Mom said the town is going to restore the boardwalk and beach," she said conversationally. "That would be good for the community."

"As long as they don't go overboard."

Margaux smiled. "That's exactly what Mom said."

He looked down the broken asphalt to the row of abandoned businesses. "I love this town the way it is. And a small arcade would be good. But if it gets too fancy, the community will be pushed aside like they are everywhere else."

Margaux smiled at his vehemence. "So they should fix it up, but just enough for the local folks to enjoy it."

"Exactly."

Nick hadn't meant to say all that stuff to Margaux. For some reason he kept saying things he didn't mean to say when she was around. Before she came, he would never have just showed up on someone's doorstep with groceries. He'd never invite a woman out with him and Connor.

The grapevine would be humming with speculation by tomorrow, and he didn't want anyone to get the wrong idea or set up expectations about him and Margaux. He especially didn't want to start getting ideas about Margaux himself, because it would be too easy to hurry down that dead end.

Connor had taken to her immediately. Nick guessed children had an instinct about whom they could trust. And it was really evident he trusted Margaux. Hell, the kid was skipping today. A few minutes before, he'd come as close to talking out loud as Nick had ever heard him. And Nick knew it was because of Margaux.

Part of him was ecstatic, the other part was filled with dread that Connor was pretending he had a mother and father again and would be devastated when Margaux left to go back to New York. He probably shouldn't encourage their friendship, but he didn't have the heart to say no.

So here they were, the three of them, walking into the Clam Shack at the height of the dinner hour. At least it was off season and the middle of the week.

Only four of the ten tables were occupied. Everyone looked up when the door opened and Margaux and Connor walked in before him.

The Thompsons froze with smiles on their faces, then Mrs. Thompson waved her fingers at them, said something admonishing to her husband and he looked away. Doug Loomey, who owned the bait shop, just nodded and went back to eating his fish dinner. Nick didn't recognize the people at the other two tables.

But Peg stopped in the middle of the floor, both hands carrying plates. Her mouth went slack. "Margaux Sullivan." She hurriedly deposited the plates and rushed forward to give Margaux a hug. "I wondered how long it was going to be until you came by. Hey, Deke," she called over her shoulder.

Deke O'Halloran slid two plates through the food window. "What is it? Oh Lord. Hi, Margaux, how you been?"

"Good, thanks."

He nodded, grinned, and disappeared from the opening.

Peg looked up at Nick with a twinkle in her eye. "I see you've met our new chief of police."

Nick swore Margaux blushed, but she said smoothly, "He was nice enough to drive me and Connor on our dinner date."

Peg chuckled. Connor pulled Margaux toward a table by the window. Nick shrugged and followed them, Peg grinning after them. They'd barely gotten Connor settled next to the window when she showed up with servings of coleslaw and pickles and three plastic glasses of water.

"What can I get you?"

"What do you want, Connor?" Nick asked, schooling himself not to answer for the boy. Keeping his fingers crossed that he might actually speak.

Connor's mouth moved. Nick knew he was saying "fish fingers." He guessed that Peg did, too. He always got fish fingers at the Clam Shack.

Margaux's hand went to Connor's hair, she smoothed it away from his forehead. "Peg couldn't hear you. Tell her again."

This time "fish fingers" came out on an expulsion of breath.

"Ah, fish fingers. Those are Ceci's favorites, too." She took Nick and Margaux's orders and went to relay them to Deke.

Nick stared at his paper place mat. While they'd been on the beach and in the woods, he'd felt totally happy to be with someone Connor liked . . . someone he liked. But in the tiny restaurant he felt uncomfortable.

Margaux seemed totally at ease. She had leaned toward Connor and they were looking out the window. She was pointing to something, though Nick only saw darkness closing in on the boardwalk.

"When did the arcade close?"

"What?" Nick wrenched his thoughts back from the long road they'd been traveling. "Last September. It stayed open but mostly empty last summer. It's up for sale."

Margaux sighed. "That's too bad. We used to love to come

play the games and ride the carousel. I heard they designated it a historic site."

"Yeah, Jake McGuire's dad owns it. Jake's planning to get it up and running by next summer. It'll take a huge amount of work and money. But Jake's determined."

"Good for him." She looked back out the window. Her hair was beginning to curl and Nick liked that promise of wildness she obviously wanted to control.

She was beautiful, but he didn't think happy. If she was here for a vacation, why had she rented space at Linda's?

Peg returned with their meals.

Connor reached for the ketchup. Margaux and Nick both turned to help him. Margaux pulled her hand back and Nick flipped open the plastic top and squeezed the ketchup onto his plate. Connor jabbed a French fry into the ketchup and stuffed it into his mouth.

They ate without much conversation. After a few desultory tries, Nick gave up. They both talked to Connor, who nodded and kept eating.

Peg came to clear away the plates. "Why don't you go on back and see Ceci, Connor, while Uncle Nick and Margaux have their coffee?"

Connor glanced up at Nick.

"Sure. Go ahead. We'll be right here."

He looked at Margaux.

"Right here," she said.

Connor slid out of his chair and squeezed past Margaux. Peg looked surprised and delighted before she turned and followed Connor to the back of the restaurant.

Nick stared after them. It was the first time Connor had willingly left to play with another child. Of course Connor knew Ceci, felt comfortable with Peg. It was a small step, he cautioned himself. But it was a step. He felt a resurgence of hope.

"He's a sweetheart," Margaux said.

Nick nodded. "It was really nice of you to come out with him today. He isn't very outgoing."

"It was my pleasure."

Peg came back with two beige mugs of coffee.

"He's fine. They're watching *The Little Mermaid*. It might be hard to drag him away, so take your time."

Nick only wished that would be the case, but he knew that when it was time to go, Connor would merely get up and leave. Sometimes he longed for a tantrum or whining or something that said Connor was a normal boy.

He'd prayed for Connor to show an interest in something or someone beyond his grandmother and uncle, but he never expected him to be attracted to Margaux. A woman who lived in the fast lane, who was a career woman, who had no children, and who was going to leave.

Maybe he should explain that it wouldn't be good to get too close to the boy and raise his expectations. Or to raise Nick's. When Connor had been skipping between them out in the sea marsh, they'd felt like a family. And even though Nick knew it was an illusion, he fell into it and let himself wonder.

He took a sip of coffee, put down his mug. "Connor's mother left him with a neighbor one day and never came back."

Margaux looked up, her face going pale. A few freckles powdered her nose, probably brought on by the sun. He imagined she used all sorts of creams and beauty products to keep them at bay. He circled his cup on the tabletop.

"That's terrible. Is she . . . dead?"

Nick shrugged. Why on earth had he blurted that out? Now, she would expect him to tell her all about it. And for the first time in the two years since Ben had died he thought he might want to tell someone. He wanted to tell her.

"I don't know. Frankly, I don't care."

"How could a mother do that?" Her hand went to her mouth. "Sorry. I'm sure there were extenuating circumstances."

"If you call a guy on a motorcycle extenuating, then yeah, there were."

He shouldn't be telling her this. He hadn't confided in anybody, just gave them the line the army gave him, husband dead, wife couldn't cope with the stress. Yada yada.

"Connor's father was deployed most of his life, and he doesn't remember much about him. I visited him when he was younger. He was a normal kid. A terrible two. It was great. But now—he's sad sometimes. But he's happy, too." *Like when he's with you.*

"He seemed to be having a good time today."

Nick realized he was shredding his napkin. He dropped the remnants. "I just don't want him to suffer any more loss."

"Of course not."

She wasn't getting it. He tried again. "You're going to be busy while you're here."

"And?"

Nick swallowed. "He seems to already be growing attached to you."

"I see." She sat back in her chair, looking hurt, and he wanted to take back everything he'd said. He'd meant to drive her away, and now that he had, he just wanted her closer.

He was afraid it was too late for Connor or him.

"You want me to stay away from him."

Just say it and get it over with. "I think that would be for the best."

"I didn't think about that when I agreed to come. He was so cute. He seduced me."

She smiled at him and Nick felt his resolution slip as everything else picked up.

"But are you sure that's the best road to take? He's going to meet a lot of people passing through his life. He must know that he has you and his grandmother." She hesitated. "Unless you're planning on leaving, too."

He automatically shook his head. "I won't leave. I have too much that keeps me here."

She smiled again but this time it didn't send his blood racing; it was a combination of understanding and compassion and it cut right to his heart.

"Anyway. The damage is probably already done."

"I agree, but I won't go out of my way to avoid him. He's a child for heaven's sake. He won't understand." She looked a little sad. "I'm not much for going to Mass, and if you don't bring him to the store, I probably won't see him again.

"But I don't want him to think I deserted him, too. You'll have to think of something to tell him, that doesn't include making me out to be the bad guy." She stood up. "I guess we'd better be going."

Peg went to fetch Connor, they said goodbye to Deke and walked across the tarmac to the parking lot. The sky was full of stars, but Nick didn't call attention to them. He just wanted to get Margaux and Connor home as soon as possible before he lost his resolution and begged her to stay.

He dropped Margaux off at the marina, then backtracked to his mother's house to drop off Connor. If she noticed that it meant an extra trip for him, she didn't say. Just thanked him for dinner, said goodbye to Connor, and walked across the street to the house.

He hoped to hell she'd be gone before he returned.

It was harder to walk away than she expected, Margaux thought as she walked up the steps of the old Victorian. She was sad and disappointed at Nick's decision to keep Connor from her.

On their way back to town, Connor had fallen asleep, his head pillowed against her arm. She had to force herself not to touch him, draw him closer, protect him against the bumps in the beach road. They arrived at Le Coif much too soon. Connor had roused enough to hug her and give her a sticky kiss before she thanked Nick for dinner and got out of the truck.

Nick didn't look too much happier than she did. He didn't

even make a pretense of walking her across the street. She felt for him and knew he was doing what he thought best. He should probably find someone to marry and give Connor a real mother.

He drove away before she even reached the steps of Le Coif.

She unlocked the front door and tiptoed across the Elvis rug to unlock her new studio. She really didn't want Linda pumping her with questions about her "date" with Nick and Connor.

She turned on the light and blinked against the glare. The first thing she saw was her "ocean" dress. *From the mouths of babes,* she thought, and sat down at her drafting table. She would design a dress the color of the salt marsh at sunset. It would be her memory of one fun afternoon with a boy and his uncle.

Several hours later, she heard the front door open and close. Heels clicked across the foyer.

"Holy moly," squealed Linda. "What happened?"

Margaux whirled around. Linda was wearing black leather pants that molded to her figure like paint. A cowl-neck sweater was covered by a poncho of red, white, and green stripes.

"You look like the Italian flag," Margaux said on a laugh.

"Yeah, well you try riding around on the back of a Harley at night. I wanted to make sure anybody coming up behind us saw me before they hit me, ya know?"

"I hadn't thought about that," Margaux said. "Good choice."

"Thanks. So how come you're working and the chief's upstairs by himself?"

"Oh, is he back?" Margaux asked innocently. She'd heard him go up the stairs hours ago, but she'd pushed him out of her mind and kept working. "I was working."

"I can see that." Linda came into the room and walked along the row of sketches Margaux had pinned on the line.

"Where's the Harley-riding hunk?" Margaux asked.

"Hell, I wore him out and came home to paint my toenails."

Linda grinned at her. "He gets up at six to get to work. Thanks and no thanks. I'm going to bed. He wore me out, too." She yawned a jaw-popping yawn. "Don't work too late."

"I'm almost ready to leave. Go on to bed. I'll lock up."

"Yuh-huh." Linda waved and climbed the stairs to her apartment.

Margaux finished her last sketch, a pantsuit that reminded her of driftwood. She had gotten so carried away that she'd stopped editing herself as she went along. Now, as she looked at the line of new designs, she wondered if they were really couture or just "craftsy."

She was too tired to make a judgment tonight. Tomorrow would be soon enough, when she had a little distance from them. She felt they were right, but she'd learned to bury that feeling when it came to bringing a project in on budget. In the back of her mind, she knew these new designs were one-of-a-kind couture and she couldn't afford that now. But she was determined to follow it through.

Because Margaux Sullivan had a dream, and come hell or high water, she was going to recapture it.

Thirteen

Margaux didn't see Nick for the next three days. She delved into work with a vengeance, creating design after design. Each time she hit on a polished silhouette and combination of colors that felt right, she rendered it on a large sheet of sketch paper and pinned it on the fishing line.

The weather grew warmer. She noticed more cars in the driveways at Little Crescent Beach when she drove home at night. Flea market posters appeared around town. Summer was upon them, but the creative juices were flowing and Margaux didn't dare stop in case they dried up.

She got up early and stayed late. She forgot about her life on hold, the career she'd lost, the money she owed, the husband who betrayed her, everything except the work. She lived and breathed design. And by the end of the week she had the skeleton of a new M Atelier line.

Grace called and invited her to meet her and Bri for a drink. "I can't." Margaux moaned. "I'm up to my eyeballs in work." "Rain check?"

"You bet, and then I'll have something to show."

She hung up and went back to work.

That night when she heard Linda's last client leave, Margaux chose four of her latest designs and went across the foyer to the salon.

"It's alive. It's alive," Linda intoned.

Margaux plopped down in one of the salon chairs. "If you have some time, I have some questions."

"I got the time, but I gotta sit down." Linda plopped down in the seat next to Margaux. "Okay. Lay 'em on me."

Suddenly nervous, Margaux spread out the four sheets. "I've been working on some new designs. These are just a few examples of what I hope will be my new line."

Linda whistled. "Yowza. Yowza."

"Here's the thing. It's not just the design. It's the fabric. I'll be able to find some decent base fabrics maybe, but some of them will probably have to be hand-dyed or hand-painted. At first anyway. I thought maybe you could give me some advice. I know dyeing hair isn't the same as dyeing fabric, but—"

Linda splayed out her hand. "Hey, my parents met in Haight-Ashbury. I wore tied-dyed clothes to elementary school. In the summers we sold my mother's batiks out of a Volkswagen van. But that was before Brooklyn. Thank God for Brooklyn. So stop babbling and give 'em here." She didn't wait, but spread the sketches out and began to scowl at them.

"Hmm," said Linda. "Hmmm."

"Is it even possible to do? Too expensive?"

"Doable. Depends on what you think is expensive. Definitely time-consuming."

"I'd need a small business loan, which I might not be able to get." Margaux sighed. "God knows my credit isn't worth crap right now."

Linda didn't comment.

"Or I could just send out some sketches and try to sell the designs."

"Yeah, if you want them to end up as knockoffs in Walmart."

"I don't." Margaux drummed her fingers on the table. "I could do a few mock-ups, hire some models, take some video footage, and try to get someone to hire me and my new line."

"You'd become a staff designer again."

Margaux rested her chin in her hands. "Pretty much."

"That's like me renting a chair in a salon somewhere."

"Yeah, I guess it is. But I'm getting ahead of myself."

"Not the worst place to be. Why don't you just get started and decide later?"

"And that's the next problem. Where do I find a place with water and a heat supply. Vats for dyeing, a place to dry the fabric. Hell, I'd need a whole damn workshop, which I no longer have."

"Sounds to me like what you need is a kitchen. I just happen to have one of those in back."

"Where would you bake your cookies? I've been living on them in case you haven't noticed."

"Hell, I got a kitchen upstairs. It's tiny and I'd have to work off all those calories going up and down the stairs all day." She shrieked. "Oh God, I might get skinny again."

Margaux laughed outright.

"I got a shitload of work tomorrow. Saturday's always my big day. But I'm done by five. You go to Hartford or New Haven or wherever you can get some swatches of fabric and some dye and we'll give it a whirl."

"Sounds like a plan." Margaux stood up. "I'll run some tests and take it from there."

But as she walked across the hall to her studio, she began to have second thoughts. She went in to consult with Linda about dyeing processes and came out with a list of supplies long enough to fill an entire page of her sketchbook. And she wasn't at all sure she was doing the right thing. She needed a second opinion. She picked up her phone.

"Hi, it's me."

"Hi," Grace said.

"Are you guys still on for tonight?"

"You change your mind?"

"Yeah, I need a second opinion or maybe an intervention."

"Great. I've got nachos and a bottle of Pinot Grigio. Second floor. 2B."

"I'm on my way."

She grabbed her bag and walked to Grace's apartment complex, a brick building built in the late 1800s. Her front window overlooked the street. The space was well lived in, comfortable with legal briefs piled on every surface.

"I bring a lot of work home," Grace explained as she carried a tottering pile of papers into the bedroom.

Bri was sitting on an overstuffed plaid couch, her long legs tucked beneath her, and sipping a glass of white wine.

"No watermelon?" Margaux asked.

"Grace said it was an intervention. I wanted to be a good influence." She smiled and Margaux saw a glimpse of the radiant face that had appeared on the cover of every major fashion magazine.

Grace returned, poured Margaux a glass of wine, and sat down on the couch next to Bri.

"Is this the interrogation seat?" Margaux asked, only half kidding and gesturing to the club chair Grace had just cleared of papers.

"Yep. You sounded serious. So sit down and spill."

Margaux sat and took a sip of the crisp wine. "Okay, here goes. I have this idea. A plan actually, but I'm not sure if I'm barking at the moon. I've been getting these images based on the ocean, sand, salt grasses." She held up a preemptory hand. "I don't know if I'm crazy or . . . crazy. Everywhere I look I see color."

"So what's wrong with that?" Bri asked.

"I don't know. Maybe nothing. I see these things and it just gets translated into fabric and then into designs. But it seems like a major commitment. And it's way out of my comfort zone."

"No more black." Bri gave her an understanding look. She

knew about starting over, and in a place and way that was completely new.

Margaux shook her head. "I'm not seeing black at all."

"So what are you asking?"

Margaux shrugged. "I'm not sure. Am I moving too fast? Would I be smarter just to eat crow and beg for a job somewhere? Go back to what I know? Am I crazy to think of starting out on my own again?

"I already clawed my way to the top once. Can I do it again? Do I even want to? Do I still have what it takes? It's one thing to have an epiphany while contemplating nature." Margaux slumped back in the chair. "It's another to actually put it to use."

"Well, hell," Bri said. "I should have brought watermelon."

"You're not being helpful," Grace told her. She turned to Margaux. "What do you want to do?"

Margaux groaned. "That's just it. I don't know."

"You always knew what you wanted to do."

"I know, but that was before . . ." She wound down, took a breath. "I want to design. That I'm clear on. But where and how? I mean you have to be in one of the fashion centers, New York, Paris, Milan, to be successful. And that was never a question in my mind."

"Until now?" Grace asked.

"Leading the witness," Bri said.

"Until now. It's a huge gamble. The first time around, I rose through the ranks and had plenty of capital to invest in a new line. Now I don't have the money for a decent start-up. Hell, I barely have enough money for lunch. And I've got a list of items to buy that's going to clean me out even with my wholesaler's card. I'd have to take out a business loan if I can even get one."

"Well, hell, I've—"

"No," Margaux said, interrupting what she knew was about to be an offer to loan her money. "I'll deal with the loan, but it all just seems so overwhelming. Can I really fight my way back?

"Just being at the shore for these few weeks has made me a different person. I don't think I'm as tough, as cutthroat as I used to be. Even with everything that's happened, with my life in shambles, with the future a big gaping hole, I feel, well, a certain kind of peace."

"Maybe that's your answer."

"But will it last or turn into boredom?"

"For some things you just have to wait and see," Bri said, intoning the wisdom of the ages.

"Why can't you start on a small scale and see how it goes?" Grace asked.

"Ever the voice of reason," Bri joked. "But for once I'm in agreement."

"You mean start out in Crescent Cove?"

Bri shrugged. "You were thinking the same thing, weren't you?"

"When I'm least expecting it, I think, *Stay here*. The space at Le Coif is perfect for a small-scale workshop."

"And you'd have a hell of a smaller overhead than you would in New York."

"And might slip into obscurity."

"Bullshit. Build it and they will come, or whatever." Bri waved her wineglass in the air, noticed it was empty, and re-filled it, topping off Margaux's and Grace's and returning the bottle to the table. "Hell, get a website."

"I have a website. Just as advertisement." Which hadn't been updated in months. "But no house is going to *buy* product off a website."

"No, but customers might."

"You mean sell direct to the consumer? Like a catalogue?" Margaux asked, horrified.

Bri gave her a look. "Or sell from the floor."

"Open a retail space in Crescent Cove?"

"That would be great," Grace said enthusiastically. "You could sell online and in person, the best of both worlds."

"You're moving too fast for me. We went from construction to retail in one huge leap."

"Why not?" Grace asked.

"Yeah, why not?" Bri echoed.

Margaux frowned while she sorted the suggestion out in her mind. "You mean open a dress shop?"

"Boutique," Bri corrected. She dropped into her Marlene Dietrich voice. "Something terribly exclusive and expensive."

"Are you serious? Hand-selling to customers instead of presenting in the fall and spring shows in Paris and New York?"

"You'd miss all the stress of the city," said Grace.

Bri sighed. "Waking up to the sea, instead of the subway?"

"Breathing in fresh air instead of the bum on the corner," Grace added.

"Dining at the Clam Shack instead of Tao?" Bri asked with a pointed look.

"Hey, I love the Clam Shack," said Grace.

"So do I. It was a metaphor."

Grace rolled her eyes. "Yeah, yeah, English 101."

Bri grinned. "But does Margaux love the Clam Shack?" She glanced at Margaux and a lifetime of hope, regret, and compassion spoke in her eyes.

"Of course she does," said Grace. "And it would be good to have you home."

Home. It was a seductive idea, but was this where she really wanted to be? Had she come home? Or had she left it behind when she fled the city. While she was sitting with Grace and Bri, she thought this might be it, but as she walked back to the workshop that night, fear bubbled up inside her. She had to be careful not to let their enthusiasm sway her. She had to listen to herself and only herself. That way she would never be taken in again, never be hurt and betrayed. Would never fail again. But there was a list in her carryall that said she was about to plunge into the unknown—again.

Saturday morning, Nick picked up Connor and drove over to work a few hours for Jake McGuire. He settled Connor on a blanket beneath the tree in Jake's backyard and dumped out the contents of his backpack. Jake brought out a box of wood scraps for him to play with.

"Stay here. Jake and I'll be right over there where the saw-horses are. Okay?"

Connor nodded and began building a tower with the wood scraps. Nick could never tell if Connor was listening or just nodding because he thought he was supposed to.

"Stay right there," he repeated, then went back to where Jake was waiting. "Sorry, but my mother had another of those flea market meetings and it just didn't seem right to make the kid stay inside all day."

"He's fine and Dad will teach him to play horseshoes later. Though it looks like he can entertain himself." Jake tossed a scraper to Nick.

"He can. I just wish he had some friends."

"Does he know any other kids?"

"Not really, my mother takes him to a couple of neighbors but he doesn't really like going."

"He probably just needs to find some kids he likes. It'll be easier when school is out. You should take him down to the beach. There will be plenty of kids to play with there."

"He can't swim. He'd have to have an adult with him every second. And you know what my schedule will be like in summer."

They went to work restoring hundred-year-old baseboards that Jake had salvaged from a house being torn down in Guilford. The sun beat down, the day grew hotter. The sound of scraping was the only noise around.

Nick kept one eye on Connor, who seemed content to sit in one place hour after hour.

"It isn't normal, is it?" Nick said.

"No," Jake agreed. "But it doesn't mean it's something irreversible. What did Dr. McKinnon say?"

"The usual. At least he said we could wait before deciding about school."

They finished two more baseboards before Jake declared a lunch break. Nick went to the truck for the cooler his mother had filled with sandwiches and cookies, carrot sticks and apples, and several cans of soda.

He looked over to the tree to call Connor.

He saw the wood scraps, but there was no Connor.

"Damn, where is he?" Nick raked his fingers through hair that needed cutting. "Do you see Connor?"

Jake looked around the yard. "I just saw him a few minutes ago. Maybe he went in the house to the bathroom." He went inside to check but reappeared a minute later shaking his head. "He must be around here. He couldn't have gotten too far."

"Connor," Nick called. "Connor, where are you?"

They checked in the workshop, went into the backyard.

"Connor!" Nick called, beginning to feel truly alarmed. "He's started doing this. Wandering off. I found him several blocks away during that last storm. Margaux Sullivan found him one afternoon close to Main Street. But that's the farthest he's ever been. Where the hell—" He stopped. "The cove."

"What?"

"Margaux and I took him down to the cove when we were here dropping off lumber a while back. What if he's gone back there?"

"Whoa. Margaux Sullivan?"

"I'll tell you later." Nick took off at a run, Jake at his heels.

Nick crashed through the bushes, following the path down to the shore. He slid on a patch of leaves as he came to the curve of the path, but he kept his feet and barely slowed down.

He called Connor's name, knowing that even if the boy answered, he wouldn't be able to hear him.

He sent up a silent prayer to a God he'd almost forgotten. "If he's okay, I'll send him to the Eldon School. Do whatever it takes to get him talking out loud again." He tripped on a root and went down on one knee and hand. He pushed himself up and kept going until he burst out into the sunlight, hoping, praying that Connor would be there skipping stones.

But there was no Connor. He looked out across the water, shaded his eyes from the sun, looking for any sign, even though he knew if Connor was out there he wouldn't be found. The sea looked calm and inviting, and it could swallow a man or a small boy without warning.

Jake skidded to a stop beside him, breathing hard. "He probably didn't get this far. He wouldn't come through the woods by himself."

Nick ignored him, but splashed through the water to the jetty, which he climbed, looking in the crevices of boulders for Connor's mangled body. He reached the top, peered down at Little Crescent Beach. There were a few people out, it was the beginning of summer weather. But no Connor.

The panic increasing, he scrambled back down the jetty to Jake.

"How could I have let this happen?"

Jake clapped him on the back. "Let's get back to the house. He'll probably be waiting for us there. If not, we'll call Finley and have him cruise for him."

Nick glanced back at the cove.

"He's not out there. He couldn't have made it this far. He's a little kid, the path here isn't easy to follow, much less navigate."

Nick wanted to believe that. He knew it was unlikely that Connor had found his way to the cove so quickly. But shit like that happened all the time. You turn your back and your kid is . . .

"Let's go," he croaked. They started back, more slowly this

time, looking out into the woods for a bit of color, any little movement.

Nick listened to every rustle, every crackle, hoping to hear a whisper, "I'm here," but the only answer he got was the squeal of a seagull high overhead.

He told himself to stay calm. Connor would probably be waiting for them back at Jake's. It would be just like him to have wandered off and come back. That's what he did.

And then he saw him, standing in the crook of the path. Arms by his side, erect like a child waiting.

"Connor!" The name exploded out of Nick on a rush of relief and he bounded forward. Connor drew back and Nick immediately stopped, moved more slowly. "Hey, buddy, you scared me. I couldn't find you."

Connor's eyes filled with tears.

Good God, he didn't know how to deal with this child. He knelt down. "Where were you?" he said as quietly and as calmly as he could.

Connor looked over his shoulder. Nick followed his gaze to a tree growing diagonally out of the ground, its roots wrapped around an outcropping of rock.

Margaux's secret hideout.

Nick remembered Connor's awe when she told him about the Grotto and how she and her friends met there in secret. Of course he'd be curious. Any kid would be. He supposed that was a good sign. That was normal in a boy. But it had scared Nick to death.

"Well, buddy, you can't go there anymore, okay?"

Connor looked at him with those big brown eyes. Finally he nodded.

"Because it's dangerous. Understand?"

Connor looked back at the ledge of rock.

Of course he didn't understand. It was an adventure. A special place. What kid wouldn't want to explore there.

Nick stood up and let out a deep breath.

"Who needs some lemonade?" Jake asked.

"I think we all do," Nick said. He took Connor's hand and they all walked back up the path to Jake's house, Connor docile beside him while Nick told Jake about Margaux's secret hiding place.

They went inside, settled Connor down with Jake's dad for a game of checkers and lemonade and sandwiches.

Nick and Jake took a couple of beers out to the picnic table in the backyard.

"So," Jake said, "Margaux Sullivan showed you her secret hiding place?"

Nick groaned. "Don't remind me."

"No. I want to hear all about it. Sounds intriguing."

"Don't get excited. Margaux's renting a room across the hall from Linda's as a studio."

"Ah."

"I didn't know it at the time. Anyway, Connor was with me, and true to form he wandered into her studio. Made a big splash with her."

"Oh man, not the old get-to-the-girl-through-the-kid routine."

"I wouldn't do that. She doesn't even like me much. She really likes Connor. Of course Linda couldn't leave it alone and said we should take her with us to Deke's for dinner. Connor wanted her, so I said yes. She didn't know how to get out of it gracefully, so she agreed.

"We came down here to drop off the lumber. She noticed the path. We all walked down to the cove and she showed Connor her childhood hideout. End of story."

"You forgot the part about where you had dinner at Deke and Peg's."

"We ate clam rolls, Connor had fish fingers, and we drove her back to Le Coif. End of story."

"Margaux Sullivan." Jake laughed. "Who would've thought it. After all this time. Won't be long before the old guys down at the marina will be laying bets on the two of you." He dodged from an imaginary blow.

"Trust me. They'll be wasting their money."

Jake shrugged. "Maybe."

"I'm not seeing her again. Connor's already too attached to her." He hesitated. "I told her to stay away."

"What?" The question exploded out of Jake. "You dumbass. She likes the kid. You've had it for her since you were fourteen at least. And you tell her to stay away? Are you a total masochist?"

"I just don't want him to get hurt."

"Well, hell, he won't get hurt if you don't let him live a little. But is that what you want for the kid? Is it what you want for yourself?" Jake scowled, punched him in the arm. "What if she doesn't leave? What are you going to do then?"

Margaux spent Saturday in Hartford and returned at dusk with most of the items on her list piled on the backseat of the Toyota. Six bolts of fabric lay wrapped in plastic in the trunk, and a bag of swatches rested on the seat beside her.

She pulled alongside the curb in front of Le Coif. Linda appeared at the door so fast that Margaux knew she'd been waiting for her. She bounced down the steps and peered in the car window.

Margaux handed her a box of dyes. "We'd better hurry. The sign says no parking."

"Don't sweat it. I have friends in high places." Linda lifted her chin toward Nick's upstairs apartment.

Margaux grabbed another box and followed her inside, wondering if he would actually come down to give her a ticket. Whether he even cared if he ever saw her again or not. She hadn't talked to him since the night they ate at the Clam Shack with Connor.

They went back to the car and began carrying the bolts of fabric inside.

They were on the last load when Nick came down the stairs.

"Shit," said Margaux under her breath. She ducked back into the trunk and lifted out the last bolt of fabric. When she stood up, he was standing next to her. She pulled the bolt to her chest and held it there like a shield.

He took the fabric from her. "Anything else?"

She looked at him warily. "Before you give me a ticket?"

Nick grunted and started carrying the bolt into the store. She watched him for a moment, wondering if she had just heard him laugh.

When she reached the workshop, he was standing with Linda, looking around in surprise.

"He's in a state of shock," said Linda, and whacked him hard on the back.

Nick walked over to the fishing line where her designs were hanging. Only now in addition to the "ocean" dress there were two more sundresses, a long gown, a pantsuit, a sarong, several blouses and shirts, a hostess pants with a wrap top. She felt unreasonably embarrassed.

"They're . . ." Nick hesitated.

If he said "nice," she would get in the car and drive back to Manhattan. Of course, what did he know about fashion? She'd never seen him in anything but a uniform or jeans and a T-shirt. So why was she holding her breath waiting for his opinion?

"You," he finished.

She blinked. Warmth suffused right through her.

"Okay, that's it," Linda said. "Your fashion sense is much appreciated, but if you're not going to start sewing, you might as well leave."

Nick grinned at her. "I'll leave that to you aficionados." He turned his smile on Margaux. "Ladies." He left.

Margaux stared after him. "Amazing."

"If you like the strong, silent, stubborn-as-a-mule type. Okay, let's see what we have here," said Linda, not missing a beat.

Margaux had to pull her attention back from the empty doorway. She began unwrapping the bolts. "A beautiful orange crinkle batik, some muslin, silk I got for a song, a nice coral Chantilly, shantung, silk chiffon in white and another one in a pale blue that I thought was subtle enough to use as a background."

"Save a shitload of work," agreed Linda, eyeing the chiffon. "Now come check out the kitchen."

The kitchen was completely transformed. A row of hot plates stretched across the counter. A nested stack of lobster pots sat on the kitchen table.

"Where did you get all this?"

"Harlan of the Harley knows a guy."

"Please don't tell me this stuff fell off a truck."

"Nah. Harlan does some work over at the vets' hall. They loaned him the hot plates. He picked up the lobster pots from the Lobster Pot." She grinned. "I kid you not. It's the name of a restaurant that's going out of business. He got them cheap."

"Thank him beaucoodles for me."

Linda flashed teeth. "Not to worry. I will."

Fourteen

Margaux agreed to go to Sunday Mass even though she really wanted to work. But as her mother pointed out, it was always good to have God on your side when you started a new venture.

They had just sat down at their regular pew when Margaux felt someone nudge her knee. She looked over to see Connor Prescott, his hair slicked back and wearing a navy blue suit, smiling at her.

"Hi," he breathed.

"Hi," Margaux whispered back, thinking Connor was probably the only kid in town who didn't need to be reprimanded to be quiet in church.

Jude leaned over. "Hi, honey. Where's your grandmother?"

Adelaide Prescott appeared behind him. "I'm so sorry he bothered you. He's been talking nonstop about Margaux, and when he saw you come in he just slipped away before I could stop him."

"That's just fine," Jude said, glancing sideways at Margaux. "Why don't you join us?"

"Oh no, that's very kind but we have our seats."

Connor pulled himself up on the pew and scooted close to

Margaux. He patted the place next to him for his grandmother to sit down.

"Connor!" she admonished.

"He's a boy with a mind of his own," Jude said, smiling congenially at Mrs. Prescott. "Please, sit with us."

At that moment organ music announced the beginning of the service. Mrs. Prescott sat down.

Connor hardly moved for the next hour except to slide off the pew to kneel, then climb back up again. He occasionally cast a shy smile up at Margaux. She was flattered and uncomfortable at the same time. She could feel herself getting attached to this strange child, and she knew she shouldn't. Especially because she couldn't separate her enjoyment of Connor from her desire to have her own children. And that couldn't be healthy for either of them. And then there was Nick.

After church Connor took her hand as they walked outside. Mrs. Prescott and Jude walked behind. Margaux was acutely aware of the interest they were affording certain members of the congregation and wondered what conclusions they would make.

"I hope you don't mind us barging in," Mrs. Prescott told Jude.

"Of course not. It was lovely to have you."

Mrs. Prescott turned to Margaux. "That was so sweet of you to go with them to Deke's. Connor has been talking about it ever since."

"Oh?" Jude glanced at Margaux.

"It was nothing. I had a good time, too."

"Thank you." Mrs. Prescott leaned over to Connor. "Say goodbye. We have to be going. Uncle Nick is coming to lunch."

"Bye," he said, and let his grandmother lead him away.

"Nick Prescott asked you to dinner?"

"Actually Connor did. We kind of got suckered into agreeing. And it was just Deke's."

They crossed the street to Jude's car. "Dottie insists we come to brunch, so don't argue. After next week, the summer crowd will descend and there won't be a booth to be had without waiting."

"Sounds good. I have a couple of ideas I want to kick around."

Dottie's was packed with everyone getting their last Sunday brunch in before the tourist season began. Dottie came over to personally take their order.

"And now it begins," she said. "Not that I'm complaining, mind you. Summer traffic keeps me in business the rest of the year."

They gave their orders, waited while a new summer waitress poured their coffee under Dottie's eagle eye. When she was gone, Dottie said, "So I hear Nick Prescott asked our Margaux out to dinner."

"Who did you hear that from?" Margaux asked.

"Lydia Braithwaite who heard it from Seamus McGuire who heard it from Doug Loomey who was there."

"He didn't invite me to dinner."

"Don't make me drag this out of you," Dottie said. "I have three new waitresses today that I have to keep an eye on."

"He came to give Linda his rent money. Connor wandered into my workshop, asked Nick if I could go to Deke's with them. Nick, being polite, asked me. And I didn't have the heart to say no to Connor."

"And . . ."

Margaux gritted her teeth. "The three of us ate at Deke's and they dropped me off at Le Coif. It was probably eight-thirty, hardly a date."

Dottie glanced quickly at Jude. *I told you so.* "Gotta go." She hurried away.

Margaux turned on Jude. "What have you two been concocting?"

"Nothing. We just want you to be happy."

"I am happy. Or at least I will be when I get back on my feet. Which is what I wanted to talk to you about."

Jude leaned forward on her elbows. "Okay."

Now that the time had come, it was hard to begin. "I've been working on some new designs."

Jude nodded.

"Well, yesterday I bought some fabric. A lot of fabric actually. Pretty much wiped out what was left of my bank account."

"Honey—"

"I thought I'd do a few mock-ups and send out a video. Maybe get a foot into a new house."

"Work for another designer?"

"If that's what I have to do. But that's not the issue at this point. I need to take out a small business loan."

"Stop right now. I'll loan you the money."

"Thanks, Mom, but I'd rather do it this way. I'm thinking twenty or thirty thousand would get me started. Then if I get any nibbles, I can decide which way to go from there."

"I have that much lying around in stocks. If you won't let me give it to you, at least borrow it from me."

Margaux shook her head. "I really, really appreciate the offer, but I need to do this myself."

Jude sighed. "Then what do you want me to do?"

"Give me some advice. What do you think the bank would require as collateral?"

Jude thought about it. "I don't know. I think we should consult Roger."

"Roger Kyle?"

"Yes. He has much more business acumen than I do. I'm sure he'll be able to guide you in the right direction. What are you frowning at? You can trust him."

"It's not that. It's just his name sure has come up a lot since I've been back."

"It has? Well, he is an old friend."

"He's not . . . You're not . . ."

"Not what?" Jude tipped her chin and looked totally guile-less.

"Nothing."

"Then shall I ask him for advice?"

"I guess." It sounded innocent enough. Maybe he could help her. And even if he couldn't and even though it was none of her business, it might give Margaux a chance to see just what might be going on between him and her mother.

Nick sat at his desk and shifted the cells of the spreadsheet that held the department summer schedule. He'd been at it all morning, feeding in staff availability and requests for vacation time. Memorial Day was only a few days away and it would mark the beginning of summer, which meant his small staff would be working overtime.

When he finally finished, it was almost noon and too late to go home and change out of his jeans. He headed straight to his mother's house for Sunday lunch. It was a Prescott tradition, as with so many other families, to have Sunday lunch together, and he guessed his mother insisted on keeping the ritual to lend some order to their lives.

She didn't comment when he apologized for his attire, just told him to go wash up and make himself presentable. Connor was watching television, the sound muted.

"Hey, sport. How was Mass?"

"Good. We sat with Margaux."

Nick leaned closer. "What?"

"We sat with Margaux."

"You did?"

Connor nodded and went back to his silent cartoons.

Nick returned to the kitchen. Looked into a pot of mashed potatoes. "Connor said he sat with Margaux Sullivan at Mass today."

"Yes, we did." His mother nudged him out of the way and opened the oven door.

"How did that happen?"

She slid a roasting pan out of the oven and placed it on a trivet on the counter. "Connor saw them sit down, and before I knew what he was doing, he'd followed them. Then Jude asked us to sit with them. Wasn't that nice? Connor is really smitten with your Margaux."

"She's not my Margaux. But that's just what people will think. Do you want the whole town talking?"

"You care too much about what people say."

"My job is kind of dependent on my reputation."

"Oh, pooh. Your reputation is clean as a whistle. And besides, what can they say? She was nice to a little boy."

"Ma, I don't know that it's a good idea to encourage this friendship with Ms. Sullivan."

"Why on earth not?"

"Because she'll be going back to New York. I don't want Connor getting attached to her and then have her leave."

She cocked her head at him, a sparrow's gesture. "Oh, Nicky, are you sure it's Connor you're worried about?"

"Who else would it be?"

She reached up on tiptoe and patted his cheek. "Go get Connor for lunch."

For the next week, Margaux threw herself into work. She knew she was setting up expectations. She'd rented a work space and worked every day. Just like a real job. Just like she was putting down roots. Just like she was going to stay.

She could see it in the looks Dottie and her mother exchanged. In the expressions of people she met on the street. The last time she'd gone into Oglethorpe's Hardware, Roy had said, "It's good to have you back home where you belong."

And even though Margaux tried not to look ahead, she found herself wandering into images of the future. Images of Crescent Cove. Images of Nick Prescott. Then she would pull herself together and remind herself to keep her eye on the prize. And the prize was New York, Fashion Week, *Vogue*.

She didn't see Nick or Connor, and she tried not to think about them. And yet she missed them both.

She focused solely on the design, ignoring all the extraneous things she'd had to worry about before: deadlines, cost bearing, competitive placement. She just drew and created, letting color and texture dictate her hand and mind.

Dyed and hand-painted swatches of fabric lay over every surface of the work space. Soon she would need a real workshop with equipment to dye large amounts of fabric.

Except that if the designs caught on and sold, they would get sent to a fabric designer and then to a professional manufacturer. And then a betraying thought would creep into her mind. *I want to do the fabric myself, not farm it out to another designer.* Not to depend on someone else's interpretation no matter how creative and brilliant it might be.

But that was totally unfeasible. For one thing, it was too time-consuming, and too expensive. It would drive the prices into the hundreds or thousands of dollars just to make overhead. Which wouldn't be bad if she had the clout to make it happen.

A few months ago she might have been able to pull it off, but now she would just have to swallow her ego, her pride, and hire on to another already established design house. Then maybe someday . . .

When she was busy, she stopped dwelling on what she'd lost. But at night when her mind was still firing on all circuits, panic would seize her, disbelief that only a few short weeks ago, she'd had everything she'd dreamed of. And now it was gone.

Strangely enough, it wasn't the money, the apartment, or the lifestyle that she missed. That loss was staggering but not nearly as bad as the career and momentum that had been destroyed. There was nothing she could do but push the bitterness aside and force herself back to her new enterprise, try to dream ahead and see her new designs taking Paris by storm. And at last she would go to sleep.

She lived on diner food and adrenaline. She and Linda cleared out the former dining room, which Linda had been using for storage, in order to create more space for the workshop. They carried boxes upstairs and took over one of the three spare bedrooms for storage.

A giant man in a black leather vest and shaved head came in to help with the heavy stuff.

"Hey, babe," he said in a deep voice any actor would be proud of.

"This is Harlan. He's the man with the muscle." Linda winked at Margaux and led him into the dining room. A minute later Margaux heard scraping and grunting. She got up to see if they needed help, but when she looked into the dining room, Harlan had hoisted a heavy chest onto his back and was carrying it into the hall. Linda followed behind him, swishing a broom and humming a song from *Cinderella*.

They hung cotton cording across the ceiling and taped a plastic tarp on the floor so that drying fabric wouldn't drip on the polished hardwood. They uncovered two unused bookcases which Margaux filled with neatly folded material.

When they were finished, Margaux stepped back and looked around the two rooms. Her mark was everywhere. And she had one thought.

This is what I want to do.

Fifteen

 On the day of the flea market, Nick rose before dawn. It was still dark when he left his apartment. His eyes felt gritty and his muscles ached. It seemed like he'd been working forever.

The light was on at his mother's house. He tapped on the door and waited. The security chain rattled, the lock clicked, and his mother opened the door.

"You're up early," he said, and gave her a kiss. The smell of baking suffused the kitchen. "More pies?"

"Muffins. I had some berries left over and I didn't want them going to waste. They'll be ready in a minute."

"Thanks, but I have to get going. I just stopped to say hi because I saw the light." She was already pouring him a cup of coffee.

"Really, Ma, I can't stay." He took the coffee. "What time are you coming?"

"Connor and I are going over a little before nine."

"Do you think it's a good idea to take him? There will be a lot of excitement and noise. He might wander off."

She opened the oven door and took out a baking pan. "I have the first two-hour shift at the bakery table. Everyone will keep an eye on him. We can't cosset him forever. He'll be safe. There are some kid activities planned that he might enjoy."

She put two muffins in a paper bag. "Eat these before they get cold."

"I'll try to come by on my break. If I get one. Maybe I can take him around the fair."

"He'd like that. It's time he started doing things. Even if it isn't comfortable at first. He'll get used to it. And maybe he'll learn to like it."

"How did I get such a smart mother?" He surprised her, and himself, by taking her into a hug and holding her there. "Do you need help getting things into the car?"

"No, you go on. Connor can help. And don't worry."

He felt better as he got into the cruiser. Dawn was just beginning to break, and the porch light created a nimbus around his mother's small frame she stood in the doorway.

St. Adelaide, he thought as he drove away.

Margaux stretched over the worktable and put the last hand-painted touches to the fabric she'd been working on for days. It was a silk chiffon of palest yellow and painted in free-form swirls, slashes, and sprays of aqua, ultramarine, rose, and coral. It had taken a lot of trial and effort before she got the tones perfect as well as colorfast. And it had turned out just as she'd imagined it.

The "Toreador Song" rang out from the foyer and a voice called out, "Mags, are you here?"

"Grace?" Margaux dropped her brush onto a rag and went out to the front room. Grace stood in the doorway, wearing khaki cargo shorts and button shirt.

"We're here to steal you away to go to the flea market," Grace said.

"Is it Saturday already?"

"Yes. So chop-chop."

"Okay. I could use a break. Give me two minutes."

Bri pushed Grace to the side and stepped into the studio. She was dressed in jeans and a white tailored shirt and looked like she'd just stepped out of a Ralph Lauren ad. She didn't speak but gazed at the designs that hung across the opposite wall.

"What do you think?" Margaux asked, mentally crossing her fingers.

"Holy Versace. This ain't your mother's beachwear."

"That's good, right?"

"Good? They're incredible."

Margaux felt immense relief. She knew Bri would never flatter her. "But will they sell?"

"Shit yes." Bri stepped over to the sketch of an A-line dress, cut on the bias and gored at the hem to fan out to a frothy hemline just below the knee. The tiny shoulder straps were finished with a row of deep folds that tumbled down the back. A range of color from light aqua to midnight blue combined in a swirl of muted colors that seemed to flow from one to the other.

"I get it. It's the sea at dusk. And those drapery things that arc around the front and back"—Bri broke into a commentator's voice—"reminiscent of the tide rolling in." She settled back into her own voice. "And that little touch of what is it? Maroon? Brown?"

"Sienna," said Margaux.

"Yeah, I don't see it myself when I look at the water, but it works; like it anchors the whole picture somehow. But what about the fabric? You can't tell me you found this pattern in a warehouse."

Margaux smiled. "Come this way." She went to the placket door at the back wall and slid it open to the dining room. They stepped into a hanging forest of silks, shantungs, tulle, and muslin whose blues, golds, and greens shimmered and billowed in the breeze from the windows she'd opened to speed up the drying process on her newest "Sunset" fabric.

"Wow," said Grace.

"Amazing," said Bri, wandering through the billowing fabric. "It's like a seraglio in here."

Margaux looked around. Her Sunset fabric lay draped over a

row of dining chairs while the fabric paint dried. The last two yards were spread across the worktable and thumbtacked in place to keep it from shifting under the brush.

"You *have* been busy," Grace said. "How long did this take?"

"Seems like forever."

"How much longer before you have enough to make something?"

Margaux considered the folds of material. As soon as the Sunset fabric dried, it would be ready to cut. Normally she'd do muslin mock-ups and then the real thing, but there was no time. There was also no extra fabric if they made mistakes. "Soon."

"Getting cold feet?"

"Just a bit. I still have a hell of a lot of work to do, so let's get going before I change my mind."

"And before it gets any more crowded. You want to lock these windows before we go?" Grace asked.

"No, I'll come back later. It's pretty safe around here and I want to dry that last batch of chiffon."

They went outside.

"We'd better walk. We barely made it down Main Street on our way here and we probably got the last parking place in town." Bri pointed across the street where a big yellow truck on monster wheels was parked next to Margaux's blue sports coupe.

"That's yours?" Margaux asked incredulously.

"Yeah, bought it secondhand. I know the tires look like overkill but on a rainy day on the north forty, they come in handy."

"You have a north forty?"

"More like a north ten and a half. But enough for me."

"Who would have ever thought."

"Hey, I have plans for that house. You have to come see it. We'll order takeout. My kitchen isn't quite finished yet. The place is a mess, but it's got great potential."

They walked down Main Street where a line of cars inched toward the elementary school. Heat radiated from car hoods, exhaust fumes wavered in the air.

"I always forget what a big deal this is," Grace said, fanning fumes from her face.

"They have this every year," Bri said. "Do you think they'll ever run out of stuff to sell?"

"They could subsist for several years on junk from our attic alone," Margaux said. "Mom and I cleaned a bunch of stuff out for it this year. It didn't even make a dent."

"Oh boy." Bri rubbed her hands together. "Just so you know, I'm looking for kitchen stuff. Antique or close to antique linens that are in good enough condition to be rejuvenated." She hesitated. "And play stuff. For the girls. On the outside chance I get them before they're forty."

"How's that coming?"

"Slow as sludge in the Yangtze. The paperwork is ridiculous. Just when I think I'm done, it seems to start all over again."

"Why China?" Margaux asked as they waited for a minivan to pass so they could cross the street to the school.

"I couldn't get two children in the States. Especially not with my history. China was my best bet. It'll be worth it when they finally get here."

They turned onto Pine Street where more cars were waiting to park. The field behind the school was a sea of tents and wooden stands. Trucks and cars were parked side by side, merchandise piled in their open trunks and spread on the grass in front of them. Here and there a trail of smoke cut through the air where souvlaki, hamburgers, clam rolls, and hot dogs were being sold. The sun beat down and people were already lined up at the lemonade and soda stands.

They stopped at the gym entrance.

"Inside or outside first?" asked Bri.

"Inside," said Margaux. "I should say hi to Mom. And I know she'd like to see the two of you."

"We see her all the time."

Margaux stopped.

"Duh, we live in the same town," Grace said.

"And Jude is in my reading group," Brianna said.

"Oh," Margaux said, feeling a twinge of jealousy.

"Well, I still need to say hello. Want to meet up later?"

"We'll just mosey ahead of you and you can catch up," Bri said. "Most of the good linens will be inside. If we get separated, meet at the Skilling's Ice Cream cart in an hour."

"Okay, keep your eyes open for garment racks, sewing forms, stuff that I might need."

Margaux stopped at the Beach Auxiliary table, surprised when she saw who was manning the table with her mother. A man about five-eleven, in good shape, a suntanned face with crinkles around the eyes, receding hairline, and white silky hair. Even though she hadn't seen him in years, Margaux recognized Roger Kyle.

He was selling a pair of ice tongs to a lady wearing a Mexican sombrero.

Roger and Margaux exchanged hellos.

"He's phenomenal," Jude said fondly. "He's sold more stuff than I have and I know most of these people."

Dottie waved from the coffee machine. Margaux's stomach rumbled.

"I've got to catch up with Bri and Grace, but I have to peruse the bakery table before I go."

She was deciding between a lemon bar and a pecan swirl when Connor's head appeared over the edge of the table.

"Well, hello there. What are you up to?"

He thrust a pad of paper at her. She took it from him. It was a picture with a big yellow circle and a strip of yellow at the bottom of the page. "The beach," she guessed. "It's very beautiful."

He said something. She leaned across the table to hear him better.

"It's not finished yet."

"Well, I know it's going to be wonderful. You'll have to show it to me when you're done. Okay?"

He nodded and smiled up at her. He was so sweet she wanted to take him home with her. *Bad way to think,* Margaux told herself.

She bought a blueberry muffin from Mrs. Prescott. "Has Connor gone on the Moonwalk yet? There are some fun things to do in the children's area."

"Nick said he'd come take him when he gets his lunch break."

They both looked around at the crowd, understanding clear between them. *If he gets a lunch break.*

Margaux lowered her voice. "Why don't I check back before I leave, and if he hasn't come, I'll take Connor . . ." She remembered that she was supposed to be staying away. "Or I could watch the table while you take him."

Mrs. Prescott beamed. "You are so sweet. But I'm sure Nick will come for him."

"Okay. See you later, Connor."

Connor grinned and waved goodbye, then disappeared from view.

When Margaux caught up to Bri and Grace, Bri had already filled one of her tote bags with tablecloths and doilies.

"This stuff is great," she said. "Oh, look over there, blue glass."

They followed her to the next booth where she bought several apothecary bottles. Grace shrugged at Margaux and they moved on. By the time they made their way outside, they were all carrying loaded tote bags, most of the items bought by Brianna.

They stopped by the Beach Auxiliary table where with a laugh and a shake of her head, Jude allowed them to store their purchases while they continued shopping.

"I hope you didn't buy any of the things we just donated, Margaux."

"Not me, most of this is Bri's nonsense. I'm looking for more practical things for the shop—the workshop."

"Ah." Jude put the tote bags beneath the table.

They bought fresh-squeezed lemonade and drank it sitting at a picnic table under the shade of a large tent. Then they hit the rows of vendors outside.

They wandered down the fairway while the day grew hotter and the crowds got bigger. By the end of another hour, Margaux was tired and hungry, but she'd scored two dress racks from the Baptist Ladies' Auxiliary.

She wondered if Nick had gotten a chance to take Connor to the children's area. She could see it across the way; there was face painting, spin art, a fishing booth, and an inflated Moonwalk where swarms of children jumped up and down squealing with delight.

She was about to suggest they pick up their purchases from Jude and find a nice air-conditioned place for a late lunch when Bri said, "Omigod. Look at those hats."

She picked her way across the trampled grass to a square booth with hundreds of old-fashioned hats for sale. Grace rolled her eyes and followed. Margaux took one last look at the kiddie area, that familiar pang of longing cutting deep inside her. She should ask Bri about the adoption process.

She didn't have to be married to have a child. Once she got her finances back in order, she could adopt. Of course, she'd have to work double time to be able to afford a child in the city and that wouldn't be fair to the child. The same old argument. One that Louis had often used whenever she suggested it was time to start a family. But if she lived here . . .

She felt someone tug at her jeans.

She looked down to find Connor looking up at her. He had an American flag painted on his cheek, there was a red ring of cherry snow cone around his mouth. He was holding a piece of drawing paper in a sticky hand.

"Hey, where did you come from?"

He glanced over his shoulder. She followed his gaze to a booth but she didn't see Nick or Mrs. Prescott.

He nudged her with his piece of paper.

She took it from him while she perused the area for one of the Prescotts. She looked down at the paper. It was his picture of the seashore. He'd added a strip of blue sea. Three stick people stood on the beach, two big ones with a little one between them, holding hands.

Margaux swallowed her reaction. "Is that you and Uncle Nick and Grandma?"

Slowly he shook his head.

"Connor!"

She'd know that voice anywhere. Connor pressed close to her side. She instinctively placed her hand on his hair.

Nick strode toward them looking like thunder. He shot Margaux a searing glance before he dropped to one knee. "How many times do I have to tell you, you can't run off like this."

Even Margaux cowered under his anger. Connor began to tremble.

Nick immediately calmed down. More quietly, he said, "I didn't mean to yell, but you scared me. You need to stay with someone you know, not wander off. Understand?"

Margaux felt Connor's slow nod beneath her hand, then his head turned up at her.

"He wanted to show me his picture."

Nick stood up.

"Don't be mad. He knows me, he must have thought it was all right."

"I'm not mad." His jaw was set so tightly she thought it might shatter.

She lifted her chin. The man was going about this the wrong way. *Don't get involved,* she warned herself. *Not your problem.* But she couldn't ignore the small boy trembling beside her.

Nick's mouth tightened even more. He took a controlled breath. "You're right. I probably didn't make it clear."

Bri and Grace walked up at that moment and came to stand by Margaux, a united front.

"Come on, Connor. Let's go back to Nana."

When Connor didn't move, Nick scooped the boy up and carried him away. Connor looked back over Nick's shoulder, his eyes round and sad.

Margaux realized she was still holding his picture with its yellow beach and happy family.

"Wasn't that Nick Prescott? What was that all about?" asked Grace.

"Connor wandered away from him. He was upset."

"Huh," Bri said. She was wearing a wide-brimmed lavender hat with butterflies dancing at the end of narrow satin ribbons.

"Now there's a fashion statement," Margaux said, but Bri wasn't listening. She was staring after Nick and Connor.

"Well, well, well," she said. "I think we just met Margaux's merman."

Sixteen

 "So is it true?" asked Grace, sipping her Mojito at the Sea Dog Pub. "Is Nick Prescott your merman?"

"No. Yes." Margaux twirled her glass of Pinot Grigio around on the table. "I was out drawing on the jetty when he came out of the woods and went for a swim."

"Commando?" asked Bri.

"He was wearing shorts."

"Too bad. Then what happened?"

"He swam around. I was in a fanciful mood, so I drew that picture. He got out and left."

"A golden opportunity missed."

"I don't know." Grace paused to take a sip of her Mojito. "He's downright scary. No wonder that poor kid was shaking in his boots."

"That poor kid," said Bri, "is Ben Prescott's son." She sighed. "It's a damn shame. Life is weird, you know? Some die, some live. It just doesn't make any sense."

"No, it doesn't," said Grace.

They all ruminated on that for a moment, then Bri broke the silence. "But to get back to the police chief. I always thought he had the potential to look good if you just got rid of the uniform, dressed him up, and took him to a good stylist. Too spit-and-polish to be fun. But him all sleek out of the water and covering you with that burning gaze he was laying on you at the flea market. Now that's an image a girl could get her teeth into."

"Then go for it," Margaux said.

Bri held up both hands. "Not me. I have enough on my plate. Besides, I'm not going down that road again."

"What road?"

"Letting a man back in my life. I just don't trust myself to have the discipline to do what I need to do when there's a man around. I get distracted easily." She glanced over at the lavender butterfly hat.

Grace laughed.

Bri shrugged. "It was a spur-of-the-moment thing. Anyway, it'll make a good dress-up hat for when I get the girls."

"So tell me how this all came about," Margaux said.

"The girls?" Bri took a sip of her martini. "While I was in Switzerland recovering from my accident, I got involved with Smile Train, this organization that treats facial deformities in Third World children. There were so many children who needed someone to love them, so I put in the paperwork."

Grace lifted her glass to Bri. "A very compassionate attitude."

"It's not all altruism on my part. They said I probably would never be able to have kids from all those years of not eating, and all those other things I did to stay thin. These days I can eat whatever I want and I stay thin. Go figure."

"Just out of curiosity. Have you tried to have children?" asked Margaux.

Bri leaned back for the waiter to place her chicken Asiago in front of her. "Not really. Never found anyone I thought I wanted to wake up to for more than a couple of days in a row."

"Me either," Grace said, and tucked into her chopped salad.

"And I met the wrong man," Margaux said.

"No offense," Bri said, "but that asshole is beyond wrong. He's just plain out evil."

"Is he? I keep thinking that he must have just gotten into something over his head and things snowballed."

Bri pointed her fork at Margaux. "Do not start making excuses for him."

"I'm not. Right now, I hate him and don't care what happens to him. I guess it's just that I want to exonerate myself for making such a huge mistake."

"Oh, honey. We all made mistakes. Okay, maybe not Grace. But look at me. I wrecked my life and I can't even blame it on a man. Well, I could, but . . . Oh yeah, I see what you mean."

Grace called for another round of drinks and by the time coffee and dessert arrived, they'd passed onto brighter topics.

They walked arm in arm back toward the marina, dropping Grace off at her apartment on the way.

Margaux put Bri and her packages into her truck.

"Are you sure you're all right to drive?"

Bri gave her a look. "Trust me. I won't make that mistake again."

Margaux yawned as Bri drove away. She'd meant to go back to work, but between the flea market, the wine and food, and the fact that it was almost eight o'clock, she was exhausted. She'd start again tomorrow after a good night's sleep.

Jude slipped her hand into the crook of Roger's elbow as they walked to the parking lot.

His other hand closed over hers. "It's been a productive day. Are you too tired to have dinner?"

"Of course not."

"Good. We never had two minutes to ourselves today. Do you have a place in mind? Shall we take one car or two?"

Jude hesitated. "I thought we might eat in tonight."

"Your place?"

"Why not? We don't always have to go to a restaurant."

Roger's elbow tightened. "Sounds nice."

They drove separate cars back to Jude's condo. They waited for the elevator without speaking, and Jude thought how much like the embarrassment of a first date the situation was. There shouldn't be anything unusual about inviting an old friend to dinner, but she couldn't stop the nerves that had been let loose in her stomach.

She'd lived in her condo since she moved out of the beach house ten years before. She'd never invited Roger inside until now. It was time.

They took their drinks out to the balcony and leaned against the railing while they watched the sun go down. A breeze drifted up from the water, and Jude thought how comfortable it was standing here, two old friends, alone, and being good companions to each other.

Good heavens, she was thinking like an old woman. She was young, energetic, wanting to be loved. But not wanting to commit to something new.

"Sunset becomes you," said Roger, then laughed. "Sounds like a song, but I mean it. The sun sets off your hair until it positively glows." He put his drink down and turned to face her.

"I'd better start dinner."

He grasped her shoulders, gently but firmly. "You know, Jude, I'll always love Alice. Just as you will always love Henry. That will never change."

Jude cleared her throat. It felt thick and uncooperative. "You think they would want us to move on?"

He shrugged slightly and smiled. "It doesn't matter what I think. It matters what you think."

When the lights of the gym were finally turned off, the trash was carted away, and the last van had pulled out of the parking lot, it was after midnight. Nick climbed into his cruiser and drove across town to drop off the car at his mother's.

It had been a shit day. He'd yelled at Connor, he'd snapped

at Margaux, and when he took Connor back to his mother, her look of disappointment made him want to howl at the moon. And there was a full one tonight.

Things were slipping out of his control. No matter how hard he worked with Connor, the boy just didn't seem to come around.

And now he'd attached himself to Margaux Sullivan, which ordinarily would have made Nick happy; he liked having her around. But he was afraid that Connor would backslide once she left him. So he'd practically ordered her to stay away.

Was he a fool? He wanted to see more of Margaux himself. But that was selfish, and there was no room in Nick's life for that.

He walked back to his apartment, the moon lighting his way, his hands shoved in his pockets. His feet hurt, his back hurt, even his soul hurt. He'd reached the stairs to his apartment when he noticed a window open on the first floor.

He sighed and started to walk around to the front door to lock things up when a noise came from inside. Instantly alert, Nick unsnapped his holster and eased around to the front of the house.

The front door was ajar. Damn Margaux. She was just asking for trouble by being so lax and now she'd gotten it. Though what some punk thought he could steal in a gobload of material and sketches was beyond him.

He crept up the porch steps, slipped into the dark foyer. The studio door was also ajar. He pulled his pistol, held it ready, kicked the door open, and yelled, "Police, freeze."

A voice yelled back, "Don't shoot. It's me."

Nick slowly eased his finger off the trigger and holstered his .45, his pulse pounding. "Margaux?"

"Yes." She appeared out of the back room, looking ghostly in the light coming through the window.

"Jesus H. Christ, I could have shot you. What the hell are you doing here this late with the lights off?" He clicked on the overhead.

She blinked. "I forgot to close the windows when I went to the flea market. I was planning to come back and work, but I didn't and I forgot about them until I was almost asleep. So I came back. And the reason I didn't turn on the lights is because I didn't need them, I didn't plan on staying."

"Go lock the windows now," he said, fighting nerves and adrenaline and thanking God he hadn't killed her.

She went back inside the second room and he heard the windows scraping down. He should probably go help her, but he could only stand with his back against the wall, shaking and trying to draw breath.

When she came out again, she had more color, but looked worried. "I'm sorry," she said. "About everything."

She walked past him and pulled out a ring of keys. He followed her out and waited for her to lock up. He followed her to the porch and waited while she locked the front door. Then he walked her across the street to her car, which in his tired state, he hadn't noticed in his rush to apprehend the burglar.

She opened the driver's door.

Nick gritted his teeth. "You should always lock your car, especially at night."

He leaned forward to check her backseat just as she turned around. Right into his arms which automatically closed around her. He didn't let go. Couldn't let go. She was tense beneath his touch, but she didn't pull away.

"I'm sorry about the way I acted this afternoon," he said, so close to her that his breath ruffled her hair.

"Forget it."

"It's just that I'm worried about Connor getting attached."

"I understand, but I'm afraid it might be a little late for that. Maybe if I explain to him that I might—"

He wanted to tell her not to leave. For Connor. For himself. But he had no right. He eased away and for a second it seemed that she came with him. Then there was space between them, the night air cool around them.

"Maybe I can help," she said.

"How?"

"I'm not sure. But at least he's reaching out to someone . . . even if it is me."

He turned away from her and leaned against the car. He was afraid she might be right. It was hard for him to admit he needed help. He'd depended on himself and himself alone for so long, he wasn't sure he could depend on anyone else. And he wanted to be the one Margaux could depend on, not the other way around.

"Why don't you bring him to the beach. I could introduce him to some of the other kids. Or you could come and introduce him yourself if you'd rather."

"I've taken him to the park, to the playground, I tried to get him to play with other kids."

"I'm sure you're doing everything you can. But you'll be busy soon and the beach might be fun."

"More fun than me."

"No, of course not. I'm sure you're a lot of fun. I mean, I'm sure Connor thinks so."

"No he doesn't." Nick laughed, dry and without humor. "Just when he starts to have fun, I say something too loud, or lose my temper, or move too fast, and he crawls right back to where he was before."

He closed his eyes, felt her hand on his arm.

"You know what they say about it taking a village. Maybe you shouldn't try to do it all yourself. You don't have to." Her hand moved away and he felt oddly bereft.

"Just think about it. Good night." She got into the car.

Nick roused himself in time to shut her door. "Drive carefully."

She smiled up at him and left him standing alone under the streetlight.

Seventeen

 "Ask the girl out on a date," Linda said the next morning as she handed Nick a cup of coffee.

"I can't go on dates. I'm the chief of police."

"Exactly my point."

"What?"

"You're not the pope. Chiefs of police can date. It's expected."

Nick shook his head, imagining the talk if he went out with Margaux. If she'd even go out with him, though there was definitely something between them.

"For a big tough guy you can be a real wuss. You want me to ask her for you?"

Coffee sloshed in Nick's mug. He grabbed a napkin to soak up the spill. "Don't even think about it. I mean it, Linda. Don't mess in this."

She was standing on the other side of the table, hands on her hips, giving him her cheeky grin.

"I mean it."

The grin just broadened.

"I'll never forgive you."

"Never?"

"No. Never." He stood up. "I've got to get to the station.

Thanks for the coffee." He left by the back door. As he walked
down the drive to the street, she threw open the window and
sang at the top of her lungs, "Can't get no . . ."

Margaux parked across from Le Coif and checked to make sure
the police chief was nowhere in sight before she got out of the
car. Which was stupid, because she really wanted to see him
again. And at the same time she didn't—and shouldn't.

She hurried across the street and went inside. Linda poked
her head out. "Hell's bells, it's eight o'clock. You sleep in or
something?"

"Or something. You're open early."

"Yeah. I had to mainline the chief with some joe this
morning."

"Your tenant almost shot me last night."

"I heard. You sure have that man rattled."

"He thinks I'm an idiot and he warned me to stay away from
Connor."

"He didn't."

"Well, he did, though to give the devil his due, he did apologize later and said it was because he doesn't want Connor to
get attached and then have me leave."

"And are you leaving?"

Margaux frowned at her. "No. Not right away, but as soon
as I get a line to show, I'll have to."

"Uh-huh. Is that my phone ringing?" Linda popped back
into the salon.

Margaux unlocked the door to her studio and stepped inside.
What had been an empty space days ago was now filled with
bundles of fabric, both dyed and waiting to be dyed. Fabric
hung from coat hangers, was draped across tables, was folded
and stacked on the bookshelves. Her work had eaten up the
second room and threatened to need more.

And she still didn't have one design constructed. She could

draft her own patterns, but she was not a seamstress. She needed a staff. And she had no way to pay them.

She sat down at her drafting table and called her lawyer while she looked out the window at the marina. There had been no progress in the money search, nothing about the where-abouts of her erstwhile husband, even though it seemed he was a person of interest in a hedge fund scheme.

"If they do find him, can you make him sign a divorce agreement? I don't relish being married another year to the creep while I wait for the abandonment limitations to run out."

"I'll talk to some people; in the meantime, go out and have some fun. There is no way that jackass can touch anything you have, not if you paraded a hundred lovers before the court. He's in deep, Margaux. I'll make sure you get a divorce before he becomes a felon."

"I can't pay you right now."

"But you will. I can wait."

But how long? Margaux wondered as she hung up. Even if she gave up and got a normal job with a salary or hit the streets of New York and begged for any position in a studio, she would barely make enough to live on, much less pay her expensive lawyer.

As much as the idea of running her own business appealed to her, the only way she could get back on her feet was to come up with a production line. Either way, she had to start work. She called Jude.

"Of course I'll help. I already offered. I'll be your silent partner."

"No, Mom, I need to be totally responsible for this, but I could use some advice. I'll need someone to construct the clothes. I don't even know if I can find someone locally who can do that kind of work."

"Well, I do. Adelaide Prescott."

"Nick's mother?"

"She used to work in the garment district before she married Cyril and moved here. She's an excellent seamstress."

"I don't know if that's a good idea."

"I know what you're thinking, but she told me the other day she was going back to work when Connor was in school. Between you and me, they need the extra money and this would be perfect."

"But what about Connor?"

"She can bring him with her. He won't be in the way. He sat at a three-hour meeting the other night so quietly that I forgot he was there. Any more arguments?"

"No."

"Then shall I call her?"

"Would you mind? It might be better coming from you. I'm not sure Nick would want his mother working for me. He seems kind of sensitive that way."

"I'll call and bring her by this afternoon if she's amenable."

"Maybe we should wait to make sure the loan goes through."

"Nonsense. The loan will go through. Now don't worry. I'll call Adelaide, you make an appointment at the bank, and we'll ask Roger to come and advise us."

"We don't need a man to do this for us," Margaux said.

"No, we don't. But it makes things easier. Trust me. Besides, he worked on the state planning board for years. He knows about costs and accounting and returns and that kind of stuff. I confess I don't."

"Neither do I," Margaux admitted reluctantly. Until a few months ago, she'd had an accountant to do those things.

"He's just going to advise. Not dictate, if that's what you're worried about."

"All right, ask him. And Mom. Thanks."

She hung up, opened her notebook and studied her ever-lengthening list. She had temporary space. She had the fabric and the designs. She was about to hire a seamstress. She'd need additional staff, more equipment, which meant more space, and models. She'd present an invited runway showing, which meant she would need to find an appropriate venue, and a videographer to make a decent demo tape.

A giant money pit with no guarantees.

That afternoon, Jude brought Mrs. Prescott to Le Coif with Connor. Her hair was twisted neatly at the nape of her neck. She was wearing a summer suit, beautifully made, but a few years out of date. Chanel maybe, thought Margaux.

Connor stood quietly at her side, but he smiled at Margaux.

Mrs. Prescott held her purse aside while she bent over the worktable. "This shantung is exquisite." She glanced at the design board. "For the pantsuit?"

"Yes," said Margaux. "How did you guess?"

"It's perfect for it."

"You're hired," said Linda, coming into the room, frosting brush in her hand.

"Well, I . . ." Mrs. Prescott looked doubtfully at Margaux. There was a faint pink to her cheeks that hadn't been there before.

"Don't you have a head to dye?" Margaux asked.

Linda looked down at the brush in her hand. "Oh yeah, but don't close the door. I want to hear everything."

"Sorry about that," Margaux said. "Linda isn't the most patient soul in the world."

Margaux took Mrs. Prescott around the room, showing her fabric and the designs and explained what she envisioned. Jude stood out of the way, but Connor wedged himself in between his grandmother and Margaux.

"Would you be interested? I'm not quite ready to set up. I have no machinery yet and . . . And it would only be for a few weeks until I can get enough designs to hold a show."

"Wouldn't you like to see samples of my work?"

"Like the suit you're wearing?" Jude asked.

Adelaide blushed rosily. "I copied it years ago from a Chanel suit I saw in *Vogue*."

"It's beatifully made," Margaux said.

"We'd be in your debt, Adelaide," Jude said. "I can't think of anyone we could trust more to manage the workshop. We really need your help, if you think you could find the time."

"Well . . ." Mrs. Prescott hesitated, then looked at Margaux. "You'll need space to begin with. I don't have enough room at my house for cutting, sewing, and fitting. I do have an industrial Pfaff. It isn't new. It's in good working order, but we'll need a serger. Silk thread. Are you going to use premade binding?" She wrinkled her nose. "I'd advise against it. Using the original material as binding is time-consuming and not cost-effective, but gives a much nicer look."

"I agree," Margaux said, imagining her expenditures soaring into the stratosphere. Cost-effective? She'd be lucky if she didn't go bankrupt. Again.

"Would you like to think about it and let me know?" asked Mrs. Prescott.

"No-o-o," came Linda's voice from the salon. "You're hired. Give me a minute and I'll come over."

They continued to talk about fabrics and construction until Linda popped her head in. "Last one's cooking. I've got twenty-five minutes. Walk this way."

She led them upstairs. *"Wal-lah."*

"What do you mean, Voilà?" Margaux asked. "This is your apartment."

"Yeah, but I still have two empty bedrooms. She opened a door on her right, reached in and turned on a switch. "Wow, look at that. Looks like a sewing room to me."

It was empty except for a pile of cardboard boxes.

"I'll just move those . . . somewhere and it's yours."

"Linda you can't—"

"Of course I can."

Mrs. Prescott stepped inside. "Good. There's room for at least three sewing machines, a steamer. We could put a cutting table in that corner. Cramped but workable."

The woman knew her stuff.

Linda went back to finish with her client, and Jude, Margaux, and Mrs. Prescott sat down to organize. Feeling sorry for Connor, who hadn't spoken a word since his initial whispered "Hi," Margaux found a scrap of rejected chiffon and tied it around his neck like a cape. She tied a narrower piece around his forehead.

"Now you're a bona fide pirate," she said.

Mrs. Prescott looked on, her expression so wistful that Margaux was afraid she'd done something wrong.

"If your grandmother says it's okay."

"You look mighty fierce," Mrs. Prescott said, and Connor grinned and brandished an imaginary sword.

They were going full steam when a cell phone rang. Mrs. Prescott reached for her purse. "Sorry, Nicky insisted I get this." She opened it. "Hello?"

"Because Connor and I aren't at home," she said to the phone. "We're both at Margaux Sullivan's design studio. It's across the hall from Linda's." She smiled at Margaux and Jude and looked at the ceiling. "We're talking about the possibility of me working for her." She moved her ear away from the phone. "Yes. We'll be here when you get here."

She hung up. "Just like his father. Has to take care of everything and everybody all the time."

Margaux didn't need to ask who she was talking about. "Will he object to you working here?" The last thing Margaux wanted was to cause a rift in the Prescott family.

"He'll come around. Now about that cambric. It will have to be hand-finished if you want it to look seamless."

Nick walked in five minutes later. He looked hot, flustered, and spoiling for a fight.

Just what Margaux didn't need.

"Hi, honey, come look at the fabric Margaux's designed."

"I've seen it. Could I talk to you for a minute?"

Mrs. Prescott's lips twitched, much as her son's did when he was trying not to smile. "Nicky, where are your manners. You didn't say hello to Jude or Margaux."

"Hello." Nick looked from one woman to the other. "Where's Connor?"

They all looked around. Margaux had forgotten all about him.

"Here I am, Uncle Nick." Connor crawled out from under the table wearing the chiffon cape and bandanna Margaux had made him.

Nick blinked and Margaux realized that Connor had spoken in a normal voice. "Nana's going to work for Margaux making clothes."

Emotion flickered across Nick's face, but Margaux couldn't tell if it was surprise or anger.

They all stared at Connor, who suddenly looked frightened.

"Isn't he a great pirate?" Margaux said, thinking, *Please don't scare him.*

"The best," Nick said, sounding bemused.

Connor didn't move, he seemed to barely breathe.

"A great pirate," Nick repeated, and knelt down to take a better look at the chiffon costume.

"Actually," Jude said, "we've been begging your mother to run the construction department for us."

"What?" Nick stood up.

"Margaux is designing a new line and she needs someone who can construct them for her."

"What about Connor?"

"I'm going to help," Connor said, back to his whisper voice.

"Do you have any objection?" Mrs. Prescott asked, the balance of power somehow shifting from her son to her.

Nick shook his head slightly as if it were all too much for him. "No. If that's what you want."

"It is. When would you like me to start?"

"I was going to start cutting patterns on Saturday. Is that too soon?"

"Not at all. Ten o'clock?"

"That would be great. Thank you so much, Mrs. Prescott. This really relieves my mind."

"My pleasure and please call me Adelaide."

They left soon after that. "Well," Margaux said to Jude, "now all I need is a way to pay her."

Nick walked into the studio around five that afternoon. Margaux braced herself for a tirade about hiring his mother and thinking she was better than they were. The man had issues, which was too bad because other than his streak of stubborn, my-way-or-the-highway attitude, he was just the kind of man she respected. And any woman would be glad to have at her side.

Or in any other position. Margaux blushed hot. She was not here to have those kinds of thoughts about the police chief. It was bad enough that her heart gave a little lurch every time she saw him. Not good at all.

"Hi," she said. "If you're upset about your mother coming to work—"

"I'm not. It's her choice."

Somehow that didn't relieve Margaux's wariness. "Then—"

"I'm here to . . . ask if you wanted to go to dinner. Sometime."

Margaux's mouth opened, but if she had meant to say something, it flew right out of her head.

"I'm off Friday night. If you're not busy."

"She's not busy," echoed from the beauty salon.

Nick shut the door.

"I'm not busy," Margaux said. He was asking her out? On a date? She hadn't been on a date for thirteen years. And from his hesitant invitation, he sounded like he hadn't either.

"Do you have a place you'd like to go?"

Margaux shook her head. "I'm kind of out of the loop."

"Okay I'll—"

The door opened. Linda stuck her head in. "You're killing me here. I got a date tonight and you're making me late. Take her to the Cove Inn, they have great *ambi-ants*. Steak ain't bad, either." She grinned at them. "He'll pick you up at seven-thirty. Wear something sexy. Whew, that's settled. I gotta run."

She shut the door, Margaux looked at the floor, feeling like a gawky teenager. She listened to Linda bound up the stairs; when she heard a door closing on the floor above her, she looked up at Nick.

There was a slash of color across his cheekbones, accentuating their contour and making him look sexy and adorable at the same time.

Wrong, she admonished herself. *Adorable isn't a word in your vocabulary.* And it was something she was pretty sure Nick Prescott had never been, even as a baby.

He laughed uncomfortably. "Well, I guess I was making a hash of this. I'm a little out of practice."

"Me, too."

"So would you like to have dinner on Friday?"

"I'd love to."

Jude opened the sliding glass doors to her balcony and stepped outside. Margaux was up and running and she felt at loose ends. And lonely. Roger had been gone for less than twenty-four hours and her apartment felt empty without him.

She looked out at the vista as she did every morning and every night. Below her, the water of the sound sparkled with sunlight. The beach was alive with sunbathers and romping children.

Once, it had been her down there, reading in her beach chair, waiting for Henry to come home from his commute to Hartford while Danny and Margaux played at the water's edge.

Life had been good then, their future spreading before them like the water below her. Henry would come straight from the train station to the beach with his suit jacket thrown over his shoulder. Danny and Margaux always saw him first, and as soon as they began to run toward the house, she knew that when she turned around, she would see Henry smiling at her as they pulled him to the chair next to hers.

Emotion welled up inside her—threatened to spill out. Her children had grown into beautiful young adults. Then Danny was gone.

Henry was never the same after that. They still came to the beach in summer and returned home to Hartford in the fall. He went through the motions and he still loved her and Margaux as he always had. But he aged rapidly. His hair turned grayer and his shoulders stooped. Then Margaux married Louis. Jude still sat at the beach every afternoon, but it was she who saw Henry first—and last.

And then Henry was gone, too. It seemed as if the longer she lived, the more was taken from her. Not gradually, as old age fell into the inevitable, but lobbed off in great chunks, the healthy branches sacrificed along with the frail.

Life was about loss. One minute standing on the promise of your dreams, then free-falling backward into nothingness. Is this what it meant to grow old? To gradually be stripped of all you cared about. And then what? Were you supposed to spend the rest of your life, dreaming about the past while you waited to die?

Or did you start a new life, set the cycle in motion once again. Take the chance of losing that, too. And if you did, what happened to the old life? Did it die away from lack of attention?

Her love for Henry was like a rock in her gut. Growing heavier and larger each day. It only hurt sometimes—set off by a smell or a color or the unfurled wings of an osprey. But it was always there.

She had lost Henry and Danny, and she was afraid of losing

Margaux, too. Not to death—she quickly crossed herself—but to bitterness.

What shall I do, Henry? Tears dropped onto the backs of her hands where they grasped the railing. *I know I can't go back, but I'm afraid to go forward. What should I do?*

Eighteen

 On Friday, Margaux met Jude and Roger in front of the bank.

Roger smiled and held open the door. "I know you must be anxious, so let's get this show on the road."

"And I'm going to cosign," Jude said. "So no argument."

"Mom, no." Margaux's stomach turned sour. "I'm a bad risk. Maybe I should forget it."

"We are not," Jude said. "I have total faith in you. And it isn't fair not to let me do this." Her jaw jutted out.

Margaux heaved a sigh. "Let's go for it."

Two hours later, when they walked out of the bank, Margaux had a business loan and a new checking account.

"Congratulations, sweetheart." Jude hugged her.

"It was all you and Roger. Thank you. I won't let you down."

"You've never let me down. And I'm so happy that I could help."

"Can I take you two ladies to a late lunch?"

Margaux shook her head. "I'd love to, but I'd better get back and tell Linda the good news. She'll be ecstatic. Thanks, Mom. Roger, you were incredible." She reached over and kissed his cheek. He looked pleasantly surprised.

The salon was crowded. Linda was just putting someone under a hair dryer when she saw Margaux. Margaux gave her a thumbs-up.

Two minutes later, Linda stuck her head in the doorway. "Great. Now go get ready."

"For what?"

"Your date."

Margaux jumped up from the drafting table. "Oh God, I forgot. What time is it?"

"Two o'clock."

"Oh." Margaux sank back on her chair. "Plenty of time."

Linda rolled her eyes. "You have two hours to work, then come across the hall and I'll wash and blow you out."

"You don't have to."

Linda pulled her glasses down to the tip of her nose and peered over them. "You look fine, but you don't look great, you don't quite have the knack of blow-drying down. And you're not taking my hairstyle to the Cove Inn with crinkles. Two hours." She pushed her glasses up and disappeared.

Margaux was too excited about her loan to do any work, she just walked from sketch to sketch dreaming about the finished product. And if she were honest, a few of those jitters were because of the upcoming date with Nick.

Which was really stupid. She partied with international moguls, celebrities, rich Upper East Side investors, jet-setting sheiks, Parisian playboys. But she was tied in knots over dinner with a small-town police chief.

Nick did weird things to her peace of mind, not to mention the flash of heat he aroused in her whenever he was near, or she heard his voice, or—*not going there.* She had a career to jump-start . . . tomorrow.

She forced herself to concentrate for the next two hours and was actually grateful when Linda came in and strong-armed her across the hall. By the time she left Le Coif, she was washed, dried, styled, and bullied. And she was feeling a little dizzy.

"And if you get lucky, just remember, I'm not listening." Linda gave her a cheeky grin.

"Not to worry. We're going to dinner. And I have a feeling it wasn't even Nick's idea." She raised her eyebrows at the hairdresser.

"Of course it was his idea. Does he look like a man easily coerced?"

"No, but I don't underestimate your powers of persuasion."

"I predict this is going to be the start of something big."

"Don't start singing or getting expectations. It's dinner. And that's all."

"We'll see." Linda pushed her out the door. "And don't get your hair wet when you shower. You do have a shower cap? Here, better take one of these." She thrust a plastic cap at Margaux. "You do have a slinky dress, don't you?"

"I just happen to have a new one. A nice sea green sheath."

"Great with your hair."

Margaux worked her way to the door. "See you tomorrow."

Linda stood at the door and watched her walk across the street, half mother hen, half Mae West, and all grins.

Nick cursed and yanked the knot out of his tie, pulled the tie from his neck, and threw it on the closet floor. He chose another one.

Navy blue with a thin gray stripe. Did this tie even go with his jacket? Was the jacket formal enough? He knew zip about fashion.

The Cove Inn was way too elegant for Nick's taste, but thanks to Linda he would be sitting beneath a crystal chandelier trying not to spill his wine on the white linen tablecloth. He'd rather take Margaux to some place where they could just relax, talk, maybe reminisce a little, get to know each other without having an overattentive waiter hovering nearby waiting to fill his water glass every time he took a sip.

It was going to be a disaster, not to mention setting him back a bundle, which he didn't begrudge at all until he thought about the Eldon School tuition. But it seemed he'd waited his entire life to have dinner with Margaux Sullivan. This would get it out of his system. He'd make a fool of himself, a bull in a china shop, and she would be thoroughly disgusted.

And if she had a horrible time, then things would be tense between her and his mother. Was he crazy? He was going on a date with his mother's employer.

He didn't even want his mother to work. He wanted her to enjoy life. Go out with the girls. Get her hair done at Le Coif. Play bridge or whatever ladies her age did.

He didn't want her slaving like she'd slaved her entire life to make ends meet. To give her family an extra little something. And he especially didn't want her working for Margaux. His motives were partly selfish. He didn't want the difference between them brought constantly to attention.

And he had to pick her up in a truck, he thought morosely. He couldn't very well use the police cruiser or his mother's old Buick.

Jesus. It was going to be a disaster.

Margaux was ready half an hour early. She considered having a pre-dinner glass of wine to calm her nerves, but in her state, she might get rip-roaring drunk by the end of the meal. She sat down on the couch to wait. Her new knit dress began to creep up her thighs.

She should probably have stuck to something more subtle. A black pantsuit. But she was done with black; besides, what kind of date omen would that be? Strange how her attitude toward black had changed since she'd been in Crescent Cove. In the city, black was chic, de rigueur for evening. It had been the impetus for her success. Here it was depressing.

She looked good in her green sheath. She'd found a pair of stilettos in her suitcase, but she wasn't wearing hose. Not because she was thinking of getting out of them later, but because she hadn't brought a pair to the beach.

Besides, she wasn't trying to seduce the man. That was a

laugh. She hadn't tried to seduce a man in years. Probably couldn't even remember how. Not that she wanted to.

Except was that true? Wasn't that what she did every day with her designs? Promise beauty and desirability? Every time she met a new designer or retailer or potential client at a party, didn't she go about seducing them into buying her clothes, giving her floor space, wearing her latest creation. Of course, that was what the business was about; glamour and façade and watching your back.

Wowing Nick should be a piece of cake. And yet, she was as nervous as a girl going to the prom. It was ludicrous. It just showed her how far away from her true self she'd come. Because she was looking forward to spending the evening with him.

She liked him and respected him for taking care of his family and for his work ethic. And if she were truthful, she was attracted to him physically. Bone-deep attraction. Every time he was close, she had to force herself not to find reasons to touch him.

And that might be difficult tonight.

It was just dinner, a table between them. But what about after dinner? Would he kiss her? Would he expect more? Or would they end the evening awkwardly shaking hands at the door.

She jumped off the couch when she heard his truck pull onto the graveled parking area. Stood there until she heard his knock at the back door. She straightened her skirt, smoothed back her already smooth hair, and forced herself to walk calmly to answer it.

He was wearing a light gray jacket and charcoal gray trousers. His hair had grown since she'd arrived a few weeks ago, and she could see just the beginning of curl against his forehead.

Definitely symbolic of the man, she thought. Was he beginning to lighten up from his no-frills attitude? It was charming. Was it because of her?

She'd like to think so. She smiled at him, invited him in, and thought, *Girl, you are in deep trouble.*

The Cove Inn was a columned mansion built in the mid-nineteenth century. It was painted white with dark green shutters and sat behind a manicured lawn surrounded by a stack stone wall. The grounds were filled with trees lit with tiny white lights à la Tavern on the Green.

Nick drove through the wrought-iron gate and around the circular drive to the entrance where a valet took the truck with a sheepish look at Nick.

"I gave him a ticket once," Nick explained as they walked into the restaurant.

They were met by the maître d'. "Good evening, sir, madam."

Margaux did a double take. The maître d' was a large man with a shaved head and a deep voice. He filled out his tuxedo beautifully.

He led them to a table at the far end of the restaurant that overlooked the water.

"Michael will be your waiter this evening," he said. "Enjoy." He nodded slightly, winked at Margaux, and walked away.

Margaux stared after him, then looked across the table to Nick. "That was Harlan."

Nick grimaced. "Hence the secluded table."

"You gotta hand it to her. Linda knows how to get what she wants." And Linda obviously wanted the two of them together.

Michael came with the wine list. Nick consulted her about preference, then ordered a Napa Valley Cabernet that made Margaux blink. Either he knew his wines or someone had prepped him before he came. She appreciated his effort. It was a sweet thing to do.

She looked at Nick, but when he looked back she turned her attention to the twinkling trees outside.

Michael returned with the wine and poured. They touched

glasses, "To your new endeavor," Nick said. "Linda said you got the loan."

"Yes, the bank came through, thanks to Jude and Roger Kyle." Margaux decided to get it out and over with at once. "I hope you don't mind me hiring your mother. Her reputation as a seamstress and finisher preceded her. It's hard to find that kind of talent anywhere, especially outside of New York. So I feel especially lucky that she agreed."

Nick half smiled. "I wasn't real thrilled with the idea at first. But she really wants to do it." He paused, looked out the window, then back at Margaux. "She actually seems younger and more animated since she decided to go back to work."

"But you still don't like it."

"I guess I'll have to get used to it."

The conversation stalled. Normally Margaux would fall back on some current event in the fashion world, but she didn't know where to start with Nick. She went through society functions by rote, she realized. And now that she thought about it, she couldn't remember a time when she'd really enjoyed one, just for itself, and not as a means to an end.

"What?"

"Hmm?"

"You sighed. Is the wine no good?"

"It's excellent."

"Would you rather go someplace else?"

"No, this is wonderful. I . . . I was trying to remember the last time I had been to dinner just to have a pleasant evening. And I am . . . Having a pleasant evening. More than pleasant."

"Well, that's a relief."

Margaux laughed. "You weren't worried, were you?"

"Me? No. You?"

"No . . ."

"I'm sensing a but here." Nick put down his wineglass and leaned forward. "Is there a but?"

"Not anymore. I was afraid that it might look weird. I mean, I'm still officially married, and you're the police chief."

Nick gave her one of his rare but unique smiles. "Were you afraid for my reputation or yours?"

Margaux laughed. "Both, I guess, but I'm over it." She sat back while Michael placed arugula salads in front of them. "Have you always lived in Crescent Cove?"

Nick frowned, hesitated. "Until I was twenty, then I joined the army."

Margaux wrestled with a smile, remembering her initial response to Nick and his sunglasses.

"What?"

"Nothing. It's just that I can tell."

He narrowed his eyes. "How?"

"Just can."

"You think I'm uptight and hard-nosed and don't know how to have fun."

Margaux laughed and held up a hand. "Okay. I did when we first met. The operative word here is *did*." She grew more serious. "Now I think you're a man who takes care of his family. It's a rare trait where I come from."

"I thought you were from Crescent Cove. You told me you were three-quarters townie."

"I am. I meant from where I've been lately." She picked up her wineglass, mainly to have something to do. She suddenly felt like crying, not for what she'd lost but for the time she'd wasted. She took a breath and it passed.

"Dottie says you just came back last year. Were you in the army all that time?"

Nick shook his head, looked out the window into the night. "I lived in Denver. I was . . . a teacher."

"Really? What did you teach?"

"History. At a college there."

"Ah, a history professor. You're full of surprises, though I guess I should have guessed from your reading material."

Nick winced.

"What? Is the *Ostrogoths in Italy* a big secret? Who were the Ostrogoths anyway?"

"Do you really want to know?"

"Kind of. I could Google them, or you could just tell me about them."

"Okay, but tell me when you get bored." And Nick gave her a concise history of the Ostrogoths until Michael took their salad plates away.

"I bet you're a good professor."

"Was, maybe. Does the bank loan mean you're staying in Crescent Cove?"

It was such a non sequitur that Margaux was speechless.

"I was just wondering." He paused, swallowed. "If I should make arrangements for Connor . . . if my mother is going to be working a lot."

"Adelaide and I already discussed this. The job is temporary, but I can't say how temporary. It depends on a lot of things. I have to get back in the thick of things to stay viable." She hesitated. "But there are a lot of factors, and strangely enough, I'm kind of settling in. I know I can't stay, but the longer I do, I know that it will be harder to leave."

"So why can't you stay? I mean, aren't there designers who don't live in Manhattan?"

"Sure. They live in Milan. Paris. Tokyo. London."

"But not in Crescent Cove."

She shook her head. "It's tempting, but I worked all my life to get where I am."

"I know."

"You do?"

Nick looked away. "I can imagine."

"Of course. You had to study to become a historian. And you have to be—" She broke off. He must have given up his teaching position to return to Crescent Cove and take care of his family.

"Where the jobs are," he finished.

Michael returned with their entrées, which ended the subject. She bet anything Michael would be getting a big tip for his timely interruptions, if not for the impeccable service.

After dinner, they walked out to the patio at the back of the mansion where tables were set up for alfresco dining. Nick seemed lost in his own thoughts, and she wondered if he was ready to end the evening. She wasn't.

He led her across the patio and beneath an arbor to a brick path that followed the shoreline. It was lit by lanterns that hung from wrought-iron posts.

At first they walked side by side, not touching, but after a while Nick took her hand and linked it through his elbow. It was such a gentlemanly, old-fashioned gesture that Margaux's heart melted toward this brusque stubborn man.

They were so mismatched. And yet, it felt right. She let herself move closer to him. They walked in silence, looking out to the Sound, listening to the gentle lapping of the waves against the seawall.

As they walked farther from the inn, the lanterns became more sparsely spaced until the path was lit only by the stars. They came to the end of the path where it widened into a patio with benches facing the sea. Nick led her over to one of them and they sat down. Close enough to feel his warmth, not close enough to feel intimate.

He pointed to the sky. "Look."

She looked. Thousands, millions of stars hung fragilely in space, as if a breath could shake them loose and set them falling toward earth. And she thought how daily dramas were played out against a world that was near perfect, that adapted and changed, but never broke under the weight of its own importance. Accepted all without judgment. Her. The man sitting next to her. Even Louis.

She shivered.

"Cold?"

"No, it's just so beautiful." And she could see the fabric in her mind's eye. Silk velvet in a blue so deep as to be almost black. And the stars . . . not glitter, not diamantes, something she hadn't found yet. But she would; she only had to look.

They sat for a while longer, then Nick stood up. "We'd better get going."

Margaux tried to read his expression in the shadows, but it was impossible. Was he anxious to go home? Get rid of her?

"I've had a really nice time," she said.

He looked startled. "I'm glad. So did I."

They started back toward the Inn. They'd just reached the lit portion of the path when Margaux stopped. Off to her right was a large terrace, part of the inn that had been hidden by trees until they turned to retrace their steps. It was lit only by the lights coming from the inn, but even from where she was standing, she could see it was large enough for a banquet-sized crowd. And she suddenly, vaguely remembered attending a wedding there years before.

It was long enough to hold a decent-sized runway and wide enough to fit a hundred people or more. Large enough for an experienced videographer to get a good tape. And the French windows of the inn and the surrounding twinkling trees would be the perfect backdrop.

Unfortunately it was probably reserved through the next decade. And the fees would be astronomical. But maybe not if she held it on an off night, or even an afternoon. It didn't have to be an "event." She just needed a few models and enough people to look good on film. The back of a few heads. Well-styled heads. And she bet between Linda, Jude, and her, they'd have no problem filling the house.

She became aware of Nick watching her curiously. He might decide she was nuts, might never ask her out again, but she would always be grateful to him, because she had just found the perfect venue for catapulting her back to success.

"Thank you," she said, and threw her arms around his neck.

Nineteen

 At first Nick was too shocked to move. He was pretty sure she wasn't giving in to passion. It had to be some gut-level response to whatever she was thinking.

But he wasn't going to argue. He let her hug him. His arms went around her waist. He knew he shouldn't do it.

He didn't care. He basked in the feel of her, memorized every curve, every scent. He drank her in and knew he'd gone off his rocker, because he couldn't get enough of her. Knew he would never get enough of her. Wanted to ease her down on the bricks and make her his.

She loosened her grip as if she just realized what she was doing. His arms fell away, and he prayed that she hadn't felt his heart pounding or any other reaction he was having to her.

He struggled for breath. Tried to think of something to gloss over the awkwardness while chastising himself for not kissing her when he had the chance.

"Sorry," Margaux said. "I got carried away. This is the perfect place for me to set up a showing of my new line." She smiled, embarrassed. "As soon as your mother constructs them." She sighed. "If I can rent the space and if I can talk Brianna into modeling for me."

The mood was broken, but he was glad that he'd been part of her excitement. He just wished it had been over him. But it didn't matter what he wanted. You played the hand you were dealt and that was that.

The valet brought the truck around and he helped her in. When he climbed into the driver's side, she smiled at him and she looked so right sitting there beside him that it hurt. He tried to ignore the rush of desire that pulsed through him as he drove toward the entrance.

"You probably think I've got a one-track mind," she said, sounding apologetic.

"I think it's great. I can appreciate someone being wedded to their work." God, why had he chosen that word?

"So which work are you wedded to, Nick? Teaching history or being chief of police?"

Sucker punch. He hit the break too hard and they both rocked against the seat.

"Did I hit a nerve? Sorry, I didn't mean to pry. It just sort of popped out. Because I'm interested in you. I mean. I care about . . . Oh shit. You know what I mean."

"This is just an interim position. I needed the job for . . . well, you've seen what for. No big deal."

"Sounds like a pretty big deal to me."

"That's where you're wrong." He hadn't meant to sound so harsh. She was watching him with an expression he couldn't read. Wariness. Anger. Pity. But hell, he didn't want her to think he was some heroic person. Women did that kind of thing. Made huge leaps of faith. And he wasn't like that. But he did pay his debts. He couldn't bring his brother back, but he sure as hell would take care of his son.

He felt her touch on his arm. She did that when she wanted to communicate. He'd miss that when she was gone.

"I've seen how much you care about your family. Not every man would make his family first priority. I should know."

He cut his eyes toward her, but didn't comment. He knew she was getting a divorce. But not why.

He turned onto Salt Marsh Lane. They were almost at her

house, and he knew he should let the subject drop. He didn't
want the evening to end on an angry note, with her thinking
about her husband and him thinking about all the shit he'd
done wrong in his life—a wedge hammered between them.
But he couldn't seem to stop himself.

"I know you're getting a divorce. Your husband must be an
idiot."

"Oh, he's much worse. And I was a fool. It's hard to admit
you've wasted a huge amount of your life on a lie."

He stopped the truck in the middle of the street and turned
to her. "That's bullshit. You didn't waste it. You're famous. I
saw all those magazines."

"All I ever wanted to do was design dresses. But I took a
wrong turn when Danny died. I was desperate to do something to take away Mom and Dad's pain. I married Louis. I
was going to fill their lives with grandchildren, give them so
much that it would ease their loss. And look—no husband, no
children—" She broke off, her face looking ghostly white in
the dark.

"I wanted kids, too. Now I have one." His words sounded
sharp almost bitter.

"Connor is a sweetheart."

"Yeah." He put the truck in gear and continued down the
street. He'd confessed enough for one night.

"But what about a wife?"

The truck swerved, he steadied it. "Is this a proposal?"

"No," she said on a laugh. "It's just me being nosy. Forget I
asked."

"There was the army, then teaching. Time passed and I
never got around to getting married. Never found anyone—
never a lot of things."

"Never found anyone you wanted to marry?"

"I loved a girl once, I think."

"You think?"

"It was a long time ago. I was young. She was younger. I didn't appreciate what she meant to me until years later. By then I was in the army and she was . . . somewhere else."

"Did you ever try to find her?"

Nick shook his head. "No. But things have a way of working out for the best." Or not. At least he'd finally said what he felt, even if she didn't understand it.

"You mean that you might be disappointed if you met her again? Maybe she'd be really fat or something?"

"Or something. Here we are." He pulled into the drive and cut the engine. She probably thought he was going to try to hit her up for a nightcap, but he wasn't that smooth. Best to just open her door, give her a kiss on the cheek, and damn himself for cowardice on his ride home.

She was already getting out of the truck by the time he got there, making him redundant, but he followed her to her door.

She opened the screen and opened the door.

"Margaux, don't you ever lock anything? There are all sorts of thieves and predators out there."

She huffed out a sigh. "I triple-quadruple locked every door and window when I lived in the city. We never had to lock anything here. And please don't tell me times have changed. I know they have. And now you've spooked me."

"Do you want me to come in and make sure the house is empty?"

She smiled and he realized what a transparent excuse for coming inside that sounded like. He did want to come inside, wanted to pick her up and carry her caveman-style through her unlocked back door. "You can wait in the truck until I'm done."

"I'll be perfectly fine. Though if . . ." She turned to him. There was an awkward moment while some unseen force drew them together.

Nick stepped toward her. He meant to kiss her cheek and

leave, but just as he leaned forward she shifted and his mouth found hers. The air rushed out of his lungs and his arms went around her.

She melted against him, conforming perfectly to his body as if she were made for him. Her lips opened and he explored her mouth with his tongue. She responded even better than he could have imagined, and while the kiss lasted, time stopped, his problems floated away. He was lost in the moment and damn the consequences.

With a murmur, she pulled away. He didn't want to let her go, but he did. She looked up at him with wide expectant eyes, but he saw the uncertainty behind the desire.

"I'd better get going."

"I know." She stepped into him.

The next time he let go, Margaux stumbled. He shot out a hand to steady her. He knew exactly how she felt. He was pretty damn weak in the knees himself. And he had the mother of all erections.

"Good night," she said, and went inside.

Nick just stood there. He couldn't think clearly. Could barely think at all. It was all he could do to get into the truck and drive away.

He hadn't wanted to stop at the kiss. Might not have been able to if it had gone on much longer. And that would just be a huge complication, though he bet it would be one hell of a night.

Or she might not have wanted that at all and told him to go to hell. He wasn't quite ready to take the chance.

In a way it was better not knowing. Some things were better off left in the imagination, than to have them killed in reality.

Margaux waited at the door until the truck was out of sight, then turned back to the kitchen. She'd forgotten what it felt like to be swept off her feet. To have someone really pay attention to her when he was making love to her. Okay. A kiss wasn't exactly making love, but it sure felt close.

She knew he would have stayed if she had given him the slightest reason to, but she was afraid. There it was. Margaux Sullivan, who faced the backbiting, backstabbing world of high fashion without a blink of an eye, was afraid of a small-town cop.

That wasn't entirely true. It wasn't Nick Prescott she was afraid of. It wasn't even the chance of getting hurt or disappointed again. It was the fear that if they had gone further, she might not want to pull back again. And she would start making excuses to stay in Crescent Cove instead of getting back to her career, a career that couldn't include a gruff taciturn man, or a darling little boy who desperately needed a mother to love him. It would be professional suicide.

She reined in her thoughts. She was jumping way ahead of herself. A couple of kisses, as good as they were, weren't an invitation to happily ever after. Not that she'd fall for that fairy tale again.

So why did being with Nick feel different? Was it just because she was starved for affection or was it real? And if there was something special between them, would she give up everything for it?

The answer had to be no. As much as she wanted a family, she just wasn't ready to give up designing. Maybe when she was at the top of her game again, but not now, when she was down and had nothing to offer.

All the same, it was going to be damn hard to walk away from Nick and that sweet silent boy who had already won a place in her heart.

She turned out the lights and walked down the hall to the stairs. The house was so quiet she thought she could hear the distant sounds of the past. Only the present was silent. Margaux was alone.

★ ★ ★

Margaux reached Le Coif before Linda had opened the salon for the day. She found her in the kitchen, hunched over a paperback, a cup of tea hovering near her mouth, but never quite making it.

"Good morning."

The tea sloshed, the book erupted into the air. "Holy moly, you scared the crap out of me."

Margaux picked up the book. *The Wench's Secret Lover.* She handed it back to Linda. "Sorry. I came in just to thank you for suggesting the inn."

"*Ambi-ants* got to you, huh?"

"Did you know Harlan was the maître d'?"

"Well, of course. You didn't think I picked him up in a biker bar, did you?"

"He's very impressive in a tux."

"Just one of his many charms." Linda gave her one of her toothy grins and knocked back the rest of her tea. "So you had a good time?"

"Very."

"That's nice, though I gotta say, I couldn't help but notice that I didn't hear any sneaking upstairs to Nick's apartment going on, and since I heard him coming in at some ungodly early-bird-special hour, I'm guessing that the only dessert you had was at the restaurant."

"It was our first date."

"Of many, we can but hope."

"I don't know about that, but I do have to thank you for suggesting the inn. Have you seen that big terrace off the side of the restaurant?"

"Um . . ."

"You have."

"No I haven't, only the little one in back. Honest Injun." She raised three fingers in the air and it reminded Margaux of the Selkies' solemn oath.

"Well, it's a perfect venue for a runway show—if I can get the space for a price I can afford. I figure most weddings and graduations are held on weekends, so maybe a weeknight. It's perfect."

"You should be so excited about your date with Nick."

Margaux frowned. "We had a good time. He's intense, but a gentleman."

Linda rolled her eyes. "I gotta talk to him about that."

"I've got work to do. Just wanted to say thanks."

"You're welcome."

Margaux closed the door to Linda's mumbled "Hopeless, hopeless, hopeless."

Mrs. Prescott came in midmorning with a carpetbag of sewing supplies and Connor, wearing his cape and headband from the day before.

"He would have slept in it if I had let him," Mrs. Prescott said. She settled him on a stool at the drafting table while Margaux rolled out paper on the larger worktable so they could begin pattern cutting.

"Nicky put my sewing machine in the trunk. He said he'd come over on his break and carry it inside for us."

Margaux blushed. From the way Mrs. Prescott was smiling at her, she must know that the two of them had dinner together the night before. This could get dicey, Margaux thought. She should never have gone out with Nick knowing that his mother was about to become her employee.

Excuses, excuses, she told herself. *This isn't a sudden revelation. You knew what the situation was and went ahead and did it anyway. So deal with it.* She erased the smile that had crept onto her face.

They spent the morning planning and cutting. Margaux told Mrs. Prescott about her ideas for using the inn for a runway show.

"It must be very expensive."

"I'm sure it is, even if they have an available time. At first I thought about having a showing here, just one or two models walking around in the clothes, but this way I could get a good video to send out at the same time."

Margaux stood and stretched. "Let's take a break. I could use some tea and I bet Connor would like a snack. Where is Connor?" Margaux looked around the room, no Connor. She leaned over and looked beneath the table, not there.

"Oh dear. Connor, honey, where are you?"

"Look in the back room. I'll go see if Linda has seen him."

Margaux found him sitting in one of Linda's styling chairs, turning in circles while Linda combed out Dottie Palmer.

"Hi," Dottie said. "Didn't want to bother you, you seemed so busy, but I do want to come in and peek."

"Sure. Though there's not much to see yet. Connor, your grandmother's looking for you."

Connor slid off the chair, head bowed.

Margaux, Linda, and Dottie exchanged looks.

"It's okay if you come across the hall, but just tell us so we won't worry, okay?"

He nodded.

"We're going to have a snack. Are you hungry?"

He nodded.

"Cookies in the cookie jar," Linda said. "Connor knows where it is, don't you, luvbug?"

Connor smiled at her, took Margaux's hand, and led her toward the kitchen.

"Let's get your grandmother first," Margaux said.

She called in at the door to her studio. "Found him."

Mrs. Prescott came out, looking chagrined. "Connor Cyril Prescott, you know better than to run off without telling anyone."

Connor leaned into Margaux. She crouched down by him and pushed a curl off his forehead. "It's because we don't want anything to happen to you. We'd be really sad if you got lost or hurt and we couldn't find you. Now, let's go get some cookies."

She stood and saw Mrs. Prescott. There was a strange look in her eye.

"Sorry, I didn't mean to overstep."

"You didn't. He needs a—someone to—I won't bring him again. He can stay with my neighbors. They don't mind watching him."

Connor leaned closer to Margaux. He was warm and nearly weightless against her.

"Of course you can bring him. We'll just have to find some things to keep him occupied."

When they went back to work, Margaux pulled Connor's stool to the worktable. She drew some shapes on scraps of brown paper, found some snub-nosed scissors in his backpack, and set him to cutting out the shapes.

When Nick arrived, lugging a massive sewing machine, the three of them were working at the cutting table, heads bent over their work.

"Where do you want this?" he asked, glancing at Margaux and letting his gaze slide away.

Margaux looked at Mrs. Prescott for directions but she was looking at her son. "Can't you say hello?"

"Hello. Where do you want this?"

"Upstairs."

He turned around and clumped up the stairs. Connor tugged at Mrs. Prescott's dress and whispered to her. She nodded and Connor ran after his uncle.

Mrs. Prescott stared after them, her eyes glistening. Margaux knew she should back away from this family. They had all sorts of issues she really didn't have the time to get enmeshed in. But she was afraid it was already too late.

While they stood there, Dottie and Linda came out of Le Coif.

"Was that Nick's voice I heard?" Dottie asked.

Linda opened her mouth but Margaux cut her off. "He brought Adelaide's sewing machine."

"He also took Margaux to dinner last night."

"Linda!" Margaux snapped.

"Really," Dottie said.

Mrs. Prescott looked pleased.

Margaux glared at Linda, willing her to shut up, but she just grinned back, and said with fake innocence, "It wasn't a secret, was it?"

Nick and Connor appeared at the top of the stairs to find four women looking up at them. Three smiling and one ready to spit nails.

"Anything else you want me to do?" he asked warily.

Margaux shook her head.

"Actually," Linda said, "can you wait here for just a second? I want to show Dottie and Adelaide something. You, too, Connor." She shooed them all toward the kitchen, leaving Margaux and Nick alone.

Nick came down the stairs and looked back at the kitchen. "That was subtle." He shoved his hands in the pockets of his uniform and looked uncomfortable. And who could blame him. Linda had the finesse of a sledgehammer.

"Your mother is a fantastic pattern cutter," Margaux said, trying to gloss over the awkwardness.

"Is she? I'm not surprised. She tends to do everything she does well."

Like her son, Margaux thought, but she didn't say so.

"We've accomplished more this morning than I could have done by myself in a week."

"Maybe I should go get Connor."

Okay, awkward was one thing, but he was so obviously uncomfortable and wanting to get away from her that she started getting mad. *She* hadn't herded the others out of the room. She was just as much a victim as he was. And you'd think he might be glad to see her. Those weren't bargain-basement kisses last night . . . at least not to her.

"I hope our having dinner together isn't going to make things uncomfortable for you," she said, looking for a reaction.

"Huh? Oh no. And I wouldn't care if it did. I enjoyed it." He paused. "I hope you did, too."

"I did." She moved a step closer to him. She wouldn't mind a quick taste of last night's kisses, but Nick looked about as willing as a piece of granite.

"Maybe we can do something again," he said, not looking at her.

"You and me?"

He frowned at her. "Who else?"

"Just making sure."

He relaxed into one of those rare smiles that transformed his face and Margaux had a totally adolescent response. Which really discombobulated her.

"I better get back to work," she said.

"Me, too." He started for the front door and she returned to her workshop. The moment she was inside, she raced to the front window and looked out. Nick was getting into his police cruiser.

"What happened to Nick?" Linda asked from the door-way. "I guess you're looking out the window because he just left." She slapped her forehead. "I can't work like this," she squawked, and flounced across the hall to the salon.

Twenty

 "Don't let Linda make you feel uncomfortable," Adelaide said when they'd returned to work. "You and Nick are both adults and it's your business." She glanced toward Connor, who was sitting on the floor reading a picture book.

"I won't take time away from Nick and Connor."

Mrs. Prescott smiled fondly at the boy. "You'll be lucky if you can get away from him. Now, we'd best get back to this pattern."

Margaux sent them home at two o'clock. Connor had fallen asleep on the floor and Mrs. Prescott was showing signs of fatigue. She'd been on her feet all morning.

"We've made a lot of progress and I have another batch of dyeing to do. And some hand-painting I want to experiment with."

She helped Mrs. Prescott gather up Connor's toys and his cape, which was looking a little frayed.

"Connor, honey?" Mrs. Prescott said in a soft, soothing voice. "It's time to go home. Connor?"

The boy came awake all at once. Sat up, alert, and looked around as if he didn't know where he was or what to expect.

"Say goodbye to Ms. Sullivan."

Connor got up slowly, like an old man, Margaux thought, or a mime moving in slow motion.

"Bye, Margaux," he said on a breath. He let his grandmother slip his backpack over his shoulders, waved a little wave to Margaux as his grandmother led him away.

Margaux followed them to the door. "Adelaide?"

"Yes, dear?"

"Would it be okay if Connor came down to the beach tomorrow after Mass? Unless you already have plans. I could take him crabbing and there might be a few children there he could meet."

She realized her mistake immediately. Never ask in front of the child, because Connor was looking at his grandmother with those big eyes. She saw his lips move. Knew he was saying "please."

"If it's okay with your gran and you don't have plans with your Uncle Nick."

Adelaide Prescott looked from Connor to Margaux, clearly torn.

"I'd love to have you both. Nick's welcome, too. I'll call Jude and invite her. If you think it's a good idea."

Connor tugged at his grandmother's skirt. A small movement, no jumping up and down, no pleading. It was eerie and Margaux knew it wasn't normal. And yet he was such a sweetheart.

"Thank you. That would be lovely."

"You got the loan yesterday and you waited to call us until today?" Bri pushed the cheese plate across the table to Margaux. She and Grace had shown up at the beach house with champagne and hors d'oeuvres an hour after Margaux called them with the good news.

The night air was balmy and not too humid, so they'd taken snacks and wine out to the porch to watch the sunset. And talk.

"It was kind of a hectic day. This chèvre is delicious."

"So tell us about it."

"It was for more than I'd meant to ask for, but Roger thought we should have some pad."

"Smart man," Bri said.

"And I found the perfect venue for a runway show."

"Where?"

"The Cove Inn. There's a patio that is just the right size and can be dressed very nicely."

"The Cove Inn? Perfect. Why didn't I think of that?" Bri said, cutting off a slab of Gruyère and balancing it on a cracker.

"I wouldn't have thought of it either, except—" Margaux stopped, not sure that she was ready to share about her date with Nick. It seemed a little like kissing and telling. But boy, what kisses.

Bri stopped with the cracker halfway to her mouth. "Margaux?"

"Hmm?"

"I'm sensing a story here. How did you think of the inn?"

"I went to dinner there."

"With Jude?"

"Well, actually . . . I went to dinner with Nick Prescott."

"The merman? Holy cow. Tell us everything." Bri leaned forward; Grace scooted over closer to Bri and they gave Margaux their full attention.

Margaux slipped from her perch on the porch rail and pulled up a wicker chair to face them. "He invited me to dinner. I think Linda put him up to it. But I went. And I had a nice time."

"Nice?" Bri sighed. "He was a dud."

"Not at all," Margaux said. "Are you going to eat that cracker or just point it at me?"

Bri put the cracker down.

"You like him," said Grace.

Margaux hesitated. "Yeah, I do. Most of the time. But he's really intense. Not very relaxing to be around."

"Hell, you can relax at the old folks' home," Bri said. "Did he, did you . . ."

"Bri, really. It's none of our business," Grace said, but she looked hopeful.

Margaux took a sip of her champagne, twirled the stem in her fingers. "After dinner we walked by the water and when we were coming back I saw the patio."

"And then?"

"And I was so excited I threw my arms around his neck." Margaux rushed through the last words and looked at the floor.

"And then?"

"I realized what I had done. It was a shade awkward. I thanked him for dinner and he drove me home."

Grace blew out air. "Come on. If you're going to tell us, get on with it. I'd hate to have to use my cross-examination technique on you."

"He kissed me good night—twice."

"And?"

Margaux smiled. "It was pretty damn good."

Bri collapsed back on the settee. "I take it that means he left after that."

"Yeah. Though I think he would have stayed if I had en-couraged him."

"But you didn't."

Margaux pushed her fingers through her hair. "I can't get involved with anyone now. For starters, I'm not exactly di-vorced yet."

"A technicality," said Bri.

"I'm trying to restart my life, my career, I can't take time to . . . you know."

"Have sex? Have an affair? Fall in love? What are we talking about here?"

"I don't know," said Margaux. "I just don't know, but what-ever it is—was—it felt pretty damn good."

"Then go for it."

"It's out of the question."

"I don't see why," Grace said.

"It's complicated."

"No it isn't," said Bri. "That's just an excuse. Go for it." She huffed out a breath. "But the merman aside for the minute, you have a shitload of work to do if you want to get something built and shown in the next month or so."

"I know it. Keep your fingers crossed that I can pull it off."

"Hey. How can you fail with me and Grace by your side. Selkies forever, remember?"

Sunday was sunny and warm. Adelaide and Connor arrived at the beach house around one. Nick wasn't with them, and Margaux felt a shaft of disappointment mixed with relief.

She told herself it was because if he came, she wouldn't have to take full responsibility for entertaining Connor. She wasn't ready to admit that she'd hoped he'd come for her own enjoyment.

"He had to go in to help Finley. One of the other officers called in sick. I'm not sure he would have come anyway. Though you were very nice to include him in the invitation," Adelaide added hastily. "He just doesn't come to the beach much."

Margaux remembered him swimming in the cove and had to stifle a reminiscent shiver.

Connor was wearing X-Men swim trunks and a large T-shirt. A man's baseball cap with the Crescent Cove Stingrays logo on the front was shoved down to his eyes.

Margaux thought it must have belonged to his father.

They all went out to the porch, where Jude had set glasses and lemonade.

Connor dropped his backpack on the floor. Adelaide walked out to the edge of the porch and stopped, looking out at the beach.

Everybody looked where she was looking. The lifeguard tower.

The breath stuck in Margaux's lungs. She'd seen that same look on Nick's face when they'd climbed the jetty and he'd looked down—on the old lifeguard tower. How could she have been so insensitive to have Mrs. Prescott spend the day with the memory of her dead son looming in the background.

She glanced at Jude, whose expression was stricken.

Adelaide pulled Connor close to her and leaned over, pointing to the lifeguard stand. "You see that white tower on the beach?"

Connor nodded.

"Your daddy used to sit up there. It's a lifeguard station and it was his job to keep people safe."

Connor looked out at the tower, his eyes round, his mouth slightly open as he exhaled a long breath. "My daddy?" he whispered.

Adelaide nodded. Margaux doubted that she could answer, because Margaux could barely swallow the lump in her own throat. Adelaide straightened up. "Now you and Margaux go have fun."

"Let's go," Margaux said. "I've got pails and string all ready for us by the back door. But first we need sunscreen."

When they were lathered up, Margaux handed Connor a pail, took one for herself, and the two of them set off across the beach toward the jetty.

Connor stopped to watch some children building a sand castle, but when Margaux asked if he'd like to play, he shook his head and began walking again.

He held Margaux's hand up the rocks. The tide was out, but the jetty was still wet and slippery. She searched the crevices until she found a promising pool, then set down her pail and lifted out a baggie of fish parts.

When she opened the baggie, Connor wrinkled his nose and made a face.

"I'll have you know that this gunk is a delicacy to a crab."

She mashed a piece onto the end of one string and handed it to Connor. "Now slowly lower the end into the pool. Try not to move so the crab won't know we're up here."

Connor leaned over the pool and lowered the string into the water. Then he froze.

"You don't have to be that still."

He looked at her, confused, and Margaux didn't offer any more advice. She leaned over the pool with him until she saw movement in the water. "Look," she whispered.

A crab sidled up to the bait and latched on. "Pull the string straight up."

Connor pulled the string up. The crab hung on almost to the end, then dropped back into the pool and darted out of sight.

Connor frowned.

"That's what they call paying your dues."

Connor's frown deepened.

"Never mind. It's hard to catch crabs. Let's try another pool." They climbed along the jetty. Margaux picked another pool and they squatted over it, patiently waiting for a nibble.

"It's coming," Connor whispered.

"Okay, now wait . . . wait." The crab bit. "Pull it up gently."

The crab hung on, and Margaux slid the pail underneath it just before it let go of the string.

"Ta-da," she crowed.

Connor grinned, his new tooth just beginning to show, and he held up his string for Margaux to bait again.

As their crab collection grew, Margaux's back began to ache and she was worried about Connor getting a sunburn.

She pointed out some of the other creatures left in the pool by the tides. One even had a little minnow swimming in the shadows of the rock.

"They're called tide pools," Margaux explained. "The tide brings them in, and when it goes out again, it traps them in these pools of water."

Connor peered into the pool, leaning over so far that Margaux grabbed the back of his shirt.

"Are they going to die?"

Taken aback, it took a moment for Margaux to answer. "No. The tide comes in and washes them out to sea again." *Usually.*

"I want to put them back."

She leaned closer. "What did you say, sweetie?"

"I want to put the crabs back. I don't want them to die."

"Don't you want to show your gran and Uncle Nick?"

He shook his head. "I want to put them back. There." He pointed across the far side of the jetty to the cove where they had skipped rocks.

"I don't think we should go there. These rocks are very slippery and your gran would be sad if you skinned your knee or elbow."

He didn't argue, just kept looking down into the cove. Then he turned to her, so close that their foreheads almost touched. "That's where the Grotto is."

"Yes, it is. What a smart boy you are to recognize the cove."

"Can we go there?"

"Not today. But sometime maybe, from Jake's house. Okay?"

"Okay."

"Let's go see how the sand castle is doing." Margaux helped him down the rocks and onto the sand. The kids were gone so Margaux and Connor poked around the sand castle, Margaux pointing out turrets and the moat and the windows made from seashells.

When they got back to the house, Roger had started the ice cream maker, and Jude and Mrs. Prescott were sitting on the front porch.

At Margaux's insistence, Connor showed them his catch. "Now can we put them back?"

"Of course," Margaux said. "Shall I take a picture of them first?"

He nodded.

She went into the house for her cell and took a picture of Connor holding the bucket, and then a couple of close-ups of the crabs. "Want to see?"

He nodded again and grinned when he saw his picture on the screen.

"Can we put them back now?"

"Yes, I'll just go out and dump them in the waves."

"Will they drown?"

"No, they're crabs. They live in the ocean."

"Okay."

Margaux trekked out to the water's edge, Connor tagging along, carefully overseeing the bucket. She walked out into the water and lowered the pail, and let the surf rinse it clean and carry the crabs away. Then she held up the empty pail.

"Goodbye, crabs," she called.

"Goodbye, crabs," Connor called after her.

Margaux stopped, the pail suspended in the air. She could hear him; he was standing on the shore with the shore noises around him, and she could hear him. This was the second time he'd spoken out loud. That had to be a good sign. She had to force herself to stay calm. She was thrilled, but she didn't want to call attention to it and risk driving him back into silence. "Let's see if Roger has finished making the ice cream."

She took his hand and they ran back to the house, Margaux's feelings soaring at Connor's small breakthrough.

They celebrated the crabs' release with softly frozen ice cream. Mrs. Prescott and Connor got ready to leave.

"What do you say?"

"I had a nice time," he whispered.

"Connor, honey, she can't hear you."

Connor looked like he might cry.

Margaux knelt down. She wouldn't force him to speak.

"I had a nice time." He threw his arms around Margaux's neck. He whispered something in her ear. It sounded like, "I love you."

Her heart constricted; she gave him a quick hug and stood up. "I'm very glad you could come."

"It was so kind of you," Mrs. Prescott said.

"My pleasure. See you tomorrow?"

Mrs. Prescott nodded and trundled Connor out the door.

Margaux sank into a kitchen chair, still shaken by what she thought she'd heard.

"Tired?" asked Jude.

Margaux groaned. "Kids are exhausting."

"Yes, they are," Jude said. "No matter how old they are."

"We caught crabs with a string," Connor said.

"You what?" Nick asked as he came over to where Connor sat at the kitchen table.

"We caught crabs with a string."

Nick was tired and frustrated; it had been a long day and he wished for once he could hear Connor without having to hunch over like an old man. At least Connor was more animated than Nick had ever seen him. That was something.

He pulled a chair over, sat down next to his nephew, and leaned close to him.

"Crabs, huh?"

"Margaux took pictures with her phone and she's going to send them to Nana."

"Cool. What happened to the crabs?"

"We put them back in the ocean."

"Live to be caught another day."

Connor frowned at him.

"So you had a good time?"

Connor nodded. "We climbed on the big rocks. I wanted to go to the Grotto, but Margaux said we had to ask you."

"Thank God for that."

"Can we go, Uncle Nick? I want to make a wish."

"What?"

"I want to make a wish," Connor said on a big expulsion of air.

"Bud, the Grotto can't make wishes come true. It's just a rock. It's dangerous. And I don't want you going there. Understand?"

"It does, too. Margaux said."

"Well, Margaux was mistaken."

"She said."

This time Nick could barely hear him. And the disappointment in Connor's small face cut right to his heart. But he couldn't have the kid running off to the woods every time his back was turned. God only knew what could happen to him.

His mother put a penny on the table before Connor. "Why don't you make a wish in the birdbath out back?"

Connor looked skeptical but he took the penny and slid off his chair.

"Hurry back, dinner's almost ready."

She turned on Nick.

Nick raked his fingers through his hair. "I know. I know. You don't have to tell me. But he can't go around thinking that his wishes are going to come true. Especially not if he thinks he has to go to that . . . I already found him there once. I thought he had just wandered off into the woods."

He braced his elbows on the kitchen table and felt his mother's hand on his shoulder. "Let him have his dreams, Nick."

"I don't want to take them away. I just want to keep him safe."

"I know you do. But a boy needs to dream."

Delicate fingers stroked his hair.

"I need a haircut," he said, grasping at the mundane.

"I like it longer. You have your father's hair."

And Ben's. "I have to go."

"Supper's almost ready."

"I'm not hungry."

"Nicky, I wasn't chastising you."

"I know, I'm just tired."

"Nicky."

"Later, Ma."

He practically stumbled out the door. *A boy needs to dream.*

Margaux had finally seen Jude and Roger off and she'd just sat down with a much-needed glass of Pinot Noir when there was a knock at the back door.

She pushed out of the cabbage rose chair and went to the kitchen. She could see a large form behind the screen door. She recognized him immediately and her stomach did a little shake, rattle, and roll.

"Come on in. Are you on duty or can I offer you a glass of wine?"

"Neither."

She stiffened. So not a social call. "Then what can I do for you?"

"You can stop filling Connor's head with ideas that his wishes will come true."

"What are you talking about? We went crabbing. Your mother was here the whole time. We ate ice cream. *C'est tout.*" She narrowed her eyes. "That's French for that's all."

"Don't condescend to me. I have a degree. I can even under-stand a modicum of French."

He glowered at her, the intensity of his eyes making her take a step back.

"Oh, for crying out loud. You came all the way over here to read my beads over being nice to your nephew and then top it off with the undeserved accusation that I think you're stupid."

He'd started to pace but he stopped. Margaux swore she could hear him grinding his teeth. He was a man so close to the edge that she should be afraid of him. But she wasn't. Because all that anger was coming from a man who was hurting.

She'd done the same thing herself when she'd first found out about Louis. "I'm sorry. Could we please just start again?"

Nick took a deep breath and Margaux half expected his next

words to come out in a whisper like Connor's. "Look, the kid has had a rough time. Just don't tell him his wishes can come true."

"I didn't. We didn't even talk about wishes. Just crabs."

"He said you told him the Grotto would make his wishes come true. You know what he wants, don't you. He wants his father and mother, but he can't have that. What will happen when they don't come back?"

Margaux tried to remember their conversation.

"He wanted to go to the Grotto. I said he'd have to ask you. That's all."

"Then where did he get the idea?"

"I don't know." But she did. She vaguely remembered the day she'd shown them the Grotto and told him it was where they played pirates and dreamed their dreams. But what was wrong with that? "Dreams, not wishes. I told him that's where we dreamed our dreams."

"He's six. He doesn't know the difference. Do you understand what you've done?"

Margaux had been feeling guilty, but now her temper flared. "Who the hell are you to tell me how to act and what to say? The kid should be allowed to dream. Everyone should. Maybe you don't know how to, but it doesn't mean the rest of us can't."

"Why can't you just—"

"Butt out? I'll stay away from Connor, but you have to tell him why. And you'll have to figure out what to do with him when Adelaide is working, unless you plan to make her quit, too. No wonder the kid doesn't talk. You're so heavy-handed, he's probably afraid to."

She heard her words and couldn't stop them. She saw his face and knew she had hurt him. "I didn't mean that. You're not like that. It was spite talking." She stretched out her hand.

"No. You're right. I'm—" He turned abruptly. The door slammed behind him before she could say "I'm sorry."

Twenty-one

Margaux was hollow-eyed when she set off for work the next morning. She hadn't slept. Several times in the night she considered getting in her car and waking Nick up to tell him what she really thought. But she wasn't sure what she thought.

She just knew that she loved that kid and she was afraid she was beginning to love Nick.

Adelaide was already working when Margaux did manage to drag herself out of bed and go to the shop. Connor was sitting on the floor wearing his pirate cape, which was looking the worse for wear, and playing with a row of Matchbox cars.

Well, at least Nick hadn't gotten to his mother yet.

Of course, it was never too late for him to throw his weight around. She'd best let Adelaide know about what had happened the night before.

Making sure Connor was occupied, Margaux motioned for Adelaide to follow her into the other room.

"Your son isn't very happy with me right now. Actually, he told me pretty much to leave his family alone. I don't know how you want to handle it. I just wanted to tell you that I'd really like you to keep working, but I don't want to make trouble between you and Nick and Connor."

Mrs. Prescott pursed her lips. "He's not very happy with me, either; I take it he came blustering to you after he left me. You don't have to answer, I can tell somebody had a sleepless night. He'll come around if you just give him some time."

Margaux tried for a smile, but stifled a yawn instead. "You need to know that I said some things that I didn't really mean. I was pretty harsh."

"You two will work it out. He's not an easy man. He had too much responsibility thrust on him at too early an age, and now with Connor. But he's a good man. A caring man, one who takes care of his family before anything else."

"I know." Margaux tried to swallow, but her throat was dry. "He wants me to stay away from Connor."

"He's afraid Connor will become too dependent. Will come to expect more from you than you are able—or willing—to give. He's just trying to protect him."

"I understand that. I really do. I like Connor but I don't want to complicate his life. And I don't want to disappoint him when—"

Adelaide patted her arm. "Let things take their course. Don't let Nick bully you. He doesn't want to. He just doesn't know how not to. Now let's get to work. I think we're ready to drape that lovely shantung."

Adelaide's cell rang and she stepped into the foyer to take it. Her cheeks were flushed when she came back inside.

"That was my son. I told him I was working late and if he wanted to apologize to you he knew where to find us."

They had worked side by side for several hours when Connor held up a piece of green construction paper.

"Look. I made a dinosaur."

Margaux looked up. She pushed a smile on her face while her mind reeled. She'd heard him speak and she was on the other side of the table. "That's . . . wow. That's a fantastic dinosaur. Is it a T. rex?"

"No. It's a stegosaurus. It has spikes."

"I'll say." Margaux glanced at Adelaide, who was staring

at her grandson, her expression arrested in surprise. She had heard him, too.

"See, Nana? I cut out a dinosaur."

Adelaide nodded, her smile wavering. "You sure did."

Her voice was unsteady and a frown began to creep on Connor's face as if he had just realized he'd done something wrong. He still hadn't told anyone why he wouldn't talk, but that didn't matter anymore. Connor was talking and Margaux was determined to keep him talking.

"Why don't we hang up Steggy on the fishing line?" Margaux said brightly, hoping to give Adelaide time to recover.

"With the clothes pictures?"

"Yes. Right in the middle."

"Oh boy." Connor slid off the stool and ran over to the line of renderings.

Margaux lifted him up so he could pin it to the line. Then they stood back and studied it.

"Very cool," said Margaux.

"Very cool," Connor agreed.

"Why don't you go get Linda? I bet she'd love to see."

Connor took off across the hall.

Adelaide fumbled in her purse for a handkerchief and wiped her eyes. "It's a miracle. I don't know how to thank you."

"It isn't me. He's just deciding to come back to us. On his own terms."

"Maybe. And maybe he's found someone he can trust."

Connor came back with Linda in tow.

"I hear there's a vicious dinosaur loose in here." Linda widened her eyes at Margaux.

"There it is." Connor pointed to his picture.

"Eek!" Linda screeched. "Get my broom. I'll protect you."

Connor giggled. "He's not scared of a broom."

Linda stuck out her lip and crossed her arms. "Are you sure?"

He nodded.

"Well, dee and tarnation. I guess he'll just have to stay."

Once Adelaide and Connor left for the day, Margaux gave up trying to work. It had been a wild forty-eight hours. She drove by the police station hoping to gather her courage to go inside and apologize for the things she'd said last night. She wanted to be the one who told Nick that Connor had spoken aloud, but his cruiser wasn't there.

Disappointed, she drove home, poured a glass of lemonade, and curled up in the cabbage chair.

It was turning dusk when she heard a car pull into the drive. Not Jude, she always honked. She quickly smoothed back her hair, wishing she hadn't changed into cutoffs and a T-shirt. Nick had decided to forgive her. Without waiting for him to knock, she hurried through the kitchen and mudroom to the back door.

There was a silver Mercedes parked on the gravel. A man got out and came to the back door. Margaux stopped breathing. She stepped back and tried to shut the door, but he was too quick for her.

"So this is where you got to." Louis pushed her into the kitchen and shut the door.

Nick took the beer Jake handed him and perched on the edge of the picnic table in Jake's backyard.

Jake pulled over a lawn chair and sat facing Nick.

"You know, for a smart guy, you can be pretty dumb sometimes."

"Tell me about it."

"So why don't you do something to fix it? Stop acting like an ass and go apologize. She'll forgive you. She obviously likes you. God knows why."

"Liked me."

"And whose fault is that?"

"Mine. I admit it. I'm an ass."

"Then go apologize. Tell her you're an idiot and you need her."

"I don't need her."

"Of course you do. Or you wouldn't be moping around here like you haven't moped since the last time she left twenty years ago."

"It's complicated."

Jake took a long pull of beer and regarded his friend. "You know, Nick. I've known you for as long as I can remember and I would never take you for a coward."

The beer turned to acid in Nick's throat. *Ben was the hero. The hero who'd killed himself rather than go back into battle. The boy Nick had sent to the army, the man who couldn't live with what he'd seen and done.*

Jake appeared beside him. Nick hadn't seen him move. "Sorry, man. I didn't mean it. I was just trying to get a rise out of you. You know, light a fire so you'd hightail it over to her house and get laid or something. Really."

Nick blinked at his friend. "What? Oh, I know. I was . . ." He heaved a sigh.

"It's more than just Margaux, isn't it?"

"No. You're right. I'm letting everything jerk me around. She should be home by now. I'll go over there. Apologize and hope she forgives me."

But Nick didn't apologize. When he arrived at the Sullivan house there was a late-model silver Mercedes parked by her blue coupe. New York plates. Margaux had company and his apology would have to wait. He drove past the house and turned back toward town.

Margaux took a step back. "What do you want, Louis?"

"To see my wife. What else."

"Not your wife for long. I've filed for divorce." What had she ever seen in this man? He was wearing an expensive summer-weight wool suit. He was good-looking in that Wall Street way; lean, suave, with the chiseled features of a magazine ad and just as shallow. She had never seen a face she hated more.

"But while you're here, would you like to return the money you stole from me?"

"I can explain."

How many television-movie losers began in the same tired old way. *I can explain.*

"I'm not really interested in explanations. You stole our savings, stock holdings, and the 401Ks. They repossessed the apartment and shut down my business. I lost everything. All because of you."

"I know, I know. I meant it for the best."

Margaux barked out a disbelieving laugh.

"I invested it. I had a tip. It was a sure thing. We would have had so much money we could have gone anywhere, done anything. We could have made your business skyrocket, or you needn't work at all. But it went sour. The market. The timing. It wasn't my fault. I did it for us, for you."

"So there really is nothing left?"

"Nothing. But I can make it right."

Margaux threw up her hands and walked away, which was a mistake. He followed her into the living room. She began to get apprehensive. A man who would do that to her might not stop at the money. Would he get violent? He'd never hit her or even threatened to. But he must be desperate to have come after her.

"I did it for us."

"Bullshit."

"Be reasonable, Margaux." He gestured for her to sit down. Like he was the goddamned host. "Let's just discuss things . . . rationally." He lifted both eyebrows in the way she had grown to dread, a belittling, condescending expression that made you want to confess to anything.

"There's nothing to discuss. I want you out of here. Now."

"Come on, sweetheart. Just listen to me. I can get us out of this fix. I've got a deal lined up. Really big. I could get back everything we lost and more. I'll make us very rich. You could start your clothing line again, bigger and better this time. The two of us. Like we always wanted."

"You just don't get it, do you? There is no us, Louis. You killed us. If you didn't come to return the money you stole, then there's no reason for you to be here. Please leave."

A tinge of red broke out along his razor-edged cheekbones. And to think she had always loved his cheekbones. Now, they made him look villainous.

"You don't mean that, baby."

"Baby? You must have me confused with someone else." Margaux glowered at him. Crossed her arms and sank into one hip. A posture Louis despised. He broke.

"Margaux, dammit." He grabbed her by both shoulders. "I need money. I need it now. You can get it. You can take out a mortgage on the beach house."

"I would never risk this house, not for you or anybody." She tried to wrench away, but his fingers dug painfully into her arms.

"Ask your mother for the money. She has a bundle, I know."

"Get out of here, Louis. I don't care what kind of trouble you're in. You brought it on yourself and you can sure the hell get out of it on your own. If you can. Now leave or I'll call the police."

His grip tightened and Margaux began to feel afraid.

"You owe me."

"The hell I do. You took everything, you bastard. Now get out."

He pushed her away so hard she fell on the floor. He turned and began rummaging through the papers on her desk. He would find the bank loan. She struggled to her feet.

"Get out!" she screamed.

But she was too late, he held up her bank statement.

"Now what's this? You managed to land on your feet after all."

Margaux's blood turned cold. This greedy sleazebag was the

man she married? Wanted to have a family with? He hadn't always been this way, had he? Or had she just missed it.

"Just give me the money and I swear I won't bother you again."

She couldn't think of a thing to say. She could only look at him with nausea rumbling in her throat.

He frantically pushed papers around the desk and found her checkbook. He tossed it at her. "A check will do."

She grabbed the checkbook and threw it behind the couch.

"Goddammit." He moved so quickly she didn't have time to dodge away. His hands wrapped around her throat. "Don't make me hurt you. Now, get the checkbook."

Vaguely, she heard the screen door slam.

"What the—"

Louis's hands fell away and the rest of the sentence died in his throat. Margaux saw a blur of jeans and T-shirt before Nick came into focus. He'd slammed Louis against the wall and held him there.

Louis tried to fight back, but was as ineffectual as a bug pinned to a display case. "Who the hell are you? Let go or I'll swear out a complaint."

Nick's grip tightened. "I'm the chief of police here. So swear away."

Louis looked from Nick to Margaux and laughed, though Margaux heard the fear in it and for a second she felt sorry for him. But only for a second.

"So that's how it is. Really, Margaux. Your taste astounds me." He'd recovered that slip of self-control. He sounded cool and sarcastic; the way, she suddenly realized, he often sounded.

Nick lifted him away from the wall. "Stay inside," he told Margaux, and pushed Louis through the arch and down the hall.

After a heartbeat, she followed. They were already outside. She only went as far as the screen door, but she heard Louis's last words.

"Get your filthy hands off me. We'll see how police brutality sits with your superiors."

"We'll see how a restraining order sits on you." Nick shoved Louis toward the Mercedes. "Don't come back or there will be a cell at the local station waiting for you."

Louis stumbled toward the car, but he just had to get the last word in. He was so easy to read. "You'll be sorry, Margaux. You and your blue-collar friend here." He got in the Mercedes, gunned the engine, backed up, and screeched off in what Margaux knew was a fit of pique. Louis was too cocky to be frightened for long.

Nick came back to the door, looked at her through the screen. She tried to open it, but he held it closed.

"Are you okay?"

She nodded. Pushed at the door again. It didn't budge.

"If he comes back, call the station."

Margaux felt hot tears roll down her face—tears of shame, of anger, of frustration, and of loss.

"Do you want to get a restraining order?"

"I want you to come inside."

"I can call Jude or have Finley patrol the block through the night."

She shook her head. "You. I only want you."

"You're sure?"

"Yes, I'm sure." She stepped back and he came inside. He opened his arms and she walked into them.

"I'm sorry . . . about everything," he said.

"Me, too. Especially about what he said." She hiccuped.

"I've been called worse. I need to call Jude or she'll be on her way over here."

"Mom?"

"Seems Dottie saw the Mercedes pass the diner. She recognized him and called Jude, Jude called me. I was . . . in the neighborhood. I told them I would take care of it and to stay put. Which I've discovered doesn't mean shit."

Margaux gave a watery chuckle.

He called. "He's gone. She's fine. Don't come. Call Dottie. You're welcome."

He hung up, dropped his cell on the table, threw his discipline, his honor, and his good intentions to the wind, and kissed her. He wasn't even sure if she really wanted him or if it was just the adrenaline of the confrontation with her husband, but he wasn't going to ask her again.

"Look at me." He let go of her long enough to lift her chin until she was looking into his eyes and what he saw there made his decision. He lifted her off her feet and kissed her so deeply he thought he might drown.

She pulled away with an expulsion of air. "I want you . . . but not here in the kitchen."

"No."

"Upstairs."

He took her mouth, his hands splayed across her back, pulling her closer even as he walked her backwards toward the hallway. By the time they reached the stairs, neither of them was leading or following. She let go of him long enough to open a door and Nick followed her inside, not knowing if this was a dream come true or if he was making the worst mistake of his life.

Twenty-two

Margaux melted into Nick. Heat radiated from him, and she wanted to be closer, her moth to his flame. Colors filled her head as she tugged the T-shirt from his jeans, pushed it up his chest so that she could splay her fingers against him, hard, strong, safe.

His hands seemed to cover her back and she wanted to feel them on her bare skin. She grasped the edges of his shirt and pulled it upward; he lowered his head so that she could yank it over his head. It left his mouth close enough to nuzzle her neck. She was on fire, impatient, ready and eager. She pulled off her own T in one movement.

Nick growled, low like an animal, and a thrill shot through her. He cupped her butt and pulled her up to him until she wrapped her legs around him. His jeans were rough on her thighs, the friction sent shock waves through her body. He unclasped her bra; she leaned backwards, and they toppled onto her bed together.

In a flurry of movement, they shed their clothes while Nick spread kisses over her lips and breasts, nipped at her collarbone, and finally settled himself above her.

And stopped—hovering there like a film when the projector breaks.

"What?" Her question was almost a wail.

"I—are you—?"

"Dammit. Don't think, don't analyze, don't be responsible. Just love me."

He pushed her knee to the side and drove into her. Margaux's breath caught, then he began to move, slowly, rhythmically, braced on his elbows, his eyes open and staring deep into hers.

And they climbed together, him setting the pace, leading the way; and she let him, reveling in him, soldier, policeman, historian, uncle, son.

And her lover. Selkie and merman, together, spiraling tighter, driving, driving to that one moment when the world winked out, turning the dusk to black, frozen in time, before it shattered and burst into light.

Slowly they descended, slick with each other's sweat, sweet from their kisses, until they lay together, heaving bursts of heated breath, synced, in tandem.

Nick rolled off her, pulling her with him. He wrapped her in his arms and pressed her head to the hollow of his shoulder.

She curled into him and began to cry.

She felt him stiffen, ease away so he could see her face, alarmed. "Are you okay? Did I hurt you? What?"

She shook her head, tried to tell him, but words didn't come. She just cried, feeling like a fool, afraid that he would hate her, would get up and leave. That she had ruined everything.

"Margaux, talk to me."

"Stupid. That's all. Just cathartic nonsense. Sorry."

"I won't let him hurt you. I won't let anybody hurt you."

Cold water couldn't have moved her faster. She slapped her hand over his mouth. "Let's forget everything but now."

She felt him relax but he held her tight. "Everything will be fine."

She settled into him.

"Better now?"

She nodded, enjoying the rasp of his chest against her cheek.

"That was good. Really good."

They slept.

Nick propped himself on one elbow and watched Margaux sleep, half covered by the sheet, which they must have pulled up somewhere during the night. One arm was flung out above her head, wild and abandoned in sleep. It was late, close to midnight, and he knew he should be going, but he wanted to kiss her. Make love to her again. He wanted a lot of things.

It was dark in the room, but the sliver of the new moon seemed to shine right through her window. It turned her skin luminescent. There was a dusting of freckles across her nose that he hadn't seen in daylight. He smiled, she'd probably be pissed. He'd bet anything freckles weren't chic.

He thought they were damn cute and he wanted to kiss every one of them. Which made him a certifiable nutcase. He touched her hair, she stirred in her sleep, and he pulled his fingers back. He should leave.

"Nick?"

He looked down, her eyes were open, sleepy, sexy, and heartbreaking.

"Yes?"

"You're not about to do a hit-and-run are you?"

He laughed. It was just what he'd been thinking. "That depends."

"On what?"

"On if you want me to stay."

"I think I can convince you." She slid beneath the sheet; he felt a supple, warm hand on his thigh; fingers trailed up his skin, leaving goose bumps when they left. Her fingers found him.

"I'm convinced," he said on a strangled breath. "I'm convinced." And he slipped beneath the sheet to join her.

It was still dark when Nick got out of bed and dressed. He leaned back to kiss Margaux and murmur, "I have to leave."

Her lashes fluttered open. "It's still dark."

"I've got the early shift."

She smiled and stretched. "You just don't want anyone to see your truck in my driveway."

"I'm pretty sure it's too late for hiding." He sat down on the edge of the bed. "Do you care?"

"Not in the least. Do you?"

He thought about it. "No. Not at all."

She sat up, belatedly pulled the sheet up to cover herself. Nick frowned at her.

"What?"

He moved her hand from the sheet, pulled it toward him, and looked at her arm.

"What?"

He reached over and turned on the bedside lamp. Margaux shut her eyes.

"Damn him," Nick said tightly.

Margaux cautiously opened her eyes against the light, and looked down at her shoulder. Five finger marks bruised her upper arm where Louis had grabbed her.

"I swear, if he so much as shows his face around here, I'll take him out."

Margaux captured his hand and pulled it from her shoulder to kiss it. "Don't think about him."

He leaned over and kissed her. She was so tempted to pull him down and make him late for work. It had been a long time since she'd slept with someone who warmed her, who cared about her.

But he had the early shift, and she didn't want to be the reason he was late . . . probably for the first time ever. She watched as he hurriedly dressed in the shadows of the lamplight. Returned his drugged goodbye kiss and stretched languidly. When she heard his truck back out of the drive, she reached over and pulled his pillow close, breathed in the scent of him, and went back to sleep.

* * *

"Morning, Chief," Finley said, fighting a grin.

"Finley." Nick refused to look him in the eye. Dee had already beamed at him when he walked into work. It was probably no secret that he'd spent the night with Margaux. The whole damn town probably knew and were casting their votes of approval or not.

He'd just opened a big can of worms, but hell, it wasn't like he'd been on duty with the cruiser parked there all night. He wasn't the pope. He had the right to a life.

"Sure you do. Nobody's saying you don't."

Nick stared at Finley. "What?"

"You were kinda talking to yourself. Out loud," he added in case Nick didn't get it. "In fact, most of us are glad to see you finally getting some action."

Nick shot him his most quelling look. Finley walked nonchalantly out the door. "Oh, by the way, I gave myself the night shift this week. Hope you don't mind." He closed the door before Nick could think of anything to say.

He caught up on paperwork for an hour, then went out to give the updates to Dee Janowitz.

Dee looked up from her knitting. "You're looking awfully chipper today," she said innocently.

Nick gritted his teeth. "I'm going on patrol."

"Have a nice day."

He barely got out the door before his cell rang.

"Did you apologize?"

"Hi, Jake. Yes, I did."

"So did she forgive you?"

"Yes."

"And? I don't want to appear nosy, but what the hell happened?"

Nick sighed, his life was a fishbowl. But of course he owed all this to Jake. He'd still be angry and alone if Jake hadn't badgered him into apologizing. "Her husband was there trying to extort money from her. I threw him out. She asked me in. And the rest is history."

"I hope not."

"Me neither. I hope it's just the beginning."

"Attaboy. Have you seen her today?"

"Not since I left."

Jake whistled. "Stayed all night, did you. Good for you. Now, listen, don't wait to see her, because the longer you wait the more awkward it will be."

"Is this the voice of experience? As I recall, you're not much luckier at this than I am."

"Yes, and the reason I'm dumber than you is that I didn't learn my lesson the first time. Go take her flowers or something."

"Thanks for the advice, but I'm pretty sure we're past the flower stage."

"Women are never past the flower stage, unless you've moved onto the jewelry stage."

"Where do you get this shit?"

"From my sister Pat. Trust me, she's a pro."

"Duly noted. In the meantime, I do have the law to uphold. I'm on patrol for the next four hours."

"Just make sure you patrol past the flower shop." Jake paused. "Good luck, man. You deserve it."

At eight o'clock Margaux woke up for real. And for the first time in months, she faced a new day without worry clenching her gut.

But she'd had her fun. Now, it was time to get her life on track. She grabbed a notebook and went to the kitchen to make coffee and a list. By nine o'clock she had a plan.

Linda was waiting for her with a cup of tea and a grin. "Well, at least you didn't come in together. That would have just been too obvious. Take this." She handed Margaux the tea, cackled, and broke into a happy dance.

"Cut it out. Did Nick tell you?"

"Mr. What-the-hell-are-you-talking-about? Nope, but he had that warm fuzzy glow when I waylaid him to give him a cup of coffee."

"To pump him for details," Margaux added. "And I don't think Nick has ever had a warm and fuzzy glow in his life."

"Yeah he did, kinda like the one you're wearing." Linda shot her a saucy look.

"Do not make jokes around Adelaide."

"Honey, how do you think Nick got on earth? Adelaide's no fool. I bet she took one look at him this morning and has been smiling ever since."

"Oh God," Margaux groaned, remembering that Nick kept the cruiser parked at his mother's house. "This is so embarrassing."

"But was it good? No, don't tell me. I just want to imagine. Feelings," Linda warbled, and swept into the beauty salon.

Margaux went into her workshop and closed the door, looked around and smiled. Damn, she felt good. The patterns they'd cut the day before were clipped together waiting to be transferred to fabric. The fabric was folded in the other room.

It was time. She picked up her cell and called Bri. The call went to voice mail.

"Hi, I'm probably out feeding the chickens. Leave a message."

"Bri, it's Margaux—"

"Mags." She sounded out of breath. "What's up?"

"I think it's time to hold an organization and projection meeting. Are you really interested in helping out?"

"Absolutely. Grace is in court today, some zoning thing, but she'll be out by four. How about then?"

"Perfect. We'll meet at the workshop. Thanks."

"I'm in," Linda called from across the hall.

"I'm counting on it," Margaux called back.

Adelaide and Connor arrived at ten.

"Margaux. Uncle Nick isn't mad anymore."

Adelaide smiled contentedly. "And all is right with the world."

"It certainly is," agreed Margaux. "Let's cut some fabric."

Together they spread the yellow, painted chiffon on the worktable. Tested ways to fit the pattern pieces and decided on a bias-cut skirt.

"It takes more fabric," Adelaide said, "but the movement is worth it."

It was exactly what Margaux had planned. She and Adelaide were going to be a good team.

By the time Adelaide was ready to leave for the day, the Sunrise dress was pinned to the dressmaker's dummy. The bodice lay in graceful folds from a thin halter top. The skirt billowed with each tiny breeze that came through the half-open window, swirling the colors gracefully across the fabric.

Adelaide made one more adjustment to the neckline and stood back to study the finished product. "Well?"

Tears sprang to Margaux's eyes. "It's just as I imagined it. Thank you."

"You're on your way."

"We're on our way. I think we'd better hire some more seamstresses."

"I'll go home and begin calling some local ladies." She and Connor left a few minutes later.

Margaux's cell phone rang.

"Hi," Nick said. "I just thought I'd call and . . . see how you were doing."

Margaux made an exasperated face at the phone. "Great. We draped the first piece today and I'm really pleased. Your mom is a genius."

"Uh, yeah. How's everything else?"

Margaux looked at the ceiling. Well, if she was sick of suave, shallow men, she'd come to the right place. Nick was deep and caring and strong—and about as rough around the edges as she could imagine.

"Everything else is good, too."

"I was wondering if you'd like to do something again, some-time, tonight maybe. I'm off. Finley volunteered for night shift all this week."

"Bless him. Yes, let's do. I'm meeting Grace and Bri for a planning meeting around four o'clock. You saw them at the flea market. We should be finished by six or seven. How about dinner at my house?"

Silence.

"If you're worried about people seeing your truck two nights in a row, you could walk." She bit her bottom lip, trying to keep the smile out of her voice.

"I don't care about that."

"See you at eightish?"

"Okay. Can I bring anything?"

"Just you." She hung up. She was feeling way too giddy for her own good and she did have business to take care of.

She called her lawyer. "Louis was here last night, demanding money and threatening me."

"That explains a lot. I just got back from the precinct. The Feds picked him up this morning for questioning. They let him go, but not before calling me. While he sat there sweating, I—with a little help from my friends in the agency—strong-armed him into signing the divorce papers. I just sent them to the judge. It's a done deal, you should be officially divorced by the morning. I'll send you a copy."

"I don't know how to thank you. Besides paying you of course. As soon as I can."

"Like I said, I can wait. Besides, I got a great deal of pleasure nailing his ass. What a scumbag."

Things were suddenly moving fast, snowballing, amplify-ing the urgency of getting her show mounted and her name back in the workforce. But this latest news was welcome. Not being divorced wouldn't have stopped her from seeing Nick, but being divorced made it a lot more justifiable.

Bri came in at four. She went straight to the back room and stopped in front of the Sunrise mock-up. She frowned at it, cocked her head, lifted the hem of the skirt, and let it fall while Margaux held her breath.

She turned to Margaux. "Girl. You're back. Magsy, you're back. This is fabulous."

Margaux exhaled. "Not back yet, but I will be."

Linda joined them just as the "Toreador Song" played from the foyer. "Damn, this better not be a walk-in."

Grace walked into the workshop; blue suit, sensible two-inch pumps, and leather briefcase.

Margaux introduced her to Linda.

"You ever consider red highlights?"

"Uh." Grace took a step back.

"Don't worry," said Margaux. "She's enthusiastic, but harmless."

"And I know my highlights. Shall we retire to the kitchen?"

As soon as everyone was seated at the kitchen table, Margaux cleared her throat. "Before we begin, I have an announcement. I'm divorced. Well, I will be by tomorrow."

"Forget coffee," Linda said. "I'm breaking out the sparkling cider."

"Does this mean the merman is a real possibility?" asked Bri.

"Bri," Margaux warned, and cut a look toward Linda. It was too late.

"The merman? What merman?" Linda snorted a laugh. "You mean Nick? Yowza. Margaux and the merman. If that ain't a happily-ever-after." She wiped her eyes.

"Margaux?" Grace said. "Are you holding out on us?"

Margaux shrugged.

Grace slapped the table. "Wow. He's already had his day in court and you didn't tell us."

"You sneaky little so-and-so. What was the verdict?"

Margaux smiled slowly. "Guilty as sin."

They all laughed. Linda poured a round of cider, and Margaux got down to business. She outlined her plans for the runway show, the effect she wanted to create and her intention of using the show to produce a video she could send to established houses. "And if the video is good enough, someone might pick up the whole line and the designer."

Bri raised her eyebrow at the last idea. "I thought you were going to be true to thine own self."

"I'm still considering it, but it might be more feasible to be true to myself with someone else footing the bill and taking the losses. I just want to keep my options open."

Grace stopped writing and opened her mouth.

Margaux held up her hand. "There are more immediate things to be dealt with. Jude talked to Joe Mangioli at the inn. They're pretty booked for the weekends, as you expected. But he has several openings on weeknights in July and August. Mondays are cheapest. Thursdays cost more. She told him I'd get back to him by the beginning of next week."

"Not Monday, dead day, and August will be too late," Bri said. "You don't want to get lost in the fall collection madness."

"My thoughts exactly. I was thinking the last Thursday in July."

"Can you be ready by then?"

"Adelaide is hiring more seamstresses. It depends on how many she can get and how quickly they can get this up and running."

"You need to do it early enough to create some buzz and get people into the showroom before the season is over," Bri said. "You'll have to have the grand opening right after the runway show."

"Showroom?"

"Well, you can't sell these designs out of your trunk. You have to have a showroom."

"I can't afford space in New York."

"Who said anything about New York? You can do it here. There are enough upscale summer people to create a buzz if you give them a place to view things."

"Let nonprofessionals in?" asked Margaux incredulously.

"Excuse me, where is the woman who was talking about hand-selling one-of-a-kind designs?"

"You're the one who suggested it."

"But you weren't against it."

Margaux frowned. "I've given the idea a lot of thought, and it might be a good idea, but down the road. Once I've made back some capital."

"You mean once you've wowed them, then sat on your success while the momentum dies and they've forgotten all about you, and then you have to start at square one again?"

Margaux sank her chin on her hand. "I know, I've been through this in my head every night since I've been here. I just want to take things one step at a time. I can't afford to get overextended."

"Contrary to popular belief, life doesn't happen one step at a time."

Linda hopped up and salsaed out the door. "We're having a grand opening . . . having a . . ."

The others followed her to the workshop, where she threw up her hands diva-style. "We gotta get some mannequins. Labels. Shit. And a sign. Something arty-farty. Hell. You better come up with a name."

Margaux laughed. "I've been working on that, too, but I haven't come up with anything that really reflects my new look. I thought Au Naturelle by Margaux Sullivan. But it sounds mediocre."

"What about Dress-scapes?" asked Bri. "You know landscapes, dress-scapes. Nah, it doesn't mention the designer. Which is fine if you're Ralph Lauren and Polo, but not if you're Margaux Sullivan. You need more of a brand."

"I could go back to M Atelier."

"Bad karma. No offense."

"Plus . . ." Grace glanced at Linda.

"She's knows the whole story."

"M Atelier may have some legal problems attached to it. I can check and see what liens might still be held against it."

"I didn't think about that. And I appreciate your offer, but Bri's right, I need to shed the past and start fresh."

"Well, then," Grace said, "I can at least help get you incorporated. How about something like Margaux Sullivan Originals?"

"It's a good thing you're a lawyer," Bri said.

Grace grimaced. "Too dry and to-the-point?"

"Too."

"What's wrong with plain old Margaux's?" asked Linda.

Brianna made a face. "Did you call Le Coif 'Linda's Beauty Parlor'?"

"Okay, okay, I get it."

"Besides, Margaux's sounds like gingham potholders and cinnamon potpourri. We need something . . ." Brianna circled her fingers in the air. "Something *je ne sais quoi*."

"*Margaux,*" said Margaux. "How about just plain *Margaux*? The spelling has been a pain in my butt since first grade, it might as well do something good for a change."

Grace looked thoughtful.

"Hmm," said Bri. "*Margaux*. Exotic and yet inviting. Makes everyone think they should know it. And those who don't will want to find out. And it rolls off the tongue." She dropped into her sultry Marlene voice. "*Dahling*. It's a *Mahgaux*."

"I like it," Grace said.

"And it'll fit on the sign," said Linda. "I bought two when I first opened up. They were on sale."

"We'll get the sign," Brianna said. "But thanks."

"I like the name and I like *that*." Grace pointed to a design for a capri pantsuit. Subtle colorations of the sea at dusk played along the pants and soft kimono jacket that partially covered a midnight blue chemise. "I'll place my order now. I'll be your first customer."

Margaux quickly wiped away tears that for some stupid reason rushed into her eyes. "You would look fabulous in it."

"You can wear it at the grand opening," Brianna said. "But we'll have to do something about your hair and shove those sensible feet into some come-and-get-me stilettos."

"Red highlights," Linda said. "Definitely need some red highlights."

"Then it's settled," Margaux said. "I'll consult with the Cove Inn and with Adelaide and we'll take it from there."

"I'll get on the legal stuff," Grace said.

"Thanks. That leaves one crucial thing." Margaux's eyes met Bri's.

"You need models."

"I was hoping—"

"No. You need young and hip. Not sagging and gimpy."

"Oh please," Grace said. "You're still gorgeous."

"And I need someone I respect and who knows how to make the clothes come alive. I'm done with scowling, slouching models. You can just stand in place and we'll turn the wind machine on you. Let the clothes do the work. You just have to be beautiful elegant you."

Bri's mouth twisted. "No. I'll make some calls. See if I can round up three or four girls. Maybe find some students I can whip into shape, but I won't go out there."

Twenty-three

 Margaux stood at her kitchen sink arranging freesias in a milk jug.

"What's the matter?" asked Nick. "I hope it's not the flowers."

"I love the flowers. They were very thoughtful."

"Hmm. So what's with the sigh?"

"I was just thinking about Bri. I asked her to model for me but she refused."

"Can you blame her?"

"No. It's just that she was so good. She'd be perfect for this."

"Except shit happens."

Margaux remembered Bri's words, *Some die, some live.* Bri was given a second chance, Nick's brother hadn't been so lucky.

She placed the vase of freesias on the table where he was sitting and kissed him. "Did you know she used to have a mad crush on your brother?"

"Bri? Really?"

"Really, a big one. She even wrote about him in our secret diary."

"He said she liked him, but I didn't believe him. I thought she was just flirting, you know, slumming with a townie."

"You were wrong."

"I was wrong about a lot of things."

She waited for him to continue, but he just fiddled with the flower stems.

She brought him a glass of wine, then squeezed between him and the table and sat on his lap.

"You miss him."

"I—yeah."

He didn't elaborate and Margaux changed the subject, but he was subdued during dinner.

Later in the night as they lay in bed satisfied and content to look through the window at the starry sky, Nick began to talk. "Ben was a hotheaded kid. Our father died and he just went wild, I couldn't get through to him. He got in some trouble while I was away in the army.

"He and some other guys robbed the bait and tackle store. Dumbasses. They got away with twenty-three dollars and change. Ben had turned nineteen; he would be tried as an adult. I convinced the proprietor not to press charges if Ben enlisted.

"I took him down to the recruiting office. Signed him up."

Nick fell silent, and Margaux waited, sensing there was more.

"The next week I put Ben on the train. The last words he said to me were, 'I hate you.' "

"Oh, Nick. He didn't mean it."

"No. He didn't mean it." He took a breath. "I made him enlist to keep him out of jail, but also I thought it would straighten him out."

Margaux said nothing, just let him talk.

"He was a hero. He won a whole bunch of awards, three Bronze Stars, a Medal of Honor for extraordinary bravery. That was in Iraq. At the end of four years he could have come home. He had a wife and kid by then but he re-upped and was deployed to Afghanistan.

"He was never much one for calling or writing, especially not to me. But I got a letter. Said he was glad he was there, but it was brutal, and he wouldn't be coming home. His exact words. 'I'm not coming home.'

"I could tell something was wrong, something mental. I tried to get him out, but it took too long. He walked into open fire and was killed. He was awarded the Purple Heart." Nick's voice cracked. "He didn't *want* to come back and he made sure he wouldn't. I should never have sent him."

Margaux turned into him and he loved her with a ferocity she knew had as much to do with pain as with desire. And she accepted it willingly and felt her heart melt for the man she was quickly coming to love.

Margaux wasn't surprised when Jude walked into the work-shop the next morning. She was carrying two lattes and a wide smile.

"What's the occasion?" Margaux asked, though she thought she knew.

"You're divorced and Sarah Thompson said Nick Prescott's truck was outside your house two nights in a row."

To Margaux's chagrin, her cheeks heated.

"And that he bought you flowers."

"Sarah Thompson should get a life."

"I'm so happy for you." Jude put down the cups and leaned over to hug her daughter.

"You don't think you're being premature?"

"Absolutely not. We all adore Nick and he's not that willing to be adored."

"Whoa. It's only been two days. This is just . . . I don't know what it is." *Just that it's been really good.* That she'd never felt so close to anyone as when they'd made love the night before. That now she realized she and Nick had been drawn together from the beginning.

"I think it's a little early to start working up your expecta-tions."

"We only expect the two of you to have a good time."

"We?"

Jude shrugged. "Your coffee's getting cold."

"Mom."

"Just me and Dottie, oh, and Sarah Thompson, of course. And Adelaide."

"Adelaide? Who told her?"

"No one as far as I know. But a mother knows these things." Jude flashed her a complacent smile. "I also hear you're getting some more seamstresses."

"And I thought the fashion-industry grapevine was fast. They've got nothing on Crescent Cove."

"That's because we care. You know what they say, small towns . . ."

"Big noses?"

"I was going to say big hearts." Jude glanced at her watch. "I'm late for my hair appointment. Gotta run."

"Mom, I almost forgot. I've booked the Cove Inn for the last Thursday in July for the runway show. They had a cancellation."

"Oh, honey, that's so exciting. Congratulations."

Margaux waited until the door closed behind Jude, then she smiled. She trusted Jude to get the news out. You couldn't buy publicity like the Cove grapevine.

Three seamstresses arrived on Thursday, bringing their own sewing machines. The serger and two industrial sewing machines Margaux had rented from a machine shop in Hartford were delivered, and Adelaide moved the construction department upstairs.

The workshop was suddenly empty and quiet. Margaux sat down at the drafting table. She'd finished the designs for the show but she wasn't content. The idea of showroom and possible boutique kept niggling at her mind. If she was to open the showroom to the public, she would need more items for sale. Jewelry and accessories she could order from other designers.

She had someone in mind. But she needed to fill out the line with pants, skirts, camisoles.

By midafternoon she had several designs she liked. She took them upstairs to consult with Adelaide. Connor was playing with Matchbox cars out in the hallway, but he jumped up when he saw Margaux.

"Look what Uncle Nick bought me." He held up a new police car. His voice dropped to a whisper. "Can I come downstairs with you, if I don't bother you?"

Impulsively Margaux pulled him close. "Of course you can. You never bother me." Realizing what she'd done, she let go, but Connor wrapped his arms around her legs and hugged her.

"Pick up your cars first so nobody falls on them." He released her and hurriedly scooped up the toys and put them in his backpack. All but the new police car, which he put in his shorts pocket.

Margaux stepped into the sewing room. The ladies were all busy, Adelaide hovering over them, more like a mother hen than a factory boss. They each looked up just long enough to nod and went back to work.

Adelaide motioned her back into the hallway.

"Things seem to be going well," Margaux said.

"Yes. I'd like to get most of the pieces ready to begin the finishing by the Fourth."

The Fourth of July. It was only a week away, Margaux realized. Time was galloping forward.

"Excellent. Then we need to discuss whether we can build enough to display one in each size for the showroom, then maybe augment what we have with a few additional pieces. Take a look at these." She handed Adelaide her recent sketches.

Adelaide perused each sketch. "I think there are enough large scraps of blue to turn into camisoles. And maybe some of the white silk."

"Good. I was thinking raw silk for those capris. Upscale but still comfortable and beachy." She pointed to the rendering. "A seamed pleat down the front and a set of diagonal darts from below the knee to above the ankle. Piecemeal something for a few sarongs. I'll make another run to Hartford for fabric, if you think we can do it."

"Of course we can."

Her cell rang. "Hi, it's Bri. Just wanted to let you know that I haven't been able to get any professionals, the notice is too short. But I did get a commitment from Annalise Ghi to send me four of her top students. For free. If they can use you as a reference. I told them fine. I hope that was okay."

"Absolutely."

"I told her we didn't want anorexic angst. She promised to work them like the devil and send them three days early so I can finesse them. Don't worry about room and board. They can stay at my house, God knows I've got the room."

"Have you thought any more about—"

"If you put me in a pantsuit, I'll emcee. But I won't walk. That's my best offer."

"It's the best offer I've had in years."

"That's sad. If you're going to try to open the boutique in conjunction with the show, you'd better start looking for a manager now."

"I hadn't thought about that. You amaze me," Margaux told her. "Where did you get all this business acumen?"

"I told you, I went to college. I'm not bad at it, either."

"In that case, would *you* like that job?" Margaux asked, only half joking.

"It might look good on my résumé. I'll let you know."

"Accepted. You and Grace are invited to the beach for the Fourth."

"You're taking the day off?"

"Under duress. Jude said I might get away without going to Mass, but no way was I going to miss the fireworks."

"I like the way she thinks. We'll be there."

"Great. And Bri, thanks. I mean it."

"No walking."

"It's a deal." Bri hung up and Margaux began designing an outfit to end all outfits for her new emcee.

The Fourth came all too soon. The alarm woke Margaux at five. She slapped it off and was drifting back to sleep when she felt the bed dip beside her.

"Do you have to go?"

"Double shift. It's a holiday, remember?" Nick bent down and nibbled her neck.

She slipped her arms around his neck. "You shouldn't have done that, Chief. Now you'll have to pay before you go."

"I have to be out of here in twenty minutes and I need to shower."

"No problem." She heaved out of bed. "I'll wash your back."

The shower took seventeen minutes. "See, time to spare," Margaux said as she watched Nick shave, but you'll have to get coffee from Dottie, I don't have time to cook."

"That's okay, I don't love you for your culinary skills." His hand stopped as he realized what he'd said. Margaux recovered first. "It's a good thing. I could sew you a shaving sarong, but it would be a shame to cover up those assets."

"Enough," he said, washing off the disposable razor and giving her a quick kiss. "See you at midnight. With any luck."

"The bewitching hour. I'll be waiting." She followed him downstairs and smiled until he drove away, then she dropped into a kitchen chair. Surely, that had been just an expression. He didn't love her, did he? Of course not, it was much too soon. He'd just been kidding her about her lack of interest in cooking.

And it was too early for her to even think about anything permanent. The ink had barely dried on her divorce decree. And she had a career to revitalize.

She'd meant to sleep in since the workshop was closed for

the holiday, but she knew that was out of the question now. She made coffee and watched the sunrise. When the first family arrived at the beach, she went back to bed.

She awoke to noises from outside. She put on her new swimsuit and went downstairs. Roger and Jude had set out beach chairs and umbrellas to claim their spot on the beach just like the dozens of other families who lived in the community.

Bri and Grace arrived a few minutes later.

"Hallelujah, you got a new suit," Bri said. "I wonder who—I mean what—inspired that?"

Margaux threw a towel at her.

Mrs. Prescott dropped off Connor before lunch. She was spending the day with some of her friends in town, but promised to keep her cell phone nearby in case they needed her. Margaux assured her they would be fine and hoped she wasn't being too optimistic.

She saw a patrol car pass by and she ran to the back door, but it was only Finley. He gave her a thumbs-up and continued down the street.

The beach was swarming with kids and Margaux hoped it wouldn't be too much for Connor. At first he stayed on the porch watching the other kids playing. He was fascinated by a group of boys who were running with sparklers, but he didn't seem inclined to join them, thank God.

Finally Margaux retrieved the crab pail and a plastic shovel she'd unearthed in the shed and took Connor to play in the sand. She eased him to a place about six feet away from two children who seemed about his age and who were filling their pails with sand and dumping them out. The boy had a big plastic dump truck.

Margaux sat down on the sand, handed Connor the shovel, and began dropping handfuls of moist sand in the pail. When it was full, Margaux turned it over and patted the bottom. She lifted the pail up, leaving a tower of sand. Soon she and Connor were surrounded by pail-shaped mountains.

The two nearby children wandered over and sat down. The little boy and Connor began filling the dump truck while the girl scooped out tunnels in the mounds Margaux had made.

Feeling she'd made big headway, Margaux slipped away to the porch where she could see all three children.

"Is it too early for one of those drinks with a paper umbrella in it?"

"How about some lemonade," Jude said. "Afraid we don't have any umbrellas."

"Sounds good. How did you manage day after day with us on the beach? I'm afraid to take my eyes off Connor. He might feel shy, get scared, wander off. It's exhausting."

"You seem to be enjoying it."

Margaux nodded. She was enjoying it, but a part of her felt it should be her and Danny's children out there, Jude's grandchildren instead of a little boy she'd only known for a few months.

Jude squeezed her shoulder. "He's a sweet boy."

"Yeah, he is."

The two kids left and Connor came back to the porch. His nose looked pink. Margaux slathered more sunscreen on him and made him put on his T-shirt and hat. He had lunch—hot dog, chips, and an orange soda—sitting on the steps in the shade of the porch overhang.

After lunch the two kids from the morning came over to see if Connor could play. Jude promised to watch him while Margaux, Bri, and Grace went to the kitchen to whip up a batch of watermelon martinis.

Margaux was standing at the kitchen sink when she caught a glimpse of a patrol car moving slowly down the street. It might be Finley again, but—

"Back in a sec," she said, and ran out the back door.

Nick slowed the cruiser to a stop.

"Hi." She leaned in the open window. "Are you allowed a little fun while you're on duty?"

"A very little."

She kissed him and moved away.

Nick groaned. "You are such a tease."

"You said a little fun."

"Then you shouldn't be wearing that suit."

Margaux looked down. She'd forgotten she was wearing her new bikini. Aqua and gold and tiny. "It's new. At least I'm not wearing the one with the ruffles and strawberries."

"True. I've got to go. Think you can keep that on until about midnight?"

"I'll try."

"Is Connor here?"

"Yes, and he's been playing with two other kids all day."

"You're kidding."

"Nope."

He reached out the window and pulled her over, claiming a longer kiss that left her breathless.

"You better hope you don't get reported for enjoying your job too much."

"You're right. Don't forget me. I'll be back." He drove off.

Smiling, Margaux turned to find Bri and Grace, noses to the kitchen window. They disappeared in a flash.

They were waiting with martinis. Bri handed her one. "Now that was definitely an inspiration."

Adelaide picked Connor up at four. He had to be bribed with ice cream to get him off the beach. Margaux walked them to the car. When Margaux buckled his seat belt, Connor pressed sticky hands to her cheeks. "I love you."

Margaux smiled. "I love you too, sweetie."

Bri and Grace left around six, Bri to feed her animals and Grace to meet friends at the public beach and boardwalk for the fireworks.

Roger and Jude left soon after. "We're going to watch the fireworks from the comfort of my balcony. You're sure you don't want to come?"

"Thanks, but I think I'll just take a shower and a nap."

"Busy day. You've done wonders for that child. I'm proud of you."

"Thanks." She walked them to the door. Jude kissed her goodbye, and to her surprise so did Roger.

Margaux showered and changed—leaving the bikini out in case she needed it again—and went to watch the fireworks from the porch steps. She could have gotten the full effect by walking to the jetty or even sitting on the sand. But both were dotted by couples or groups of friends or families, and though Margaux didn't feel alone, she didn't feel like joining in.

The first spray of fireworks had just lit the night sky when she was startled by Nick, changed into jeans, walking across the porch and sitting down beside her.

"Charlie Briggs needed the overtime, so I let him have the rest of my shift." He unclipped his pager and set it on the step. "I'm on call."

Another boom reverberated in the air, followed by silver medallions that exploded into pink and green. Margaux barely noticed, because Nick had pulled her close and was kissing her like she couldn't remember being kissed before. And she didn't want to remember any kisses before Nick.

She wasn't aware that the fireworks were ending until the last barrage of explosions lit the whole sky.

"I hope Jude's watching the fireworks," said Margaux against Nick's mouth.

"Why?"

"She usually has her binoculars trained down here."

"I say we go inside."

"Good idea."

Twenty-four

"What we have here," Linda said, gesturing to the bare walls of *Margaux*, "is a freaking empty dress shop."

"Boutique," Margaux, Bri, and Grace said in unison.

Linda grinned. "I don't see no *boo-teek* anywhere. Just some dust bunnies and a secondhand armoire."

"She's right," Margaux said. "I've been so focused on the show that I let the *Margaux* opening slide."

"Maybe you could postpone the opening until after the show and decorate then," Grace suggested.

"Product. We're talking about product here." Linda walked away from them, turned back abruptly, and threw her hands wide. "They see product, they want to buy it. They don't want to see product, make a memo in their BlackBerry to go buy it in a couple of weeks, maybe three, if they're still in town whenever we get around to opening this joint. Uh-uh. That's not the way it works."

"Thank you." Bri high-fived her. "At least two of us know what's what."

Margaux threw the legal pad she'd been making notes on at her. "I get the point." She looked around. "We could use the garment racks I got at the flea market in a pinch."

Linda groaned. "The Baptists didn't even want them. Anyway, we need them upstairs. Try again."

"You're right. I should have ordered fixtures, but hey, I'm new at this."

"It's too late to order things," Bri said, looking around. "Besides, maybe you'll be better off without the standard accoutrement."

"You mean untraditional displays?" Margaux said. "I've been thinking of that myself."

"So how can we help?" Grace asked.

They discussed it over lunch while Margaux made lists and handed them out. "Let's see how far we get with these and meet back here at six."

"Better make it eight," Bri said.

It was almost nine before everyone returned. Nick and Margaux were unpacking baskets she picked up at several import stores. They were surrounded by a dozen more shopping bags and an assortment of distressed bookcases they'd found in a local "antique" furniture store.

"How about these?" Linda asked as she wrestled two metal baker's racks through the door. Nick relieved her of both of them and placed them in the center of the floor.

"I got the white ones 'cause I thought they would fit in with the atmosphere better than the shiny ones, but they'll exchange them."

"No, these are perfect," Margaux said.

"Good. 'Cause there are two more in my car. Come on, Chief, Harlan is working tonight." Nick followed her outside.

"She's amazing," Bri said.

"She is that," Margaux agreed.

Grace came in a few minutes later carrying two large boxes. "Sorry I'm late but I got stuck in traffic."

"Traffic? I thought you were going to the party store to get tissue paper and mesh bags."

"I did. Here's the paper and the bags, I got large and small ones." She slid the top box on the floor next to Margaux. "Then I got to thinking." She put the other box down and opened it.

"Grace Holcombe, there's hope for you yet," Brianna said, taking one of the delicate tissue sheets from the box.

"It's beautiful," said Margaux.

"Made from mulberry fibers or something. Anyway, I talked to the manager at EcoPapier. I helped her with a zoning problem once. She has enough of the paper in stock to get us started. She can order more." She opened one of the shopping bags. "They also had these nifty little gift boxes, made of something natural, I forget what. Anyway, these are brown and green but they come in different colors."

"Yowza," said Linda. "Those are expensive. I hope she gave you the saved-my-ass lawyer discount."

"She did."

"Perfect," said Margaux. "I'll call her tomorrow and place an order."

Grace puffed up. "See, Ms. Bri, I do have an artistic bone in my body." She exhaled. "Though I think I just used it up."

They moved bookshelves, unpacked bags, and considered where to put things. It was after midnight when Grace lifted an unwieldy bundle from one of the bags. "What's this?"

"A fishing net." Margaux shrugged. "I might have gotten carried away on that one."

"Not to worry," Bri said. "You can always open a branch of *Margaux* in Palm Beach. Add a few seashells and they'll eat it up. And pay a fortune. Hmm. Let me crunch a few figures." She wandered away muttering to herself.

The next day, Nick brought his friend Jake McGuire, a master carpenter and woodworker, to build dressing rooms. Margaux had seen his work. It was exquisitely detailed and expensive.

When she tried to ask him about his fees, he shrugged. "Nick and I have been friends since forever. He's happy. I owe you."

As pieces were finished, they were brought downstairs. Margaux marveled at how much had gotten done as the shelves and racks filled with her designs. It seemed that each remnant had been transformed into a camisole or a scarf and without looking like they were anything but carefully conceived.

Margaux sometimes just sat in the center of the room, amazed at herself and her friends and the staff of seamstresses she hadn't even met until a few weeks before. She was grateful, but also a little stultified when she overheard them talking about the fall and how they would soon need a larger workspace.

"You're really making this work," Nick said as he looked around the finished boutique.

"Yeah." It was happening and Margaux suffered new moments of terror. Not the gut-wrenching disappointment and fear she'd brought home, but the exhilarating butterflies that attacked right before you stepped into the unknown.

He kissed her. "Gotta go. Don't worry." He passed Bri on her way into the shop.

"I'm here for my fitting." Bri's voice held less attitude than usual and Margaux wondered if she was having second thoughts about emceeing. She wasn't about to ask. "Come with me."

They went up the stairs. Adelaide took her into the last unused bedroom and shut the door. After what seemed like an eon, Adelaide came out. "She's taking a moment."

Margaux frowned. "Is she—"

"She's beautiful."

A few minutes later, Bri stepped out into the hallway wearing Margaux's specially designed "Storm." Silver iridescent harem paints, overpainted with mauve, deep purple, and eggplant. The pants buttoned at the ankle and were cinched at the waist by a flowing double scarf encrusted with crushed prism stones. It was topped by a sheer clinging camisole in heliotrope and an open jacket of the same fabric as the pants. She looked incredible.

Margaux burst into tears. "You're beautiful."

Bri nodded and she started to cry.

"Come get out of that outfit before you get it all wet," Adelaide said, and sniffed as she trundled Bri away.

That afternoon, Margaux locked herself away with Adelaide. She had come in early to dye one more length of fabric, one she intended to make into a dress for herself.

"A simple sheath," she told Adelaide. "Do you think you'll have the time?"

"Of course. It's beautiful and so simple, but what is that?" She pointed to a place on the fabric.

"Something special for Connor. It goes front left near the hemline."

An hour later they had the fabric draped.

"It's perfect," Adelaide said. "Perfect."

Three days before the opening, the models arrived. Bri brought them by the store to introduce them and schedule fittings for the next day.

"Annalise is a genius. I described what kind of girls I wanted and she nailed it."

An African-American with close-cropped hair, a blonde, straight and long, a brunette, short and curly, and a redhead, wavy and silky. Pretty girls, not too harsh but not too wholesome.

Margaux and Bri sat over coffee in Linda's kitchen and scripted out the descriptions of the clothes that would be modeled.

"I'll do hair and makeup," Linda offered. Her coal black hair was spiked more than usual that day. She was wearing purple eye shadow and false lashes and carrying her ever-present cup of tea.

Bri's eyes widened in horror.

Linda sprayed a mouthful of tea. "You should see your face." She pulled the lashes off and dropped them on the kitchen table. "I really had you going. Don't worry. I can do *sub-tile*."

Margaux nodded. "Hard to believe sometimes, but she can."

* * *

The show was scheduled for a Thursday night. On Tuesday Margaux and Bri oversaw a professional photo shoot with the models at the inn. There would be other photographers at the show but Margaux didn't want to take a chance of not getting any usable stills.

Wednesday morning, Margaux woke up to storm clouds. "No," she pleaded.

Nick stirred beside her, then jolted upright. "What?"

"Look." She pointed to her bedroom window.

"Oh. It won't rain." He pulled her down and captured her arms and legs.

"How do you know?"

"I just know."

"How?"

He groaned, propped himself up on his elbow, and looked down at her. "AccuWeather. Now let me show you how to relax before you go to work."

That afternoon they carted everything to the inn. Joe Mangioli, the manager, showed them to a banquet room where they could dress and leave their supplies. While Bri and the models tested the runway the hotel had constructed, Margaux went over the hors d'oeuvres list with the kitchen. Catering was part of the package. And it wasn't cheap.

The dress rehearsal was held the afternoon of the show. Not in the dark and not in time to fix anything major, but it was all Margaux could afford. It was a disaster, but as Margaux knew, a bad dress rehearsal was supposed to mean a good show. She just hoped that was what it meant this time.

When they returned to the workshop, Linda whisked a protesting Adelaide into Le Coif and shut the door. The other seamstresses went home, but would be at the inn that night in case of any last-minute snafus.

Margaux was left alone in the boutique. She had to admit it was impressive, especially considering the way it started out.

But she was shaking with nerves. What if no one came. What if no one bought. What if she was making a huge mistake.

"Mind if I come in?" Nick stood in the doorway. He was wearing his uniform; Margaux hoped he wasn't here to tell her he couldn't come to the showing.

"Of course not. I was just . . ." She ended with a gesture that took in her surroundings.

"Thinking of all the disasters that might happen?" He came up to her and slipped his arms around her.

She leaned into him. He was warm and strong and something twisted inside her.

He kissed her neck.

She shivered. "Your mother's next door."

"Hmm." He walked her over to the door and kicked it closed.

An hour before the runway show they were still hanging orchids from the lampposts. Brianna had the models ready to go, and she was giving instructions to four young women on how to keep the models dressed and on schedule.

"Who are they?"

"One works at the Sun and Surf shop on the boardwalk, one is a student teacher, and the other two I met at the feed store."

Margaux looked toward heaven.

"Not to worry. They've been drilled. Plus each model has her own seamstress—they never had it so good. And never will again. And if all else fails, we got the beautician with the mouth." She grinned. "Everything will be fine. Now, go change into something stunning."

Margaux went, but before she could change, Linda pushed her into a chair in front of the portable makeup table.

"I blow-dried it this morning. It's already looks great."

"Well, it's gonna look greater. I have my reputation to uphold." She spritzed, twisted, pulled, and curled while Margaux squirmed and sneaked peeks at her watch.

Linda handed her a mirror and twirled the chair around.

"Wow," Margaux said. Her hair had been pulled into a twist, tendrils curled loosely around her face and neck.

"I call it"—Linda struck a pose—"Tequila Sunrise with a twist."

Margaux laughed. Linda snorted and conga-lined around the chair.

"I call it fabulous. Thank you."

By the time Margaux put on makeup, changed into her dress and new heels, there was only a half hour before showtime, and she was a bundle of nerves.

"Fabulous," said Bri. "When the hell did you have time to do that?"

Bri stirred the air with her finger and Margaux dutifully turned around, displaying the sheath that she'd hand-painted that week and Adelaide had "whipped" up. It was pretty nice if she did say so herself. Celery green shantung with four shades of darker green shooting upward from hem to bust and over one shoulder. It didn't have a name yet. Somehow "Salt Marsh" didn't have the right ring to it.

"Adelaide made it. She's amazing."

"It's amazing. And that odd detail on the skirt. It works."

Grace arrived, a pair of four-inch heels dangling from one finger. "Linda," she said by way of explanation.

Jude and Roger arrived next, Jude beautiful in a silk sarong and Roger wearing a tuxedo and looking very dapper and very happy. Dottie and Tom Palmer came in right behind them, and even Quinn and Darren made a brief appearance.

The patio began to fill with people as waiters moved through the crowd with trays of hors d'oeuvres and champagne.

The Thompsons brought several families from Little Crescent Beach. Sarah Thompson introduced Margaux to a young man with a camera. "Emily Whitelaw's boy," Sarah told her in an aside. "Just graduated from Rhode Island School of Design."

Margaux let him take her picture with the model wearing the Sunrise dress.

She was standing in the hallway with Bri, counting the final minutes and wondering if Nick had been called out on an emergency, when he came in, wearing a tuxedo. He looked rugged and handsome—and lovable when he ran his finger inside his collar, setting his bow tie askew.

"He cleans up very nicely," said Bri, "but go fix his tie and tell him to stop squirming."

Wine and champagne flowed freely. By eight o'clock, there was barely space for all the guests, all dressed to the nines and having a good time.

But the hit of the evening was Adelaide Prescott. The bun was gone and in its place was a helmet of wispy honey-colored hair. The dress she wore was not one of her usual shirtwaists, but a sweep of deep purple and magenta orchids on a black background.

"Am I a genius, or what?" Linda whispered in Margaux's ear.

"A genius. She's beautiful."

Connor was almost invisible behind her, but she pushed him forward and he came toward Margaux carrying a bouquet of flowers. He looked back at his grandmother, then shoved the flowers at Margaux.

"Thank you, they're beautiful." Margaux knelt down and hugged him.

She stood up. "Do you see something special on my dress?"

He scrunched up his face in concentration. "It's grass."

"Uh-huh."

"See anything hiding in the grass?"

He studied every inch of her dress, then his face lit up. "It's my dinosaur. You put my dinosaur on your dress. Look, Nana. Margaux put my dinosaur on her dress."

"Dinosaur," said Bri. "Genius."

Margaux followed them out to the patio. Dottie, Jude, and several other ladies crowded around Adelaide. Margaux searched for Nick and found him on the edges of the crowd, standing with Tom Palmer. His eyes were on his mother, a combination of surprise and wistfulness in his expression.

He slowly made his way through the crowd and came to stand in front of her. He leaned over to kiss his mother's cheek. Mrs. Prescott glowed.

Margaux looked around the patio. Friends, neighbors, acquaintances, strangers, there wasn't a person here who didn't wish her well. Not like an opening in New York where half the attendees were praying that you'd flop. Gratitude swelled inside her.

Bri came up beside her. "It's eight."

Margaux took a deep breath. "Oh God."

"Too late to chicken out now." Bri took a breath and made her way toward the stairs to the runway.

Margaux watched her go, wondering if it was hard for Bri to be up there but not as a model, and hoping she hadn't asked her friend to give too much.

The patio lights dimmed, the runway lit up. Bri, looking majestic, took the stage.

"Good evening and welcome . . ." Bri's voice lifted above the crowd, clear and rich and deep.

The crowd quieted as if mesmerized by her voice, their attention riveted on the stage as one by one the models took the runway, each one looking more stunning than the last. As soon as a model exited, she was redressed in a new outfit and sent out again. Bri and Margaux had spent a whole afternoon working out the order and they'd nailed it. Not one glitch.

Still Margaux didn't breathe easy until the final model had finished her walk and they all took the stage for a final group pose. Margaux was swallowed by a crowd of well-wishers while several photographers crowded around the runway to take pictures for their local papers and the video people wrapped and packed up their equipment.

It was after eleven when they finally ushered everyone out.

Several women promised to come to the store as soon as it opened, but Margaux knew better than to rely on promises made after multiple glasses of champagne. It would take a few weeks before she had a clear idea if this could really work. A few months for it to build any momentum. And two years to flourish or fail.

But Margaux would worry about that later. Now she was content to bask in her success.

Jude and Roger said good night and walked out arm in arm. Nick carried a sleeping Connor out to his mother's car while Margaux insisted Mrs. Prescott go home for a much-needed rest. Margaux gave the models their checks and her thanks; they already had their luggage packed and a ride to the train station.

"They really did beautifully," Margaux told Bri. "Thanks to you. Though they can't wait to get back to Manhattan."

"That's because they don't realize that the next big fashion capital is Crescent Cove, Connecticut."

Margaux laughed. "And you were, and *are,* wonderful. I really appreciate it. I mean it."

Bri nodded. "What? Did you think I was going to get up there and forget my lines?"

"No. I just thought it might be hard, you know, not being out there yourself."

"Honey, I'm thirty-six. I wouldn't be out there anyway. Now, let's get this stuff packed up and back to *Margaux*. There's a martini there with my name on it."

Margaux. For the first time it really hit her. She'd embarked on a new life.

Nick returned from the parking lot. His tie was already untied and hanging from his collar. His collar was open at the throat. Margaux shook her head affectionately. He was rough-and-tumble and would probably never own an Armani suit, but he looked perfect to her.

"Congratulations," he said, and gave her a quick kiss. "I'll go help Harlan load the van."

An hour later they had unloaded everything into the back room at *Margaux* and hung the outfits to air. Margaux sank down on the stool behind an old wet bar Jake McGuire had transformed with pickled wood and oxidized hardware into a cashier counter.

Grace appeared in the doorway. "Okay, everybody out. There's sustenance in the kitchen."

Bri stretched. She'd changed into black stretch capris and an off-the-shoulder beige knit top.

"It better include watermelon." She pushed Margaux off the stool and toward the kitchen.

There was watermelon, a blender full of it. And Grace was waiting with a glass filled to the rim. The kitchen counter was laden with tinfoil containers, a Crock-Pot, paper plates, napkins, toothpicks, and a dozen champagne flutes. Linda was just taking a tray out of the oven.

"Don't look at me. Dottie sent this over. She said no success was complete without her cocktail weenies."

Bri looked under the tinfoil-covered dishes. "And potato salad, baked ham, artichoke dip. Spanakopita? Yum."

Harlan and Nick came in. Harlan was still wearing his tuxedo, but Nick was back in jeans and a T-shirt, the rented tuxedo probably lying on his bedroom floor. Margaux remembered her first impression of him, harsh, stubborn, uptight. He was all those things, but more.

"Let me do that." Harlan took a champagne bottle from Grace, who was struggling with the foil cover. He unwrapped the cork and pulled it out in one efficient movement. The pop set off applause all around. They drank a toast to the show, to the boutique, to each other, they all filled their plates and stood around the kitchen eating and talking.

"I used to have a dining room," Linda said, "but this is much more intimate." She fed Harlan a cocktail weiner. He chewed the weiner and licked her fingers, and the room seemed to grow quiet as everyone watched. Margaux felt a twitch in her gut and sneaked a glance at Nick, only to find him looking at her.

Grace and Bri put away the food and got ready to go. Margaux walked them out. When she returned to the kitchen, Linda and Harlan were gone.

"Some night," Nick said. "You made it. I knew you would. Smart and beautiful and determined."

"Hmm." Margaux stifled a yawn.

"Tired?"

"Yes, but I think it was the champagne that did me in."

"Need a designated driver?"

"I sure do. I'm hoping it's you."

Twenty-five

 Saturday morning, Margaux met Grace and Brianna for brunch at Dottie's. Brianna was the last to arrive. She slid into the booth and slapped a newspaper down on the table. "Look at this."

Margaux and Grace leaned over the paper. It was the *New Haven Register,* and there in living color was a picture of Margaux standing next to the Sunrise dress. The headline of the article read, *Art Meets Fashion at the Shore.*

"Omigod," Grace said.

"I don't remember the *Register* being there," Margaux said.

"It must have been that photographer the Thompsons brought."

"Emily Whitelaw's boy," Margaux said. "I was just helping the kid out. No one said he was a staff photographer for the *Register.*"

"And there's more." Bri opened the paper to a half-page spread of the photos from the show.

"Wow."

"And look at the caption," Grace said. "It announces the grand opening on Tuesday. You're going to be mobbed."

"We can but hope," Margaux said, having a hard time believing things were going this well. "I still have a lot of work to do."

"We," Bri corrected. "We have a lot to do."

"Does that mean you'll be my manager until I can find someone permanent?"

"As long as I'm off in time to feed the animals."

"Absolutely."

"And I'm in whenever I'm not in court."

"Selkies forever," said Margaux. "You guys are the best."

"Looks to me like you're on your way. Here's to Tuesday." Grace lifted her coffee cup.

"To Tuesday."

Nick helped Jake McGuire maneuver the new *Margaux* sign into place.

"Is it even?"

"A little more on Jake's side."

They shifted the sign. Nick went down to stand beside Margaux and looked up at the sign. It was a wrought-iron rectangle with filigree cutouts and *Margaux* scripted in sea green.

"It's beautiful." Margaux's eyes were shining and he wanted to take her in his arms and love the daylights out of her.

"So tomorrow's the big day," said Jake, climbing down from the ladder.

Margaux took a deep breath and let it out. "That's what the paper says."

"Well, good luck."

"Thanks."

"You're going to be a huge success," said Nick. He was so proud of her. She'd pulled herself from disaster and wouldn't give up. "You've done an amazing job."

She reached up and kissed him on the cheek. He cut his eyes to Jake, who shrugged, grinned, and began to fold up the ladder.

Margaux's cell rang. "Sorry." She walked away to take it.

Nick watched her as she listened. She was frowning. He hoped it wasn't bad news. She'd worked so hard, was just beginning to settle into the idea of staying in Crescent Cove.

Jake carried the ladder back to his truck. Margaux hung up.

"Everything okay?" Nick asked, searching her face.

"Yeah. But it was weird. That was a fashion house in New York They saw the spread in the *Register*. They want me to come talk to them."

The world went out of focus for a second. "They want to buy some of your clothes?"

Margaux shrugged. "I think they may want me."

Stayed out of focus. "What did you tell them?"

"That I'd get back to them."

"You're thinking about going back?" He was having a hard time wrapping his mind around this. He'd thought . . . but it didn't matter what he thought.

"I haven't thought about it in weeks."

"But you're thinking about it now."

"No. I don't know. No. They're a little house and couldn't possibly accommodate the things I want to do. But it is flattering." She reached up and put her arms around his neck.

She was so warm, so right, so perfect for him, that he wanted to hold on and not take the chance of losing her. But he knew you couldn't hold on to people against their will. He just hoped this call would be the last.

He gently removed her arms. "I have to get to work."

"What time do you get off? Shall I make dinner? Meet you somewhere?"

"I'm not sure. I'll call you later."

He leaned over and kissed her. Right there on Marina Street. In front of Jake. In full view of the two old fishermen lounging on the marina bench. He didn't care. Already he felt as if he were being left behind.

Margaux watched Nick get into the truck, waved when he drove away; she turned to find Jake McGuire watching her. There was something in his eyes that was suddenly darker. "Is something wrong, Jake?"

"I sure as hell hope not." He gave her a two-finger salute and got in his truck and drove away.

The call from New York had certainly put a damper on everyone's mood, including hers. Elsie Rule had a nice little distribution, a lot smaller than Margaux had generated in the last few years. It was a little insulting that they should even ask her. They were small potatoes. And she was—well, she was no potatoes at the moment, but she would be.

She should have explained to Nick about the industry. How the game was played. She'd told them she'd be in touch not because she was seriously considering their offer, but because that was the way business was done. Keep them hanging, make them come back with a better offer, it was just part of the positioning game.

Surely he realized she wouldn't just walk away from all that she'd worked for, from him and Connor, from her friends.

She'd explain it to him tonight, then show him how much she loved him. She stopped mid-stride. That pesky L word again. It was too early to talk about love, much too early. Especially after her disastrous marriage. But wasn't that just what she was feeling? If she stayed here, Nick would become a part of her life. Was already a part of it.

Margaux's stomach dropped like a roller-coaster. It seemed like yesterday that her life had spiraled out of control and she'd come limping back with no home, no future, no prospects. Now, suddenly everything was happening too fast. The store, Nick and Connor, the call from New York. She didn't want to work for Elsie Rule, but she couldn't deny that she'd felt a thrill of excitement when she answered the phone. She'd felt the same thrill just a few nights ago, when the first model walked down the runway wearing her new design, but would that thrill last?

She needed to slow down, take control, keep her mind on the now, not on the what ifs. She took a deep breath, climbed the steps, and went into *Margaux*.

Bri was sitting on the floor cross-legged folding scarves.

Margaux sat down beside her. "Selkies forever." She picked up a scarf and began folding it. "Do you ever miss your old life?"

Bri looked sideways at her. "Which one? The modeling one or the one where fast living nearly did me in?"

"The modeling."

"Sometimes. But I spend most of my time investing in my new life." She tossed a folded scarf into a wicker basket and turned to face Margaux. "Are you missing New York?"

"I don't know. When I'm here, I think I can live like this forever, then I see an ad, or someone calls, even if it's someone I'm not interested in, and part of me is envious."

"It'll pass mostly. I didn't have a choice, you do. And if you want my two cents, I think you've made the right one. Life is too short to grapple your way through it. Look around. This is you. Your business, your designs. And you have a man and boy who love you."

"It's too early to even talk about love."

"For you maybe. But that kid looks at you and sees Mommy. And Nick, well, he might play things close to his chest, but when *he* looks at you . . . honey, that's love." She wrapped her arm around Margaux's neck and pulled her in for a hug. "Count your blessings, girlfriend. Count your blessings."

Bri squeezed and let go. "Now, make yourself useful and start folding."

An hour later, the second call came. A larger house and more tempting until she looked around the half-furnished shop. "Thanks so much. Let me think about it and I'll get back to you."

Bri shook her head and kept working.

Instead of going straight to Margaux's after work, Nick drove to the promontory above the jetty. He walked out to the rocks just as he had twenty years ago, Private Nick Prescott with his whole life before him. Only tonight he was wearing running shoes and jeans instead of army regulation boots and uniform and much of his life was behind him.

As he looked down on the beach, he could almost see Ben sitting on the lifeguard stand, Margaux and her friends laughing and flirting. Elusive ghosts. Now Margaux was in his life, but would she stay? Something had shifted after that phone call. She said it was nothing, but it was. He could tell just the way her energy sparked while she was talking to them.

All day he thought about it. He was afraid she was slipping back to a place where like the girl on the beach she'd be too far out of reach.

He looked out to the horizon trying to dispel the sick feeling in his stomach. Maybe he was being too premature, as if he'd even expected her to leave all along. Because he still couldn't believe she would be interested in him.

Maybe he was acting like some lovesick teenager. She probably hadn't given that phone call another thought, while he hadn't been able to get it off his mind. It was only one call; surely she realized that her life was here with him—and Connor.

There were several women and two photographers waiting outside *Margaux* on Tuesday morning.

"Better than Filene's Basement," Linda crowed, and hurried across to Le Coif to peek out the door at the customers.

"Ready?" Margaux exhaled and shook her hands to dispel her nerves. Beside her, Bri looked cool and unruffled.

"Never let 'em see you sweat, Mags. Stand here looking generous but slightly aloof. I'll take care of the sales." She unlocked the door. "Good morning. Welcome to *Margaux*."

After an hour Margaux was still a nervous wreck. And her jaw was tired from smiling. There was a continuous flow of customers. Some of them even bought. A few of them bought a lot. But it was only the first day. Could it last?

By early afternoon, she couldn't take any more and fled upstairs to sit with Adelaide and the other seamstresses.

Adelaide looked up from the camisole she was hand-hemming. "It sounds very busy down there."

"It is, but I can't take the stress. I don't know how Bri does it."

Connor left his coloring book and came to lean up against her. "What's the matter?" He looked worried.

"Nothing at all. I'm not very good at selling things."

He patted her hand. "That's okay. You can make good clothes."

"Thanks."

He climbed onto her lap.

"Connor, get down this instant."

Connor looked at Margaux. She ruffled his hair. "You little manipulator. It's fine, Adelaide." It was better than fine. It felt just as she imagined it would be when she had kids. Connor wasn't hers, but that didn't mean she couldn't enjoy his company.

The seamstresses left at four. Margaux and Adelaide were closing the sewing room and Nick had just called to say he was on his way over when her cell phone rang again. Thinking it was Nick, she took the call.

"Margaux, Sam Breed from S and B here. I had no idea of what was happening over at M Atelier. I wish you'd called me."

Sam Breed. Sam Breed was calling her? *Stay cool,* she told herself. "Sam, what a surprise." Adelaide shooed Connor into the sewing room and shut the door. Margaux started down the stairs. "How have you been?"

"Hectic as always. Seems like the year is just one long preparation and presentation." He laughed.

Easy for him to say. He had a job. S and B was one of the most prestigious houses in New York.

"Things are hectic here, too," she said. The front door opened. Another customer, she turned her back to them.

"I saw the article and the pictures. Very interesting."

Margaux frowned, not a good word when describing couture.

"So, Margaux. Why don't you drop by my office this week. We'll talk."

He wanted to talk? She willed herself not to sound too interested. *Stay calm. Stay in the bargaining seat.* She clicked into couture mode.

"Let me see . . ." She played for time. Let him think she was checking her calendar. Should she go talk to him? She'd just gotten back on her feet. Was this an info quest or could he be seriously interested in her.

"Friday's the earliest I could make it."

"Friday's fine. Say ten o'clock."

She smiled to herself. "Better make it eleven."

"Great. Can't wait."

Margaux hung up, stunned. Sam Breed had called her for an appointment. It could only mean one thing. She was back. She was really back. Smiling, she slipped her cell into her shoulder bag and turned around.

Nick was standing in the doorway, unmoving. Like the old Nick, his eyes were hard, his jaw set.

"Hey, that was quick. You're never going to guess who just called me."

"Probably not."

"Sam Breed. One of the most important people in the industry."

"Great." But he didn't sound like he thought it was great.

"He wants to meet with me on Friday."

"He's coming here?"

"Of course not. I'll have to go down to the city."

"I thought that you . . ." He gestured to the new shop.

"I do. But this is a huge coup. Sam Breed is interested in me. This is big. It's like . . ." She searched for an example that would make him understand. "Like Yale calling you to teach."

"I could commute to Yale."

"That's not the point. It would be an offer you couldn't refuse to at least listen to."

"If that's what you think, you don't know me at all."

She did know him and she knew that if it came to his family and his duty to them, he would give up what he wanted most. What did it say about her that she was even willing to go to New York to talk to Sam Breed.

Jude was her only family and she would be happy for her. Nick had never mentioned that he wanted her to be part of his family. She cleared her throat.

"I just want to hear what he has to say. Be excited for me."

"I am." He looked past her shoulder. "Come on, Connor. I'll take you for pizza."

Connor stood on the bottom stair, a piece of dark blue construction paper in his hand, his lower lip stuck out. "You're fighting."

Margaux knelt beside him. "No, honey, we were just discussing something."

He looked at her, then looked to Nick and back. "Here." He shoved a piece of paper at her. He'd pasted Day-Glo stars across the page. "It's the Milky Way. For your dresses."

"Thank you, it's beautiful."

"Come on, sport. We gotta get going."

"Can Margaux come?"

"Not tonight. She has other things she needs to do."

"Nick," Margaux said, not believing he was cutting her off so easily.

"See you later."

He hurried Connor outside.

Bri was standing in the door to *Margaux*, her messenger bag over her shoulder. "I have to go feed the animals. Oh, Mags, think about what you're doing." She shook her head and walked out the front door.

Margaux closed up and went home to wait for Nick. She was feeling a little confused. No, angry. Why couldn't Bri and

Nick be excited for her? It wasn't like she'd deserted them. Sam Breed was big stuff. She had to see what he was offering. It could be the opportunity of a lifetime.

So why did she feel so miserable.

But not so miserable that she called him back to cancel the appointment. A few months ago when she thought she had no choice, the idea of starting over wasn't so frightening. But now that a comeback was a possibility, the idea of cutting off her final tie with the New York fashion industry filled her with dread. What if she failed here? What would she do then?

Jude called. "I heard you got some nice offers from New York."

"Yes, and everybody's pissed at me."

"They care about you and want what's best for you."

"What is that?"

"I can't answer that. Only you can know for sure."

"I have to just go see, don't I?"

"You know I'll support you whatever you decide." But she sounded disappointed. "You'll figure it out. I didn't see Nick's truck there."

"He isn't here."

"Call him. Talk things over."

Margaux hung up. She didn't call him. He knew she was expecting him. And if he didn't care enough to at least talk to her . . . *This is what you get for placing your trust in another man. Didn't you learn anything from Louis?*

Margaux clapped her hands over her ears trying to drive out those betraying thoughts. Nick was nothing like Louis. She had brought this on herself. Why couldn't she just be content with what she had? She *was* content, more than content . . . for the last two months. But would it last? Could it last? One unexpected phone call and already her new life was unraveling.

Nick came in late that night. Margaux was already in bed. She reached out for him and he came to her. They didn't speak. Margaux was afraid they had nothing to say.

Twenty-six

"I don't get it," said Brianna, frowning at a mannequin she was attempting to dress. She gestured around the boutique. "I thought this is what you wanted. Your own line, your own house. To be able to experiment and not just stick to trends."

"I did. I do. But this is Sam Breed. He has access to huge distribution. We could have Sunrise dresses and Driftwood pants in every boutique and department store in the States, maybe overseas. Aren't you the least bit curious about what he wants?"

"No, I'm not. I know this business, too. Lots of talk. It doesn't mean shit."

"I know, that's why I'm just going to talk to him. Nothing is decided. But I have to do whatever it takes to get back on top, and if that means farming myself out to the highest bidder, then—"

Brianna turned so quickly that the mannequin toppled over. "A lot of people have come to depend on you here. Just remember that. Not to mention Nick and that little boy. Are you going to walk away from them, too?"

"It doesn't mean it's over."

"Doesn't it? The fact that you're even contemplating going back says something."

Margaux began gathering up her designs. *Her* designs with the finished products surrounding her. And she was leaving them. She dashed away a tear and started to close her briefcase, saw Connor's Milky Way picture and put it in with the rest.

She'd been so happy a few days ago. She'd felt back on track until the lure of Manhattan raised its head. She didn't want to leave Crescent Cove, but she didn't know if she was ready to give up everything she'd worked her whole life for.

Bri turned on her. "You have a chance to start life over with all the things important to you, and you're throwing it back like it was garbage. Do you know how many women, hell men, would kill to have what you have?"

Margaux could only shake her head.

"Nick is one thing. He's an adult and can fight for you if he wants. But what about that poor child? He's totally attached to you. And you let it happen."

"Stop! You don't understand. I have to do this. I have to just try. I don't have a choice."

Brianna laughed, a harsh angry sound. "Oh, I understand. I used to tell myself that every time I took a diet pill or a line of cocaine: I have to do this, I don't have a choice. Well, I had a choice. And I made the wrong one. I wrecked my career and I came damn close to wrecking my life.

"You have a choice, Margaux. Just make sure you can live with the one you make."

Margaux closed her briefcase and picked it up. "Success in New York doesn't mean I have to give up Crescent Cove."

"I'll tell Grace you said goodbye."

Margaux nodded as she ran for the door. Being a New York designer was what she'd always wanted. They all knew that. So why were they acting like she was a traitor? What was the harm in looking at her options?

She made the mistake of looking back as she got in the car. The new sign, the dressed window. Her line, her store.

And if the options panned out, how could she walk away from all she had here?

Margaux sat on the jetty, hugging her knees and wondering how her life had gotten so messed up. She should be packing, checking her portfolio, but she'd been too upset to concentrate.

She should be happy, but she felt sick. How could something flip from wonderful to pure hell in the blink of an eye—in the space of one phone call.

She rested her cheek on her knees and watched the sunset, red, yellow, and orange, the hot colors on the palette, but today they felt cold. Slowly a figure emerged out of the sun's glare, a black silhouette, and for a second Margaux's heart stuttered and the world seemed to right itself. Then she realized it was too small to be Nick.

As it neared the jetty, the silhouette took form; Margaux sighed. Coming to vent more anger as though Bri's outburst hadn't been enough. She gave in to the inevitability and didn't even attempt to avoid the confrontation.

"I thought I'd find you here." Grace sat down beside her and gazed out at the Sound. "Bri told me you're leaving."

Margaux nodded, her throat was so tight she could hardly speak. "I guess you're pissed, too."

"No. Just confused. I thought you were happy here."

"I was."

"What happened?"

"Sam Breed called, he wants to talk to me. He's at one of the biggest houses in New York. It could put me back in business."

"I thought you were back in business. What about *Margaux*? You seemed so excited about opening your own place."

"I was. I am. It's just . . . I don't know. I like working here, love the work I've done here. It's been crazy but so satisfying, the hand-dyeing, the hectic schedule, the zany everyday things that happened that you never see when you're stuck behind a drafting table, light-years away from the finished product."

Margaux shook her head. "I've been so happy with you and Bri and Jude. All of us together again. And Nick and Connor. And I love the designs I made here . . . the runway show. I loved it all."

"But you're going back to New York."

"I just want to hear what he has to say. I told Bri that. I told Nick. They just assume I'm leaving for good. Nick has already written me off, Bri practically kicked me out of my own store. And if they're so ready to throw me under the bus for one phone call, how can I trust them to stand by me when the going gets really rough? Oh God. I wish he'd never called."

"Pretend he didn't."

"I can't. I've failed once, and I don't think I can stand to fail again. I can't afford to make any mistakes. What if *Margaux* is a dead end? Becomes just another upscale boutique, selling overpriced clothing during the summer and limping along during the winter months until the next tourist season begins."

She buried her head in her arms. "I'm afraid I won't be able to pull it off."

"Yeah, fear," Grace said. "Fear is a great motivator, but not a good one."

Margaux looked up. "I know, but it isn't just that. New York is what I know, what I do, I don't know if I'm cut out for this."

"You thought so a few days ago."

"That was before— How do I know if staying here is not really the beginning of something new, but settling for less? A copout, the coward's way out?"

"You'll figure it out."

"I don't have time to figure it out. I leave on Friday. At this point I'm not even sure I have a reason to come back."

"At the risk of sounding pedantic, let me tell you a story. One that I don't tell so listen up; you won't hear it again. When

I graduated from law school, my father insisted I go with his firm. I always wanted to be a small-town lawyer, but I caved because I thought it was the respectful thing to do."

"Plus your dad could be pretty persuasive."

"That, too. That's where the fear came in. I was more afraid of his disapproval than of losing what I wanted most. I mean, what if I struck out on my own and failed? Sound familiar?

"On my first case, I was part of a team that defended this sleazebag rich kid accused of armed robbery. He didn't need the money, he just got a thrill out of holding people up. I got him off on a technicality. Me, the newest and youngest member of the team.

"He went right back to robbery. Only the next time, he killed a convenience store clerk.

"His father was a big client, and when they put me on the team to defend him again, I refused. My father said that was the way the law worked; I said it wasn't my way. I quit on the spot and came back to Crescent Cove. My father doesn't speak to me, but I'm doing what I want."

"God, how awful for you."

"Yeah, it was. I still have nightmares about it. But sometimes shit has to happen before you have the courage to do what you really want. I was torn, but in the end, I followed my heart home."

"You think I should stay?"

"I think you should follow your heart."

"How can I when it's torn in two."

Grace pushed to her feet. "Whatever you decide, remember we all love you, even Bri, who's just a little pissed right now. She's lost a lot, she doesn't want to lose you, too."

She climbed down the rocks and started across the beach. Margaux watched until she was just a small dark shadow on the setting sun. She wanted to call her back, tell her she'd decided to stay in Crescent Cove. But she couldn't. She loved them and she knew if she left, things would never be the same between them. But if she stayed she might grow to resent them all.

Margaux's car was gone when Nick came home that night, but Brianna was just coming out the front door. His first instinct was to pretend he hadn't seen her and go up the stairs like everything was normal.

But their eyes met and he could tell she had been crying.

So it was over. Margaux was leaving.

Brianna gave a disjointed little shake of her head as she passed him, but she didn't stop and Nick didn't call her back.

He stood rooted to the sidewalk as everything in his life blew to pieces. He should never have let down his guard, never allowed himself to . . . whatever it was he had done. How did he go on from here? And how could he explain to Connor when he didn't even understand it himself.

He loved her. Had always loved her. He'd even be tempted to follow her to New York knowing he would never fit into her world. But he couldn't. He had responsibilities and that was enough—had to be enough—for him.

Margaux pulled out her suitcase with all the black clothes she shut away. She might need them now. It was late, Nick should have been home by now. *Here,* she amended, should have been *here* by now. Everybody else had given their opinion about her life. And he hadn't even weighed in. Maybe he didn't care.

She sniffed. Of course he cared. He had to care, though it would be easier if he didn't. Where the hell was he?

At last she heard the truck come to a stop outside. The door slammed, but he didn't come inside. When she couldn't stand it any longer she went to the kitchen and looked out. Nick was leaning up against his truck, his arms crossed.

"What are you doing?" she asked from the doorway.

"Contemplating the meaning of life."

"Come to any revelations?" She stayed in the doorway. Something about the way he was acting kept her from taking another step. The few yards between them seemed impassable.

"Are you going to come in?"

"Are you going to New York?"

"I have to. I'd be irresponsible not to see what they're offering."

"To see if it's better than what we have to offer?"

"No. It's not like that. Why is everyone so against me going? I can be back by dinnertime."

"If . . ."

"If what?"

"If you don't decide to stay there."

She wanted to say she wouldn't, that she would be back, but she couldn't. "I have to make a living."

"And you can't here?"

"Nick."

He pushed away from the truck and came toward her.

She waited. She wanted his touch, his kiss. She wanted him to understand.

"New York isn't so far. I can commute. The city during the week and weekends here."

"Until you get busy with a show, or you're sent to Paris or Rome or any of those other places."

"You and Connor could come to New York."

"Margaux." He took her in his arms, lifted her nearly off her feet, and kissed her. Long, hard, and she gave in to him. "Isn't this enough to keep you?"

"Nick," she pleaded.

He released her. "I guess not. Go inside. Don't forget to lock your door." His voice was bleak, he was leaving her before she could leave him. But she didn't want to leave him.

"Nick. You're not being reasonable."

He opened the door, waited until she finally stepped inside, then he closed the screen and held it closed.

Just like he'd done the day Louis had come to threaten her. It was the first time they'd made love.

Only this time she knew he wouldn't be coming inside.

"Why are you doing this? You won't even consider giving us a chance. You control your mother and you control Connor, but you can't control me. So you're cutting me off. Don't you realize how selfish you're being?"

He stared at her. "Me?" he said quietly, his anger vibrating his words. "You can come and go at will and I'm selfish because I can't?"

"No, but—"

"You think I'll leave my mother and Connor to fend for themselves, or uproot Connor and follow you to New York? What happens to us when you get too busy for us, or when you get tired of us? Of me?"

"I wouldn't."

"Can you promise that?"

"How can anybody promise?"

"I didn't think so."

"I should have known," she said, so heartsick she could barely form the words. "It's your way or the highway. I was right about you all along."

Goodbye, Margaux." He turned and walked back to his truck, his steps measured, in control. *His way or the highway.*

"I have to say goodbye to Connor."

"No."

"I have to. He won't understand."

He turned on her. "You should have thought about that earlier."

"Nick, please."

"Tomorrow after lunch." He got in the truck and, without a look, drove away, unhurried, but final.

She watched until he rounded the corner. She watched until the faint lights of the truck were swallowed up by the night.

* * *

At one o'clock, Margaux pulled up to the curb in front of Adelaide's Cape.

Adelaide came to the kitchen door. "They're in the backyard," she said, and closed the door.

Margaux walked to the back of the house. Nick was throwing a ball to Connor and Margaux lost her nerve. But Connor saw her and dropped his mitt to run to her.

She knelt down, the tears already clogging her throat, and wondered how she was ever going to say goodbye.

"Hi, sweetie."

He stopped. "Hi."

"Listen, I came to tell you something."

His bottom lip began to quiver. "Uncle Nick said you were leaving. He was lying. You're not leaving."

"I have to go to New York."

"I don't want you to go."

"I have to."

"When are you coming back?"

Nick was walking slowly toward them.

"Well, I might have to work there. Grown-ups have to work."

Tears rolled down his cheeks. "You can work here."

"I can't." She was so tempted to say maybe she could, but that would be unfair, give him false hope. As much as it hurt, Nick was right, better to make a clean break. Nick had already shut her out and now she had no choice but to do what she said she wanted to do. Go to New York. She pulled him close. Put her arm around his little body and he clung to her. God, was she really about to end things?

"But I'll come to visit on the weekends. Sometimes."

She looked at Nick but he was looking at Connor. He'd shut her out completely.

Connor buried his head and clung tighter. "But we didn't see the Milky Way."

"You will, honey. You will." She stood, nearly lost her balance.

Nick pulled Connor away.

Connor looked back at her, his eyes so full of sadness that Margaux's will faltered. She glanced at Nick but he was closed off; there might never have been anything at all between them.

She didn't blame him. At that moment she hated herself.

"Bye," she managed. She turned, no longer able to stop her own tears, and stumbled toward the street.

"No!" screamed Connor. Margaux turned back to him, she couldn't stop herself. "No!" he screamed again, and ran toward her. Nick snatched him off the ground. Connor flailed, fighting to get down, but Nick held him tight.

"Go. Just go, dammit."

Margaux tried to back up, but her feet seemed stuck to the ground.

"I'll be quiet," Connor wailed. "I'll be quiet. I promise. Don't go! Don't go!"

Nick's face froze, horrified as he tried to hold the squirming boy.

Everything seemed to stop. Time, feelings, movement. *I promise to be quiet.*

Good God. She started toward them, at first against her will, then running until she was standing right in front of them.

"Is that what you think? That I'm going because of you? It isn't that at all."

But Connor was past listening. He just kept saying, "I'll be quiet, I'll be quiet," until the words were a whisper.

"Connor. Listen. Do you think I'm leaving because you make noise?"

Slowly he nodded.

"That's not true."

"Mommy did."

She looked at Nick but his face was so stricken that it hurt to see.

"No, honey, she didn't. It was something else, not because of you."

"Mommy said. And she left."

Margaux shook her head. How could a mother leave a child thinking that? How could a mother leave her child for any reason?

You are.

"I love your noise. Do you hear me? I love when you talk out loud and make noise. And I want you to practice talking loud for when I call you on the phone. Okay?"

He just looked at her, tears streaming.

"Okay?"

He nodded.

"Go," Nick mouthed.

"I love you. Both of you." Margaux turned, started down the driveway. But she stopped at the end and looked back one last time. Connor struggled against Nick's hold, his arms reaching out toward her, beseeching and totally silent.

Nick sat in his patrol car just off the road behind a copse of trees. He knew she would have to drive this way. It was the closest route to I-95. He dreaded the moment when he would see her Toyota pass by, almost as much as he dreaded that she wouldn't come by at all. That would mean she'd taken the longer route to make sure she avoided seeing him again.

Connor hadn't said a word since she'd left him. Nick should hate her for what she'd done to Connor. And he tried to, really tried. Mainly he just ached. A dull pain that was slowly squeezing the breath out of him. He wanted to scream. Drive away. Go back to Denver and forget these last few months.

But he wouldn't. He didn't run out on his responsibilities.

Maybe this was his punishment. For joining the army when his family still needed him. For not being here when Ben's hotheadedness turned to delinquency and he began to get into real trouble. For sending Ben to a war that destroyed him. For allowing himself to dream.

He sat in his cruiser, thinking. And waiting. When Margaux finally passed by, he had to force himself not to churn up the siren and go after her. But for what? For how long? So he watched her zoom away through a shield of fog and disappointment. When she was gone, he turned on the engine, pulled onto the road, and made the U-turn back to town.

Twenty-seven

The smell was the first thing that hit her. She'd gotten used to driving with the windows down, letting the hot air flow through the car, bringing the smell of salt air and living things. Now, fumes ripped at her eyes and throat. She quickly rolled up the windows and turned on the air conditioner. She sat in traffic on her way to midtown until she was afraid the engine would overheat. She parked in a garage that cost her forty dollars.

She'd made appointments with Elsie Rule and four other designers just to compare their offers with what Sam Breed would offer her on Friday. It would give her some leverage in the negotiations. Some clout.

Elsie was her first appointment, and as far as Margaux was concerned her least interesting. She walked up two flights to Elsie's combined workshop and business office.

Elsie greeted her with a gracious smile, probably forgetting the things she'd said about M Atelier's last collection in the ladies' room at Lincoln Center. Never bad-mouth anyone in a bathroom stall, it was the first rule of getting to the top.

Margaux opened her portfolio and spread several of her new designs on Elsie's drafting table. She walked out ten minutes later quietly fuming. Elsie wasn't even interested in her new designs. What she wanted was the black Atelier collection.

Margaux thanked her for her interest and flatly refused.

Three more designers, three more offers. They all wanted black.

After the last appointment Margaux walked along Seventh Avenue pondering her situation and calming the fear poking at her consciousness that she was only wanted for her black designs.

"Ridiculous," she said, startling several pedestrians, who suddenly stepped away, giving her a wide berth. She made it about two blocks before her feet, already chafing inside heels she hadn't worn all summer, began to throb.

The silk of her shirt clung to her back. She circumvented a pile of black garbage bags and went into the Korean market. She filled a tin from the salad bar, added two bottles of Evian water and an orange, and called it a day.

The apartment where she was staying belonged to a former colleague who was out of town. She didn't have air-conditioning. Margaux opened all the windows. Took off her clothes and walked around in her underwear, eating salad out of the tin.

She wondered what everyone was doing back in Crescent Cove. If Bri had put up a *Closed* sign and walked away.

She kept checking her cell to see if Nick had called but of course he hadn't. She'd pretty much said he couldn't count on her to be all the things he wanted, maybe needed, her to be. And though his words stung, she recognized the truth in them. He had sacrificed his dreams to take care of his family. The thing that had first attracted Margaux to him had been the thing that had also driven her away.

And she'd called him selfish. She was the selfish one. With a groan, she slumped on the hard futon couch and lifted her hair off her neck, hoping that a breeze would whip in through the half-raised window. But the air stayed still, muggy and heavy, bringing no relief to her heated skin. And no relief to the shame and chagrin that burned at her heart.

She thought about calling Jude to see if she'd seen Nick

or Connor. She was worried about Connor. She railed at the timing that had separated them so suddenly with no time for him to get used to the fact that she was leaving.

But maybe it was better this way. One clean break, he would soon forget her; kids were resilient, they bounced back.

Who was she kidding, Connor hadn't bounced back from his first traumas.

She jumped up off the couch, paced the small living room. Reached for the phone. Put it down. She'd wait a few days until everyone calmed down. Someone was bound to call. Jude at least would want to know that she made it safely.

And what about the boutique and the seamstresses she'd hired. She'd at least have to call someone with instructions. She glanced at her watch. After eleven. Bri would be asleep. She had animals to feed in the morning.

She'd have to wait until tomorrow. She took herself to bed.

It was too hot to sleep and she spent most of the night sitting on the windowsill listening to the sounds of traffic and arguing street people that drifted up from the street.

She finally forced herself to go back to bed. She couldn't face Sam Breed with bags under her eyes.

She stared at the ceiling, closed her eyes, imagining the rush of the tide and the sea breeze lulling her to sleep. She awoke the next morning between sheets damp with sweat. Without thinking, she reached out. But there was only an unused pillow.

She took a cool shower and dressed in her Driftwood slacks and jacket over a Sunrise camisole. She looked in the mirror, smiled at her image, and chickened out. She changed into something more appropriate for a fashion-industry job interview. Something cutting-edge. Head of the pack. Competitive. Black.

She hit the streets with confidence; by the time she reached the S and B building she was a nervous wreck. She stood in the lobby clutching her portfolio and trying to breathe.

She pressed the elevator button and rode upstairs.

S and B was slick, urban chic, with wide halls and large airy offices decorated in muted silver gray. As she stood in the reception area, waiting to be buzzed into Sam's office, she felt a thrill go up her spine. She was back.

"Margaux, darling. You look divine." Sam greeted her with an air kiss and a smile. He was handsome, cultured, and impeccably dressed. The things she'd come to expect in men. Sam had probably never had to rent a tuxedo in his life.

"Come on in and let's have a little chat."

He offered her a seat in one of the leather barrel chairs clustered around his desk. Margaux sat and placed her portfolio by the side of the chair. Sam then sat down on the other side of the desk.

His smile was confident, made perfect by years of expensive dental work.

Leverage, she thought. *Clout. Stay calm.* She smiled her own perfect smile.

"Everyone is extremely excited about having you come on board."

Let him talk. Wait, though her heart was hammering in her chest so hard it hurt.

"So let me see these designs the *New Haven Register* called 'evocative.' "

Margaux smiled. A little jab behind the compliment, but it said so much more. He wanted her, but he was going to try to hardball her. But how much? And what did he really think she was worth?

Margaux opened her portfolio, handed him several of her sketches.

Sam nodded, frowned, tilted his head, moved on to the next while Margaux thanked heaven she'd decided to change to black. It wouldn't show the sweat that was trickling between her breasts.

"Very nice, inventive, a certain *je ne sais quoi,*" said Sam Breed as he handed back her designs.

What he wanted was her little black dress.

Margaux managed to conceal her disappointment. But maybe he was right. She had worried from the beginning that her new line of designs was too craftsy, not couture.

"We've got a place for you. Your own office, your own production schedule. We'll even call it M Atelier by S and B."

The offer was good, better than good. She told him she'd have to think about it. It wouldn't hurt him to sweat a little. And she needed to be sure she wasn't making the wrong decision.

"Great, it will give you time to work up some new designs for S and B. Something cutting-edge."

They made an appointment for the following Thursday.

She walked back through the plush lobby, down the hallway lined with sparkling glass doors. It was all upscale and it could be hers. For a few black dresses.

The interview had not gone as she'd hoped, though she was sure she could make it work if she played her cards right.

She headed back to her borrowed apartment to work up some haute couture designs.

She had to give her life here a fighting chance. It was hardly fair to compare the ocean breeze with a hot blast from a subway grate. They each had their own charm. Sort of. And anyway, she loved the city. Loved the energy. Loved the in-your-face attitude of its inhabitants. Did not love the smell of the bum who seemed to be following her. She stopped at the corner and waited for a chance to rush across the street.

All she had to do was decide.

She spent the afternoon designing at the kitchen table. When she got too hot to think, she stood in front of the open refrigerator door, then went back to work.

After a handful of designs, she still couldn't seem to capture the right feeling, a compelling edge, the wow factor.

She was trying to force the process. She should probably call some friends and see if they wanted to go out to a bar or something. Start to reestablish her life. But the only friends she really wanted to see were in Crescent Cove.

If Nick had been more understanding, supported her, she could call, talk to Connor, tell them she missed them and would be back soon. But that might be a lie. If she took the job Sam offered, she'd be too busy to go back to the shore for a long time.

Maybe Nick had been right after all. It wouldn't be fair to Connor, or Nick, if they tried to make a go of it on her terms. She flushed to think of her last recriminatory words to Nick. She'd said things she didn't really mean, because she was so hurt and disappointed. Words they'd both remember for a long time.

She decided to take herself out to dinner. She went to one of her favorite neighborhood bistros, but a table for one didn't exactly improve her mood. It was hard to keep your mind on eating while all around you, lovers sat, heads nearly touching, talking about whatever lovers talked about, and she tried to remember what she and Nick talked about before that last terrible argument. And she wondered what Nick and Connor were doing. If Nick had been able to soothe him, or if he had crawled back into his silent world.

And if he had, that would be her fault.

Out on the street, she checked her phone again. No missed calls.

She stopped in the deli and bought a pint of Häagen-Dazs sorbet, a comfort food with minimal additional calories. God, she hadn't thought about calories since she'd left the city. Now she'd have to keep aware, keep ahead, stay sharp.

By the time she climbed the stairs to her apartment, the sorbet was beginning to melt. She ate it out of the carton and looked over the designs she had made that afternoon. They weren't whimsical or fanciful, they didn't have a *je ne sais quoi* feel about them. They were black. And boring.

She'd have to do better than this if she was going to hold her own in the industry.

She kept thinking about Nick. She missed him, she wanted to hear his voice, ask about Connor. Tell them both . . . what? What could she possibly say after what she'd done to them?

She replayed their last meeting. Nick saying, "Isn't this enough to keep you?"

How much money did she need? How much fame would make her happy?

Sam's offer was more money than she had ever hoped for. Certainly more than she'd been making before M Atelier was taken from her. Ten times more than she could possibly make in Crescent Cove. All she had to do was design a few black numbers. When she'd reestablished herself, she'd gradually begin to reintroduce color into the line.

But what about the other things, the friendship, the camaraderie, the love of a boy and a man. Did she have to lose all that to follow her dream?

She looked down at her sorbet. It had turned to soup. She tossed it in the sink. Paced the kitchen, shot her fingers through her hair, and was surprised when her hair settled back into place. She'd miss Linda, the mouth, the enthusiasm, hell, the help and the belief she showed to a stranger.

What should she do?

Say yes and be back in the game, or walk away from everything she'd ever dreamed of. She was excited, afraid, and still indecisive. And she missed Nick.

She picked up the phone and pressed his number, not sure what she'd say. And not caring.

"Stay right there," Nick told Connor, who was sitting on the tire swing in Jake's backyard. He gave him a push. "I'll be inside the garage for just a second."

Jake came out of the house and handed Nick a beer and led him into the extra room in back of the woodworking shop. "You sure you want to do this? I mean you're welcome to stay here anytime, you know that."

"Thanks."

Jake nodded. "Hard going home at night?"

"Night. Day." Nick stopped to drink some beer and looked around the small room.

It had a bed and a tiny bathroom. It would do. And he needed a place to stay. He'd started dreading going to his apartment at Linda's, even to change clothes.

The boutique was still open, but only because Brianna had taken over running it, supposedly until Margaux came to her senses. But Nick knew better. Why would she want to come back here once she got back on the road to success?

"Dad says you should use one of the extra bedrooms and not the room out in the workshop." Jake grinned. "He only thinks that because this is where my mother used to send him when she was mad at him." He laughed. "She was one tough lady. Had to be. Like Old Mother Hubbard, a kid in every spare space. It's actually pretty comfortable for a bunkhouse. But you're welcome to come inside."

"Thank him for me, but this is fine. It's just until I can find another apartment."

"You got it," Jake said, turning off the light and heading back to the yard. "But that's not going to cure what ails you."

"If you start talking about time healing all wounds, I'll crack this bottle over your head."

Jake sat down on the picnic bench. "Shit. I wasn't gonna be so understanding. I don't get why you didn't fight harder to get her to stay. I've been around the two of you enough to know that you were pretty close. You're in love with her, no way to get around that, and she loves you. Even someone as bad at relationships as me can see that. And even someone as bad at relationships as you should have done something.

"Did you even ask her to stay?"

"Sort of."

"Sort of? Did it in any way sound like, 'Margaux, I love you. Connor and I need you. Will you marry me?'"

"Hell no."

"Maybe that's the problem. Maybe she thought you wouldn't commit and she cut her losses when she had the chance."

"Shut the hell up. You can't even get a date. You're not exactly an expert in commitment."

"No, but that's no reason you should make the same mistake."

"It wasn't a mistake. She couldn't stick it. Didn't care enough. Christ, what more could I do? Hit her over the head and carry her to my cave?" Nick winced, thinking of the Grotto.

"I was thinking maybe a phone call would do. Don't be stupid and wait for her to call you. This is not the time for playing games."

"I'm not."

"Does that mean you called her?"

Nick shook his head.

"Why not? How hard is it to say, 'Hi, how's it going?'"

Nick barked out a laugh that hurt.

Jake's eyes narrowed. "Has she called you?"

Nick didn't answer.

"She did. Dammit. What happened? Please don't tell me you blew it."

"I didn't pick it up."

"What? Are you freaking crazy? Or do you just love the pain?"

Nick had wanted to answer it, but he knew he would do something stupid like beg her to come back, then she'd feel sorry for him, and it would just be too humiliating when she turned him down.

So he'd walked away from the phone, stood looking at it from the far side of the room while it continued to ring. When he couldn't stand it any longer, he hurried back and snatched it up, but the ringing stopped.

"And you didn't call her back."

"No."

Jake growled in frustration. Took a couple of steps away and turned back. "I guess you didn't really love her after all."

"I did. I do. But my first responsibility is here. Connor hasn't raised his voice above a whisper since the day she left, if he bothers to say anything at all, just wears that stupid scrap of material around his neck. I've enrolled him in the Eldon School. They have a pre-fall orientation program."

"She brought Connor out of his shell."

"And put him right back there when she left. Made it even worse. Look at him."

They both looked toward the swing. There was no Connor.

"Goddammit." Nick was off the table and running toward the swing. "Connor!"

"I'll look in the shop." Jake ran inside and came out a minute later. "Not in there."

Nick scanned the yard until his eyes came to rest on the woods and the path that led to the cove. "Dammit. I know where he's gone. I shouldn't have brought him here. I didn't think."

He took the path at a run. He was vibrating with fury by the time he came to a stop in front of the rock ledge. "Connor, are you in there?"

Nothing. He squatted down and looked inside. Saw the white T-shirt Connor was wearing. "Come on out, buddy."

Connor didn't move.

"Connor, please come out. It's time to go home."

Connor shook his head.

Clinging to the ragged edge of his patience, Nick ducked under the ledge, grabbed the boy by the arm, and pulled him out. He didn't resist, didn't cry, didn't make a sound.

Nick backed out and put him on his feet.

Jake bent over to look under the ledge. "What was he doing in there?"

"I don't know. He saw it one day when we were with . . . you know."

Connor didn't resist when Nick took his hand and the three of them walked back to the street.

As soon as they were in Jake's yard, Nick knelt down. "I don't want you to go there again. I want you to promise or I can't bring you with me anymore."

Connor stood there. Quiet. Just standing.

Nick raked his fingers through his hair, hair he was wearing much longer these days. He'd get a haircut first thing tomorrow.

Jake gave Nick a look and knelt down. "What were you doing in there?"

Connor turned his head toward Jake and whispered, "Making a wish."

"Making a wish?" Jake looked at Nick for clarification.

"Margaux told him that it was where they used to make wishes or some nonsense like that."

"It's not," Connor said on an expulsion of breath. "My wish will come true. Margaux said."

"Well, Margaux was wrong. Get in the truck."

Connor glared at him but walked slowly toward the truck.

"Nick," Jake said. "Cool it. He's just a kid."

"Cool it? Let him keep thinking his wish will come true? He's wishing that Margaux will come back."

"Ouch."

"I'll bring my stuff over when I get off from work tomorrow."

"Sure. See you then. And Nick, try not to be so hard on the boy or yourself."

Nick raised a hand and got into the truck. He buckled Connor's seat belt; Connor refused to look at him. "I'm sorry, champ. I miss her, too, but missing and wishing won't bring her back." He'd been right twenty years ago. He'd known it, but that hadn't stopped him from falling for her all over again.

Twenty-eight

 Margaux spent the next two days designing and fretting. She stopped only long enough to eat and call Bri. The first time she was with a customer—at *Margaux*— and didn't have time to talk. When she called back, Margaux was in the shower. She left a message. "Hope you're doing okay. Jude said we should keep the store open until further notice."

Store? Bri had called *Margaux* a store, not a boutique? She was still pissed.

"So let Jude know, so we can decide what to tell the seamstresses and Linda will know what to do about the rent."

Margaux didn't call her back. She called Jude.

"Am I making the right decision? Sam's offering good money, my own line, a chance to get back in the game."

"Only you can decide," Jude said. "Go with your gut."

"My gut hurts. Everybody's mad at me."

"They're just disappointed that it didn't work out. You have to do what's best for you."

"Have you talked to Nick? He never even returned my call."

There was a pause. "No, actually I haven't seen him."

"Why?"

"He hasn't been around."

"What about Connor?"

"He's been coming to work with Adelaide, but he's going to a preschool term at the Eldon School, starting Monday."

"That's good, right?"

"We all hope so."

"This is what I've always wanted," Margaux blurted out, trying not to think of Connor alone at school.

"I know, Mags. And it's all right, whatever you decide."

She thought of Nick, punishing everyone because he was mad at her. He probably wouldn't even let her see Connor if she went back. "I'm taking Sam's offer."

Silence.

"But if Bri doesn't mind, she can keep *Margaux* open until everyone can find other jobs."

"I'll tell her."

"And don't worry, Mom. I'm good for the loan payments. I won't let you down."

"Sweetheart, you've never let me down."

Was it Margaux's imagination that she heard the unspoken "until now" in her mother's voice?

"Well, stay in touch. Let us know how you make out."

Margaux's throat tightened, her eyes stung, she'd burned her bridge, it was onward and hopefully back upward.

"I will. Bye," she said, and hung up before Jude could hear her cry.

Nick climbed down the outside stairs of his apartment. He was still recovering from his conversation with Linda when he tried to pay her an extra month's rent for the inconvenience of his leaving without notice.

She refused to take the money. As he left, she began singing: "Money can't buy you love."

He turned on her, pushed to the limit. "Maybe you should tell that to Margaux."

"Maybe you should tell her yourself. I'm calling the hippies to see if they want the apartment. I'm out of yak butter." And she slammed the door in his face.

He was just putting the last box of his possessions in the back of the truck, and thinking he'd made it out of his apartment without any more scenes, when Brianna came running out the front door. She was wearing one of those Driftwood pants and a flowing top and it made his throat tighten.

Holding the rail, she took the steps two at a time, marched over to his truck, and planted her hands on her hips. "What are you doing? Is this the move to New York?"

"What move? No. Don't be stupid."

She sank into one hip and he knew he was in for it.

"As long as we're name-calling, you can own the 'stupid' and add the 'stubborn' and the 'selfish' to go with it."

Nick dropped the box and turned on her, ready to give her back insult for insult. He was fed up with everyone ragging on *him* for what Margaux did.

Then she smiled. Slowly. Beautiful, distant, and accusing. How the hell did she manage all that at once?

"Go get her."

"Right." Nick moved toward the driver's side but Brianna stepped in front of him. She had to be close to five-ten, but hell, she seemed about seven feet tall as she scowled at him, almost eye-to-eye.

He slipped past her, she punched him in the arm as he passed. "Goddammit."

Nick turned on her. "Why? Why would she come back? What can I offer her that New York can't?"

"Gee, I don't know. Maybe yourself and Connor?"

"That wasn't enough."

"Are you sure?"

Jake's question needled at him. "Did you tell her you loved her and wanted to marry her?" He'd come close, but it had stuck in his throat . . . because he knew what her answer would be.

"She was sure," he said, but he began to wonder if he'd been a coward. "Hell, she didn't even stick around for this store, and it was way more important to her than we were."

Brianna rolled her eyes at him; he cut her off before she could say something painful.

"She threw it all away. For her old life."

"Jeez. You can't be as dense as you sound. She got scared. Haven't you ever been scared, Nick? Forget I asked. I can see it; sense it on you. You're scared now."

"I'm—"

"She went back to what was familiar, where she knew the rules."

"It's what she wants."

"Maybe. Or maybe she just needed to go back to make sure she was doing the right thing by staying here. Did you ever think about that? Did you do anything to convince her she had a life here?"

He flushed. He could feel it and he couldn't stop it. "I thought I did." But he could hardly get the words out.

"You know, sometimes it's easier when you don't have a choice. Take me, there was no going back, I had to make a new life for myself. She's torn, afraid of making the wrong decision, taking the chance of losing it all again."

He heard her words, but he was having a hard time focusing. He'd been so besotted, so . . . happy, that he'd forgotten she was still reeling from losing everything she had cared about. "They're the same here, make a dress, sell a dress."

"Oh sure, she's got that part down, it's the you-and-Connor part she doesn't know what to do with."

"Exactly. At least now you get it." He moved her aside, opened the truck door, and climbed in.

She held the door open. "You forced her hand."

"How so?"

"She asked you to come to New York."

"How am I supposed to do that? What about Connor? His life has been about loss. I can't pick him up and go to a city that's frightening, where he has no friends, I have no job, and what about my mother, should I just leave her here?

"Jesus, Bri, what does she want from me?"

"Oh, please. Connor has more sense than you do and *he's* supposed to be the child."

"She didn't want us." Nick started the truck. "Everything was fine until she came back."

"Call her, butthead." Brianna slammed the door.

Nick revved the engine and drove away. He wouldn't call her. She'd called him. And left a message. "Hi. Just wanted to see how Connor is doing. I just . . . just hope things are okay. Okay. Bye."

Hardly the words of someone who wanted to come back, to be a part of his life, to love him till death did them part.

Margaux threw herself into her new designs. By Wednesday afternoon, she had a stack of false starts and four or five designs that would pass muster. She spent a good amount of time staring out the kitchen window to the brick wall of the apartment building next door. Found herself sketching the brick pattern, pulled over the latest rejected design, went into the bedroom, rummaged for her pastels, and brought them back to the kitchen table.

Black with a hint of brick red. Nothing too extreme, just a pop of color. But after several attempts, she had to admit defeat. Brick red was not doing it for her. She longed for ocean sunsets and marsh grasses. Her fingers itched to pick up her pastels and just doodle something . . . just for fun. But she wouldn't have time for fun once she went back to work.

Already the colors were fading, the sunsets, the salt marshes, the midnight sky turning to grays. She could recapture them. She had once. She could do it again. After her first season, maybe her second. Once she was back on top.

But how long would that take? It had taken her twelve years

to find the style that established her in the business. It had only taken three months to find her voice in color.

Wednesday night she carefully packed her portfolio. Deliberated about what to wear, and at nine Thursday morning, she was riding up the elevator to S and B.

She didn't have to give her name to the receptionist this time. She was greeted with a "Good morning, Ms. Sullivan. Mr. Breed is expecting you."

Margaux nodded, smiled, read the woman's name tag. Doris. For a brief second she thought about her own secretary and wondered if she could steal her back from the competition.

"So can I show you to your new office?" Sam said once they'd gone through the obligatory air kiss.

"We've put you in a large office back here." He led her through a sea of desks, piled high with swatches, daily books, spreadsheets. Phones rang; staff hurried through the maze of aisles, heads down, energetic, tense, determined.

She didn't see any completed designs, not one draped dressmaker's form. Because all that work was done on another floor, another building, city, or country.

She slowed as she recognized Lisa Raul, a young designer who had been a bright star on the horizon for several years before she fizzled. She was back on the floor, designing as part of the pack. Margaux smiled slightly and Lisa turned quickly away. Margaux could feel her humiliation across the room.

"I've appointed Joey Carlin as your assistant," Sam said as he led her through the room. "He helped us on the Paris show. We stole him from Lagerfeld. But if you have someone else in mind, no problem."

"Joey's perfect."

"Here we are."

Sam showed her into a freshly painted and carpeted office where Joey was standing by a large desk and smiling. He pumped her hand. "So glad to have the opportunity to work with you."

"Well, I'll let you get settled. Then we'll take a look at your new line."

"Thanks, Sam," she said, trying to sound more at home than she felt.

"Uh, Mr. Breed, Production said they wanted to have the new Atelier drawings by noon." He turned to Margaux. "If you've got something finished."

Sam looked a question at her.

"Of course." She placed her portfolio on the desk and spread several of her latest designs out on the desktop. Sam leaned over, studying them closely, pushed two out of the way. Chose two others. "What else do you have?"

Margaux showed him two more.

"Okay this one, and . . ."

He pulled the next one across the desk and turned it around. Margaux had included a design of one of her ochre and ecru Driftwood sarongs . . . Just as an experiment.

Sam nodded, reached over to snag a pencil out of the pencil caddy, and scribbled something across the page and a huge arrow pointing to the dress.

"Love it. Joey, call over to the warehouse and see if there's more of that black shantung. Perfect for this cut, don't you think?" He glanced at Margaux.

"Perfect," she said. And it *was*. For New York, for the runway, for the fashion industry.

"And Joey, I want full mock-ups by tomorrow's meeting. Margaux, these are dynamite. I'm wondering if we could bump the production schedule up? I'd love to see at least a couple of these in the fall show.

"Joey, check with Cynthia on what spots we can lose. If we can get these constructed, I'll pull a couple of pieces from the fall show, put these in their place. It'll be tight, but I think we can get it done."

Joey's mouth opened. "But—"

"Get going."

Joey left the office.

"Yell if you need anything. Welcome back."

Alone, Margaux looked around her new office. A steel and glass desk, drafting table in the corner. Natural light as well as work lights.

She set up her supplies and got to work.

It was after seven when she left that night. As she walked across the main room, lights shone from at least half the cubbies. They were gearing up for Fashion Week. And with a little luck, M Atelier would be part of it.

She picked up takeout Chinese and went back to the apartment to continue work. Suddenly the kitchen table seemed too small, the air too hot and still, the brick wall outside the window too claustrophobic. She'd have to start looking for her own place. A studio, possibly a small one-bedroom, but she'd have to wait to get paid first.

The next week passed in a blur. Margaux arrived early, stayed late. Everyone was working overtime and on overload. Tempers flared, diva attacks were the norm. It was intense, exciting. Exhausting. And relentless.

She'd turned in several designs that had gone to assembly. She'd okayed fabrics even though she knew it was more of a nod to her reputation and she had no doubt that they would change the fabric in a flash if the costs went too high. Or dozens of other reasons.

At the end of the week, she ran into Lisa Raul as she was coming out of the ladies' room. Lisa stumbled past her, she was crying.

Déjà vu. Margaux's stomach burned in sympathy as Lisa rushed into a stall and retched. Margaux tiptoed away, leaving her to break down without an audience. It was a cutthroat business, Margaux just hoped the girl was having a stress meltdown and hadn't just gotten fired.

Joey was waiting in her office, with fabric swatches for her to okay.

Sam stuck his head in the door. "Got a minute?"

"Sure."

He stepped inside. "You're in the fall show, you need to sign off on these right away."

"Great," Margaux said. Then she remembered Lisa Raul. Had she been dumped to make room for Margaux? Her stomach turned.

"Sam, I just saw Lisa Raul. She seemed pretty upset. Do you know what happened?"

Sam waved a dismissive hand. "A big disappointment. She just couldn't compete, flat designs, no imagination. She showed such promise three years ago. We paid big bucks for her, and she just wimped out."

"Did she get bumped from the fall show to make room for me?"

"Hell, I was going to have to do it anyway. I would have had to scramble to get something else, so if you want a full line in the fall show it's yours. But we'll need more. What do you have?"

Lisa's career had been deep-sixed with a shrug—to make room for Margaux. It was the way things worked. Had always been that way. Would always be that way. No one's fault and Margaux's chance.

She mentally reviewed the things she'd worked on that week. They all just melded into one big gray area, nothing stuck out. She reached for her portfolio. Pulled out the top design. Handed it to Sam.

"Mmm, don't love it," Sam said.

She handed him another.

"That's more like it. We'll place it up front. Dynamite." He held out his hand for more.

Trying to remember what else she had to show, she reached for the rest of the sketches.

As she pulled them out of her portfolio another paper floated to the desktop.

A crumpled piece of blue paper and Connor's Day-Glo stars. Her breath caught and she gripped the edge of her desk.

"Margaux? Is something wrong?"

Here was her chance to be back in the game. To make a success of her life. To set the runways ablaze with her designs—her black designs. She wanted to say she was fine, but she couldn't get the words out.

He was willing to move mountains to get her. Screw the scheduled designers to keep her. But she didn't want to be responsible for someone else's failure. That's not how she wanted to live her life. Not her designs at the expense of another's.

Something *was* wrong. Terribly wrong, she thought as she gazed down at that crumpled sky with Connor's stars. The Milky Way. For her dress. The dress she hadn't designed yet. And the one, she finally realized, she needed to make.

She closed her portfolio, looked up, smiled. "Thanks, Sam. This is such a great opportunity, but before this goes any further, I'm afraid I'm going to have to pull out."

Sam's face didn't change. "I see. What if we sweeten the —"

"No. It's a wonderful offer and opportunity. But to be fair to S and B, I'm really committed to what I'm doing now. Put Lisa back in the show. She's got talent, she just burned out for a minute. I've done that. We all have. But she's talented, she's got a great future ahead of her. Take a chance on her."

"Margaux. What will it take? You want to do a few pastels, I understand. But pastels just aren't in this season. Maybe next year."

This season. Maybe next year. Pastels. He didn't get it. But Margaux did at last. The colors she saw weren't on the design palette, the clothing she made was whimsical, wearable, and maybe, just maybe, affordable without being shoddy. They weren't haute couture. Maybe never could be. Maybe that's not where she belonged.

Actually she knew it wasn't where she belonged. It was sad to admit, but it set her free.

"I'm sorry, Sam. I've made my decision. Keep the designs I made for you. I don't have use for them. I wish you all the best for the fall show. Goodbye."

She turned and left. No air kiss, no one-armed hug that wouldn't wrinkle suits or mess makeup or hair. Just two impeccably dressed men, staring in disbelief as she packed up her portfolio and grabbed her purse.

She made her way back through the chaos, smiled at everyone, nodded at the receptionist, and took the elevator downstairs.

She was hit by a blast of heat and the pungent smell of truck exhaust. There had been a time when she craved the energy of the city, of the industry. But she was a different person now.

Or at least she was the person she was meant to be. It may have taken a taciturn policeman and a silent little boy for her to get it. But she got it now. She just hoped she hadn't waited too long.

She began to walk faster. If she hurried, she could beat rush-hour traffic and be home before dark.

Twenty-nine

Margaux drove straight through Crescent Cove and stopped in front of Le Coif.

"Moved out the day after you left," Linda said.

"You're pissed," Margaux said. "You have a right to be. Raise my rent to take care of what you're losing without Nick."

"You think that's gonna fix things?"

"Do you want me to find another place for the boutique?"

"Do you want me to slap you upside the head? Brianna and Grace and Jude have been playing round-robin keeping this place open so you'd have something to come back to when you woke up and realized what a horse's ass you were. Now I suggest you start working on an ad campaign. Put an ad in the paper for some retail help. And get your butt over to Adelaide's and beg her to come back to work."

"I can do the first two, but I don't think Adelaide will be so easy."

"Won't know until you try."

"Is Nick staying with her?"

"Nope."

"Do you know where he's staying?"

"Nope."

* * *

A week went by. Margaux made her peace with Bri, Grace, Linda, Dottie. Everyone welcomed her back, though it took some longer than others. She went back to work . . . on her beach designs.

And she was almost happy.

"So I'm a slow learner. I just had to make sure," Margaux told Bri and Grace over a batch of watermelon martinis. "Now I know for sure. This is where I belong."

"You don't sound too happy about it. Have you seen Nick?"

Margaux shook her head. "He knows I'm back. If he wanted to see me, all he has to do is come to the store."

"Ask Adelaide."

"I can't. What if Connor sees me? Nick won't let me spend time with him. It will be awful."

"Oh hell, Margaux. He's not some kind of ogre. He's just a guy who went out on a limb for you, probably a first in his controlled, organized life. And you cut it out from under him."

"This from his worst critic," Grace said, and poured another round of martinis.

"God, I've messed up everything."

"Yeah, but you can fix it," said Bri, and raised her glass. "Now go talk to Adelaide. We need her."

We. They were *we* again. Margaux felt a shred of hope that she might be able to rectify things with Nick and Connor. "Okay, I'll do it."

It wasn't easy. Adelaide wasn't at home the two times Margaux tried to visit. She even considered marching into the police station and demanding that Nick see her. But she didn't. She hoped he'd come around, forgive her and take her back, but she didn't hold out much hope. She'd hurt him, harmed Connor, and disappointed Adelaide. She had a lot to answer for, if they would even listen.

She'd given up a future for one she thought she wanted, and by the time she'd discovered her mistake, she had lost both.

She was sitting at the counter of *Margaux* when the "Toreador Song" let her know that a customer was on the way. She dragged herself up from the stool and pasted on a smile.

Jude and Roger came into the store. They had that look. The look of promise, of happiness. Her stomach flipped over.

"Hi."

"Hi," said Jude. "Roger and I have something to tell you."

"I know. Congratulations."

"You don't mind?" asked Roger. "If you feel—"

"Not at all. Welcome to the family." *Family,* the word echoed through her mind and settled in her heart.

Jude was eyeing one of the new hostess gowns that had just come down from the sewing room, but she said, "I don't know if I'm speaking out of turn."

Margaux laughed. "It never bothered you before. Is it something bad?"

"That depends. Adelaide said you and Nick weren't seeing each other."

"He won't see me. He doesn't want to have anything to do with me and I can't blame him." Her mouth twisted. "I have everything I wanted now, but I lost the one thing that I need."

"It isn't too late."

"Yeah. It is. He won't take a chance again. I can't blame him. And I don't even know where he is. He isn't staying at his apartment."

"He's staying at Jake McGuire's until he can find a new place."

"Oh great. I've hurt him and driven him from his home. What kind of person am I?"

"You're a lovely person. And so is Nick. But you're both wary and stubborn. Somebody has to make the first move."

"I guess that someone would be me."

Jude nodded. "Come on, Mags. Nick needs you. Connor needs you. You just have to convince him you're here for good. You are here for good?"

Margaux nodded.

"Be absolutely sure before you do anything."

"I'm sure. Even if Nick never speaks to me again, I'm home for good."

"Then get going. Roger and I will mind the store."

"Go where?"

"To Adelaide's. She's home. I just saw her car in the driveway. Go on." She gave Margaux a quick hug and shooed her toward the door.

Margaux prayed that Adelaide would see her. She breathed a sigh of relief when she saw the Buick parked in the driveway, and another sigh of relief that there wasn't a white truck parked there.

She got out of the car, smoothed her hair, and walked up the driveway to the kitchen door.

She knocked, called, "Adelaide, could I see you for a minute? Please?"

It seemed forever before the door opened and Adelaide looked out at her.

"Can I come in?"

Looking resigned, Adelaide opened the door and let Margaux in.

"Say what you have to say. If you've come to fire me, think we can't work together because of what's happened between you and Nicky, I understand."

"No, no," blurted Margaux, taken off guard. "I need you. I couldn't run *Margaux* without you. I was afraid maybe you had quit, because of how stupid I've been."

Adelaide turned away and Margaux was afraid she was about to get kicked out, but Adelaide merely poured a cup of coffee from the carafe, put it on the table and motioned her to sit. Margaux saw the other cup already sitting on the table.

"Where's Connor? Is he okay?"

"He's over at the Eldon School, and no, he's not okay."

"The Eldon School. Isn't that—"

"Hopefully it's just temporary. Now that we've learned

why he was so quiet, the therapist is hopeful he'll be ready for school, maybe not in September but soon. We owe you that."

"You have every reason to hate me. I know I hurt Nick and I hurt Connor. I didn't want to, but sometimes I'm a slow learner and what I thought I wanted wasn't what I wanted at all. But I had to find that out in my own way. Being a famous designer has always been my dream." But that wasn't true. *To design clothes that made the people who wore them feel good about themselves,* that's what her diary entry had said. There was no mention of "famous."

Adelaide put down her cup. "Nicky had dreams, too. But when Cyril died he put them on hold to take care of Ben and me. Nick's always taken care of his family. Never neglected his duty. Never put himself first. Those years he was at home, he closed off a little piece of himself."

"The part that dreamed."

"And then Ben died and Connor came to us. And again Nick gave up everything for his family. It's a rare thing for a man to do. A thing to be proud of." Adelaide sighed, a weight seemed to settle across her shoulders. "For a while this summer, I thought he might get it back, that little piece, but . . ." She turned away, but not before Margaux saw the glimmer of sudden tears.

"It's my fault."

"Enough with fault," Adelaide said vehemently. "Life is what it is. We do the best we can. The two of you could do worse than each other. You both started out with dreams. There's no reason you can't fulfill them. You might accomplish it alone. But it's a much better thing to share it with someone you love."

Margaux hung her head, fighting her own tears. "It's too late for us. He would never let us try now. Too many years, too much baggage."

"Fiddlesticks. Baggage. I don't know what all this talk about baggage is. Just excuses for lack of courage. You and Nick could be happy if you would only try."

"He doesn't want to try. He hates me."

Adelaide shook her head. "He has loved you since he was a boy."

"What—what do you mean? I didn't even know him then."

"No, but he knew you. At least I always assumed it was you. And then when I saw you together this summer, I knew."

"But I don't remember."

"I know. Even then, Nick didn't talk much about his feelings, kept it all inside, like his father. But he let things slip without knowing it, in the way boys will do. Forever rushing through his chores to go to the library. He loved his history books, but I always suspected that it was because of a red-headed pixie who sat at his library table who he was forever talking about."

"Nick was the boy in the library? He couldn't be."

The boy at the library. Sitting there day after day, never making a sound.

"He never even talked to me."

"I expect he didn't want anything to change. It was a hard time for our family and especially for Nick. He didn't have much to look forward to. His books and you sitting at that table every summer were special to him."

"Why didn't he tell me?"

Adelaide shrugged. "You know Nicky. He keeps things to himself. I don't mean cold, but reserved. Not like Ben, who always wore his feelings for the world to see. It doesn't mean he doesn't feel, deeply."

"What should I do?"

Adelaide gave her a long searching look. "That's up to you, but I have to pick up Connor from school now." She stood up, put her cup in the sink, and picked up her purse. "You can ride along if you want."

The Eldon School was out on the highway about twenty minutes away on a large wooded lot. School was just letting out when they pulled into the long drive to the one-storied building. Cars lined the drive; teachers stood with small groups of children, releasing them to their parents. It was overwhelming to see children with so many different challenges, and Margaux vowed to do whatever it took to make Connor happy.

Adelaide parked the Buick and they walked toward the entrance. A young woman was herding a line of four students out the front door. Connor was among them, his head bowed, his feet scuffing the sidewalk. He looked up, searching for his grandmother. Saw Margaux and stopped. The teacher urged him on but he didn't budge.

Margaux smiled. Waved.

Connor stood perfectly still. His expression didn't change. And she wondered if she had done irreparable harm.

"Connor." She held out her hands.

He began to walk slowly toward her, stopped, then he began to run. He flew into her arms. "I knew you would come back. I went to the Grotto and wished it."

"And I'm here." She lifted him up and hugged him.

They drove home, Connor sitting in the front seat, holding on to Margaux as if he were afraid she would leave again. "I'm losing another tooth." He wiggled it to show her.

"I see."

"And school is fun."

He chatted happily, quietly at first, getting louder and more animated as they drove. Margaux didn't notice that Adelaide had turned into the police station until she pulled to a stop behind Nick's cruiser.

"You go on inside and talk to Nick."

Connor clung to her.

"Connor, let go." Adelaide pulled his hand from Margaux's sleeve. "Let Margaux go now. She needs to talk to Uncle Nick."

"You're coming back?"

"Yes, I promise." She licked three fingers and held them in the air. "That's a special Grotto promise."

Adelaide looked over his head to Margaux. "Don't take no for an answer. We'll be waiting at home, won't we, Connor?"

Connor nodded. "Don't take too long."

"I won't." Margaux waited until they drove away, then she walked into the police station.

"Not here," Finley Green said. "Left about an hour ago."

"But his cruiser is still here."

"Huh. Maybe he went to Dottie's for coffee."

Dee Janowitz stood up from the switchboard. "Hi, Margaux. Heard you decided to give us another chance. Nick had that big old history book with him. My guess is he's over at the library."

"Thanks, Dee."

She started toward the library. If Nick wasn't there, she might not have the courage to do this again. If he was there, she hoped he would at least hear her out.

She hesitated outside the library door to make one final, silent plea. *Don't walk away, give me another chance.*

She pushed open the door and went inside. The library was a small building, one main room and a side room that had been converted to a computer room. There were two tables on the far side of the room. The one where she always sat as a young girl was occupied by a man.

A man whose mere presence made her overflow with love. His head was bent over his book; his hair was longer than it had been when they first met, and she was hit with an image so strong that she staggered back.

That same head bent over his book years before. As steady and predictable as the tide. She hadn't understood what that kind of steadfastness meant. Had given it no thought. She was too involved in her plans for her future. But she understood now. And she remembered the sense of loss she'd felt the summer he hadn't been there. Every day for the rest of that summer, she went to the library, looked at their table, hoping he would be there, but after several weeks, she had to admit he was gone for good.

She stopped by the magazine rack, quietly lifted out the

latest issue of *Modern Bride*, and walked slowly to the table, almost afraid to disrupt this fragile moment. She pulled out the chair across from him and sat down. She opened her magazine to a page filled with bridal excess and smiled at the girl she had been and prayed for the woman she'd become.

Nick looked up.

"Hi, I'm Margaux. What are you reading?"

He hesitated, then slowly turned the book so that she could see, *A History of the Ostrogoths in Italy*. She took his hand. Kept it.

"It sounds interesting. Will you tell me about it?"

His eyes narrowed. He was going to look away, stand up, and leave, and she knew if he did, he would never come back.

"I have a dream," she said.

He flinched and tried to pull his hand away. "Yeah. I heard."

She held it tighter. "I have a dream," she continued, afraid to even look at him, "I have a dream to live at the shore, to design my own clothes, and sell them from a little boutique on Marina Street."

The tension was so compelling she thought it might suck her right across the table.

"Are you sure it's the right dream?"

"Yes."

"Does this dream include anyone else?" he asked, his voice a gravelly whisper.

"I want it to, I hope it does. But I can't control that part of the dream."

"Who can?"

"You." She waited, hardly daring to breathe.

"I'm not sure I believe in dreams."

"You have to. You believed in them once. Believe in them again." *Please say yes, please don't turn away, you need me, Connor needs me, and I need both of you.*

"Connor believed. He went to your Grotto and made a wish. He believed it would come true."

"Let's make it come true, Nick."

"First I want you to answer a question."

"Okay. If I can."

"Will you marry me?"

"Yes."

"And promise to never leave us again?"

"I promise. I've been really stupid. I was confused but I'm not now. This is what I want."

Nick closed his book and they both stood up, their hands linked across the table.

"Let's go home, Nick. Connor's waiting for us."

SHELLEY NOBLE is a former professional dancer and choreographer. She most recently worked on the films *Mona Lisa Smile* and *The Game Plan*. Shelley is a member of Sisters in Crime, Mystery Writers of America, Romance Writers of America, and Liberty States Fiction Writers.

She has two children and lives near the New Jersey shore. In her spare time she loves to discover new beaches and indulge her passion for lighthouses and boardwalks with vintage carousels.

Shelley Noble